Dear Reader,

Arabesque is proud to publish the **At Your Service** series, a fictional account of four courageous and committed heroes serving in the Air Force, Army, Navy, and Marines. We know that you will come to admire and fall in love with these proud African-American military officers: Major Zurich Kingdom in *Top-Secret Rendezvous*, Colonel Neal Allen in *Courage Under Fire*, Captain Haughton Storm in *The Glory of Love*, and Colonel Nelson Wainwright in *Flying High*.

The **At Your Service** romance series is the story of their lives and the women they love . . . filled with patriotism, camaraderie, romance, passion, and intrigue! Each novel will draw you in and not let you go, as you come to appreciate the honor of each hero, as well as the commitment of the people they care about. The series is a fictional account meant to capture the essence of those serving our country, and as such we have taken creative license with the cover photography and the stories we know you will enjoy.

BET Books began planning this unique series honoring African Americans serving in the military in the Spring of 2002, not knowing that events would unfold in the war with Iraq in "Operation Enduring Freedom."

Now, more than ever, we hope that you enjoy this series yourself, or buy the books as gifts for someone special. We welcome your comments and feedback, and invite you to send us an e-mail to **BET Books@BET.com.**

Best regards,

Linda Gill
Vice President and Publish

BOOK YOUR PLACE ON OUR WEBSITE AND MAKE THE ARABESQUE ROMANCE CONNECTION!

We've created a customized website just for our very special Arabesque readers, where you can get the inside scoop on everything that's going on with Arabesque romance novels.

When you come online, you'll have the exciting opportunity to:

- View covers of upcoming books

- Learn about our future publishing schedule (listed by publication month and author)

- Find out when your favorite authors will be visiting a city near you

- Search for and order backlist books

- Check out author bios and background information

- Send e-mail to your favorite authors

- Join us in weekly chats with authors, readers and other guests

- Get writing guidelines

- AND MUCH MORE!

Visit our website at
http://www.arabesquebooks.com

FLYING HIGH

Audrey woke up the next morning and grabbed her head. How much champagne did she drink?

When she finally sat down with a cup of coffee and was about to ignore the ringing telephone, she remembered that, as a doctor, she couldn't do that.

"Hello," she said, having scalded her throat with the first sip.

"Hi. How do you feel this morning?"

Good heavens, it was *him*. "How do I . . . Maybe I'd better ask you how *should* I feel."

"Pretty rotten, I would think. Did you get some coffee?"

"I just got one swallow before I had to answer the phone."

"Sorry about that. Next time I won't let you drink that much."

"You mean I didn't disgrace myself? You want us to go out to dinner again?" His laughter sent pain through her head. "Well, did I?"

"Of course not. You were sweeter than I dreamed you could be."

"Nelson! Please don't tease. I remember your buckling my seat belt when we left the restaurant, and that's all."

"Really? What a pity! I'll never forget that kiss, and you don't even remember it."

"Now, you look here. I did not kiss you."

"No? Then come on over here and look at my face."

"You must have gone somewhere after you left me."

"Come on, now, Audrey. No woman could follow you."

"Ohhhh," she groaned. "Nelson, I do remember thinking you were a gentleman. I think I may have made a big error."

"I wouldn't lie to you, Audrey. You kissed me and told me I was sweet. I practically fell down the steps."

"*Steps? What steps?*"

"Uh, the ones in your house. You weren't sure you could walk up the stairs, so I carried you."

"I don't want to hear any more. This gets worse by the second. Nelson, promise you won't mention any of this to me again."

"Well, I'll try, but when I think about that kiss, there's no telling what I might do. And then, there's—"

Other Books by Gwynne Forster

Sealed with a Kiss
Against All Odds
"Christopher's Gifts" in *Silver Bells*
Ecstasy
"A Perfect Match" in *I Do*
Obsession
Beyond Desire
"Love for a Lifetime" in *Wedding Bells*
Fools Rush In
Swept Away
Secret Desire
Scarlet Woman
Once in a Lifetime

Published by BET/Arabesque Books

FLYING HIGH

Gwynne Forster

BET Publications, LLC
http://www.bet.com
http://www.arabesquebooks.com

Flying High is a work of fiction, and is not intended to provide an exact representation of military life, or any known persons. The author has taken creative license in development of the characters and plot of the story, although military bases and conflicts referenced may be actual. The cover photography is meant to evoke each branch of service, and may not be an exact representation of military uniform. BET Books/Arabesque develops contemporary works of romance fiction for entertainment purposes only.

ARABESQUE BOOKS are published by

BET Publications, LLC
c/o BET BOOKS
One BET Plaza
1900 W Place NE
Washington, DC 20018-1211

All Kensington Titles, Imprints, and Distributed Lines are available at special quantity discounts for bulk purchases for sales promotions, premiums, fund-raising, and educational or institutional use. Special book excerpts or customized printings can also be created to fit specific needs. For details, write or phone the office of the Kensington special sales manager: Kensington Publishing Corp., 850 Third Avenue, New York, NY 10022, attn: Special Sales Department, Phone: 1-800-221-2647.

First Printing: September 2003
10 9 8 7 6 5 4 3 2 1

Printed in the United States of America

ACKNOWLEDGMENTS

I am deeply indebted to Marine Corps Gunnery Sergeant James F. Simms for guiding me through the morass of Marine Corps standards, rules, and regulations, and I thank Linda Hudson-Smith sincerely for introducing me to Sergeant Simms. I am also indebted to my husband whose love, support, and encouragement are indispensable to me.

One

Nelson Wainwright, Colonel, United States Marine Corps, glanced at the overcast sky, dropped his briefcase, and switched on the television. He hated getting wet when he was fully dressed; in fact, he disliked untidiness and considered a wrinkled uniform the epitome of it. He turned on the television to check the weather and read the news beneath the picture: Sixty-eight and cloudy. Rain likely. Cooler than usual for May

"What will a man endure to achieve his aims?" the motivational speaker said, as Nelson reached to switch off the television. The question mocked him, enticed him to linger and listen. "How much will he sacrifice? What will he give? What will he gain? And what can he lose?"

Ordinarily, Nelson did not allow media gurus or self-styled motivators to impress him, but those words hounded him as he drove from Alexandria, Virginia to his office in the Pentagon. He had spent twenty-four of his forty-five years in the Marine Corps, and as recompense for working so hard and shaking hands with death more times than he wanted to remember, he intended to retire with four silver stars on his collar. He'd love to retire with five stars, but nothing less than becoming a four-star general would satisfy him.

Nelson knew two reasons why, even with good

fortune, hard work, and shrewdness, he had a less-than-even chance of retiring as a full general. His superiors did not know that an injury to his neck pained him sufficiently to make him unfit for duty, nor did they know of his failure to report a corporal whom he'd discovered asleep while on guard duty in Afghanistan. He didn't doubt that if his superiors knew of the unremitting pain he suffered, they would force his immediate retirement. And if he managed to camouflage that, he could be dismissed or at least disciplined for not having reported that marine's misconduct. Either meant he would finish military life as a colonel.

He parked in the space reserved for officers of his rank, and as light raindrops spattered his shoulders, he dashed inside the Pentagon. But as he entered his office, an eerie feeling settled over him, and every pore of his skin jumped to alert as if he were back in Afghanistan anticipating a missile strike. He rushed to answer the telephone even as dread washed through his system.

" 'Morning. Wainwright speaking."

"Good morning, Sir," a female said. "This is Lieutenant McCafferty in the Commandant's Office, and I'm sorry I have to give you this sad news."

Nelson leaned forward, mentally bracing himself, and listened as she told him that his brother had perished in an automobile accident that morning.

"You're listed as next of kin, Sir, and as guardian for Commander Wainwright's child, Richard Wainwright. Let us know what we can do for you. This office will send you an order for two weeks' leave effective immediately."

He sat there for an hour dealing with his emotions and collecting his thoughts. Joel, his younger brother and only relative other than little Ricky, had been looking forward to a great future in the Navy, and now . . .

Well, what was done was done. The Navy would take care of Joel; he had to look after four-year-old Ricky.

As the days passed, Ricky didn't respond favorably to the succession of foster mothers with whom he placed the boy, and Nelson couldn't help noticing negative changes in the child's behavior, from bright and cheerful to sullen and quiet.

"That does it," he said to himself when, on one of his daily visits, Ricky clung to his leg in a fit of tears and wouldn't let go. He picked the child up, paid the foster mother for the remainder of the month, and took Ricky home with him.

He wasn't a religious man, but he gave sincere thanks when Lena Alexander, whom his secretary had recommended, walked into his house. She greeted him, looked down at Ricky, who loitered behind, dragging a beach towel, and her face lit up with a smile as she bent to the child and opened her arms.

"My name is Lena, and I love little boys. What's your name?"

When Ricky smiled at her and told her his name was Ricky Wainwright, Nelson relaxed. Seconds later, Lena was giving Ricky a hug and the child was telling her about his imaginary friends. The next morning, Nelson moved her personal belongings to his home and settled her in a guest room.

It had been years since he had shared his living quarters, not since the four months during which he'd lived with Carole James, the woman who had brought another man—his closest friend—to the bed they shared, and had cared so little for Nelson that she let him catch her cheating. The woman who would have been his wife within six weeks. In the more than five years that followed, he enjoyed the quiet, though not the loneliness, and hearing Ricky's joyful noises and Lena's humming as she worked buoyed his spirits. Home was suddenly a pleasant place, especially at dinner when Lena and the boy were company for the delightful meals Lena prepared.

"What's the matter with your neck, Colonel?" Lena asked him at breakfast several days after joining his household. "Looks to me like you always favoring your neck. Better get it looked after. Trouble don't stand still in this world; either gets better or worse. You know what I'm saying?"

He did, indeed. Didn't the pain in his neck get worse daily? "I'm dealing with it, Lena. Don't let it bother you."

"Ain't bothering me none, Colonel. You the one that's uncomfortable. I declare, I wish somebody'd tell me why men so scared of a doctor. In the almost thirty years that I worked as an LPN—you know, licensed practical nurse—I never yet saw a male patient who didn't wait till he was half dead before he went to the doctor. You better do something before you get a problem with your spine."

He didn't have to answer her, because she left the breakfast room humming what he suspected was her favorite hymn.

"What's the name of that tune, Lena?" he asked when she came back with a carafe of hot coffee.

"If you don't know that song, you in trouble. Even the devil knows 'Amazing Grace.'"

He held his breath, watching while she filled his cup to the brim. He bent over and sipped enough so that he could raise the cup to his lips without spilling the coffee.

"That surprises me, Lena. I would have thought the devil was more creative than to . . ."

He stopped. Her expression amounted to wonderment at his obtuseness. "Colonel Wainwright, I never said he sang the song; I said he knew it."

She walked with him to the door, holding Ricky who enjoyed telling him good-bye and getting a hug at more than six feet and five inches above the floor. "You go see a doctor today, Colonel."

"See a doctor, Colonel," Ricky parroted.

"Ricky, you have to call him Uncle Nelson," he heard Lena say as he headed for his car.

"You sit down here and build your castle or read your book while I tend to a little business," Lena said to Ricky one morning about a month later as soon as Nelson left home. Ricky talked to the pictures in his books and pretended to read.

She dialed the hospital. "Let me speak to Dr. Powers, please."

"Dr. Powers speaking. How may I help you?"

"Audrey, honey, this is Aunt Lena. I love my boss. He's a wonderful man, so good with his little nephew. I wish—"

"Aunt Lena, I am not interested in your matchmaking. I'm glad the guy is a good father, and I'm glad you like your job. Now—"

"Hear me out, Audrey. Something is wrong with this man's neck. If he's not holding it and rubbing it, he's got something wrapped around it, and I can't get him to see a doctor. It's free for officers at Walter Reed Hospital, but I can't get him to go. Last night, he stopped eating his dinner, got up, and put something around it. I hate to see him suffer like this. Come over one night or maybe this Sunday when you're off and have a look at it. He's such a good man."

"If it bothers him enough, Aunt Lena, he'll do something about it. I'd rather not meddle in that."

"Well . . . I, I just don't know what to do. It's not like he was hiding from the law." Lena hung up. She would find a way to get him to a doctor, he could bet on that.

"You didn't commit no crime, did you, Colonel?" she asked Nelson one night at dinner. When he stopped eating and stared at her, she pretending not to notice. "I mean, you not hiding out or something. You know what I mean, don't you."

He half-laughed and pointed his fork at her. "No, Lena, I don't know what you mean, and stop needling me." Then he laughed outright. "It just occurred to me that you're a blessing to my ego. I get so damned much deference at the Pentagon that I've started to believe I deserve it, but I can count on you to bring me down front and keep my feet to the fire, so to speak."

She turned her back in order to get the piece of celery that had lodged in the gap between her front teeth, then turned back to him. "I didn't mean to get familiar, but—"

He laughed, and he wasn't bad-looking when he wiped that stern expression from his face. "I don't believe you said that."

"Well, truth is I care about what happens to you, and I've had plenty experience with people who've been injured, so I know that neck of yours is a serious problem."

"That's right. Sometimes I forget you're a nurse.

Lena, I'm not entirely foolish. A missile hit the helicopter that I was piloting in Afghanistan and when the copter crashed, I got some injuries, and this whiplash was one of them. My other injuries healed; this one is taking a little longer. That's all."

"Hmmm. You had that before I came here, and I've been working for you over three months. That's more than long enough for a whiplash to heal. Why don't you go over to Walter Reed and let them take care of it?"

"I can't do that, Lena. If my superiors find out that my neck is still giving me trouble, they may force me to retire. It's bad enough that I'm still on desk duty."

"Oh, dear. I see what the problem is, and if you go to a private doctor, it'll be reported. Well, I'll pray for you. I sure will."

He seemed relieved to get that subject out of the way, but he didn't know that she wasn't used to accepting defeat. She put Ricky to bed, and while Nelson read the child's favorite story to him, she called her niece.

"Audrey, could you do me a favor?" she asked after they greeted each other. "I want to go on my church's outing Saturday, day after tomorrow. They're going to Crystal Caverns down in Strasburg, Virginia, and I always wanted to go. Year before last when they went, I couldn't get away from work. Could you look after Ricky"—she didn't dare mention Nelson—"for me Saturday? Just give him lunch and read him some stories. He's no trouble, and sweet as he can be."

She listened to the silence until she thought she would scream. Finally, Audrey said, "What time do you think you'll get back there?"

"Around seven."

"All right. I'll do it this once, but you know I don't cook."

"Sandwiches will do just fine." She hadn't planned to

take the excursion, but she phoned the organizer and got her seat. Maybe she could kill two birds with one stone. Nelson Wainwright was a catch for any woman.

Audrey Powers did not relish the thought of baby-sitting, not even for half an hour. But her aunt had been so supportive during her struggles—first to get through college and then to complete her medical training—that she couldn't think of anything she wouldn't do for Lena. She stuffed half a dozen Chupa Chups into her handbag and stepped out of her house at barely sunup. The drive from her house in Bethesda to Alexandria, circling Washington on the Beltway, took her only twenty minutes in the sparse Saturday morning traffic. She parked in front of the beige-colored brick town house at 76 Acorn Drive. Lena greeted her at the door.

"You're just in time. My taxi will be here in fifteen minutes." She turned around and pointed to the little boy. "This is Ricky. Ricky, Audrey is going to stay with you today."

Audrey looked down at the child who stared at her with an almost plaintive expression, and her heart seemed to constrict as she knelt beside him. "Hello, Ricky."

"Do you like little boys? Miss Lena loves little boys." His expression had changed to one of challenge.

"I love boys, especially little ones, and since I don't have a little boy, I can love you, can't I?"

He nodded, but kept looking at her. Suddenly, he smiled. "You can play with my bear and my blanket."

Realizing that that meant acceptance, she hugged and thanked him.

"Nelson will be down for breakfast around eight-thirty," Lena said as the horn blast signaled the arrival of her taxi.

"He'll be . . . Well, if he's here, why am I . . . ," Audrey said as the door closed after Lena.

Audrey took Ricky's hand and followed him to the refrigerator. When she opened it, he pointed to the milk. "Chocolate milk, please."

She poured the milk, thinking that she couldn't wait to give her aunt a piece of her mind. "I've been had," she said, when she didn't see any cooked food in the refrigerator. "I'm thirty years old, and I let my aunt hoodwink me."

He held the glass up to her. "Sugar, please."

"I don't believe anybody puts sugar in your milk, but since nobody gave me any instructions, have a field day."

She put a teaspoon of sugar in the milk, stirred it and watched his eyes sparkle with delight. Now what? Her search for cereal or anything else a child would eat for breakfast proved futile.

"What do you eat for breakfast, Ricky?"

"Cake."

"Don't even think it. Try to bamboozle me, will you." She found some bread, toasted it, and, aware that he had a passion for things sweet, slathered the toast with butter and raspberry jam, poured a glass of orange juice, and sat Ricky down for breakfast.

"How old are you, Ricky?"

He held up four fingers. "Five."

She wondered if that was another of his games aimed at addling her, and it occurred to her that she might have to spend ten or twelve hours dealing with Ricky's little shenanigans. While he ate, she looked around for a coffeepot and the makings of a good cup of coffee. She didn't remember having gone so long after waking

without her caffeine fix. As soon as the smell of coffee
permeated the kitchen, Ricky held out his glass.

"Can I please have some coffee, Audie?"

She would look back one day and know that was the
moment when he sneaked into her heart. "You little
devil," she said, as laughter spilled out of her. A light-
heartedness, a joy, seemed to envelop her, and she lifted
him from his chair and hugged him.

"No, you can't have any coffee, and you know it."

His lips grazed her cheek in a quick, almost tentative,
kiss, delighting and surprising her. "Now be a good boy
and finish your milk."

"Okay. I'm four."

She was about to thank him for telling the truth when
the sound of heavy steps loping down the stairs reminded her that they were not alone, and her belly
tightened in anticipation.

Nelson stepped out of the shower, and as he dried his
body, it occurred to him that a man of his height had to
spend twice as much time on ablutions as a did a shorter
man of slight build. But he wasn't complaining; he liked
his six-foot-five frame. He slipped on a red short-
sleeved T-shirt and a pair of fatigues and followed the
aroma of coffee, his spirits high as he anticipated getting in a solid day's work at home.

He was used to Ricky now, and thought nothing unusual as he strode down the hallway enjoying the sound
of the boy's chatter. He stepped into the kitchen.

" 'Morning, you two. What's for break . . . What
the . . . Who are you, and where's Lena?"

"Unca Nelson, Audie gave me toast. I love toast,
Unca Nelson."

She looked up at him, her lips parted in what was

surely surprise, and immediately her lashes covered her remarkable dark and luminous eyes. *Who was she?* Jolts of electricity whistled through his veins, firing him the way gasoline dumped on a fire triggers powerful flames. He thought he would explode.

"I said . . . Who are you?" Her grudging smile sent darts zinging all over his body; poleaxing him. He groped for the chair beside Ricky where Lena usually sat, and slowly lowered himself into it.

"What are you doing here? If I may ask."

"I'm Audrey Powers," she said. "My Aunt Lena had to go to a church outing today and asked me to fill in for her. I can't believe she didn't get your approval."

Dignified. Well spoken. Yes, and lovely. "Lena get my approval for something she wants to do? She tries, and if she doesn't succeed, she deals with matters in her own way. Thanks for helping out. I have a lot of things to do around here today, and it's good that you're here to look after Ricky. Any chance I could get some breakfast?"

Her reticence didn't escape him. "Cooking isn't something I'm good at, Colonel. I noticed some grits in the pantry. If you can handle grits, scrambled eggs, and toast . . ."

She let it hang, and he knew it was that or nothing, so he didn't mention the sausage or bacon that had to be somewhere in that refrigerator.

"I'd appreciate it, and if you wouldn't mind sharing your coffee . . ."

As if seeing him for the first time, or maybe questioning his temerity, her eyes narrowed in a squint, and suddenly he could feel the tension crackling between them. *Good Lord, I don't need this. I don't know a thing about this woman.*

She got up from the table, exposing her five feet,

eight inches of svelte feminine beauty, rounded hips, and full bosom emphasized by a neat waist. He gulped air as she glided toward the kitchen counter, got a mug of coffee, and handed it to him.

"If you want a second cup, the carafe is over there beside the sink."

Her message didn't escape him; she wasn't there to pamper him, but to take care of Ricky. "Thanks. I'm not much good before I get my coffee."

"Somehow I find that hard to believe, Colonel. I'd bet you do what you have to do, no matter the circumstances."

His left eyebrow shot up. "I try to do that, but how do you know?" He gripped his neck with his left hand as the familiar pain shot through him, took a deep breath, and forced himself to relax. Thank God Lena wasn't there to start her lecture. "When it comes to duty, a man ought to set personal considerations aside. And call me Nelson. Do you mind if I call you Audrey?"

"No, I don't."

"I like Audie, Unca Nelson."

"After conning me into putting sugar into your chocolate milk, I guess you do." She looked at Nelson. "He told me he eats cake for breakfast."

He couldn't help laughing. "Ricky is skilled at getting what he wants. He doesn't get sugar in his milk, and I hope you didn't give him any cake."

"He got the sugar, but I knew better than to give him cake."

"I like cake, Audie. Miss Lena makes cake, and it's good, too."

Her gaze lingered on Ricky, and it was clear to Nelson that Ricky had won her affection. "I'm sorry, Ricky, but I have never made a cake in my life. Excuse me, Nelson, while I get your breakfast."

"It's okay. Miss Lena will make the cake," Ricky called after her.

If only his neck would stop paining him. He had to finish installing the bookcases in his den and get some work done on the paneling in his basement.

He finished his breakfast, started upstairs to his den, and glanced around to see Ricky following him with his "blanket," a navy-blue beach towel, trailing behind him.

"Rick, old boy, you're going to have to give up that blanket. Wainwright men do not romance blankets." He looked up to find Audrey's gaze on him. "They romance women." Now, why the devil had he said that? He whirled around and dashed up the stairs feeling as if he'd lost control of his life. And he always made it a point to control himself and, to the extent possible, his life and everything that affected him personally.

She's not going to detour me, I wouldn't care if she was the Venus de Milo incarnate. And I'm going to give Lena a good talking-to when she gets back here.

Damn! He jerked back his thumb, dropped the hammer, and went to the bathroom to run cold water on the injury. If he had been paying attention, if the picture of Audrey Powers sitting at his kitchen table smiling at Ricky hadn't blotted all else out of his mind . . .

I don't care who she is or what she looks like, I'm not getting involved with her. He laughed. Getting involved was a two-sided thing, and she hadn't given any indication that she was interested. He corrected that. She reacted to him as man, that was sure, but the woman displayed her dignity the way the sun displays its rays. And she kept her feelings to herself. He'd give a lot to know who she was, but he was not going to let her know

that. She was here for one day, and he'd make sure that
was all.

Audrey cleaned the kitchen, something she seldom
had to do at home, and tried to figure out what to do
with Ricky. Finally she asked him, "Where's your room,
Ricky?" Perhaps she could read to him or he could play
with his toys.

The child beamed with glee, grabbed her hand, and
started with her to the stairs. "Up the stairs, Audie. I
have a big room."

She started up with him then stopped. She did not
want to encounter Nelson Wainwright right then, for she
hadn't reclaimed the contentment that she'd worked so
hard and so long to achieve, the feeling that she belonged to herself, that her soul was her own. One look
at Nelson Wainwright—big, strong, and all man with
his dreamy eyes trained on her—and she had nearly
sprung out of her chair. Like a clap of thunder, he jarred
her from her head to her toes, an eviscerating blow to
her belly. She thanked God she'd been sitting down.

"Can you play my flute?" Ricky asked her as they
walked into his room, a child's dream world.

Her gaze fell on a full-size harp, and her heart kicked
over. She'd studied the harp and once had played it well,
but hadn't touched it since her father died. He loved to
hear her play and would sit and listen for as long as she
played.

"I'm sorry, Ricky, but I've never played the flute."

"Unca Nelson can play it. Can you read me Winnie-
the-Pooh?"

She told him she could, and he handed her the book,
surprising her when he climbed into her lap and rested
his head on her breast while she read to him. The

prospect of motherhood didn't occupy much of her thought, because her one experience with love and loving had erupted in her face. And since she wanted nothing more to do with men, certainly not to expose herself in an intimate relationship, she blocked thoughts of motherhood and children. But she couldn't deny that Ricky stirred in her heart a longing for the joy of a child at her breast.

When the story ended, Ricky scampered off her lap, ran across the room, and put a compact disk on his player. Then he ran back and looked up at her, waiting for her response as Ella Fitzgerald's "A Tiskit A Tasket" filled the room. To let him know that she appreciated his gesture, she sang along with Ella while he clapped his hands and jumped up and down laughing and trying to sing along with her.

"Hey, what's going on in here?"

She settled her gaze on the door and the man who stood there wearing a quizzical smile and a soft, surgical collar around his neck.

Ricky ran to his uncle and tugged at his hand. "Audie read my book for me and I'm playing my CD for her."

He picked the boy up and hugged him. "Don't wear her out, now."

"How old is Ricky?" Audrey asked Nelson.

"He'll be five next week." His left hand went to the back of his neck. "He's made tremendous progress since Lena's been with him. I had him in foster care for a couple of months after my brother died, and that experience set him back considerably. I brought him here to live with me, and I could see an improvement within a week."

She watched as he held his neck without seeming to give the act conscious thought. It was not a good sign. "I'm sure he feels the difference. Some foster parents give a child love and understanding as well as care; others don't, often through no fault of their own. Tell me, do you play the harp?" She pointed to the instrument in Ricky's room.

He lowered his head. "Wish I could. That one belonged to my brother, Ricky's father. He played it very well indeed. I put it here in case Ricky takes an interest in it."

Speaking of his brother obviously saddened him, and she found that she wanted to know more, but didn't dare invade his privacy with a personal question.

"I'm hungry, Audie. Can I have some ice cream?"

"May I have some ice cream?" Nelson said, correcting the child. "No, you may not. You get ice cream after you've eaten all of your lunch. You know that."

His face a picture of innocence, Ricky turned to her. "Don't give me much lunch."

She stifled a laugh and got up, surprised by the realization that she had spent half a day enjoying the company of a four-year-old. Still holding Ricky in his arms, Nelson didn't move from the doorway as she attempted to leave the room. Her nerves skittered as she neared him and when she couldn't help glancing up at him, he looked down directly into her eyes and caught his breath. She managed to pass him, but only the Lord knew how she did it.

Something in him, something hard and strong, blood-sizzlingly masculine clutched at her. An aura like nothing she'd experienced jumped out at her and claimed her. And all he'd done was stand there. How she got downstairs she would never know; he blurred her vision and sabotaged her thoughts. Worse, her heart threatened to bolt from her chest. She leaned against the kitchen counter. Nelson Wainwright was just another man, and she had no intention of making a fool of herself over him. A long sigh escaped her. One piece of her father's wisdom claimed that the road to hell was paved with good intentions.

"Girl, you need to get out more," she chided herself. "Stuck in that hospital all the time, you forget what it's like out here."

Within a few minutes, she called up to him. "Lunch is ready, Nelson, such as it is."

He took a long time getting downstairs, and she couldn't help wondering why. "Thank you for taking care of this, Audrey," he said. "I get the feeling this is aeons away from what you normally do."

He stared at the food before him. "I take it you don't cook much. These look good, though," he said of the tuna salad and cheese sandwiches.

"I cook not at all."

Ricky clapped his hands and laughed. "No potatoes and no veggies, Unca Nelson. I like this. I want Audie to stay with us all the time."

He seemed to wince as his hand went once more to his neck, and this time there was no mistaking his pain. Without considering her action, she rose from the table, stepped behind him, and examined his neck.

"What the . . . what are you doing?" he demanded as her fingers began the gentle massage that she knew would bring him relief. "I said . . . Look here. You're out of line."

"No, I'm not," she said, without pausing in her ministrations. "I'm a physician, Nelson, and physical therapy and sports medicine are my specialties. This will make you feel better."

"You're a *what?*"

"A physician. I can't help noticing your problem, and it's clear to me that the pain is killing you."

"Look here! You can't—"

"Don't you feel better already? Fifteen minutes of this and you'll feel like a different man. Just relax and give yourself over to me."

"What kind of—"

"Shhh. Just relax."

"Does it hurt, Unca Nelson?" Ricky's voice rose with anxiety, and she hastened to assure him that she was helping, not hurting, his uncle.

"I'm making him feel better, Ricky. Go on and eat your sandwich. Isn't the pain easing already, Nelson?"

Her fingers, gentle, yet firm, kneaded his flesh. "Relax," she'd said, but how could he, tense as he was with the pain that was his constant companion. He thought of pushing back his chair and leaving the table, but if he did that, he could hurt her. How could Lena betray him so blatantly?

"Relax. Drop your shoulders," she whispered.

No one dictated his life, as Lena was trying to do, and he wouldn't have it. He attempted to move, but with deft fingers Audrey soothed him, easing the pain, giving him the first relief he'd had in nearly a year, reducing the throbbing to a dull ache. Her hands massaged him with soft circular movements, squeezing and caressing. He lowered his head and luxuriated in the relief that her gentle strokes gave him. Then, with his eyes closed, he saw her fingers skimming his entire naked body, caressing and adoring him, preparing him for the assault of her luscious mouth.

Good Lord! His eyelids flew open, and he gasped in astonishment. He'd been within seconds of a full erection. Better put an end to that bit of heaven, and fast. He put both hands to the back of his neck and gripped her fingers.

"Thanks. You're right, I feel better, but can I finish my . . . my sandwich now?"

She went back to her chair, but she didn't sit down. "You're not angry, are you? I know it made you feel better. The problem is that the relief is very temporary. Massage is not a cure."

He didn't attempt to depreciate the comfort she gave him; Audrey Powers obviously knew her business, and anyway, he didn't want to seem ungrateful. "How could I be angry? I feel better right now than I have in a year."

She sat down, her eyes wide and a look of incredulity on her face. "You've been suffering like this for a year? How could you stand it? "

He let the shrug of his shoulders communicate his feelings. "You do what you have to do. Simple as that."

She leaned toward him. "But it isn't necessary for you to suffer like this."

"It is, Audrey, believe me. The Marine Corps is a unit of men in perfect physical and mental condition. We are the crown of the service, the cream of the crop. If you can't hack it, you get a letter of thanks, and that's it. I can handle it, and I will."

"But can't you go to Walter Reed or the Navy Medical Center?"

"Sure, if I want an honorable discharge. I'm not ready for that."

"But . . . You mean your superiors don't know about this?"

He stared at her, and if he seemed threatening, he didn't care. "No, and nobody's going to tell them."

Not many men stood up to him, but he could see from her demeanor that if he pushed her, she would shove right back. Apparently having thought better of

an alternative response, she nodded and said, "I see.
What a pity."

Even at the tender age of four, Ricky appeared to
sense Audrey's concern, for he attempted to pacify her.

"I'm eating all of my sandwich, Audie."

She smiled and stroked Ricky's cheek, though Nelson could see that her thoughts hadn't shifted from him
to the child.

"Am I going to get my ice cream, Audie?"

It amazed him that Ricky had so quickly warmed to
Audrey. Maybe he just liked women; if so, Nelson
wouldn't blame him, and he certainly understood the
boy's preference for this one. She'd gotten to him the
minute his gaze landed on her. Not that it would make a
difference in his life. He meant to give Lena a stiff lecture about her underhanded little trick, and he didn't
expect to see Audrey Powers again.

"If your Uncle Nelson says you may have ice cream,
I'll get you a nice big scoop," he heard her say to Ricky.

With a smile obviously aimed to captivate Audrey,
Ricky said, "Miss Lena always gives me two nice big
scoops."

Laughter rumbled in his chest, and he felt good. He
couldn't remember when he'd had such a light . . . He
pushed the word back, but it returned, and he admitted
to himself that he felt happy. He looked from Ricky to
Audrey, and tremors shot through him at her unguarded
expression as she caught his eye. It was there only for a
second, but he didn't mistake it; she wanted him. It was
there when they met. He'd had enough experience to
know that an attraction as strong as what he felt for her
couldn't be one-sided.

Questions about her zinged through his mind. Why
would a medical doctor baby-sit even for one day?
Where was her office? She wasn't wearing a ring, not

even a diamond, so why was a woman with her phe-
nomenal looks single? He voiced none of them. He
didn't like revealing himself, and therefore he didn't request it of others. He pushed back his chair.

"Thanks for my lunch, and especially for that great
massage. I'd better get back to work while I'm still pain-
free."

He looked at Ricky and marveled that the child didn't
jump from the chair and trail after him as he usually did.
Ricky ignored him.

"After you give me my ice cream, Audie, you can
play with my robot."

He went upstairs, almost reluctant to leave them. As
he worked, their chatter and laughter buoyed him, but
after a time quiet prevailed. He walked over to Ricky's
room to find them both asleep, Ricky in Audrey's lap
with his head on her breast and she with both arms
around him. The longer he stared at them, the lonelier
he felt. Disgusted with himself, he put on a leather
Eisenhower jacket, went out in his back garden, and
busied himself building a fire in the brick oven. He
couldn't say exactly why he did that, but he was certain
of his need to change the scene and recover that part of
himself that, within a split second, Audrey Powers had
stolen. He sat there in the cool and rising wind until
after dark warming himself by the fire and reminding
himself of Carole James, the one woman, the betrayer,
he'd allowed himself to love. Thoughts of her brought
the taste of bile to his mouth.

"I'll die a bachelor," he said aloud, shoveled some dirt
on the coals, and went inside.

Audrey prowled around Ricky's room, fighting a
vexation at her aunt that was rapidly escalating into

anger. It was time Ricky had dinner, she didn't know what to give him, and his hotshot uncle was nowhere to be found.

"I wanna eat, Audie. I'm hungry."

She looked at her watch for the nth time. Seven-fifteen. Of course he was hungry; so was she. She heard the back door close, grabbed Ricky's robot, and rushed to the top of the stairs.

"Who's there?"

"Sorry, Audrey. It didn't occur to me that I might frighten you. Lena isn't back?"

"No, she isn't, and Ricky's hungry. Maybe you'd better phone a restaurant and have something delivered."

He reached the top of the stairs where she stood holding Ricky's hand, or maybe Ricky was holding her hand. The cloud covering her face and the set of her mouth told him to tread carefully. He didn't enjoy tangling with women in the best of circumstances, and this one was angry. Moreover, she had a right to be.

His hands went up, palms out. "I'm sorry about this. I was out back, thinking Lena—"

"She isn't here, and—"

He wasn't accustomed to being interrupted, but he thought it best not to tell her that. "As I was about to say, if you'll tell me what you'd like to eat, I'll order dinner. I know a great seafood restaurant that will deliver full-course meals within forty minutes."

"I'll take shrimp and whatever goes with it."

A deep breath escaped him. Thank God for a woman who didn't feel she had to wash his face with his errors. "Great, so will Ricky. Be back shortly."

He went into his room and ordered dinner for the four of them. He had a few things to tell Lena, but that didn't mean she should be deprived of a good meal.

His hunch told him the less Audrey was required to

do, the better her mood would be, so he set the table in the breakfast room and opened a bottle of chilled chardonnay.

"Would you like a glass of wine while we wait for dinner?" he asked Audrey.

Suddenly, she laughed. "I may be furious with my aunt, Nelson, but I won't bite your head off."

"Thanks for the assurance. You've got such a dark look on your face that I wasn't sure I should say a word to you. This wine is usually pretty good."

"Thanks, I'll have half a glass. I don't drink when I have to drive. Say, that's the doorbell, isn't it? Mind if I answer it?"

"Uh, no. If it's Lena, give her a chance to explain before you blow her away."

She rushed to the door with Ricky and his blanket trailing behind her. "Oh. It's the food," she called to Nelson, looking up to find him beside her. He paid the delivery man and took the food.

"Come on, you two, let's eat."

They sat down, and the doorbell rang again. She moved as if to get up, but he raised his hand. "I'll get it. You should have cooled off by now."

"I never cool off till I get my due," he heard her say as he headed for the door.

"Sorry. Forgot my key. How you doing, Colonel? I know Audrey's mad by now, but I got back quick as I could."

"Audrey? What about me? I'm the one you've got to reckon with."

"Now, now, Colonel. Give me a chance to get in. I bet your neck feels better."

The audacity of the woman! "Dinner's on the table. I'll speak with you later."

"Miss Lena. Guess what. I had toast this morning,

and I didn't have to eat any veggies for lunch. Audie gave me san . . . sandwiches."

"I bet she did. Audrey, honey, I'm so sorry."

"No problem," Nelson said. "Audrey's mad at you, but you two can deal with that later. Right now, she's going to smile if it kills her. We're going to enjoy our food."

They listened to Lena's tales of the famous Crystal Caverns and her picturesque account of the view along the highway as they approached it. He knew she meant to placate both him and Audrey, but he didn't think she achieved either.

"I'd better be going," Audrey said, when they finished eating. "Be sure and take care of your neck, Nelson. My judgment is that if you don't, you will have serious trouble down the road."

It struck him as silly; he didn't want her to leave. "Uh, thanks. I . . . It was good to meet you, Audrey."

"I want Audie to stay," Ricky said. "I don't want her to leave, Unca Nelson. Please don't let her leave."

Audrey knelt beside the child and placed an arm around him. "I have to go, Ricky. I hate to leave you, but I have to go home."

"No!" Ricky ran and stood with his back against the door. "No, you can't go."

Nelson looked down at his nephew and wondered whether Audrey had sprinkled some kind of dust over him and the boy. He reached to lift Ricky into his arms, but the child evaded him.

"I don't want Audie to leave." Then he sat down on the floor and began to cry. "Unca Nelson, don't let her leave. I don't want her to go."

Lena bent to take the child into her arms. "Ricky, darling," she said. "It's time for bed. Kiss Audrey good-bye and off we go to bed."

He twisted away from her. "No. I want Audie to stay."

"I'll come back to see you, Ricky. I promise."

Nelson stared at her. "Don't tell him that if you don't mean it."

She squinted at him, and a frown clouded her face. "I wouldn't dare lie to a child. If you don't want me to come see him, say so."

"I'm sorry." He picked up the recalcitrant boy, hugging and comforting him. "It's all right, Ricky. She said she'd come to see you, and she will. Now give her a big kiss and let her go home. She's tired."

Ricky reached out to kiss Audrey. "I'm sorry you have to go, Audie. Bye."

Ricky didn't usually hold on to Nelson so tightly, and it struck him with considerable force that the effect of so many losses in the child's young life lay close to the surface of Ricky's emotions. He wondered if Audrey reminded Ricky of his mother. She didn't bring to his mind any other woman he'd ever met, and he doubted he would forget her soon, if ever. Remembering her promise to visit Ricky, he turned and, still holding the child, loped with him up the stairs to his room. Who was this woman who had changed both their lives? He put the boy to bed and stood looking down at him as he dozed off to sleep. *You will forget her long before I will.* For the first time in seven hours, pain streaked through his neck.

TWO

Audrey took the Capitol Beltway, bypassing the city to avoid traffic on her way home to 68 Hickory Lane in Bethesda, Maryland, a Washington suburb. The day had been less stressful that she'd anticipated, though she certainly had not expected to meet Nelson Wainwright. She drove into the garage, as she usually did when getting home after dark, and entered her house through the kitchen. Faced with the choice of an apartment in the District or a town house in Bethesda, she hadn't hesitated to take the latter. She loved her home, a gray two-story brick with green shutters set among evergreen trees and shrubs, and she had a special fondness for her garden and the woods beyond.

She walked into the kitchen, turned on the light, and hurried to the hallway to answer the phone.

"Well," Lena said, without preliminaries, "what did you think? Is the problem with his neck serious?"

Audrey rested her left hip against the walnut, marble-top table on which she kept the phone, and took a deep breath. "Aunt Lena, you have a lot to account for. Nelson Wainwright is perfectly capable of taking care of his nephew for one day. I could have been doing I don't know how many things I've been postponing. You didn't need a substitute sitter."

"Yes I did, too. I wouldn't be shouldering my responsibility if I just upped and went off for a day."

"You told me last week that you weren't going on that trip."

"I changed my mind. Besides, his neck's been getting worse. How bad is it?"

"I don't know. Without an MRI or a CAT scan, I wouldn't be able to make a diagnosis. I think it's a problem, and he'd better have it diagnosed and treated."

"That's what I've been telling him. Did you at least examine it?"

And she had almost lost herself in the process. "I did, but I gave him a good shock. I think he thought at first that I was coming on to him. I eased the pain for a few hours."

"What did you think of Ricky?"

Where was all this leading? "You created a problem for me, you know that? I didn't have a reason to go back there till I had to promise Ricky I'd visit him. I'm not happy about that, but I have to keep my word to him."

"Cute little tyke, and sweet as he can be. Don't you think he's handsome?"

"Ricky? He's too little to be handsome."

Lena's sigh of exasperation reached her through the wire. "Not Ricky. The Colonel. Girl, where're your hormones?"

Audrey rolled her eyes and looked toward the ceiling. "Under lock and key."

"Now, child, don't let one little experience sour you on men. Nothing is sweeter in this life than the love of a good man. You're thirty and in the prime of your life. You ought to have a . . . a nice man, Audrey."

One little experience, indeed. That one had been catastrophic. "Right you are, Aunt Lena. We'll talk again soon. I'm pooped."

She hung up, took a shower, and crawled into bed with a mystery novel, but the story wouldn't engage her attention. A nice man. Any normal woman would want one. But the "nice" man who'd sworn he loved her had courted and seduced her, taking her most priceless possession from her, and *then* confessed that he hoped he hadn't made her pregnant because he couldn't marry her. He had a wife, two children and another one on the way, something he kept secret until after he took her virginity.

She sat up in bed. *One of these days, I'll get even with him. If it's the last thing I do, I'll make him pay.*

Nelson Wainwright. Everything about him bespoke honor and integrity. Surely he wouldn't . . . "He's a man, isn't he?" she said aloud. But, heedless of her admonition to herself, her mind's eye flashed into her memory the way he'd looked at her when he stood in the doorway and let her pass him. His eyes . . . as seductive as soft June moonlight over a garden perfumed with roses. Beguiling and . . . She got up, downed a glass of wine, got back in bed, and fought the covers until, exhausted, she fell asleep.

The following Monday morning, Audrey arrived an hour early at her office in the Howard University Hospital. With the files of some of her patients, videotapes, and several relevant research papers, she studied possible causes for Nelson's discomfort, because she didn't believe it could be attributed to a whiplash or that a whiplash would take so long to heal. She was deep into her research when her first patient arrived at nine-thirty.

It's just as well you got out of my head, Nelson Wainwright. She cleared her desk, but Nelson remained in her thoughts. *My interest is purely professional.* She recited it as if it were a mantra. *Purely professional. If nothing else, any man that good-looking is bound to be a ladies man, and I never could stand those.*

"Ms. Carmichael, I'll see Mrs. Blanchard now."

That night when Nelson sat down to dinner with Lena and Ricky, he could hardly bear the pain in his neck, though he wore a soft collar in the hope of easing the discomfort. The memory of Audrey Powers' fingers soothing his neck only made the pain worse. Lena said grace and then asked Ricky to repeat it. The ritual meant as much to Ricky as the evening meal, and he prided himself in being able to say the grace without making a mistake.

"I see your neck's got you again," Lena said. "Here, have some of this salmon paté. I know you like it, so I made a big batch. If you don't do something about that neck, you're gonna be in serious trouble. I declare—"

"Lena!"

She didn't stop eating. "What is it, sir?"

"You always call me 'sir' when you know you're out of line. I don't want this conversation at the table again. And I haven't told you what I thought of your little scheme to get Audrey Powers over here."

She chewed more slowly. "You didn't like her?"

"Lena, you could twist the Bill of Rights till it read like an indictment. *Of course I liked her.* Why wouldn't I? I'm a living, breathing man, aren't I? And for goodness sake, get that satisfied look off your face. I just made a statement of fact."

"I ain't said one thing, Colonel. Me and Ricky just sitting here watching you lose it. All I did was ask her to come stay with Ricky."

"Audie said she's coming to see me, didn't she Miss Lena?"

"Yes she did, darling, and she will, too."

"Watching me . . . Lena, would you please pass me that salmon paté?"

She looked askance at the dish and then at him. "Why, yes. But that's the first course. We supposed to be on the entree now. Have some of this roast pork. It's delicious."

"I'm sure it is. Pass me the salmon paté, please." He loved roast pork, but he was damned if he'd let her tell him what he couldn't eat. "And would you please give me Dr. Powers's telephone number? I want to thank her and apologize for the inconvenience you put her through Saturday."

"You going to call Audie, Unca Nelson? Can I talk to her?"

"When I call her you may, but tonight you're going to bed early, and I am not going to read *Bobby's First Kite* ten times tonight, either."

"How many times can we read it, Unca Nelson?"

"You and Lena are intent on ringing my bell tonight, but it won't happen," he said at the end of the meal. "I'm oblivious to both of you."

He picked Ricky up, hugged him, and gave his bottom a playful swat. "Come on." In a little over three months, the child had become a part of him. And as overbearing and motherly as Lena tended to be, she made his house a home, endearing herself to him in so many ways.

As he left for work the next morning, a feeling, warm and satisfying, pervaded Nelson, a sense that he was leaving, not the empty house that had been his for years, but a home that protected the loved ones who would greet him when he returned. As he headed down the corridor to his office, he greeted several young officers with a smile that reflected his sense of belonging, and noticed the look of amazement on their faces. Surely they didn't consider him a sourpuss just because he didn't grin at them. He dealt with war and espionage, and that did not inspire him to walk around there with a smile on his face. He went into his office and got busy.

Nelson knew he was blessed with an intuitive sense about human beings, an insight that, to his knowledge, had failed him only once—and what a crucial failing it was, misjudging Carole James.

"That's because I let my emotions rule my head," he told himself as he began to search through the thirty personnel folders on his desk. He needed five officers for a mission in sub-Saharan Africa, and the act of choosing nearly unnerved him; they had to be the best, but they had barely any chance of getting back home.

"It's like playing God," he said to himself. "I don't like it." After several hours, his mind made up, he telephoned Captain Jack Jefferson. He believed the man had the stuff that constituted bravery under intense pressure, but he had to be sure.

"Good morning, Sir. Did I make the cut?"

Nelson stood and shook hands with the officer. "First one. This is voluntary, Captain. If you decline, it won't be on your record."

"That bad, huh?"

He leaned back in his chair and summoned the willpower not to grasp his neck. "We'll do all we can to protect you and to rescue you if you get into trouble. You're not married. Would you be leaving a woman behind?"

He watched the man's demeanor and was relieved

when Jefferson shrugged. "There's someone I like, but it's nowhere near serious. I'm free." He leaned forward. "I want to go, Colonel. I've been studying and priming myself for this for the past year. I'll get what I'm going after. Believe that."

Nelson did believe him. The man lived up to his notices. He shook hands with him. "You'll get your orders in a few days. Good luck." He'd almost said, "God bless you," but that would have been out of character, and he didn't want to sound ominous. He chose the other four, sent their names and serial numbers to the Commandant, and called it quits. He had warred with his nerves for ten hours, and it was enough for a day. He headed home, looking forward to Ricky's laughter and Lena's mothering.

Audrey sat on her back porch enjoying a warm evening in late May and thinking how wise she had been to add the porch after she bought the house. She had planted honeysuckle vines, but, to her dismay, that variety didn't have a sweet odor and cutting them down only guaranteed she'd have more of them. She'd have to dip up the roots. The scent of magnolias coming from a neighbor's garden teased her olfactory senses and, when the breeze shifted, a profusion of sweet smells— roses, magnolias, white irises, and heather—rustled her way. She tucked herself into the big chair and dozed off to sleep.

Now who could that be? she wondered, awakening with a start and, praying that it wasn't a patient with an emergency, dashed inside to answer the phone.

"This is Dr. Powers."

"Hello, Audrey. This is Nelson Wainwright. I'm calling to—"

She sat down. *Control, Girl. Control.* "What a surprise! I hadn't expected to hear from you. How's Ricky?"

His silence probably wouldn't have unnerved her if it hadn't lasted so long. She didn't know whether to hang up, ask if he was still there, or just wait.

"Audrey, this is my call," he said after a while. "Thank you for spending your Saturday with us and for helping out. And I apologize for Lena's underhanded way of getting you to do it. I also want to know how you are."

"Whew! Get your money's worth yet?"

"Now look, Audrey. I didn't call to create a misunderstanding where none exists. How are you?"

Cut and dried, was he? Well, if he was after plain truth, she'd give it to him. "You woke me up, so I don't yet know how I am. I was sitting on my back porch sleeping peacefully and almost fell on my face getting in here to answer the phone. How are *you?*"

His laugh, deep and throaty, seemed to rise from the pit of him. "You're murder on a guy's ego. Fortunately, I didn't call to be cajoled. How am I? Rotten. I just sent five good men off to their dooms, and what's more, they know it. I called you because I figured a conversation with you would get it off my mind, at least while we were talking."

She hadn't expected that, and it was on the tip of her tongue to ask why he didn't have a nice warm woman to give him comfort when he needed it, but she thought better of it.

Remembering some of her own frustrations at work she said, "That's got to hurt, and I'm sure it's the part of your job that you like the least. If it wasn't so late, we could go to the annual Mount Vernon Wine Tasting Festival. I've heard it's like being back in the eighteenth century."

"I've never thought of going, but I think I'd like it. We could go tomorrow right after work. What do you say?"

Why on earth had she brought that up? She was being nice, and the idea was convenient because she thought the festival lasted that one day. She didn't want to encourage a relationship with him, but she couldn't back down, could she?

"You still there?"

"Uh . . . okay. I'll . . . It ought to be fun." She said that more to console herself than to be congenial. "By the way, how's your neck?"

"'Bout like it was when you first saw me."

"Oh. I *am* sorry."

"Where are you, Audrey? I mean where is your home?"

"I'm in Bethesda, and I'm home."

"Whoa, there. Didn't mean to suggest otherwise. It's only a quarter of eight. How about meeting me at the Omni Shoreham on Calvert at Connecticut. It's almost midway between us, and I can talk to a person rather than a voice, nice as it is."

"The Omni Shoreham *Hotel?* Is that what you said?"

"The lounge, Audrey. The lounge." She imagined that he'd begun to pace the floor in exasperation, but she rubbed it in nonetheless.

"Sorry. Can't be too clear about these things. Many a gal went for a ride and ended up walking . . . if you see what I mean."

"I wish I could have been looking at you when you said that," he said in a low, almost surly growl. "I don't try to bamboozle women. If I want something from them, I ask."

She leaned back and swung her left leg over her knee. "Nicely, I hope."

"You bet," he growled. "Otherwise, how would I always get exactly what I want?"

"Whew!" she said. "Honey, I'm fanning. Can't you feel the breeze?" His laughter curled around her. "Hmmm. You're a lot looser than I thought you were."

And, whether he knew it, he'd piqued her curiosity and revved her feminine engine. She ought to stay home. Her father, God rest his soul, had always said the way to avoid trouble was to go the other way when you saw it coming. *I'm in no danger. Only a fool would have to learn a lesson twice. And I could use some diversion.*

"Me loose?" he asked in a voice that hinted at surprise. "Just depends on who you are and where you catch me. I can be as loose as they come. How about it? We've already wasted fifteen minutes."

"Okay. Meet you at the Omni lounge in half an hour, and be prepared to watch me eat a sandwich; I haven't had dinner."

"See you there, Audrey, and I'm looking forward to it."

He hung up, and for a full minute she sat there staring into space. What had she let herself in for? Nelson Wainwright had served notice that he was not the one-sided, straitlaced man she'd thought. She hurried into a long, narrow red, gray, and black paisley skirt with a side slit to the knee, topped it with a sleeveless red silk cowl-neck sweater and matching cardigan, and inspected herself in the mirror. Displeased with what she saw, she combed her hair out to fall carelessly on her shoulders and put a pair of large silver hoops in her ears.

"I don't care what his reaction is," she told herself when she recalled how that outfit heightened her sex appeal. "And what *can* he think if I didn't put on any lipstick?"

Although she left home quickly and drove directly

there, Nelson was sitting in the lounge when she arrived. A point in his favor. He didn't allow her to look around for him but went to meet her.

"Thanks for coming. Our table's in the corner, and I got a menu for you. The food here is good."

"I bet you've already eaten," she said, and gave the waiter her order.

"We eat early for Ricky's sake. That boy really is taken with you." He pulled a piece of paper from his pocket. "He drew this this morning, I'm told, and asked if I would mail it to you."

She looked at what she assumed was a little boy and a bird. "This is . . . I don't want to seem maudlin, but it's so dear I could . . . Tell him I love him."

His gaze drilled into her. "I will."

Just that, and nothing else. And why was he looking at her like that? "Is . . . uh, something wrong? I mean . . ."

"You're a beautiful woman, and I'm talking about the inside. I like the way you look in this . . ." he waved his hand around as if he were at a lost for words. "This get-up. But that isn't what I'm talking about. I got an inkling of your caring and concern for others when you were at my house, and I'm more certain of it now. Your patients are very fortunate."

He'd knocked her for a loop. So direct. She was that way herself, but being on the receiving end of such candor shook her a bit. "Thank you . . . I'm embarrassed."

"I see that, and I didn't mean to make you uncomfortable. Certainly not that." His fingers strummed along the beige marble that served as a table top. "I don't often see compassion in my work—that's not what the Service is about—but I value it."

The waiter arrived with her shrimp salad, relieving her of the necessity of replying and plunging them more deeply into a topic that would ultimately lead to intimate disclosures.

"This looks great," she said. "Want some? They put enough here for a family outing."

His gaze bore into her. "I don't have a fork."

She beckoned to the waiter. "Would you bring me another dinner fork, please?"

"Why didn't you ask for a plate?"

The waiter brought the fork, and she handed it to him. "You eat from that side, and I'll eat from this side. Meet you in the middle."

He continue to look at her. "Go on," she said. "Eat. It's good."

He put a forkful in his mouth and savored it. "Yeah. It *is* good. Tell me. What do we do when we reach the middle?"

Bait her, would he? "I haven't figured that out yet. I thought of this . . . our starting from different sides, I mean. You figure out about the middle."

She stared in amazement as his cheeks curved slightly, releasing the beginnings of a smile that drifted slowly toward his eyes and lit sparkles in them. Then his long silky lashes hid his eyes and with his elbow resting on the table supporting the hand that held his head, he erupted in a laugh that seemed to tax him because he couldn't explode in that public place. She thought she would have to pound his back.

When he sobered he said, "Figuring that out won't cost me one bit of sweat. Audrey, learn right now not to hand me those double entendres. I can't resist setting them up to suit my own funny bone. You going to Mount Vernon with me tomorrow afternoon?"

"I said I would, didn't I?"

"You said it would be fun. I hope the people working

and volunteering there are wearing period clothes. Tell me where, and I'll pick you up."

"I'll be driving."

Leave your car at Howard, take a taxi, and meet me at the entrance of Macy's in the Pentagon. Can you do that?"

"Taxi all the way to Arlington? Sure, but—"

"It's on me. You won't have to worry about parking or fighting the traffic, and I'll take you back to your car. How's that?"

She wished he wouldn't look at her like that. Or maybe it was just her, but his eyes seemed to possess her. She felt like pulling off her sweater. Both sweaters.

"I'm not yet sure I should go anywhere with you," she blurted out. "You're dangerous."

He leaned back, hooded his eyes with his long lashes, and let a smile play around his lips. "You should know better than to tell a man he's dangerous. If he wasn't, he damned sight will be."

"Well, now that you've warned me, showed your hand, I mean, I feel perfectly safe."

He laughed, and how she loved the sound of that deep, masculine rumble that seemed to start in a bottomless pit and sneak its way out. "You're as safe with me as you want to be, Audrey. What do you want me to tell Ricky tomorrow morning?"

She stood. "Let's see if the gift shop is still open." She reached for the bill, but he grabbed it first.

"Next time, you pay. This one is on me."

They walked around to the gift shop, where she found a white rabbit that sang "Twilight Time" when squeezed. "Think he'll like this?" she asked Nelson.

"He'll like anything you send him."

She had it wrapped, gave it to him, and they walked

outside to her Mercury Sable. When she reached for the door, he stilled her hand.

"What's your favorite place in Washington?"

Surprised, she said without hesitation, "The Tidal Basin. Any time of year."

"And what perfume are you wearing?"

"I didn't put on any—"

He interrupted. "Maybe not tonight, but earlier. What is it?"

So now he knew she hadn't put on any perfume for him. "Fendi. It's the only one I wear."

He stared down at her. "I like it. It becomes you. Thanks for getting me out of the doldrums tonight. See you tomorrow at four o'clock."

She told him good night, and he stood there until she drove out of the parking lot. She took a short cut through Rock Creek Park; though she didn't like driving that long, unlighted stretch of road, it saved a lot of time. As she reached her house and was about to drive into the garage, she heard a horn toot several times, looked to her right, and saw Nelson as he waved and drove by. *How did you like that? He tailed her home to assure himself of her safety before taking that long trip back to Alexandria. Another point in his favor.*

Nelson took his time getting back to Alexandria. He had plenty to think about, not the least important of which was his powerful attraction to Audrey Powers. He shouldn't have called her, and it made even less sense to inveigle her into meeting him for chat. Admittedly, he needed diversion, but choosing her for it didn't make sense. He parked in front of his house, got out of the BMW, and leaned against the hood. An unbelievable night. A blanket of stars, and not a cloud. And the breeze soft and warm. . . . "Damn!" he said aloud when demon libido began its predatory gallop through his body. "If I had any sense, I'd cancel that date with her for tomorrow. I'm not getting emotionally involved with her or any other woman." He straightened up, went inside, and headed straight for the telephone. But when he started to dial her number, he couldn't make himself do it.

"That you, Colonel?" Lena called from upstairs.

"If it isn't, Lena, you're in serious trouble." He wouldn't be surprised if she asked him for a record of his daily activities. It wasn't that she was meddlesome. She cared about him and Ricky. He met her at the top of the stairs.

"You should be asleep, Lena. Ricky doesn't let you sleep after he wakes up."

"I don't mind. Poor little thing don't like being alone. Sometimes I wonder what he went through before he came to live with you."

He leaned against the edge of the bannister and folded his arms across his chest. "I often wonder the same thing. After my brother was widowed, he had a woman taking care of Ricky, but I knew he'd wanted to change that arrangement, so I did. I placed him with three different foster mothers, and he hated them all, especially the last one. He and I both are happy with our present arrangement."

"Thank you, sir. I'm happy here, too. I never was contented at home after my husband passed. Just couldn't get used to being there by myself. And those big-shot RN's I worked with at the hospital didn't help none. I tell you they were so hinkty, you know, ornery and acting like they were better than us LPNs, that I got fed up and quit."

He patted her shoulder. "You have a home here for as long as you want it." Halfway down the hall to Ricky's room, he stopped and turned around. "Lena, we'll get along fine if you don't try to regulate me."

She laid her head to one side and braced her right hip with her fist. "Y'all can't be serious, Colonel. Ain't a man been born that don't need a little regulating sometime. I was married for almost forty years, and I can testify to that."

He could feel his lower lip sag and his eyes widen. No point whatever in trying to deal with that kind of logic. He'd take it as it came.

"Good night," he said, then checked on Ricky and turned in for the night. If the Commandant didn't need to know every sweep of his eyelash, neither did Lena, and she'd soon learn that it was useless to try.

He got to work around eight-thirty the next morning, his mind full of the evening to come. Thinking that it had to be time for lunch, though he wasn't hungry, he looked at his watch and, figuring that it may have stopped, put it to his ear. He looked at it again. Four minutes after ten. His regular lunchtime, one o'clock, finally arrived at what seemed like quitting time to him. The day dragged until, in exasperation, he began to pace the floor. The phone rang and he rushed to it. Anything, he thought, if it will make time move.

"Hi," she said when he answered. "I'm leaving now, and I should be at the entrance to Macy's in about forty minutes."

He exhaled a long breath. "Great. Are you in a taxi?"

"I decided to take the metro. It stops there, and I won't have the hassle of getting a taxi at rush hour. I'm a five-minute walk from the metro. Oh, and you can pay my metro fare."

"I can pay . . . Whatever. See you shortly."

He had a feeling that her cussedness was deliberate. Hell, he didn't care; he just wanted to see her. His mind told him to slow down. "I can handle it," he said aloud.

He got to the appointed place seconds before she arrived, and gave silent thanks that he had. He didn't want her to think him rude or that he didn't value her company.

"Hello," he said, and smiled to add warmth to his greeting.

"Hi. I made it," she said with a gasp. He wondered if she was short of breath because she had run or because of a health problem.

"I didn't want to keep you waiting. Would you believe I ran up those steps?"

He took her hand and started for his car. "You shouldn't have. I'd wait for you indefinitely."

A smile lit up her face. "You're just saying that to make me feel good. You'd get fed up."

He had to laugh at that. "No doubt about it. I'm a patient man, but I'd know if I was being had, and I'd leave." They reached his car. He opened the passenger door, seated her, strapped her seat belt, and got in. He wondered if she realized he'd been holding her hand.

"I hope the sunset is as beautiful over the Potomac as it was last night over my garden," she said. "It's still light, so the setting should be breathtaking."

"Let's hope so. I love beauty, especially the beauty of nature."

"Me, too. I bought my house because of the garden and the park behind it. It's beautiful."

"Are you going to invite me to enjoy it?" he heard himself ask.

After a few minutes of telling silence, she said, "I don't know. I kind of hope I do."

In the process of starting the ignition, he stopped and

turned to face her. "You *hope* so? It's not within your power?"

She sank down in the leather cushion, crossed her knees, and folded her arms. Comfortable. "It is, but . . . who knows, Nelson? If I ever think enough of you to invite you to my home, I would have gone further with you than is probably wholesome for me."

"But you hope you will."

If her shrug was meant to suggest that the idea was of little importance, it missed the mark. "Well?"

"If I got that far, it would mean that you are an exceptional man. If you are, I wouldn't mind knowing it."

"That's some roundabout thinking if I ever heard any." He started the car and headed for the George Washington Memorial Parkway. "I wouldn't expect a woman like you not to have a man. How important is he to you?"

Communicating with her wouldn't be a simple matter; she seemed reluctant to answer every question he asked. Finally she said, "I don't have one, and what's more I have a contract with myself that says I'm not ever going to have one again, which is why I don't know what I'm doing here with you."

He switched to the center lane and tuned the radio to the classical music station. "That makes two of us, babe. But from the look of things, you and I may not be running this show. If we were, we probably wouldn't be together right now. But we are, so let's enjoy ourselves."

They entered the Mount Vernon estate from the back. Although they didn't consult each other about that choice, each preferred it. The back of the main house faced what had once been a thriving farm: smaller buildings that included the presidential office, smoke

house, mill, outdoor kitchen, stores of harvested and
preserved foods and grain, stables and, of course, slave
quarters. It didn't surprise him when she refused to
enter a slave cabin. Fearing that that reminder of their
country's shadowed past would make her morose, as it
had him, he took her hand and walked more purpose-
fully toward the mansion.

"You making this a habit?" she asked him.

"What? Am I making *what* a habit?"

"Holding my hand."

He looked closely at her, hoping to judge the import
of that comment, but her expression bore the innocence
of newborn child. He decided not to press his luck. If
she didn't like it, she could always move her hand. He
didn't have her handcuffed to him. She left her hand in
his as they entered the house and followed an attendant
to the guest registry where they signed their names.

"Have you ever signed a registry with a man before?"
he asked her.

She released his hand and stepped away from him. "I
have never married, Nelson. I hope that's what you
meant."

Both of his eyebrows shot up. Did she think he was
asking if she'd shared a hotel room with a man?
Stunned, he grabbed the hand that she'd removed seconds earlier.

"Audrey, that was my way of asking if you'd been
married. Period. Nothing more."

"I'm glad to know it. Wouldn't have been the first
time I misjudged a man. Let's see what kind of wines
George Washington produced."

He noticed with not a little satisfaction that she didn't
move her left hand from his right one. After tasting several of the wines, he concluded that Virginia Blush

wines didn't quite measure up to the Sonoma Valley
wines.

"We'll have to come back," she said. "It's closing
time, and we haven't even been through the mansion."

"Does this mean you'll come back with me?" he
asked her.

"Uh . . . Why, yes. This is wonderful, and we've seen
hardly anything."

He squeezed her fingers to be certain he had her full
attention. "It is . . . great, and we haven't seen much.
Granted. What I'm asking is whether you want to see it
again with *me*." He poked his chest with his left index
finger.

Man, could this woman give a guy the once over! Her
gaze seemed to catalogue every pore on his face, trav-
eling from time to time to his eyes.

"What's the verdict?" He almost added, "Judge."

"Sorry, Nelson, but I feel as if I'm in the middle of a
minefield. I like being with you, but you're capable of
confusing me. First, at your house, I got two impres-
sions. You were no-nonsense military brass with no
sense of humor, and you were a sexy . . . a stud."

"What?"

"Let me finish. The other night, I said to myself, he's
a gentleman and he's considerate, but he's a bit more
laid-back than I'd thought. He'll play if I let him."

"Go on."

"Tonight, you've ditched those other Nelsons, and
you're just plain sweet. I'd be smart if I took a bus home
and never saw you again, because I have no idea which
one of these guys you really are."

He looked down into her open, honest face, a face he
liked. "You aren't as tough as I thought you were at first,
either, Audrey. I reacted to your outward feminine attributes and something in your personality that I found

riveting, but there's much more to you. A hell of a lot more, and it pleases me."

She continued to look at him. After a short while she said, "We don't need to go into this right now. Let's find a place to eat."

He stopped himself as he was about to put his arm around her. "If you can handle a Colonial meal, we could eat at the Cedar Knoll Inn. I've heard it's rather nice."

This time, she took *his* hand. "Let's go there."

"Let's leave through the front," he said, examining his watch and hoping they hadn't missed the spectacle. They stepped through the door and with her left hand in his right one, she grabbed his arm with her free hand as she gasped aloud.

"I don't think I've ever seen anything so beautiful."

"Same here," he said, equally awed by the sight of the big round disk in the blazing sky above the vast expanse of the Potomac River. "No wonder George Washington loved this place so much. He lived here for the last forty-five years of his life, you know."

She nodded. "Imagine waking up every day and looking at this breathtaking scene!"

But his gaze had shifted from the beauty that Washington once saw to the sparkles in her eyes and the joy of her smile. "Yeah. I can just imagine."

They walked the several blocks to the restaurant, and since she didn't talk, he left her to her thoughts. He liked the Colonial charm of the Cedar Knoll Inn and imagined that if it were winter, and there was a fire in the hearth and a lighted Christmas tree beside it, he'd do something stupid like asking Audrey Powers if he could see her on a regular basis. But since it was May and he still had all of his faculties, he banished the thought and beckoned the wine steward.

When she frowned and assumed a serious mien, he realized he'd been holding the back of his neck. "It's nothing I'm not used to, Audrey. Let's not let it spoil our evening." She shifted her gaze downward, and he knew she would let it pass as he wished, but that keeping her mouth shut about it didn't please her.

"Did you like the Virginia Blush wine we had at the estate," he asked her, "or should we get something else?"

"Uh hum . . ." The wine steward cleared his throat as if they had forgotten his presence. "We have some excellent estate-bottled champagne, sir."

He looked at Audrey. "Would you like that?"

She nodded. "Why not? I'm not driving."

"I am, which means I'm only going to have one glass of it."

"Hmmm. Prudence becomes you." With her head angled slightly to one side, she patted the back of it and rolled her eyes in the manner of someone experiencing pure delight.

He wondered at her playfulness. "It can be a hell of a handicap, too." After the steward filled their glasses with the bubbling liquid, he raised his glass to Audrey and winked. "Here's to Prudence, whoever that may be."

Seemingly preoccupied, she ate little but enjoyed a second glass of champagne. When she accepted the wine steward's offer to pour a third glass, he wondered if she was being reckless.

"Sure you want to drink that? It tastes great going down, but it can rattle your cage if you're not used to it."

She squinted at him, held the glass to her lips and let all of the champagne stream down her throat. "You won't let one single thing happen to me. If you can be trusted with the entire United States of America, I'm in perfect hands."

What kind of thinking was that?

"You wait right here," he said as they walked out of the restaurant, "I'll get my car. Be right back."

"It's such a pretty evening. I'm going to—"

He interrupted her. "Please. I won't be gone but a couple of minutes. Okay?" Not wanting her to use up any more energy than was necessary, considering the amount of alcohol in her system, he walked away without waiting for her answer.

Fortunately, no traffic detained him, and he returned to her within minutes. They got into the car and, as he always did for the women who rode in his car, he buckled her seat belt.

"Did you have a good time?" he asked her.

"Uh-huh. It was great. Makes me realize I spend too much of my time working. I love music, but I don't know when I last went to a concert. Work. Work. Sometimes ten or eleven hours a day." She rested her head on his shoulder. "Hmmm. This is nice." Within minutes her deep breathing told him that she had gone to sleep.

He parked in front of 68 Hickory Drive, cut the motor, and looked down at the woman who had unwittingly drawn him into a act of intimacy by using his body for a resting place. For a long while, he gazed at her face, relaxed and beautiful in childlike repose.

He swore beneath his breath. "Get thee behind me, Satan." He didn't want to wake her up, but the longer he watched her the more he wanted her. And he wanted her. He thought of his pledge to himself that he'd die a bachelor. Then he let himself believe that if Audrey Powers wanted a man in her life on a permanent basis, she'd have one. But only for a minute. He was where he was because he kept his own counsel and didn't depend on anybody, male or female, to do his thinking.

He eased her head from his shoulder, got out of the car, and walked around to the passenger's side. Opening the door, he reached in with both hands and slipped her to the edge of the seat. As if he'd touched a live wire, he jerked away his hands. Her body, soft but firm in his hands, was like a jolt of electricity, kicking his libido into high gear. She opened her eyes and looked at him.

"What're you doing? Am I home?"

He blew out a long breath. "You are, and I was trying to get you out of the car without waking you, but since you're awake . . ." He let it hang.

"Goodness. I slept all the way, didn't I?"

Her voice was softer than he'd ever heard it, gentle and sweet. He had to get her into that house and leave her without . . ."

"Want to get out? I'll see you to the door."

She held out her hand and stepped out of the car. Even tipsy, her graciousness and feminine charm beguiled him. He grasped her hand and walked with her along the winding cobblestones to her front door, and when he held out his hand for her key, she surrendered it without hesitation. He opened the door, walked in with her, and waited for her next move.

"The light," she said in a rising voice that caused him to wonder at her panic, as she clutched his arm.

He found the switch, flicked it, and a soft glow illumined the foyer. "What's the matter?" he asked her.

"I'm scared to death of the darkness if I'm in a building. Thanks."

"You all right now?"

"A little unsteady, but I can walk up the stairs."

"Want me to carry you?" He said it jokingly, but she looked up at him as if she wasn't sure.

"Okay, I'll carry you up, but you have to get out of your clothes by yourself because I have not yet achieved sainthood."

"You have so," she said. He carried her up the stairs thinking that, for a tall woman, she didn't weigh much.

"You are so sweet," she said when he set her on her feet and flicked on the hall light. He stared down at her. What he wouldn't give to hold her and love her into a stupor! As if she knew he had to come back to earth, she reached up and kissed his cheek.

" 'Night."

"Uh . . . 'Night. I'll lock the door." He raced down the stairs, extinguished the foyer light, turned the automatic lock, got into his car, and breathed deeply. How strange! Tipsy as she was, it apparently hadn't occurred to her to detain him. And that kiss on his cheek was so puritanical it could have been intended for Ricky. He looked up, noticed a light in what he assumed was her bedroom, and started the car. He hoped she didn't make it a habit of testing his decency.

Three

Audrey woke up the next morning and bolted upright in bed. After rubbing her eyes, she grabbed her head. *Oh, no! What on earth did I do to myself?*

Gingerly, as if to avoid contact with the air around her, she raised her head and looked around. Surely she hadn't dropped her blue silk designer suit in a heap on the chair. As she climbed out of bed, she remembered the previous evening—or part of it—with Nelson, and sat down. For the first time in her life she couldn't recall events that might be of the utmost importance. Thoroughly annoyed with herself for having drunk so much wine . . . She slapped her forehead with the palm of her right hand. Good Lord! How much champagne did she drink? One glass was her limit and that with desert after a full meal. What kind of woman called a man to ask what happened the night before? She padded to the bathroom, showered, brushed her teeth, and wished she'd made coffee first.

When she finally sat down with a cup of coffee in front of her and was about to give herself the luxury of ignoring the ringing telephone, she remembered that, as a doctor, she couldn't do that.

"Hello," she said, having hurriedly scalded her throat with that first precious sip of black coffee.

"Hi. How do you feel this morning?"

Good heavens, it was *him*. "How do I . . . maybe I'd better ask you how *should* I feel?"

"Pretty rotten, I would think. I asked you if you were sure you wanted to drink that third glass of champagne. Suffice it to say you drank it. Did you get some coffee?"

Third glass. He had to be kidding. "I just got one swallow before I had to answer the phone."

"Sorry about that. If you have any Alka Seltzer, take a couple. Next time I won't let you drink that much."

"You mean I didn't disgrace myself? You want us to go out to dinner again?" His loud laughter was not what she wanted to hear. Besides, it sent a pain shooting through her head. "Well, did I?" She didn't try to hide her annoyance.

"Of course not. You were sweeter than I dreamed you could be."

"Nelson! Please don't tease. I remember your buckling my seat belt when we left the restaurant, and that's all."

"Really? What a pity! I don't know when I've been with such a loving woman. I'll never forget that kiss, and you don't even remember it."

"Now, you look here. I did not kiss you."

"No? Then come on over here and look at my face. I haven't washed it yet."

"You must have gone somewhere after you left me."

"Come on, now, Audrey. What do you take me for? No woman could follow you."

"Ohhhh," she groaned. "Nelson, I do remember thinking you were a gentleman. Not last night, but earlier. I think I may have made a big error."

"I wouldn't lie to you, Audrey. You kissed me and told me I was sweet. I practically fell down the steps."

"Steps? What steps?"

"Uh, the ones in your house. You weren't sure you could walk up the stairs, so I carried you."

She looked at the cup of cold coffee and closed her eyes. "I don't want to hear any more. This gets worse by the second."

"Not really. You aren't very heavy, you know, for a tall woman. I thought I'd have to stagger up those stairs, but you couldn't weigh more that a hundred and twenty-five. A delightful armful."

"A hundred and thirty. Nelson, promise you won't mention any of this to me again."

"Well, I'll try, but when I think about that kiss, there's no telling what I might do. And then, there's—"

"Stop it! Whatever else I did, please forget it and don't ever mention it to me."

"I'm sorry, sweetheart, but there are things a man *never* forgets. If you don't want me to mention it to you, I'll respect your wishes, but I will always remember."

"*Sweetheart!* Oh, Lord, are we that chummy? If it turns out you're pulling my leg, you'll look for a good undertaker."

"If you're in that frame of mind, you can bet you'll never know. However, under certain conditions, I won't remind you of this wonderful evening we had."

"Blackmail, huh? All right, what will it cost me?"

"I'll let you know. Think you can make it in to work? Remember you car's down at Howard, so you'll have to call a taxi about half an hour before you want to leave home. I have an appointment first thing this morning, or I'd go get you."

"Thanks. I expect I would have gone into the garage, failed to see my car there, and called the police. Uh, did we have a good time yesterday? I mean serious now?"

"Yes. And after dinner, we got into my car, you put

your head on my shoulder, went to sleep, and woke up after I cut the ignition in front of your house."

She'd been holding her breath. "What else, Nelson?"

"I opened your door with your key, we walked into the foyer, and you almost panicked because it was dark. I turned on the light, carried your upstairs, and, at the second floor landing, you told me I was sweet and kissed my cheek. I left you right there, but I will never know how the hell I did it."

"Thank you. And you are sweet. You really are."

"Don't rub it in. Sweetness is not an attribute that I ever tried to acquire. Mind if I call you this evening?"

"Uh . . . no. I don't mind. Have a good day."

"You, too."

She threw the cold coffee into the sink, refilled her cup from the coffeemaker, and drank it while she dressed. She had better watch herself with Nelson Wainwright. He didn't want to get involved, and neither did she. But neither of them was acting like it.

She got to her office on time to find her ten o'clock appointment waiting for her. By then, the woman should know that arriving an hour early only meant that instead of spending forty-five minutes at the clinic, she stayed there for an hour and forty-five minutes.

"Good morning, Mrs. Blanchard," she said, and waved as she passed the waiting room. None of that Ms. stuff for Mrs. Blanchard; she wanted the world to know she was married.

A little after ten when she had begun to feel more like herself, the voice on her intercom advised her of an urgent call from her Aunt Lena. Fearing that something might have happened to Ricky, she left Mrs. Blanchard in the therapy room and hurried to her office to take the call.

"What is it, Aunt Lena? What's the matter?"

"Who said anything was the matter? Honey, I need to be off Saturday, and I was wondering if you could keep little Ricky for me."

"Aunt Lena—"

"Hear me out. Little Ricky fell in love with you, and love is not something he's had a lot of, and the Colonel's got things to do. So if you could—"

For the next forty-five minutes, with her head the size of a watermelon, she had to deal with the back, neck, and shoulder pains as well as the imaginary aches that plagued Mrs. Blanchard, and she was not in the mood for her aunt's shenanigans. Further, Mrs. Blanchard would not take kindly to having been abandoned during her treatment.

"Aunt Lena, nothing you can ever do is going to get me tied up with Nelson Wainwright or any other man, and if you knew what I went through with that last one, you'd back off. Get Pamela or Wendy to do it. They're teachers, they should love children, and Wendy is single. Please excuse me now. I have a patient in there on that table who is probably freezing to death and mad as the devil."

And the less I see of Nelson Wainwright, the less likely I'll wind up in his bed.

In that respect, at least, she and Nelson were of one mind. At about the same time, he sat at the conference table, one officer removed from the Commandant— more an indication of his status than of his rank—and forced his attention on the prospective meeting of the Marine Expeditionary Unit (MEU). Audrey Powers spent too much time in his thoughts, and he had to do something about it.

"I want you to go to the strategy meeting, Wainwright,"

he heard the Commandant say. "You've got plenty of time
to prepare for it. See me in my office after this."

"Yes, sir." He didn't want to go to that meeting, but
sending him was the Commandant's way of letting him
know he was in for a promotion.

He left the Commandant's office feeling as if his hard
work had begun to pay off. He had the man's confidence, which meant that unless he faltered, he was on
his way to becoming a four-star general. Better get this
star first, he thought as he headed for home that afternoon.

He had prepared himself to spend the evening im-
mersing his mind in MEU matters, but Ricky met him
at the door squeezing his Audie rabbit, as he called it,
and opening his little arms for a hug and a toss in the air.
Nelson went through the ritual, greeted Lena, and got
into his room as quickly as possible. Inside, he looked
around the room . . . at his king-sized walnut sleigh bed,
the huge desk facing the picture window, the Isfahan
carpet that had cost him a fortune, and all the little
things sitting around that spelled his personality. And he
thought of Ricky and his loving greeting, of Lena and
the efforts she made to make him comfortable.

"Is being married so different?" he wondered aloud.
"I have a woman and a child who depend on me for protection, well-being, and care. But I don't have the joy
that this life is supposed to give."

He sat down at his desk and tried to work. He didn't
remember a time when work hadn't been the drug that
pacified him when nothing else would, but instead of
opening the bulky confidential file, he stared out the
window, not knowing what he saw.

The patter of Ricky's feet in the hall outside his room
brought him to the present and the duty that lay before

him. The door opened, and he swung around in the swivel chair.

"Unca Nelson, Miss Lena said Audie isn't coming to see me Saturday. Can I call her, Unca Nelson?"

He picked the child up and sat him on his knee. "Audie is a doctor, and she may have to take care of patients. She's very busy."

"If I hurt my finger, she'll come. Won't she?"

If there was ever a mixture of guilelessness and deviltry, Ricky possessed it in good measure. Nelson didn't want to encourage that kind of devious plotting, but he couldn't keep the smile off his face.

"If she was taking care of another bad little boy, she couldn't fix your finger, so see that it doesn't get hurt."

"But she said she was coming to see me."

"And she will. I'm sure of it. We can't call her now, but if I talk with her, I'll tell her you want to know when she's coming to see you. All right?"

"I guess. I gotta go help Miss Lena shell the beans."

He raised an eyebrow. "You know how to shell beans?"

"Yes, sir, and I can pull the ends off the string beans, too. Idle hands are the devil's workers."

He stared at the child. "Run that past me again? Oh, well. You're smart, and I'm proud of you."

He was about to turn around and attack the work on his desk when Ricky suddenly ran to him and hugged him, smiled, and ran off before Nelson could react. In his mind's eye, he saw Audrey reach up and kiss his cheek.

"Oh, hell," he said, and reached for the telephone.

"Hello, Audrey," he said when she answered. "This is Nelson."

"Hi, I remembered that you said you'd call me this evening, but I thought you'd call later. How are you?"

"Work is staring me in the face, and Ricky just laid

out a devious plan to get you over here. Plus, I'm dealing with something I'm not familiar with."

"What's that?"

"Well, two things actually: this woman who keeps fooling around in my head, and this sudden procrastination. I suspect there's a connection."

"At least it's *your* head."

"Still got the effects of that champagne? Maybe if you hadn't drunk it after you had that Virginia Blush wine—two glasses, I think—it wouldn't have done you in so thoroughly."

"Whatever, Nelson. You witnessed a first and a last."

"I believe that. Ricky will be five day after tomorrow. Think you could pop by and say hi to him? That would make his day perfect."

She didn't answer immediately, and he wondered at her silence. "Thanks for telling me. Of course I'll come. But didn't you think I'd like a chance to get him a present and wrap it nicely?"

"You just bought him a present. He doesn't need . . ."

"You said it's his birthday, and I'm not going to visit a five-year-old on his birthday without bringing him a present."

"All right. All right. Don't get uptight. I just remembered it a few minutes ago."

"Isn't he having a party?"

"I guess I should have planned one, but Lena takes him to preschool, and I don't know the children or their parents."

"Never mind. We'll give him a party. I'll be over around four-thirty."

"I'll be waiting to see you." It was the truth, but he could have kicked himself for telling her.

"Uh . . . me too."

He didn't care for the grudging way she said it, but if

he mentioned that, he'd give away his feelings. He said, "See you in a couple of days," and hung up.

To his amazement, the Commandant's words came back to him and, when he opened the file and began to read, what he saw there piqued his interest. Immediately, solutions to the problems presented to him began to swim around in his mind. He couldn't write fast enough, got his mini-recorder and made notes. Nearly two hours later, he heard Lena banging on his room door.

"I declare, Colonel, Ricky has to eat his supper, and it's been done I don't know how long. You all right in there, sir?"

Reluctantly, he stored the tape recorder in its case, locked the file in his desk, opened the door, and gazed down at the distraught woman. "Sorry, but I didn't hear you knock earlier. I was working."

Her face, open and reflecting the caring that she never expressed in words, made his heart race. How had he been so lucky as to have this woman in his home, lightening his burdens and loving Ricky as if he were her own child? Money couldn't pay for that.

"You're a blessing, Lena," he said, careful not to sound emotional. "You're just what this house needed."

Her smiles were his thanks. "You're a good man, sir, and you deserve the best I can do."

He walked with her down the stairs and on to the breakfast room where Ricky jumped from his chair and went to meet him.

"We're not having beans, Unca Nelson, 'cause I only shelled three." He held up three fingers. "I was in Miss Lena's way, so I drew this for Audie."

He looked at what he supposed was a tree with a bird in it. Ricky always drew birds. He'd have to take the child to a bird sanctuary. The thought that came to him brought a smile to his face; if *he* had to draw something for

Audrey, it would probably make her blush. How did you draw a kiss? He brushed his fingers over Ricky's hair.

"You did good. Never let a woman forget that you think she's precious." And never forget where that leads, a niggling voice reminded him.

Audrey had looked forward to Nelson's call, but she had anticipated talking with him after she had finished her dinner, enjoyed a long, delicious bath, and could lounge in comfort while they spoke. *There I go, wishing for trouble. It's better this way.*

After dinner, she called her younger sister. "Wendy, did Aunt Lena call you today?"

"Yes, and I'm suspicious. Aunt Lena thinks something's wrong with you if you don't have a man in your life."

"You're telling me? I'll bet she was a femme fatale in her day."

"I'm sure of it. She painted such an idyllic picture of Nelson Wainwright, his home, and his little nephew that before I knew what she was doing, she'd inveigled me into spending all day Saturday with a five-year-old. Not a five-year-old ready to turn six, mind you, but one's who's having his fifth birthday between now and then. I can hardly handle those ten-year-olds I have to deal with every day much less a five-year-old."

"Not to worry, Sis. Five minutes after you meet Ricky, he'll have you eating out of his little hand."

"Girl, you're fantasizing. Why'd you refuse to do it? Don't tell me she didn't ask you first, 'cause I know she did. There's an eligible man over there. Pam's married, and you're next. What happened? Did he lay an egg with you?"

She stifled a laugh. "I'd be surprised if Nelson Wainwright had any experience with eggs other than what he found on his plate. That man does not inspire disrespect, and mentioning him and eggs in the same breath is tantamount to exactly that."

"Whew! He must be some brother if he made that kind of an impression on *you*! I gotta see this one. Aunt Lena can definitely count on *me*. I'll be over there Saturday morning on time."

"You do that. If you're smart, you'll leave your heart in your car."

"I'll leave my . . . What do you mean? Do you have a stake there, or is he bad news for a gal who wants a family?"

She pondered that for a moment and decided to let it pass. If she answered truthfully, she would say yes to both, but she'd keep her thoughts to herself. In any case, she knew she could depend on Nelson to steer her sister in the right direction.

"You're own your own, and you be sweet to Ricky. You hear?"

"Of course I will, and I'll give you all the details, including what I think of the Colonel."

For reasons she couldn't fathom, after hanging up she wanted to call Nelson. Wanted it badly. She cleaned and polished the bathroom mirrors, dusted the Venetian blinds, washed the lingerie and stockings she'd worn that day, and wrote out a check for her credit-card bill. As she wrote, she had a sudden understanding about her desire to phone Nelson. Proprietary as sure as her name was Audrey. That call would be an act of possessiveness, of establishing her right to phone him, detain him, and talk with him. And why? Because another woman, a very good-looking woman, would ring his doorbell Saturday morning at eight o'clock.

I'd laugh if I thought it was funny. And I'm getting off this merry-go-round before the thing starts turning.

As if she'd never made that pledge, she got in bed with a copy of Thomas E. Ricks' study of Marine Corps life, *Making the Corps*, and fell asleep reading it.

Two afternoons later, when Nelson reached home after his day in the office, he parked in the garage in order to get Ricky's birthday present into the house without his seeing it. He'd have to maneuver that when Ricky's attention was centered on something. Audrey. That would do it. He'd bring it inside when she came.

As usual, Ricky greeted him as if he were the most special person on earth. It gave him a feeling of relevance that neither flying that Super Cobra AH-1W copter nor crippling or destroying enemy targets gave him. Nurturing and caring for his nephew for only four short months, receiving and returning the child's love, had sustained him as rain nourished plants, and had made his life meaningful. Somehow, responsibility for Ricky validated him.

He picked up the boy, tossed him in the air, caught him, and delighted in his happy giggles. "You stay down here with Miss Lena while I change my clothes."

"Will I have a birthday tomorrow, too, Unca Nelson?"

"Sorry, no. We get one birthday a year. Your next one comes when you get to be six years old. Stay where Miss Lena can see you."

"Okay. I could help her, but she said I have to get a little bit bigger before I can make biscuits."

The seriousness of Ricky's expression made him suppress what would have been a laugh. He ruffled the child's hair. "That's a fact." He dashed up the stairs.

"And Unca Nelson," Ricky called up after him, "She said I don't have any business downstairs in the family room. I stayed up here."

"Good boy. I want you to obey her."

"I do, Unca Nelson. Just sometimes she talks so much I can't remember everything I'm supposed to do."

"As you get older, you'll manage," he said, and ducked into his room as laughter finally escaped him. When she put herself to it, Lena could really talk. He'd have to tell her that giving a five-year-old ten different instructions in five minutes confused the child and guaranteed his disobedience.

He changed into a collared, yellow T-shirt, khaki trousers, and a pair of Reeboks, and got downstairs just as the doorbell pealed. As he opened it, he worked at settling his pounding heart. He wanted the caller to be Audrey.

"Eeeow," Ricky squealed when he glimpsed Audrey. "Eeeow! Audie! Audie!"

"Ricky, darling!" She knelt and gathered him into her arms, stroking and hugging Ricky as he plastered her face with kisses.

Nelson gazed down at them, his heart constricting in his chest. Steeling his willpower, he shoved his hands in the pockets of his trousers and shifted his gaze to the carpet on which he stood. "I wonder how long I'll manage to stay out of her?" he asked himself, knowing he couldn't count on her, that she lost herself in him whenever they came together. "It's hooked both of us."

"Hi." She smiled up at him. He couldn't bear it and, in self-defense, looked toward the door where he saw two girls and a boy about Ricky's age edge into the half-open door, evidently having tired of waiting for their cue to enter. Behind them, a red-nosed clown followed. Audrey released Ricky so that he could see who she'd brought with her. Obviously curious, but pleased as well, Ricky gazed up at the clown, a twelve-year-old boy who lived next door to Audrey's sister Pam. When the children introduced themselves to Ricky, joyous noise signaled the beginning of the party.

As he observed Ricky's self-assurance and his ease with the other children, he thought of the child he'd brought to his home a mere four months earlier: solemn, sad, withdrawn, and fearful. He knew then the miracle of love. Only the love and caring Ricky had received from Lena and himself could have changed the boy in so short a time.

"I love you, Audie," he heard Ricky say. "I love you a lot."

"Y'all, let's go downstairs now," Lena said to them.

Ricky stared up at her, his face mirroring his confusion. "But Miss Lena, you said I couldn't go down there."

"You can now."

"When did you do all this?" Nelson asked Lena as he looked at the balloons floating from the ceiling and rising—on strings—like trees from buckets of red, green, and yellow sand.

"Audrey helped me this afternoon while Ricky was taking his nap." She gave each child a paper hat and a noisemaker.

He figured Ricky's sense of awe matched his own, as the child stared in wonder at his surroundings. Nelson went to the baby grand piano, the material possession he cherished most, and played the first two bars of "Happy Birthday." Lena, Audrey, and the children joined him in singing it. If he had ever been happier, he didn't recall it.

A delighted Ricky opened gifts from each child, a

covered wagon train set from Audrey, and a wigwam
from Lena.

"You not supposed to overlook your Indian side, son,"
Lena said. Ricky thanked her, running in and out of it,
laughing and bubbling with joy.

"You're right, Lena. My maternal grandmother was a
Seminole, and my mother was proud of that heritage."

He looked at the wealth of gifts surrounding Ricky
and decided to give him his present after the children
left; he didn't know their financial circumstances and
didn't want them to feel as if they lacked something.

Ice cream, cake, lemonade, the tooting of horns, and
the strumming of little fingers on his precious baby
grand gave him a strange, unfamiliar high, something
beyond contentment and a desire to share his blessings.
He would take any risk to protect his country's children,
to provide a safe haven for their innocence and their development into mature individuals. He wondered if his
fellow Marines knew why they wore the uniform, if they
had a personal reason—as he did—for wanting to defend their country. He hoped so. He hoped that every
one of them knew the love he witnessed in the children
and in Lena and Audrey as they showered each child
with affection.

After an hour and a half, Audrey told him she had to
take the children home. "I promised their parents I'd get
them home by seven, and it's six-thirty."

So much that was inside of him wanted to spill out,
words that would let her know his feelings and, because
of their power, would demand that he know hers. But it
wasn't the time. Too soon. Maybe ill-conceived. Maybe
just not appropriate. Maybe it was only the moment,
seeing what she did for Ricky and, by extension, for
him. He hoped she couldn't read his thoughts, but it
seemed to him that if a discerning woman looked at him

right then as carefully as she did, that woman could see the pattern of his soul. He settled for thanking her for helping to make Ricky's birthday so splendid.

Instead of holding her as he wanted to, he knotted his left hand into a fist and caressed her cheek with it. Her eyes sparkled, and he wasn't sure, but it seemed as if her head tilted toward his fist returning his gesture. He stepped away from her and jammed his hands into his pockets. Yet he didn't doubt that his eyes mirrored both his desire and his ambivalence, his feelings as well as the effort he was making to control them.

"We'll talk," he said, not trusting himself to say more. She nodded, hugged Ricky, and left after the children got Ricky's promise to come and play with them.

Ricky hugged his leg in loving tribute. "Do I have to eat dinner, Unca Nelson? Can't I just have some more ice cream and cake?"

Nelson couldn't help grinning as he looked down into the child's face. Five years old and already aware that if you had things going your way, that was the time to make demands.

"You've got one more present coming after you eat your dinner."

The child's face bloomed into a smile. "Okay. What is it, Unca Nelson?"

"You'll know after you eat your dinner."

He needed a few minutes to himself, some time to sort out his feelings, to understand what was happening to him. He ran up the stairs, went into his room, and closed the door. He had always been honest with himself and with others. In his head, he meant to avoid emotional involvements and to see to it that no other woman made him the butt of a painful joke. Swearing eternal love and fidelity, accepting his ring, and letting him find her in his bed with the guy who would be best man at their wedding. Oh, no. He let the closet door have the brunt of his fist. *Oh, no. I'm not going there. Period.*

After dinner, he gave Ricky his first bicycle and watched him master it within five minutes. Observing the child's happiness reminded him of the birthday party, and he had to struggle to keep his feelings about that and about Audrey in abeyance.

"I think I'll turn in," he said to Lena.

"Yes, sir. I expect you got a lot to think about."

He stared down at her. "What do you mean?"

"It was Ricky's party, but you the one that got the message. Your life ain't normal, and now you know it. Y'all sleep well." She walked off singing her favorite hymn, and he wondered if she had some magical powers that let her see inside of him.

His steps fell heavily on the stairs, and when he reached the landing his body sagged as if he'd just run miles. He still thought of himself as an unattached man, free to do as he willed, to go and come as he pleased. But he could no longer lock the door, throw his duffel bag into the trunk of his or a USMC car, and go off without a care or a thought as to when or whether he would return. He was father to Ricky and responsible for Lena's well-being, neither of which he minded, and he didn't shirk responsibility. He wanted to watch Ricky grow and to shape him into a man, but how could he do that while fighting for peace in first one part of the globe and then another? He was the delight of Ricky's life, his anchor. What would happen to the boy in his absence? He doubted that Lena would be able to comfort him. One more stumbling block in his path toward the top. But he'd get there.

"I'm developing backward," Audrey said to herself that evening, in a moment of self-reprimand for her failure to discourage Nelson's gestures signifying the existence of more than a platonic relationship between them. The tenderness with which he'd stroked her face while his eyes told her things that reduced her to a pile of mush . . . A long breath, more a wish than a sigh, seeped out of her. She had to stop thinking about Nelson. Hadn't she daydreamed herself into what had proved to be the most devastating experience of her life? What was it about Nelson Wainwright that she seemed unable to resist?

She answered the phone praying that it wasn't Nelson, but she didn't want to speak with her Aunt Lena either.

"You still refusing to mind Ricky for me day after tomorrow?" Lena asked her.

"Aunt Lena, I'd do most anything for you. You know that. But I am not going to let you make a mat of me for Nelson Wainwright. Left to you, I'd be in his path so much he'd have to step over me. No thanks. I'm not doing it."

"Suit yourself. If it doesn't happen one way, it'll happen another. You can't do a thing about the Lord's will."

"Come on, Aunt Lena. Just because you want it doesn't mean the Lord has any such plans."

"You'll see."

Nelson opened his front door at twenty minutes before eight that Saturday morning to see a woman's finger reaching toward the doorbell. Attired in a loose T-shirt and shorts, he was on his way out for a sprint around the block. Looking down at the woman, he saw at once a resemblance to Audrey. He told himself not to get mad, but he knew that was useless when he began to grind his teeth, a sure sign that he was about to show his irritation.

"Who are you?" he asked her, knowing the answer before she opened her mouth. To her credit, she gazed up at him, seemingly unflappable.

"I'm Winifred Powers. Nice people call me Wendy. I'm helping my aunt out today. She said—"

He held up his right hand, palm out. "Don't tell me what she said. I already know. She has an emergency that she can afford to take a day off to attend to because she has these nieces who have nothing to do with their Saturdays but baby-sit." He allowed himself a smile; at least he hoped it looked like a smile since the shape of his mouth was the same as when he sneered. "Are you a doctor, too?"

She didn't bat an eyelash, but ignored the taunt as one would excuse a child. "Nope. I'm a teacher. Can't stand the sight of blood. What do you do when you're not cross?"

"I do my best to avoid sharp-tongued females."

She let her gaze travel from his feet to his head and back, then she pursed her lips as if in thought. "I don't imagine you have much success. Not unless the women you meet are afflicted with extreme shortsightedness. Mind if I come in?"

She brushed by him, turned, and asked, "Where's Ricky?"

"That's a good question. I've got two floors and a family room in the basement. Have fun." Lena would be wise to have left before he got back; he had a few things to tell her, and he didn't expect her to like any of them. She had promised to give him notice when she wanted to take an extra day off so that he could choose the person who would take care of Ricky. But she hadn't done that, and no one had to tell him she had deliberately forgotten her promise. He ran down the steps. Lena could bring all of her nieces and throw in her sisters for good measure, but he wasn't going to a doctor and he wasn't going to get married. If she didn't already know that, she soon would.

The next morning, Sunday, Audrey accompanied Wendy for breakfast at the home of their older sister, Pamela, as they did at least once a month. The three sisters enjoyed a close, loving relationship, but that morning Audrey joined them with reluctance. She didn't feel like being joshed about Nelson Wainwright, and she knew she could expect it. Her mind seemed to have glued itself to him, for she could hardly think of anything or anyone else.

The nation's Capitol was most beautiful in spring, and they ate outside on the deck shaded by the elms and the willow tree that Pam's husband, Hendren, had brought as a sapling from south Florida. Pam's garden of roses released a delicious perfume, adding to the loveliness of the morning.

"Did you make grits and sausage?" Wendy asked Pam.

"I wanted waffles and strawberries," Audrey said. "Nobody's waffles taste as good as yours." It was the Saturday morning breakfast their mother always made for them when they were growing up. Pam had assumed the parental role after their mother passed and, after she married, had continued the Saturday morning breakfast ritual. But Wendy had refused to eat waffles anymore, and switched to the Southern soul breakfast that their late father had preferred.

"I cooked all of that," Pam said, "and I'll have it over

there on the sideboard in a minute. I hope you've got room in those pants you're wearing, Wendy."

Wendy sipped her coffee. "I didn't buy these pants for comfort, girl. These things are man-tamers."

"Yeah," Audrey said. "If you crossed Pennsylvania Avenue and Fourteenth at noon on a Friday, there'd be a ten-car collision."

"You said it," Pam put in. "Speaking of man-taming, what did Nelson say about your visit yesterday?"

"Nelson?" Wendy let out a sharp whistle. "Girl, you gotta go over there and get a load of Nelson Wainwright. The man oozes sex. I took one look at that brother and decided that I've been right all these years."

She turned to Audrey. "You need your brain cells repaired." She let herself contemplate the grits, sausage, and scrambled eggs on her plate, then she smiled. "Maybe you don't. Any woman with sense would stay out of that guy's way. Now of course, if he came on to her, showed a little interest . . . now that's another matter." She savored the food. "Pam, I eat grits every day, but they never taste like yours."

"That's because you're the one who's cooking," Pam said, referring to Wendy's piddling culinary skills. But Audrey knew her older sister's thoughts had not left the subject of Nelson Wainwright. Pam was one of those people who could wring a topic bone-dry.

"Why are you avoiding him, Audrey?" Pam asked. "Didn't the two of you get on?"

No point in lying about it. "We got on fine, but I've had it with these good-looking men who ooze charm and charisma and know it. One of 'em is plenty for me."

Wendy put her fork down and stared at her sister. "Bull. I saw him, remember? I'll bet anything your problem is you fell for him like a rocket hurtling through space, and you're scared to death. Seen him since the day you took care of Ricky? Huh?"

"You know I was at Ricky's birthday party."

"That's not what I meant. You gave yourself away. Ever kissed him?"

Now what did she say to that? She wasn't about to tell anybody that she'd kissed Nelson Wainwright on the cheek when she was tipsy and didn't remember doing so.

"Get off my case, will you, Wendy? I didn't come over here this morning to get the third degree."

"Okay," Wendy said, "Just drawing a few things to your attention. Incidentally, Ricky talked about you nonstop, and his doting uncle did not discourage him. I got the impression that you're evening shade and morning sunrise in that house." She slapped her hand over her lips. "Ooops! There I go running my mouth."

"Did Nelson complain about Aunt Lena getting you to replace her without his permission or even telling him in advance?" Pam asked Wendy.

"After he got over the shock of seeing me there that time of day, he was cordial to me. I don't know what he said to Auntie after I left. The problem wasn't Wainwright; it was Ricky. That child could hardly stand the sight of me. He looked up at me, poked out his bottom lip, and walked off. The Colonel apologized. Said Ricky wanted you. Let me tell you, it was a long day."

Pam put a bowl of mixed fresh fruit on the table and sat down. "This is very interesting, Wendy. You say the Colonel is the epitome of sin itself, and yet you were not affected by all that masculinity?"

"Not a crumb. I knew right off he was disappointed that I wasn't Audrey. Besides, I learned long ago to like who likes me. We haven't talked about anything this morning but the Colonel. The man's ears must be burning like wildfire. Give him a try, Audrey. He's worth it."

Sunday evening, Nelson ruminated about Lena's strange behavior. He could not understand why Lena thought he might not accept a professional woman, especially a teacher, to baby-sit for Ricky. He couldn't figure out her agenda. And surely, if she wanted him to get involved with Audrey, she wouldn't toss Audrey's sexy younger sister at him. He waited until after Ricky was asleep and knocked on her door.

"Why?" she asked him. "I had to get Wendy because Audrey refused to come. She full of notions, that one."

"What kind of notions?"

"She thinks I'm trying to palm her off on you."

"You aren't playing matchmaker? I sure thought you were."

She placed her left hand on her hip and looked up at him in a way that emphasized the differences in their height. "Would I do a thing like that, Colonel?"

He couldn't help laughing at her antics. "Lena, you would and you are. But listen to this, and I am serious. The next time you have to be away, let me know in advance. I have a right to decide who takes care of Ricky. Got that?"

"My goodness, sir. I feel like I'm back in grade school. I know how to obey orders. Uh . . . you speak to Audrey since she was here last?"

"No. Why?"

"That girl hasn't said one single solitary word to me since that night. I declare."

He wasn't going to let her change the subject. "I meant what I said, Lena. Your nieces are fine women, but I am the one who decides who takes care of Ricky."

"Yes, sir. You sure are."

He left her, thinking he hadn't accomplished one thing. Later, sitting on the deck with his feet propped against the railing, he observed the rolling clouds and the moon that flicker in and out of them. In two weeks, he would have to go to Camp Pendleton for five days and he wasn't looking forward to it. He knew the material and was confident that they could work out a program that Congress would approve. If he did his job, a recommendation for promotion was as good as his.

So he couldn't understand his reluctance. He ought to be waiting impatiently for the day, his engines revved and ready. Admittedly, he would rather not leave Ricky at a time when the child delighted so much in their bonding. A warm wind blew over him, warm and light like Audrey's kiss on his cheek. He put his hands behind his head, leaned back in the chaise longue and let the memory of her mouth on him torture him until he felt it in the pit of his gut.

"I'm damned if I do and damned if I don't," he said as he left the deck, went up to his room, and dialed Audrey's number.

Four

"Hello, Audrey, this is Nelson," he said when she answered. "How are you?"

"Oh! I wasn't expecting to hear from you. I don't know why; I just wasn't."

That rambling suggested that her nerves matched his. "I wasn't expecting to call."

"Then, why did you? Call, I mean."

"Because you won't stop fooling around in my brain. I want to talk with you."

"Gosh, I'm sorry. If you'd show me the way out of your head, I'd leave."

"Clever. But I don't want that tonight. Anything but that."

Her voice, soft and feminine as if she had dropped a mask, a personality cloak, and revealed her own self, came to him over the wires sweet and tender. "What is it, Nelson? What's the matter?"

If he could only hold her, bury himself in her and let himself live! "I need a resolution to whatever it is that's happening between us. And something is. If you tell me I'm mistaken, I won't believe you."

"Nelson—"

"Don't say it. Talk to me, Audrey. If you don't have anything to say, recite a poem. Anything. Just stay on the line and talk to me."

"Something is wrong. Can't you tell me?"

He was beginning to question the wisdom of calling her. Letting his emotions overflow was not his style; indeed it was contrary to his character. He had to come to grips with this thing he had for her and deal with his indecisiveness about her. Irresoluteness wasn't a part of his make-up. He meant to take charge of his next career move, and he'd begin to plan for Ricky and Lena in case he went on mission and didn't return. But he couldn't focus, because Audrey was in the way. There. Everywhere. A light in the distance promising to illumine his life if only he would come close. He shook his head the way a bird releases water from its feathers.

"Oh, yes," he said in answer to her question. "I definitely can tell you *that*, but I don't want to terminate such friendship as we have."

"And what you're thinking would do that?"

His half-smile wasn't one of amusement, but of self-mockery. "What I'm thinking wouldn't, but what I'm feeling . . . that's another matter."

She took her time answering, and he understood that she finally appreciated the true measure of his seriousness. "You've touched on my reason for not agreeing to stay with Ricky. I suspect my aunt of matchmaking, and . . . Nelson, I've walked down that road and I still bear the wounds."

"You're not alone. I've done the same, and believe me, the result was not an enhanced belief in human virtue. Are you saying we do nothing about it? Ignore it and wonder whether we could have made . . . what it would have been like? That's what you're suggesting?"

"I'm a strong person, Nelson, but I'm not sure I'm up to two emotional tornados in this life. If I'm going to hurt, I'd as soon not have the accompanying humiliation."

So he was right. She cared and, as candid as she was,

if he asked her, she would probably admit it. He'd have to give his next move—if he made one—a lot of thought.

"We can talk by phone, can't we?"

"Nelson, I don't think . . . All right. We can do that. I'll come see Ricky when you're not home. Is that all right?"

"As long as you visit him, I don't care when you do it. He fell in love with you, so much so that he resented your sister and let her know he wanted you."

"She told me. She also said you impressed her."

He didn't want to hear that, either. "I didn't try."

"I'm sure of that, and so was she. Uh, when you call me, let's not talk about anything important?"

Finally, he could laugh, a genuine belly laugh that thundered out of him, releasing the pent-up energy, throttling the nefarious libido that had him in hand when he called her, and turning his world right-side up. He laughed until his spirits lifted.

"Ah, sweetheart, you're so priceless. We'll talk about movies and plays we've seen, places we've been, paintings we hate, boats we've sailed on. I can think of dozens of impersonal topics, and we can discuss them with words and leave what we feel out of it."

"Oh, Nelson, I'm ashamed. I guess that sounded awful. I just don't want us to talk about our . . . uh . . . re—"

"Our feelings for each other? Then we won't, but at least you've admitted we have them. I'll call you, and I wouldn't mind hearing from you. Good night and sleep well."

"You too. Good night."

Audrey got out of bed, where she had been relaxing and trying to understand her feelings, her ambivalence about Nelson, and her growing sense that she couldn't control those feelings as she did everything else in her life. She walked around her bedroom, looking at pictures of Pamela, Winifred, and herself as children and of her late parents and grandparents.

There was so much love in our home and in my life as I grew up. I thought anyone would love me because every person I knew seemed to dote on me. Lord, was I naive! Just the inexperienced and trusting girl that such men as Gerald Latham prey on. I want to love, and I want someone to love me and care for me. I want to love Nelson; everything in me wants him, but how can I leave myself open to that kind of pain again?

She moved from her bedroom to the living room, put on a Diane Reeves CD, got a handful of Chupa Chups lollipops, and sank into the cushion of her favorite chair. With so much on her mind, she wouldn't sleep, so she might as well enjoy herself. At the end of the Reeves CD, she put on an early Billie Holiday cassette, and fell asleep as Billie's voice haunted her with "Good Morning Heartache," a song about the fruits of misplaced love.

She awoke the next morning with a kink in her neck and as tired as if she had never slept. She showered, drank two cups of black coffee, and went to work, vowing to keep her distance from Nelson Wainwright and all other attractive men.

Nelson went to the meeting of the MEU, presented the views of the command center, and did what he went there to do. Moreover, he did it in spite of the frequent divergence of his mind to Ricky, Lena and Audrey. Thus, he was unprepared for the adulation of his peers and the more senior officers.

"The Corps must be proud of you, Colonel," a three-star general told him. "I'm glad you're on our side."

"So am I, Sir. It's a thing for which I give thanks daily," he said, standing away from the shorter man so as not to dwarf him with the ten-inch difference in their height. He knew well the importance of remaining humble and respecting his superiors.

"I expect to hear more from you," the general said.

Nelson thanked the officer but kept his focus on the report he had to give to the Commandant.

He could identify success as well as the next man, and he didn't doubt that he would see a smile on the Commandant's face when he returned to the Pentagon. As he left the scene of his triumph, a restlessness pervaded him, had ever since he left home, and he couldn't banish it. After five days of conferences and forced camaraderie, he walked out of Ronald Reagan International Airport in Washington, got into his car, and headed for Alexandria and home.

As he neared the house, he began to anticipate the pleasure of Ricky's smiles, hugs, and chatter, and the joy of being *home*. The Corps did well by him, but he had yet to eat food cooked in an Army, Navy or Marine Corps kitchen that equaled Lena's gourmet fare. He parked in front of the house, dashed up the walk, and opened the door.

Not a sound. And what a letdown! His heart began a wild thudding in his chest. Where were Lena and Ricky? He dashed up the stairs, then down in the basement. *God, please don't let anything happen to them!*

He sat down and put on his officer's thinking cap. *Where would Lena leave a message, if indeed she'd left one?*

On a hunch, he went into the kitchen where he found Lena's green notepaper affixed to the refrigerator door.

"I'm sorry I had to go see about my uncle," he read. "You weren't here to ask, so I did the best I could. Ricky is staying over at Audrey's place till either you or I get back."

It didn't occur to him to telephone her. All that talk about not wanting to get involved wasn't worth the breath she used to utter it. As long as she had Ricky, she had *him*, and a woman smart enough to get a medical degree knew that. Ordinarily, he was slow to anger, but before he could reason about it, his irritation exploded into an anger bordering on rage. What did they take him to be?

He took the Capital Beltway with as much speed as he dared to drive and, within what had to be record time, parked in front of Audrey's house. *Whatever happened to front porches?* he asked himself, irritated because he couldn't pace, but had to stand still on the little landing.

His gaze fell on the brass angel that served as a knocker and its tiny replica that was the doorbell. So much like her. He rang the bell. Which one of those women was she, anyhow? And what was taking her so long? He couldn't wait to get his hands on her, to shake some sense . . . A string of expletives streamed from his mouth at the thought of squeezing her to him and sinking into her. That's what he wanted. He wasn't angry, he admitted to himself, and he hadn't been angry. He'd been nearly out of his mind for her and he'd used Ricky's being in her home as an excuse to get to her. He told himself to calm down.

She flung the door open wide, saw him, and her face glowed in a smile. All he could do was stand there and gaze at her.

"Where's Ricky?"

Her eyes widened and she stepped back from the door. "Why, he's upstairs in the guest room. I was just reading him a story. He's been busy all day, and he's wiped out. Hello, Nelson. How are you? Come on in."

He'd been upbraided before but, in his memory, not with such precision. "Hello, Audrey," he said in a voice that surprised him with its softness. "I don't suppose you and Lena planned this?"

She whirled around and left him standing there with no choice but to follow her. He took his time. He was not a rude man, and he had patience. Plenty of it. But he had limits, too. She had claimed she didn't want an intimate relationship with him, but as she stood at that open door with the expression of one who welcomed her lover, her face belied her words. He'd made her angry, but so what. Wasn't he furious? He watched her head up the stairs, her hips swaying in a look-but-don't-touch kind of sexy arrogance that sent his blood arrow-straight to his groin.

He walked up the stairs, slowly taking his time and remembering the pleasure she'd given him when he climbed those stairs before with her tucked in his arms. This wasn't the time for his libido to get out of control, he thought, as twinges of desire began to mock him. He heard the sound of soft singing and stopped. A lullaby. Brahms' Lullaby. Uncertain now as his anger deserted him entirely, he followed the low, sultry voice to the end of the hallway and stepped to the entrance of the open door.

He gasped, and nearly lost his breath, poleaxed by the scene before him. With the wall taking his weight, he stared, lost in them. She sat in the middle of the bed, her knees crossed in the lotus position, holding Ricky in her lap with his head against her breasts. She sang with her eyes closed and gently swayed. He had a sudden and powerful urge to exchange places with the child, and it cost him every bit of his will power to stave off the evidence of desire.

Evidently realizing that Ricky was asleep, she slid off

the bed, placed him beneath the covers, and kissed his
cheek. Then she placed the white bunny in the bed beside
him, turned out the light, and started toward the door.

"Oh! I didn't know you were here. I thought you
stayed downstairs. I—"

"Forgive me, Audrey. I don't know what got into me."
She looked up at him, and he could see the hurt he'd
caused her. She shook her head as if denying something.

"You . . . I wouldn't hurt you for anything. Can't you
see I . . ." He couldn't hold it back any longer. "My God,
Audrey. I need you. Baby, I need you. *I need you!*" He
ached to feel her flesh beneath the pads of his fingers.
She attempted to pass him in the doorway, and he didn't
blame her.

So close. The smell of her hair and the perfume she
wore made havoc with his olfactory sense, and with her
body less than a finger's length from him, he smelled her
woman's fragrance and thought he would lose his mind.

"Audrey!" Her eyes glistened with unshed tears, and
he grabbed her hand and folded her into his arms.
"Baby, don't you need me?"

"Nelson, please. Oh, Lord. I don't want to start—"

"We started it the minute we met. Don't you know
that? It hit you the same way it got me." He tipped up
her chin with his index finger and stared into her eyes.

Her lips quivered as he gazed at them, glistening with
sweetness, and when she moistened them with the tip of
her tongue, he said, "To hell with everything else," lowered his head, gripped her shoulders with one hand and
her buttocks with the other and, tasted her at last.

Her lips parted and he plunged into her, rolling his
tongue around in her mouth, tasting her sweetness and
anointing every crevice.

* * *

His big hand began to stroke and caress her buttocks, creating a storm within her, as his tongue danced in and out of her mouth, twirling and tantalizing until she thought she would burn. Her nipples ached and her feminine center pulsated with desire. His groans excited her, and she grabbed his hand and placed it on her right breast. At once, he lifted her to fit him, plunged his hand into her scooped-neck blouse to free her breast, and sucked her nipple into his mouth. Ah, the sweetness! The God-given pleasure! She pressed his head to her breast and arched her back, giving him all. She heard her keening cry, but couldn't help herself. The feel and smell of man intoxicated her. Frissons of heat shot through her, and her blood pounded in her ears as tension gathered in her vagina. He stepped away from the door, closed it with his foot, and pressed her body against it while he nipped and suckled her until she felt the moisture flow from her. He moved back from her, but not quickly enough. She didn't care; she wanted him to feel what she felt, to want her as badly as she wanted him.

"Nelson, honey, I can't stand this. It's . . . it's too soon for what we need right now."

He set her feet on the floor, put both arms around her, and locked her to him. "I suppose you're right. Recently, I've known we'd be like this together. I've also known that with you and me, it will be all or nothing. And that makes it look kind of bleak."

He stroked her hair and her cheek and then rubbed her back, as if substituting those gestures for what he wanted and needed. "But, baby, you move me like no woman I ever knew!"

With her hand in his, she walked down the steps to the living room. "Let's sit in here. Why were you so angry with me?"

"I don't think I was ever really angry, although I certainly reacted as if I were. Emotions can play tricks on us. I acceded to your request that we not see each other. If I'm honest, I'll tell you that anger was an excuse to see you and to get to you any way I could."

"But you still don't want a relationship with me, and I'm not willing to risk one with you or any other man."

He took her hand, turned it over, and looked at her palm. "You know, when I was at the Naval Academy, I was the hit of every party because I read palms and predicted great things for my friends." He pressed her palm flat. "What I see in here . . ." He folded her palm. "Either we stay away from each other, or we give in to it and accept the consequences. This is nothing to play with."

"Do you believe in palmistry?"

His right eyelid lowered in a half-wink. "Did I tell you I read that in your palm? I didn't have to look into your hand to know that."

He continued holding her hand, his face softened with a smile so sweet and loving that her heart seemed to turn cartwheels in her chest. When he squeezed her fingers, rivulets of heat cascaded through her body, and as quickly as the speed of sound, desire gripped her, nearly strangling her. She wanted to lower her lashes to protect from him what she could not hide from herself—the overwhelming, rampaging need to have him deep inside her, loving her.

But she couldn't stop looking at him; his gaze bore into her, reading her and possessing her until, with a hoarse groan, he capitulated and a second later she felt his tongue in her mouth, this time possessively, claiming, demanding, knocking her senses out of order, destroying her willpower. Her nipples begged for his attention, and, as if he understood her need, he pinched and caressed them until she grabbed his hand and pressed it to her breast. She didn't care if he thought her brazen, wanton; she arched her back and, with her hand at the back of his head, led his lips to her breast.

The male heat in him jumped out at her as he suckled her until she wanted to stop thinking, stop breathing. Stop everything but the feeling of what he was doing to her. Then his fingers stroked her beaded breast, while his marauding tongue slipped in and out of her mouth. Like a well drill seeking an underground spring, he laid waste to her inhibitions and fears. She thought she would die with her need of him, and her legs spread of their own will as moans streamed from her throat.

Shock waves snaked through her when suddenly he was not touching her. Her eyelids flew open to read the question on his face. *What had she done?*

"Nelson, I . . ."

His head moved from side to side. "It's all right. But you believe me now when I say it's nothing to play with. The next time, we'll make love. You understand what I'm saying?"

"I do. I should have stopped before it went so far."

"It wasn't your responsibility alone; it was ours. I wanted to stop, but if you needed something as badly and as long as I've needed to make love with you, you'd understand that wanting to wasn't sufficient. It was almost like asking an eagle to give up his wings. Audrey, if I ever love you . . . I mean, if I ever *love* you . . . !" He stood. "I'd better get moving."

She walked with him to the door, her hands locked behind her back, symbolic of her struggle for control. "If I had the guts where you're concerned that I have with the rest of my life, I'd tell you not to leave."

"When you're ready, you won't have to say a word, and we'll both know."

He ran the back of his hand across her nose, barely touching her skin. "See you."

She didn't reply but, like a robot, closed the door behind him, locked it, and trudged back up the stairs. *Thank God I don't drink to escape.*

She tiptoed into the guest room and looked down at Ricky, hugging his bunny as he slept, "Somebody should have told me that I have a maternal instinct," she said, leaning over to kiss his cheek. "I always thought I wanted no part of it. Maybe it's just Ricky."

Or maybe it's Nelson, and your desire for him brings out this maternal feeling in you, an inner voice whispered. *Nelson! Nelson!* It would be a long night.

Lena returned four days later with a black band around her arm. "What's that for?" Nelson asked, pointing to the badge of bereavement.

"I thought everybody knew what it was for. People don't go around wearing black bands for nothing. Where's Ricky?"

"Where you left him. School's out and I couldn't take him with me to the Pentagon. Lena, I don't want to go over this again. I thought we agreed that if you had to be off, you'd let me know in advance, and *I* would choose someone to stay with Ricky."

She pulled off her hat, and her hands went to her sides. "I didn't get no notice, sir, and neither did my uncle. Otherwise, I don't think he'd a gone to sleep that night."

"You mean he—"

"Right. He didn't wake up the next morning."

He put an arm across her shoulder as he looked down at her. "Lena, why didn't you try to get in touch with me? You had my cell phone number. Is there anything I can do? Are you out of pocket? I can't tell you how sorry I am."

He didn't remember having seen her so lacking in aplomb and, for once, she appeared to be speechless.

"I was real upset, sir. Uncle Claude was a father to me from the time I was ten and my own father passed. Uncle Claude was the youngest of the six brothers and the last to go." Moisture accumulated in her eyes, but she didn't let herself shed tears. "Now my generation is out there in the front."

"Don't dwell on that, Lena. Ricky and I are your family. I'm here for you."

"You know I thank you, sir." She pulled off her hat, and looked around and smiled. "Place is nice and neat. You know, Colonel, you got a lot to offer." She walked over and faced him. "I know you don't want to hear this, but your generation is right after mine and pretty close, too. You done any thinking about a mother for Ricky? He loves me, but, Colonel, you don't call your mother "Miss," and he'll soon know the difference."

He wanted to glare at her, but considering what she'd just been through, he thought it prudent to indulge her.

"It may upset you to know this, but my sense of obligation to Ricky doesn't extend to marrying for his sake, and while my appreciation for you is considerable, neither in breadth nor depth does it cover your meddlesomeness. Understand?" He patted her shoulder to soften the remark.

"Pshaw!" she said, placing her hands at her hips. "With your parents and your brother gone and no women hanging around you—least not any that I know about—that leaves me the only person who can tell it to you exactly like it is."

"And you're bound to do your duty. Right?"

"Well, sir, duty ain't something I ever shirked."

"Getting you to mind your business is like getting roosters to lay eggs." Walking away from her, he glanced over his shoulder before she had time to wipe the grin off her face and realized that she enjoyed joshing him. "Would you call Audrey and ask her to bring Ricky home?"

"Yes sir-ree. Right now."

He went to his room and closed the door. He wasn't in the mood to do battle with his emotions, and he didn't feel like going to bed hard and aching.

About an hour later, he had reason to question his sanity. Ricky's squeals made the house come alive, and an insane kind of madness skated through him. He jumped up from his desk chair, flung open his room door, and dashed to the stairs, where he saw Ricky tugging at Audrey's hand as if urging her to climb the stairs with him.

"Unca Nelson. Unca Nelson," Ricky yelled, dropping Audrey's hand and running up the stairs to meet him. He held out his arms and the child sailed into them, giggling and hugging him—and teaching him the wonder and purity of a child's love. As he held Ricky—his only living blood relative—to his chest, the measure of his love for the boy startled him, and he closed his eyes as he dealt with the moment.

Ricky's tugging at his necktie triggered a change in his mood, and he opened his eyes only to have his heart lurch when his gaze fell on Audrey, who watched them from where she stood several steps below them. His right hand gripped the bannister. All that she felt, needed, and desired of him blanketed her face. *If only he could know for certain that she wouldn't let him down!*

"Hello, Audrey," he managed at last. "Thanks for

bringing Ricky home and for taking care of him." He put Ricky on his feet.

"Unca Nelson, I wanna show Audie my room."

"She's seen your room, Ricky."

"But she didn't see my harp."

"Yes I did," Audrey said. "Hello, Nelson. Keeping Ricky was a pleasure."

He looked down at the anxious expression of Ricky's face. "I don't see why Audrey can't have a look at your harp. Ask her to come up." He looked at Audrey, making sure that they understood each other. "I'll be in my room. Got some work to do."

Pain shot through his neck and shoulders and, without thinking, he grabbed the top of his right shoulder, grimacing as he did so. He didn't know how much longer he could stand it, but he didn't see an alternative. Days would pass when he felt like a normal man, and then the gnawing ache, the piercing, stabbing, and pricking like hot arrows into his flesh would set in and torment him for a time. As soon as Audrey left the house, he'd take a hot shower and enjoy some relief.

Unable to work as the pain intensified, he waited for Audrey to leave, for he didn't want to meet her in the hall while only wearing a towel around his hips. The light tap on his door startled him; Ricky didn't knock on his room door, but called out instead. He got up and went to open it.

"Mind if I come in?"

"It isn't wise, Audrey."

"I know, but you're in pain, and I can give you some relief even if it's only temporary."

He didn't know how he would react if she put her hands on him. "It's not a good idea."

"Are you telling me you'd rather suffer than use a little self-control?"

She had to know he wouldn't shy away from that kind
of challenge. With a shrug of his right shoulder, he
stared down at her. "Okay. Shoot your best shot. What
do you want me to do?"

He could see her professionalism asserting itself.
"Pull off your shirt and stretch out on that bed facedown."

He walked toward the bed and began pulling off his
shirt. Then, for some unfathomable reason, he began to
laugh.

"What amuses you?" she asked, obviously nettled.

"I was thinking about the legion of non-commis-
sioned marines who at one time or another would have
liked to say that or something similar to me." He
stretched out. "Darling, please be gentle." The words
barely escaped his lips before he sat upright, shaking
with laughter.

"It never occurred to me that you're a nut," she said.
"Lie down."

He thought he would fly out of his skin when she
straddled his hips. Her fingers began their magic,
kneading, pressing, and massaging until the tension and
pain began to ease and he had to fight off the urge to
sleep.

"It's okay to sleep," she said. "It means you've relaxed. You'll feel better now." She moved from him,
leaving him bereft of her warmth and nearness.

"I can't thank you enough. I feel like a different
man."

"Stay there for a while and rest." Her voice seemed to
drift away, and he realized that she was leaving the
room. "I'm going to call you this evening, because I
have something important to say to you. 'Bye."

He heard Ricky at the door, got up, and opened it.

"Unca Nelson, Audie said I can learn how to play my harp. I want to."

"I'll get a teacher for you, but you may be too young. That harp is big. Why don't we start with the piano? I'll teach you."

Ricky's eyes, so like those of his brother Joel, beseeched him. "Then can I learn the harp?"

"Yes."

"One of my friends at day school wants to come play with me. Can she, Unca Nelson? Can she?"

A girl, huh? "Of course. Where does she live?"

"Down the street." Ricky rubbed the side of his head. "Her daddy works in Washington. She gave me her phone number."

"You know it?"

"It's 287-6199, and her name's Stacey."

He nodded. This business with females must be a Wainwright curse. "All right. We'll call her later," he said, wondering what he'd do when Ricky reached puberty.

"What's her last name, Ricky?" He wanted to know something about the girl's family. Not that he was a snob, but given his high-security work, he couldn't be too careful.

"I don't know, Unca Nelson."

Down the street, huh? He believed in walking carefully and, if he could manage it, leaving nothing to chance.

"Come on, son," he said. "Let's go for a ride. We'll be back shortly," he called to Lena.

Nelson headed his black BMW in the direction Ricky indicated. "You know Stacey's house?"

"Yes, sir. It's big and red, and it's got a white lion in the grass. That's it right there, Unca Nelson."

He noted the number, about three good blocks from

his home, made a U-turn and drove past it at greatly reduced speed so as to read the name on the door. Petin.
Hmmm. He thought of the World War II French general
and traitor, Marshall Henri Pétain, and wondered about
the spelling of the two names. Maybe it was nothing,
but that name didn't fit with Stacey.

"You sure that's the house?"

"Yes, sir."

Hoping to divert Ricky's thoughts from Stacey, he
drove to the Old Town and bought them each double
cones of strawberry ice cream. Caught up in Ricky's delight in sitting at an open air cafe, eating ice cream and
watching a Ferris wheel in the distance, his mind settled
on them as a family.

I don't spend enough time with Ricky, he said to himself. *If I want him to have my values, I have to be the
one who teaches him about life.*

*But what about your compulsion to get back into ac-
tion overseas?* a niggling voice taunted. He would
worry about that when he had to.

"Let's go, buddy. Your Uncle Nelson has some work
to do."

At home, he polished his report and checked it for errors. Satisfied, he printed it out on his office stationery,
locked it in his drawer, and went downstairs to the
kitchen where he found Lena and Ricky watching
Sesame Street.

"When that's over, we'll start your piano lessons,"
he said to Ricky. "I'll be downstairs." Minutes later,
Chopin's "Polonaise" filled the room as he lost himself
in the music that flowed from his fingers.

"Am I gonna be able to play like that, Unca Nelson?"

He hadn't heard Ricky enter. "Of course you will.
You can do anything you want to do if you work hard
and play by the rules."

"Gee. Can I start now?"

He slid over, placed the child's right thumb on middle C and began the lesson. Two hours passed, and neither of them noticed until Lena stepped into the room.

"I've been calling y'all for the past thirty minutes. My dinner's gonna taste like it came out of the freezer." She grasped Ricky's hand and started up the stairs. "Did you like your piano lessons?"

"I sure did, and soon as I learn, I'm gonna teach Audie how to play."

Climbing the stairs behind the two of them and hearing Ricky's cocky comment, Nelson couldn't help reminiscing about his youth, times when he thought the world was his and he could accomplish anything he put himself to. Suddenly, he laughed aloud, acquainting himself with a new kind of happiness, the joy men know when a inner light illumines them. Maybe God would be good to him, and he could have his four silver stars, his family, and a woman who loved him.

At that same time, Audrey sat on her back porch, swinging and looking at the fireflies. Very few came out that evening, and she missed the swarm that usually entertained her. Clouds soon covered the moon and stars, and the wind strengthened to cool the air. She could almost smell the coming rain. Rolling thunder sounded in the distance, then closer and closer, and when the first lightning streaked through the sky along with the cracking sound of a million revolvers, she ran inside. Since childhood, she had feared the sound of thunder and the lightning that accompanied it and now, childlike, she sought the safety of her bed.

For nearly an hour the elements tested their power,

immobilizing her. When the storm passed, drained and disgusted that at age thirty she still couldn't cope with it, she showered and got ready for bed. She had promised to call Nelson, but wasn't quite up to the inner battle that was bound to ensue, so she procrastinated a little longer.

When the phone rang, she answered it immediately, thinking it might be one of her sisters calling to console her about the storm.

"Hello." The brightness of her voice surprised her, as she had thought herself melancholy.

"Hello. This is Nelson. You said you wanted to speak with me about a matter of importance. Change your mind?"

"Hi. I was . . . uh . . . waiting for the storm to pass."

"It passed half an hour ago. Ricky sends his love to you."

At the tip of her tongue were the words "what about you?" Fortunately, she had the presence of mind not to utter them. "He's a wonderful child. He was here with me only four days, but I miss him. This place is really dull since I took him home."

"Yeah. He's changing my life." She thought she detected a wistfulness in his voice.

"Is that because you're responsible for him?"

"Only in part, and a small part at that. I never loved a child before. Oh well, what did you want to tell me?"

"Nelson, I want to plead with you to get an MRI or a CAT scan—"

He interrupted, as she'd known he would. "Look, I'm handling it, so—"

"That's the problem. You are not handling it, and what is worse, you can't handle it. What I felt this afternoon didn't appear to me to be a whiplash. I bet anything you don't have a whiplash, but the only way to be certain is to look inside. Why do you risk permanent damage that could alter your life and your lifestyle? I can envisage problems there that, if not treated, could eventually cost you your life."

"You don't think you're overstating this?"

"I gave you my professional judgment. If you want more, I care about you, and it pains me to think of what you're suffering now and how much worse it will be if you don't get it treated."

"Look, I appreciate your concern and your help too, Audrey, but I'm doing the best I can right now."

"Is that your last word on the subject?"

"Unless fate decrees otherwise. Yes."

"Well, that was the reason why I was going to call you, so I'm turning in. Good night."

"Good night?" It sounded as if he screamed it. "Hell, woman, can't you kiss a guy? You're just hanging up?"

Taken aback, she hesitated. "I can do that, but honey, I don't get a kick out of teasing myself. And knowing what you can do to a kiss, that would be torture."

"It'll torture both of us. Open your mouth." She parted her lips, closed her eyes and let him have his way with her. "Can't you taste my hunger and this awful need I have to explore every centimeter of your mouth and every facet of your body?"

She shook herself out of the trance into which he seduced her. "You listen to me, Nelson. You say you don't want to get involved with me. Sex, you would like maybe, but definitely without emotional attachment. Well buddy, if you're not going to mow my lawn, leave my lawn mower *a-lone*. And don't forget both of us can play the game of seduction."

"I'm sorry if you're ticked off because I let you use your imagination. You weren't alone. And as for my liking the sex, baby, so would you. Now let's not hurt each other. It doesn't make sense."

"I know. It's so frustrating."

"Tell me about it. We'll talk again soon."

"We will. 'Night."

She replaced the receiver with slow hands. Nobody could convince her that she and Nelson weren't headed for a powerful combustion, and she was equally sure that Nelson was hiding something. And he would pay a price for it. An awesome price.

At work that Monday morning, Nelson had much on his mind. Flushed with the plaudits of the Commandant and fellow officers following his report on the MEU, he went to his office to think about Stacey Petin. Stacey, whose first and last names didn't match. Realizing that he could start something to which there might not be an end, he dialed an officer in the National Security Service.

"Checkmate, Marilyn. This is Nelson," he said, having signaled her to secure their conversation.

"Hi there. What's up."

He related his concern. "The child didn't ask if my boy could visit her but rather, if she could visit him. Most kids want their friends to come to *their* house. I have no reason for suspicion, except that those names don't make sense to me. Maybe it's nothing, but these days I turn around if a long shadow approaches me from behind."

"And you are smart to do it. I'll check this out on the q.t. As you say, it may be nothing. Be in touch."

"Thanks." After noting the conversation in his daily log, he dictated three letters to his secretary and went to lunch.

"Mind if I join you?" a colonel with a chestful of Kosovo arena ribbons asked him.

He nodded. "Glad for the company, man. You here for a while?"

"A couple of years, maybe. My wife isn't well, so I won't ask for overseas duty and I doubt the wigs will ask me to go."

Nelson had never developed the habit of nicknaming his superiors, and he raised an eyebrow at the use of the term "wigs." "With those battle ribbons on your chest, you shouldn't have to go anywhere unless you ask. I hope your wife's health improves."

"Thanks. She's coming along. By the way, I hear Rupe Holden's being transferred back here from Afghanistan. I figure somebody thinks it's been too quiet around here and things have been going too smoothly. Holden will definitely change *that*."

Fortunately, Charlie Wills couldn't see the rapid acceleration of his heartbeat and couldn't feel the chills that raced through him. Lieutenant Colonel Rupert Holden lurked between him and his next promotion the way a river creeps along between shores. You could cross it, but you'd better have a solid boat. He didn't welcome the man's presence as a constant reminder that he teetered toward the abyss of failure.

Later, while sitting alone at home on his deck in the warm evening breeze, he catalogued his chances of rising to the top. He had paid his dues and he deserved the recompense, but in the service, anything could happen. He'd been able to move ahead because nothing weighed him down. Now he had a family, and . . . He didn't like the thoughts that had begun to nag him with such persistence. Thoughts of Audrey and how just knowing her added a dimension to his life, one that—if he were honest—uplifted him, especially when he was in her company.

He got up and walked slowly into the hallway where the wall phone hung and dialed her number. He didn't

question his deed or agonize about it. He wanted to see
her and she was unattached, as was he. They could do as
they pleased.

"Hello, Nelson."

"What? Did you install caller ID? I want you to come
for a walk with me."

"For a . . . Now?"

"Yeah. I'll come get you."

"Nelson, look here." He didn't hear outrage, but a
pleading that he suspected was born of frustration.
"What are you doing to me? You swear you don't want
a relationship, yet—"

He interrupted her. "I'm not asking for the rest of
your life, just an hour so I can feel like myself again.
Besides, it's a great night and I want to walk somewhere
peaceful. With you."

"That's very romantic. Where would we go?"

"What do you say we walk along the Tidal Basin."

"Are you serious? I'd rather walk along the Tidal
Basin that anyplace I know. I love going there, but I've
never walked there at night."

"It's my favorite spot, too. May I come for you?"

"I'm crazy, but I'd like that a lot."

She didn't invite him to come in, but met him at the
door and walked with him to the car holding his left
thumb in her right hand. He thought about the meaning
of her holding his thumb and about how he'd been a different person ever since she picked up her phone and
said hello. But he didn't consider the implications, nor
did he care about them.

"I think it's weird that we both love to walk around
here," Audrey said as they left the car and started along

the path nearest the water's edge. "Imagine being here
on a night like this. I'm glad you called me."

He stopped walking and tugged at her hand, silently
urging her to step closer to him. "Be sure you mean
every word you say. My head and my body are raising
hell with each other, and I can't even guess which will
win. So don't say anything that could mislead me, and
I'll try to be careful for your sake."

"All right. How's Ricky?"

"Asleep when I left. But let's not make small talk. If
you like we can walk quietly. Frankly, I'm not trying to
communicate, I just want to be with you."

Maybe he wasn't communicating with words, but his
behavior told her more than he wanted her to know.
Still, she had a sense of peace and contentment as they
walked in silence, her hand wrapped in his. Shadows of
the trees formed patterns of lace, knit together as only
nature could. Their El Greco–like elongated shapes preceded them, and the moon traveled with them as if eager
to bless their joining.

The sound of a stone dropped into the water startled
her, and she stopped walking and grasped Nelson's arm.
"What was that?"

"Nothing to fear. Either a frog or a fish. Don't be
afraid."

"I didn't think I was."

He stood closer and his right hand reached out and
slid down the side of her face in a caress that humbled
her with its gentleness.

"It means a lot that you came down here with me. A
lot." He whispered the last two words. "I . . . care for
you, and I'm telling you because I don't want you to
think I'm using you tonight. I'm not. I needed some
peace of mind, and I knew I'd find it if you were with
me."

She stared up at him, examining his face, softened by the moonlight. He seemed bigger and taller than ever. A strong man with the bearing of a king. Accomplished. Self-assured. Why should he need her? For whatever reason, she knew with certainty that he did. Suddenly, his left hand went to the side of his neck, and she bit back a gasp.

"Does it hurt now?"

He nodded. "Yes. I never get a warning. All of a sudden it pains me."

Her hand slid along his neck in a circular motion and pressed with increasing force into the muscles moving down to his shoulders.

"Is that a little better?"

"Anytime and anywhere you touch me makes me better."

"Nelson, don't—"

She was in his arms, and he swallowed her words as his tongue plunged into her and his fingers raced to find her nipple, his most able ally. Tremors shook her, and her body welcomed his gentle stroking of her breasts. She gripped his shoulder and sucked his tongue deeply into her mouth, feasting on it as though she were starved. His heat began to furl upward and around her the way steam rises from grilles on city streets. His hands rubbed and tormented her buttocks until she tried to scale his body, to fit herself to him. With a groan he lifted her, locked her to him, and let her feel his need. When she wrapped her legs around his hips and crossed her ankles, he set her away from him.

"Listen sweetheart, I didn't bring you down here for this, much as I needed it. You understand?" When she didn't respond, his arm tightened around her. "Is anything wrong? Are you okay?"

"Everything's wrong and I definitely am not okay. I

just can't figure out why I lose my head with you. I know you didn't plan for that to happen." She shook her head. "It didn't occur to me to put on the brakes. Explain that."

His laughter was the last response she would have expected. "If I could, I'd understand why I started it knowing how it would end. Want to head back?"

"Sure. Are you sorry you . . . that we know each other?"

He swung their joined hands. "No way. I wouldn't have missed you for the world. This song is still playing."

"You didn't tell me about your mission. Were you successful?"

"I was indeed. Thanks for asking." They rode in silence back to her house in Bethesda. "I won't invite you to come in," she said.

He showed his teeth in that wicked grin she found so enticing. "If you're afraid we'll heat up the place again, suppose you stand in the foyer while I check the house to make sure all is safe."

"Tell me something," she said when he came down the stairs. "Can you go to a private neurologist for treatment of your neck?"

He looked in the distance for a minute. "I have to trust you with this. One word of it to my superiors and I'm finished in the Marine Corps. If I went to a private physician, the report would reach the Commandant's office before I got home. I know my neck needs treatment, but I'm going to tough it out. I've worked hard, endured hell, and sacrificed aplenty to get ahead. It's my goal to reach the top, and I'll keep on till I have four silver stars on my collar."

"But it could cost you your health."

"I know, but the last words I said to my dad were, 'I

promise.' He made it to Lieutenant Commander in the Navy, as my brother did, and it was his dream to wear the admiral's gold braid and stars. I always keep my promises, Audrey. If I tell you something, you can depend on it."

"I wish you'd tell me I'm going to survive this."

"I'd be happy if I could assure myself of that. I'll call you tomorrow." He turned and ran down the steps.

Five

I'm giving Audrey mixed signals, Nelson told himself as he drove home to Alexandria, *and it isn't fair. I believe she's different, that she's honorable, but I thought that of Carole, too.*

He parked in front of his house and leaned against the hood of the car and looked up at the sky that seemed to surround him, at the blanket of stars and the moon hanging among them. Never before had he paid so much attention to nature and the beauty that met his eyes wherever he looked. He hadn't taken time for life's simplest pleasures, he realized. How often he'd walked along the Tidal Basin at evening, winter and summer, but until this night he had never seen in the water his likeness or the reflection of the Jefferson Memorial. With Audrey, his senses seemed to spring to life.

He fixed his gaze on a sapling swaying in the breeze and thought of Ricky, a tender shoot that needed care and nurturing if he would become a man. But what of his own goals? And what about Audrey? Their attraction to each other had deepened into something more than desire, and common decency demanded that he not mislead her.

He went inside and up to his room without turning on the lights. What he needed right then was not artificial illumination, but some insight into the course his life had begun to take, a course over which he seemed destined to have no control.

In the office several mornings later while working at his desk, he answered his intercom and heard Marilyn's voice. "Checkmate. Got company?"

He bolted forward. "All clear here."

"On second thought," she said, "how about a cup of coffee at Starbuck's? Say, half an hour?"

"Half an hour."

Now what? If she didn't want to discuss it over the phone or the intercom, that meant she'd found something.

She sat at a little bistro table in the corner with her back to the wall like the sleuth that she was, prepared for any eventuality.

He joined her at the table. "Seems serious. What do you have for me?"

"It may be serious. I'm not sure. We've put that house under surveillance, and we're looking hard at four visitors."

"Who lives there, and who are these visitors?"

"The house is rented to a computer scientist, who lives there with his wife and daughter, Stacey. What's peculiar about the visitors is their timing—during working hours when the man is presumably at work, and the length of their stay. Fifteen to twenty-five minutes. Hardly time enough for infidelity on the woman's part and unreasonable since the man doesn't work at home."

He gave the waitress his order for a cup of cinnamon cappucino and mused over what Marilyn had told him. "Perhaps the woman works at home. She could be a secretary, accountant, editor, or a writer."

Marilyn shook her head. "If so, she doesn't pay income tax or social security; she's not on any local, state or national roster of employees or professionals; and she doesn't have a bank account or any kind of investment portfolio."

He released a sharp whistle. If the government decided to find out about you, you needn't try to hide. "My boy can make other friendships, but I want to know why, if that family is engaged in crime or espionage, they would choose to involve my child. Maybe it's a coincidence."

She shook her head. "It isn't. Children make perfect pawns, Colonel. You know that. Besides, your boy is not the only serviceman's child with whom Stacey wants to be friends. So far, she's had no luck."

"So what you're saying is that someone wants me or wants something that I'm supposed to know."

"Looks like it."

"Any orders?"

"Watch your back and—"

He held up his hand to stop her before she said it. "I've sworn to give my life for my country, and I'll do it, but I won't risk my child's little finger. And that is not negotiable." He knew that with those words he may have knocked himself down a few pegs with his superiors, but so be it.

She looked him in the eye. "Then we won't ask you to do that. If you wish, we can put him on security watch at that school. Who takes him there and back home?"

"My housekeeper. But from now on, I'll do it when I'm here."

"Good. You'll both get security watch. Keep this under wraps."

"You bet. By the way, how much damage have I done to myself?"

For the first time, a smile settled on her face. "None. I have three children, and I wouldn't sacrifice any part

of them either. There are other ways of getting the information we need, Colonel. Have a good day."

He was relieved but not satisfied. According to his father and grandfather, chickens had a way of coming
home to roost, so he could only hope that the incident
didn't precipitate a career setback. All the same, his
mood when he arrived home that evening was bright,
even jocular.

"Where's Ricky?" he asked Lena, after greeting her.

"Upstairs, and looks to me like he's been up there a
while. Maybe I ought to—"

"I'm headed up there. I'll see what he's up to."

When he didn't see the boy in his room, he had to
resist alarm, as his thoughts went immediately to his
conversation with Marilyn, the NSS officer whose last
name was a mystery to him. However, he need not have
worried. When he stepped into his own room, he found
Ricky sitting on his desk dialing a phone number.

After recovering from the surprise, he asked him,
"Who're you calling?"

"Hi, Unca Nelson. I'm calling Audie, but I can't talk
to her. Nobody answers."

He walked over to the desk. "Dial it again." He
watched as the little fingers punched in numbers.
"That's a three, and you were trying to punch an eight.
Who gave you her number?"

"Miss Lena."

"I'll show you." After a brief period of instruction,
Ricky punched in the number and Nelson watched the
child's eyes grow big and round as he expressed for the
first time that miracle of modern technology.

"Hi, Audie. This is Ricky. Ricky Wainwright, Audie.
Can you come over? Unca Nelson showed me how to
push the numbers." He listened to her answer, his face

blooming with his smile. "You will? Gee. I love you, Audie. 'Bye."

He jumped from the desk and ran to Nelson. "She's coming to see me, Unca Nelson. Audie's coming to see me."

"Wonderful." He didn't ask when she would be there; he had to dispose of a more pressing matter. He put the boy on his knee and told him, "Son, Stacey can't visit you. I don't know her parents or their visitors, so it's best you not make friends with her right now."

Ricky's bottom lip dropped in a pout, and his eyes blinked rapidly. Then he ran into his room and closed the door. Parenting was a endless job. On his way to reprimand Ricky, the telephone rang, and he rushed back to answer it.

"Wainwright speaking. Hello."

"Good evening, Colonel," the deep, masculine voice began. "I'm Rufus Meade, syndicated reporter for *The Tribune* and other papers and media outlets. I've agreed to do a piece on Afghanistan, and I understand that you served there, crashed there, and were wounded. I'm not planning an expose, but an accurate account of what's going on there, and I'd like to speak with you. I'm told you have the facts."

He did indeed, but how could he prevent the reporter from observing the problem with his neck and shoulders? It amazed him that his colleagues at the office hadn't noticed it.

"I know who you are, and I've read many of your reports. If you want to write about the conflict there and not about me, I'll speak with you, but my life is my business."

He heard a hint of a laugh. "That will be difficult. I can say, however, that I have no interest in documenting your private life. You can trust me on that. What do you say?"

"Who else are you interviewing, if you don't mind my asking?"

"You're certainly entitled to know that. I spent an hour with a lieutenant colonel when I was in Afghanistan a few weeks ago, but I can't say it was rewarding."

His body jumped to alertness. Had Holden told the reporter about his having overlooked a young marine's serious infraction of Marine code, falling asleep while on guard duty?

"What was the officer's name?" he asked Meade, and held his breath for the inevitable.

"Holden. He's a Marine officer. When I called the Pentagon this afternoon, a lieutenant in the Commandant's office told me to get in touch with you and gave me a bit of your service history. It surprised me that Holden didn't mention you."

He allowed himself to breathe. "He's not a fan of mine."

He agreed to meet with Rufus Meade, and they set a time for the first interview. He hung up, looked down, and saw Ricky hugging his leg.

"I'm sorry I was bad, Unca Nelson. Stacey doesn't have to be my friend. I like another girlfriend at school, too."

He sat down and urged Ricky to stand between his knees. "I'm glad you have friends. Aren't there any boys in your school?"

"They're yucky. They throw pieces of paper and make noise, and they're not nice to the girls."

He pushed back a laugh. "But you are nice to the girls, I hope."

"Oh, yes, sir. All the time, and all the girls like me.

One of them was going to marry me, but I told her I would have to ask you."

He poked his tongue into his left cheek to stifle a grin. "And you were right. We have to wait a while for that. When is Audrey coming to see you?"

Ricky placed his elbows on Nelson's thigh, let them take his weight, and looked up at his uncle. "Saturday morning. We're going to the library near her house. A lady goes there and tells stories to the children. I love stories, Unca Nelson."

He wondered whether security would tail them. Marilyn hadn't indicated full security day and night, seven days a week, and he hoped that wasn't considered necessary. But inasmuch as it wasn't a school day, he wouldn't take a chance.

"Ask Audrey if she minds my going along."

"Oh, goody!" Ricky grabbed the phone, and within minutes, the coming Saturday would differ vastly from what he had planned.

With twenty minutes free before her next patient's appointment, Audrey took out her ledger to check her financial position. She had promised herself that she would open her own office before the year was over, and the previous day she'd seen precisely the space and location that met her needs. She didn't want to begin her practice heavily in debt, and the equipment alone carried a staggering price tag. If she sold some stock, she could open her office in November or December with a manageable debt. *Manageable debt!* She cupped her face with both hands. She was never free of the dread that hung over her like a dark storm ready to flood the earth. She wouldn't know relief until seven years had passed and the statute of limitation excluded a malpractice suit. All she had done was accede to an injured basketball player's pleas that he be allowed back on the court to help the university's team win the playoff. He shot the winning basket, collapsed, and had to be taken from the court unable to walk or even to wiggle his right toes. That mistake haunted her daily, and she knew it was one reason for her thoroughness and the expertise for which she was becoming known.

She put the ledger away, washed her hands, and checked the waiting room. "How's your back today, Mr. Hayes?"

"Never felt better."

"Really? Then you don't need me."

About forty years old—though he gave his age as twenty-nine—neatly dressed, and passable-looking, Leroy Hayes thought far more highly of himself and his looks than he had any right to, at least in her opinion, and his arrogance irritated her.

"Oh, I don't know about that," he said in answer to her remark, revealing his teeth in a smile that was both suggestive and arrogant. "I figured now that I'm well, you and me, we could get down to business. I don't see a thing wrong with doctor-patient relations, but my sister says it's not ethical, so I'm well as of now."

She would see about that. "You'd better let me check. Can't be to careful about these things, and we don't want problems with your insurance company."

His smile faded. "Well, if you think so, but I'm . . . uh . . . well."

Even if he wasn't, she would make sure he stayed away from her. "Go into the first therapy room, remove your shirt and shoes, please, and lie down."

After he had waited long enough to be nervous, she joined him, and began the exercises. If he was well, it wouldn't hurt; if he wasn't, the entire clinic would know it.

With her thumbs on either side of his spine and her fingers digging into his shoulders, she pressed with all the strength she could muster.

"Ow! What the hell!"

"My! I should have been more gentle, but you said you were healed so . . ." Her left shoulder lifted in a shrug. "It isn't wise to mislead your doctor. Anyway, I've done all I can for you. You're discharged."

He turned over and sat up. "I am? Then we can—"

"We can't do anything, Mr. Hayes. I'm not looking for a man; I've got one. Let yourself out."

She had primed herself for ten minutes of good cathartic fury, but the ring of the telephone put an end to the pleasure she derived from it.

"Dr. Powers speaking."

"This is Ricky Wainwright. I want to speak with Audie, please."

She greeted him warmly. "Did you dial my number yourself?"

"Uh-huh. Unca Nelson taught me how. He told me to ask you if he can go with us to the library Saturday."

"Of course. Tell him we'll be glad to have him."

"Okay. I love you, Audie. Bye."

"Hey, wait a minute. I love you, Ricky. I love you a lot."

"Okay. 'Bye."

She telephoned her sister Winifred to cancel their Saturday morning shopping trip. One thing was certain: with Ricky along, she and Nelson would keep their libidos in check. Or would they? She had learned that if he caught her unawares, she couldn't be counted on for discreet behavior. Thoughts of his dreamy brown eyes with those extraordinary lashes, and the way his lips seemed to smile while he spoke, and of that hard mouth

on her sent warm flushes throughout her body, and she
felt her nipples harden.

*I don't want to be susceptible to him but, my Lord, I
can't wait to feel his hands on me again.*

Nelson hardly recognized Audrey when she opened
her door that morning. In low-slung white linen pants,
blue-and-white sailor shirt, and sneakers to match, she
had the appearance of a teenager, and with her hair
swinging around her shoulders, she oozed glamour and
sex. He didn't for a minute think that was what she intended, but it was definitely the effect she created.

As he gazed down at her, liquid accumulated in his
mouth and he caught his breath as it escaped him in
quick, short pants. What the devil was happening to
him? *She knows I want her, but, thank God, she can't
guess how much.* He forced a careless smile. For his
peace of mind, he'd have been happier if she had greeted
Ricky and him in one of her usual buttoned-down out-
fits. The boy smiled up at Audrey and stretched his little
arms out to her, puzzling him as to the child's affection
for him.

"Looking at you puts me in the mood for . . . er . . .
sailing," he said. Halfway through the sentence, his
thoughts had swung from fun with her on the Potomac
River to a more intimate experience. "After we leave the
library, we could go for cruise on the Potomac."

"Sounds good," she said as she hugged Ricky. He
wondered why she seemed disconcerted and asked if
she was sure she wanted to spend that much time with
them.

"I've got the day free," she said. "I was a bit surprised
that *you* wanted to spend your Saturday sightseeing."

He did not, but he couldn't take the chance that they

might become someone's target and he wouldn't be there when they needed him.

He forced a grin. "Are you suggesting I wouldn't grab the chance to spend time with you? You couldn't be serious."

He sat with the two of them in the library's children's theater with only a small part of his thigh resting on the little chair. Almost immediately, he found himself engrossed in the children's reaction to the stories and, especially, in their questions.

"If the cow can jump over the moon, how big is the moon?" one girl asked.

"Silly," a boy needled, "cows are so big they can jump over anything they want to."

"They don't jump over the fence," Ricky said.

"They don't want to get out, maybe," the girl said, "but that's stupid."

Something, maybe an intuition, pricked his senses, and he shifted his gaze to the door in time to see a tall, fair-complexioned, mustached man ease away from the doorjamb and walk out of the theater.

He tapped Audrey's shoulder. "Be right back. Take care."

Outside the theater, he saw the man with his back against the wall, using his cellular phone. Marilyn wouldn't put such an obvious agent on a case. More likely, she would send a man who wore a jogging suit and sneakers and resembled a basketball player. This man's clothes would have suited an undertaker. After making a mental note of the man, he ducked back into the theater.

"Unca Nelson, can we buy Audie some ice cream?" Ricky asked him as they left the library. "At her house we had ice cream all the time."

"Now wait a minute, Ricky. We had ice cream after lunch and after dinner. Not all the time."

"I thought it was all the time, Audie," he said taking her hand.

"I think we're going to have to forego the cruise today," Nelson told them. "Something came up."

"But I want to go on the cruise with Audie, Unca Nelson. Please. Can me and Audie go?"

"Audie and I, you mean. Anyhow, we can't do it today, but I'll try to manage it next Saturday if Audrey can make it."

He had expected Ricky's temper to assert itself, but instead, the boy turned to Audrey. "Can you come with us next Saturday please, Audie? My Unca Nelson has to do something now."

"Anytime after twelve is fine with me."

The child's eyes beseeched him, begging him to promise. He picked Ricky up and looked him in the eye. "Son, a serviceman can't make firm promises. I have explained to you that my first duty is to our country. If I'm not needed for anything else, we can spend Saturday afternoon together. All right?"

Ricky nodded, his face alight with an eagerness only a child could show. Nelson glanced over Ricky's shoulder at Audrey with an unspoken question ablaze on his face, and his heart began to race, for her eyes told him that whatever he wished was his if she could grant it. At that moment, Ricky's arms tightened around his shoulders, and he gave thanks for that buffer between him and the desire that threatened to bolt out of control. Without taking his gaze from hers, he set Ricky on his feet and took the few steps that separated him from Audrey.

"Be careful about the messages you send me, Audrey.

I won't forget them, and I will definitely hold you accountable. Can we go now?"

"Fine. See you Saturday."

"Oh, we'll speak before then. Come." He took her hand. "Ricky and I will take you home." He wanted to free himself as quickly as possible. If Marilyn had a security guard on Ricky, he hadn't been able to identify the person. One thing was certain: the man he'd seen was on someone else's team.

"He isn't our man," Marilyn said when he called her, "but we know who he is. So far, he is about as effective as a tub-thumping rainmaker. However, that could be a ruse. Our gal was sitting two rows directly behind you."

He hadn't seen a woman who . . . He gasped, and then laughter rolled out of him. What a disguise! He'd thought he was fairly expert at detecting spies, hit men, and bodyguards. The woman in the chair two rows back had had the appearance of a grandmother.

"How old is she really?" he asked Marilyn.

Marilyn's laugh amazed him; he hadn't heard it before. "Thirty-four. She can also look eighty if the situation calls for it. Not to worry. She's first-class."

He hung up feeling less confident about the mystery surrounding Ricky's young admirer. Marilyn's actions were proof she suspected impending danger. He hadn't wanted to tell Lena about it, but he didn't have a choice.

Audrey looked out of her kitchen window at the gathering clouds that would wash out her jogging for that day. She didn't remember having witnessed so many storms in early June. She didn't mind the rain, but she had never overcome her childhood fear of thunder and lightning. She went to the phone and dialed her younger sister.

"I have to postpone our Saturday afternoon shopping trip again, Winifred. I had to promise Ricky I'd go somewhere with him."

"What do you mean, you *had* to promise him? You're doing it because you want to. Is tall, honey-skinned and handsome going along?"

She loved Winifred, but the girl didn't mind jumping into her sisters' personal affairs, though she kept her own to herself.

"Nelson is going with us, yes."

Audrey imagined her sister's face taking on its superior facade when Winifred said, "Sis, you are really a case. You want the guy. Nothing wrong with that. If you hadn't gotten to him first, I would have given him more than a passing glance. That brother is *it*. I mean, we're speaking fine, here. Jet black hair, skin the color of honeycomb, dark brown eyes, and those long, silky-black lashes. If you tell me you're not interested, I won't believe you."

"You sound as if you are." She didn't like the trend of the conversation.

"Not me. I don't ride bareback, so to speak, but when I see God's perfection, girl, I bow to it. The only reason that brother's single is because some stupid woman did a real job on him."

She thought of the way his voice made her tingle. "Winifred, for goodness sake!"

"Hey! Don't be so uptight. If he's got the music that makes you dance, go for it."

"Listen, Wendy, if you knew as much as you sound like you know, you'd own Microsoft, and I'd genuflect every time your name came up. What about you? Pam told me Hendren introduced you to a great guy last Sunday night. What happened?"

She knew the man impressed her sister when Winifred didn't shoot from the hip with a ready put-down. "He was . . . uh, he was okay."

Audrey couldn't help laughing. "Okay? That's a rave coming from you. I want to meet him. Something tells me the guy knocked you off your high horse. What's his name?"

"Ryan Addison, and don't tease me about him."

If a man had finally shaken her sister from head to foot the way Nelson shook her when she first looked at him, maybe Winifred would be less strident and more compassionate. Loving a man changed a woman. She couldn't put her finger on the time or incident that had precipitated it, but although she still had her personal goals and meant to see them fulfilled, the prism through which she viewed the world had altered.

She recognized in herself a gentleness that she used to think of as milquetoast, as a lack of strength and self-confidence in others. And for the first time in her memory, she didn't avoid eye contact with the bedraggled and the downtrodden.

"Let yourself get to know him, Wendy. You can't imagine how much happier you'll be if you care for someone who feels the same way about you."

She heard a gasp. "That definitely doesn't sound like you, girl."

She sat down beside the walnut, marble-top table on which the phone rested, stretched out her legs, and crossed her ankles. "That's what I'm trying to tell you. I know Nelson's honorable, that he isn't like Gerald, and I know that if I can make myself trust him fully, I'll be happy. He cares for me, Wendy, but you were right when you said some woman did a job on him. He hasn't told me, but he might as well make a sign and plaster it across his forehead."

"What are you going to do?" Though bossy and sharp-tongued, her younger sister loved her, was deeply attached to her and looked to her for guidance.

She got up, walked to the window, saw again the black clouds that were now lit by lightning streaking among them, and drew the blinds.

"I don't know, Wendy. We're not lovers, and I'm convinced I'd better keep it that way."

"Yeah? You'd better hope he cooperates."

"Tell me about it. We should hang up; it's dangerous to use a phone during this kind of storm. We'll talk."

After hanging up, she sat there musing over what she'd admitted to Winifred. *Oh, hell! I'm not going that way. Daydreaming when I should be working. The bottom falling out of my stomach every time I look at him. I must be out of my mind. When I see him Saturday, I'm going to act as if he's just another man.*

Saturday afternoon arrived and, dressed for the cruise in white slacks, yellow T-shirt, white sneakers, and yellow socks, she opened her front door and looked into the eyes of Nelson Wainwright. Her heart went on a rampage in her chest, and the bottom tumbled from her stomach.

He almost smiled. "Hi."

She didn't answer him; she couldn't, for her jaws seemed wired together when she attempted to speak. Saved by Ricky's exuberant embrace, she hugged the child, smiled, and took her time locking the front door. But before she could remove the key from the lock, his hand closed over hers and, as if programmed, she turned into his arms.

"No greeting for me?" he asked.

"Hi," she whispered, and let her lashes cover her all-revealing eyes. But he tipped up her chin with his right index finger.

"This isn't something you can shove into a corner, and there's no point in praying it will go away. Hell! I've stopped trying because I know it's going to nag us until it has its day. You have to deal with it just as I do."

She moved as far from him as the door at her back would allow. "Are you telling me you're going to pursue this . . . this—"

He cupped her face with both of his hands. "I may not have a choice. I'm beginning to feel like the criminal who's gotten tired of years on the lam and gives himself up because the price of freedom is too high."

She imagined her eyes grew to twice their size. "What an analogy! Did you hear what you said?"

A grim, gray cast settled over his face. "Yeah. I heard it. Let's go. I got us tickets for the two-thirty cruise."

"I'm taking the short cut, and say your prayers that we don't get stuck in traffic," he said as they headed down Wisconsin Avenue.

"I love the breeze back here," Ricky said, "but I can't see anything."

"You will see plenty, but you have to sit back there in your car seat where you're safe."

"Can Audie sit back here where she'll be safe, Unca Nelson?"

What was he going to do with this child when he reached the age of reason? "Audrey's big enough to be safe up here."

"Oh. I'm going to get big real soon, Unca Nelson."

At M Street, Northwest, he crossed over to Fourteenth Street and headed for the bridge that would take them to Alexandria. A sense of pride pervaded him whenever he passed the Jefferson Memorial. Magnificent by day and awe inspiring at night.

"Maybe it's because I'm a Marine officer sworn to give my life for my country," he said to Audrey, "that I almost choke up whenever I look at this or when I see the Lincoln Memorial. I think of the countries I've been in and the abject poverty of most people on this earth—in Asia, Latin America, the Caribbean and, especially Africa—and their enslavement to the past and to the despots who govern them. All that ensures they may never have a better life. Makes me humble. I'll fight anybody and anything that threatens to take this away from me."

She shifted in the seat beside him. "I never heard you voice such sentiments."

"Oh, I know there's plenty wrong with this place, and I know what it is and what should be done to fix it. But it's almost heaven compared to so many places I've been."

"Look at the birds, Unca Nelson," Ricky screamed as they passed the Waterfowl Sanctuary on the drive along the George Washington Memorial Highway.

"One day I'll bring you out here. It's spectacular on a pleasant day. He drove through Old Town Alexandria and parked. To throw the man he'd come to think of as "Mustache" off his trail, he'd had his secretary purchase their tickets. Half an hour early, at the foot of Prince Street, they boarded the Scandinavian-built schooner *Alexandria*, and he made sure they got on first. As unobtrusively as possible, he stationed himself near the entrance and watched until the boat shoved off. He could relax . . . almost; Mustache didn't board after he did, but agents had means and used them. Still, he felt reasonably relaxed.

However, as he turned from the railing, he didn't have

to be told that the man who'd buried his face in the Saturday edition of *The Washington Post* was the one he called Mustache.

Twice, "Mustache" had seen Audrey with Ricky and himself, and that made her vulnerable. Marilyn wanted the matter kept secret, but he had to tell Audrey enough to ensure her awareness of possible danger. He watched the sights with one eye on his adversary. Along the shore as the seagulls glided above them and less flight-worthy birds fluttered overhead and alongside them, the *Alexandria* took them through bits of history; past Founders Park, dedicated to the Founding Fathers; Torpedo Factory Art Center, once a gun shell factory; and past some of the town's most elegant restaurants.

As they disembarked, Ricky's yawns gave Nelson the excuse he needed to cut their outing short. Later, Audrey lingered at her door, telegraphing to him her wish to prolong their time together. With Ricky asleep in his arms, he couldn't even kiss her properly and had to settle for a stroke of his fingers along her cheeks and the promise that his eyes communicated.

"That's it," he told Marilyn as soon as he fastened Ricky into his car seat, got in, and closed the door. "I have to tell her. She can't be sacrificed, and neither can my housekeeper."

"I'll take care of it. Tell them not to widen their circle of friends right now."

He had planned to work at home that evening, but the severity of pain in his shoulders was such that he couldn't concentrate.

"Can you tell me some stories about the cow and the moon, Unca Nelson? Can I see the moon?"

He'd never been so glad for a cloudy sky. "The clouds are covering the moon. I'll tell you some bedtime stories when I'm not so sleepy," he said, fighting pain so severe that talking irritated him.

Ricky gazed up at him with trusting eyes. "I can tell you a bedtime story if you want to go to sleep," he said. "Let's see, 'The Happy Chipmunks,' 'Puss 'N Boots' . . ." His eyes widened. "I know, I'll tell you 'The Golden Goose.' Lie down."

"Ricky, come take your bath. Ricky, where are you?" Lena called.

Ricky ran to the door. "Unca Nelson is sleepy, and I'm gonna tell him a bedtime story."

Relief flooded him when he heard Lena's steps in the hallway. "You'd better take your bath first."

"Okay. Stay awake till I get back, Unca Nelson."

"I'll try." He closed his door, went into the bathroom, soaked a towel with hot water, folded it, and wrapped it around his neck. After repeating the measure several times, the pain ebbed slightly. A hot shower left him feeling like a brand-new man, so he dressed in Bermuda shorts and a T-shirt and went downstairs where he knew he'd find Lena watching a rerun of the *Judge Judy* show.

"You're not in danger," he said, after giving her a brief synopsis of the problem. "I'm telling you because you're entitled to know what's going on."

She slapped her thighs and rolled her eyes. He figured that in her younger days and before personal tragedies darkened her life, Lena had been a handsome woman. If she'd had that gap between her two upper front teeth closed, she might even have been very good-looking. "Thanks," she said. "If I catch that old vulture tagging behind me, I'll walk right up to him and tell him I'm gonna have him arrested for sexual harassment."

Lena had an off-the-wall way of looking at things. He tried not to laugh, but it poured out of him anyway. When he could recover his aplomb, he told her, "That ought to put the fear of God in him. You bet he won't want to see the inside of a clink."

"Humph. It's my intention to put the fear of Lena into him. He may not be acquainted with the Lord."

Still laughing, Nelson bounded up the stairs, looked in on Ricky, and found him asleep with his bunny in the crook of his arm. He gazed down at the boy, trying to understand when and how he had begun to feel as if Ricky were his own child. After lowering the air conditioner thermostat, he turned out the light and tiptoed from the room. He had to warn Audrey.

"Hi. I need to tell you something, and it's not for the telephone." He looked at his watch. "It's nine o'clock. Can you meet me at the Omni Sheraton lounge, or should I come to your place?"

"Is this urgent?"

What a question! "I'm beginning to think it is, and it's best I go to your house."

"All right. But Nelson—"

"Don't you trust me?"

"Oh yes, I do. I trust me, too, but I wouldn't put my money on the pair of us. Alone together, we're not trustworthy."

He could think of several dagger-sharp answers to that, but prudence dictated that he keep them to himself. He settled for, "Trustworthy? I don't remember having let myself down, so speak for yourself."

"Think harder, and you'll come up with something. Something big."

"What do you mean by that?"

"Talk to yourself, honey. Ask yourself a few strategic questions. By the time you get here, you'll be less certain. See you in half an hour."

"Yeah." All of a sudden, staring at him through his mind's eye was the picture of his beloved Carole in his bed with Bradford Stewart, his best friend. He blew out a long, tired breath. "Yeah. See you."

Her smile when she opened the door had the shimmer of moonlight, an invitation whether or not she meant to extend one. He diverted his glance in order to change the direction of his thoughts, and even then, red toenails peeped at him from between the thongs of her sandals. Pretty toes. His gaze traveled upward to bare knees punctuated with dimples and on to white shorts that covered only a small portion of thighs that were smooth, brown, and luscious. Damn! All that talk about being trustworthy. He'd better change the venue.

"Hi. Why don't we . . . uh . . . go for a ride, maybe stop at The Igloo on Connecticut Avenue, get some ice cream or something? We can talk along the way."

She knitted her eyebrows. "But I thought—"

"I did, too. But unless you're interested in spontaneous combustion, I say we hightail it out of here."

Her eyes widened. "Oh! Uh . . . Let me get my pocketbook."

He didn't want to put his foot inside, and he'd feel silly waiting outside the front door. "You don't need it. Let's—"

She cut him off. "Quit steamrolling me. I do so need it."

She whirled around, dashed up the stairs and, five minutes later, glided back down wearing an antique-gold sweater-blouse and an ankle-length black-and-gold-patterned skirt with a slit high up one side. His gaze took in her hair hanging around her shoulders in a slightly unkempt fashion that, along with the big gold hoops that hung from her ears, gave her the look of a sexy siren. And all that in five minutes.

He could feel his lips curl into a grin. "Damndest pocketbook I ever saw."

She tossed her head. "A gentleman doesn't make such comments."

His grin threatened to erupt into a laugh. "What about an ordinary guy like me? Would he say something like that?"

"You're impossible," she said, although she showed no sign of displeasure.

He drove on Wilson Lane down to River Road, turned onto Garrison and from there to Connecticut Avenue.

"You seem to know this town as well as if it were your back yard."

He brushed off the compliment with a shrug. "I've been trained to see what I look at, to be aware of everything around, below and above me, so I can't take credit for being observant. And that's as good an opener as any for what I have to tell you." He pulled up to The Igloo, parked, cut the motor, and took her left hand in his.

"Is this a brush-off?" she asked, her facial expression similar to a large question mark.

"Nothing like that." He gave her the facts, beginning with Stacey's wish to visit Ricky. "You are not in danger, but the official advice is that you shouldn't widen your circle of friends."

"You mean, go on as if this situation didn't exist? That's asking a lot."

"I know, and I'm sorry. Apart from being careful, that's what *I'm* doing. You're in this because of your association with me, and you'll be well protected, as I will. Don't doubt that."

"I won't ask what you do that has put you in this position."

Since she wasn't asking, he saw no need to volunteer an answer. She didn't speak again for a long time, merely sat there seemingly lost in thought. His arm stole around her shoulder in a protective gesture, and when she snuggled closer to him, a softening, a longing stole into his heart, generating in him a feeling he hadn't experienced in years and had hoped never to have again. She would never know how glad he was that they were not alone in her house.

"I want a double cone of peach ice cream," she said, and as the words left her lips, she eased out of his arms with a smile blooming on her face. The way a woman looked when she had a cherished secret. He wondered at that smile, for he saw nothing remotely amusing.

Later, they sat in the car eating ice cream, she peach and he black raspberry. He punched a button, and immediately the sound of Mississippi John Hurt's ancient voice and masterful guitar giving forth with "Nobody's Business If I Do" filled the air.

"I didn't know you collected folk blues," she said. "I like this, but I've always been partial to classic jazz."

"Oh, I enjoy that, too. What about opera and symphonic music? Like that?"

"Basically, I love it, but I can do without some of it. The more modern it gets, the less I like it."

"Same here." He watched her run her tongue around the edges of the ice cream and then lick her lips. He looked at the cone in his hand, closed his eyes, and expelled a long breath. If he could just get that tongue into his mouth, he'd . . .

"I think I've had enough," he told her. "Excuse me while I find a wastebasket.

"Wait a minute." Her even white teeth sank into the cone, and she turned to him. "Taste this. It's delicious."

He took the cone from her hand, tasted the ice cream

and looked into the soft brown eyes that gazed up at him expectantly. Without thinking about it, he reached across her to the glove compartment, found a plastic bag, put their cones in it, and dropped the bag on the floor.

Her gaze still rested on his face. Tremors shook him as he enclosed her in his embrace and lowered his head. Her lips opened to him and his own groan startled him as he plunged his tongue into her mouth. She gripped his head and sucked his tongue deeply into her, moaning, pulling him in deeper. When her breath came in pants, his fingers went to the hem of her sweater, so eager was he to taste again the sweetness of her beaded nipple. But his senses kicked in, and after breaking the kiss, he held her to him and leaned his head against the back of the seat.

They were in his car beneath the street light, and he'd almost committed a serious faux pas. "I didn't mean to start that here in public. That's not my style, Audrey."

"Nor mine. I forgot where we were. At the moment, you were between me and the world." She shifted to her side of the car. "Looks as if bucket seats haven't circumvented making out in cars."

He sat forward and ignited the engine. "Not by a long shot. By the way, you've given me several IOUs. Don't be surprised if I decide to cash in. Ready to go?"

"You can't 'cash in,' as you put it, without my cooperation. I'm ready to go."

"That's precisely what I'm counting on. There's nothing one-sided about this, and you know that as well as I do." He believed in calling it as he saw it. "You want me, and I want you."

Her shrug didn't fool him, nor did her words when she said, "I've wanted a lot of things I didn't allow myself to have. So don't be so sure."

"Whatever you say."

"I'm not going any farther than your front door," he said when they reached her house. "If I step into that foyer with you, I'm going to do everything I can to make sure I spend the night." She gasped and lowered her gaze. "Better get on in there. I'll wait here until I hear the lock turn."

Looking less than happy, she opened the door, walked in, and closed it. A second later, before she could lock the door, her screams pierced the air.

Six

He stopped dead in his tracks, whirled around, and raced back to the front door. He didn't ring the bell or knock, but gave the door the full force of his two hundred and six pounds, and it yielded at once. Thank God, she hadn't had time to double-lock the door.

"What . . . What on earth?" He nearly stumbled over her. Remembering her reaction to darkness, he flicked on the light and saw that she had tripped over the ficus tree that stood beside the door. He knelt, lifted her into his arms, and cradled her body to his. Perspiration beaded his forehead and his shirt clung to his damp body. He hadn't prayed since the night his helicopter crashed, but he found words to express his thanks that she was unharmed. With his eyes closed he rocked her.

"That must have scared the beejeebers out of you. What's this thing doing on the floor?" he said, when he trusted himself to speak.

She appeared calm, but her staccatolike breathing belied it. "It fell on me when I stepped inside. I thought someone had grabbed me, and with that man stalking us . . . Well, you may imagine what I thought."

He helped her to her feet, picked the tree up, and stationed it in the hall beside the telephone table. "I expect you were terrified. Will you be all right now?" He didn't want to leave her. But neither did he want to seduce a woman who was at his mercy. "Would you like to go home with me? At least you won't be alone."

"Thanks. I'll be fine."

He checked the lock. "Seems okay."

"I hadn't locked the door." She dusted the back of her pants, though he saw no reason for it. "I appreciate your concern and that you came back here to check on me, but I'm sure I'll be all right."

"If you're sure." It could have been his imagination, or maybe her usual aplomb had only momentarily deserted her, but she seemed defenseless. Exposed. Vulnerable. Seeing her that way aroused in him a need to protect her, intensifying the physical desire that had rumbled in him since she'd opened her door to Ricky and him earlier in the afternoon. He didn't need a degree in mathematics to understand that the combination was lethal for his self-control.

"Yes. I'm sure. And . . . thanks."

"I'd better check the place out," he said, when it occurred to him that someone could have moved the ficus tree from its usual place, causing it to fall when she opened the door. After checking every part of the house, including her back deck, he made his way back to her. She hadn't moved.

He observed her carefully, her facial expression, her stance, the tilt of her head, the truth in her eyes and, convinced that she meant for him to leave, he reached for the door.

"Oooh!" He grabbed his right shoulder, frowning and wincing, unable to hide his reaction.

"Nelson! Honey, what . . . let me." She draped an arm around his waist and walked with him to her living room. "Lie facedown on the carpet, and take off your shirt.

She ran hot water from the tap into a bowl, got a

towel, and applied the heat to his neck. Then he felt her straddle him, but the severity of his pain was such as to preclude the effect that her being in that position would normally have on him.

After she eased the pain with her fingers and repeated applications of the heat to his neck and shoulders, he sat up with his back against the sofa.

She knelt beside him. "Is becoming a four-star general worth this pain and the crippling disease you'll probably get from this damage?"

He leaned his head back and looked at her. "Probably not, and if I hadn't made that promise to my father, I expect I would have given up on it. But I can't. He went through so much for Joel and me. He sacrificed his own career for us and retired as a lieutenant commander when he should have become an admiral. He turned down one opportunity after another so that we could have a stable family life. After a while, the opportunities stopped coming. Joel is gone now, and that leaves me. I promised my father I'd make it to the top, and in less than five minutes after I said the words, he slipped away from us. *I can't give up.*"

He drew her into the circle of his arm. "Didn't you ever have a goal that your life revolved around?"

She rested her head on his shoulder, tentatively, as if fearing that she might hurt him. "I'm working to open my own practice. When I think of all that it entails, I get goose bumps. It means I start from the bottom with debts and the few patients who will be willing to follow me from the clinic. Most won't, because the clinic will cost them less."

"Have you set a deadline for yourself?"

She told him she'd found a place she liked and thought she could afford. "I hope to open by the end of November."

"Maybe I'll be your first patient." He shrugged, dismissing the thought. "Just kidding. You'd have to report it, and I would never knowingly put you in a position where you had to chose between ethics and loyalty."

"I'm just praying that what you're going through will be worth it in the end. But I wish you could find a way to get the tests that wouldn't be prejudicial to your career. It pains me to think about it."

She had never said the words, and he suspected she didn't plan to, but she told him in many ways that she cared for him, and it went far beyond that hell-for-leather heat they'd had for each other since they first met. It was in him, too, and deepening with each passing day.

"If you're sure you're all right alone here, I'll leave now."

She kissed the side of his neck and moved out of his arms before he could react and plunge them into fire-hot passion. As he left her, he had difficulty remembering what he was like as a man before she came into his life.

"This is dangerous," he said aloud, easing the car away from the curb in front of her house. "I'm getting in deeper and deeper, and I can't seem to stop myself." He corrected that. *"I don't want to stop myself."*

As if she and Nelson were mentally attached to each other, her mind loitered in their private hell. She climbed the stairs, wishing she trusted her judgment about men sufficiently to follow her instincts and let herself love Nelson.

How much proof do I need? She undressed, completed her ablutions, said her prayers, and was about to crawl into bed. Feeling perverse, angry at herself, and wanton at the same time, she pulled off her gown and slipped her nude body between yellow satin sheets, the latter being one of her few extravagances.

She didn't understand the unadulterated wickedness that stole over her as she reached over for the phone and dialed Nelson's number. The minute she heard his voice, she wished she hadn't yielded to the impulse.

"Hello, Audrey. Are you all right?"

"I . . . uh . . . I just called to say good night."

"You sound as if you're lying down. Are you in bed?"

She wanted to kick herself, because she either had to admit it or lie, and she hated to lie. How could he tell? She decided to finesse the question. "Whatever gave you that idea?"

"The soft, kittenish sound of your voice, that's what," he said in something approaching a growl. "If you want me to come back over there, just say the word."

She tried to decelerate the rate of her breathing so that he wouldn't be aware of her turmoil. "I called to . . . to say . . . good night, Nelson."

"You owe me better than that, Audrey. You know . . . one of these days you and I will lay our cards on the table. Secrets, fears, baggage we can't seem to get rid of. I've been wondering what we'd be like together if we didn't have all that stuff dragging us down."

"You're speaking for you, I take it."

"No. I'm speaking for us. You think I'm so stupid I don't know the reason you keep a protective barrier around yourself? Same reason that I do. Baggage. I'm going to take a good look at mine, and I think it would be good if you did the same. In my case, the damage was done almost six years ago, which means I've let someone control one of the most important areas of my life, a someone whose main contribution to my life has been pain. Isn't that what you're doing?"

"Well?" he said when she didn't answer.

"If all you've felt is pain," she said at last, "consider yourself fortunate. I have the pain, yes, but sometimes the hatred I feel is so intense, so passionate, that it's enervating."

"I'm sorry. Really sorry. For both of us. We'd be great together, but unfortunately neither of us is able to get over that hurdle. I've just had a good talk with myself, though, and I'm turning a corner. I intend to try my damndest to put it behind me."

She was sitting up now, the feline-like prowl that had beset her earlier had dissolved with the impact of his admission. His words hadn't surprised her, but she hadn't expected that he would ever utter them to her. He intended to free himself of the past. If only she could do the same.

"To promise I'll do the same would be tantamount to telling you I'll learn how to throw an elephant."

"Let me help you."

She leaned back against the headboard and looked toward the ceiling. "How can you? I need to help myself."

"Give me a chance."

"Oh, Nelson. I heard those exact words before, and I complied. To my regret. I know in every chamber of my heart that you're different, but I can't see myself opening up to a man. If you knew! If you only knew!"

"When you trust me, you'll tell me."

She exhaled a long breath. "I guess that goes for both of us." She blew him a kiss. "Good night."

"At least you didn't forget my kiss. Good night, babe."

She didn't want to get up and put on her gown, and she was no longer in the mood to sleep nude. How could you love a man if you didn't trust him not to break your heart? She didn't know if she could ever love *any* man again. And yet . . .

Monday morning following that all-revealing Saturday, Nelson sat at his desk working out a military game, a strategy for helicopter defense in the absence of other air cover, when he received a call from Lieutenant McCafferty, the Commandant's aide. In response to her request, he walked down the hall to Room 100-A, two doors removed from his own office. He entered the Commandant's reception room and stopped. If his hair had stood straight up on his head, he wouldn't have been surprised. However, he strolled over to the man whose presence shocked him, and offered his hand.

"Good to see you again, Colonel Holden. I'm sure you're glad to be back."

Rupert Holden, known in the service as Rupe, had just returned from Afghanistan, where he'd served in the unit that had once been under Nelson's command. A Lieutenant Colonel, and thus one rank below Nelson, he, too, commanded respect.

"It's good to be back, too. I'm hoping for a lengthy tour stateside, but I don't think there's much chance. I'm told my office is a few doors down from yours, so we'll be seeing each other."

The officers stood, and Nelson looked around to see that the Commandant had entered the room. The Commandant introduced them to Rupe Holden in a briefing that lasted about three minutes, after which they were dismissed. Nelson shook hands with Holden again and hurried back to his office. Rupert Holden was the last person he needed in his life, the man who might know about the one time he broke Marine Corps rules and who, given the opportunity and a chance to curry favor, would delight in reporting it.

Holden didn't mind ratting on his fellow officers and had done so several times. His superiors ignored the incidences Holden reported, claiming that such matters were personal and unrelated to the officers' responsibilities. Nelson didn't believe in infidelity, but he didn't think Holden should have reported the officer who commited the act.

Nelson wasn't certain, but in an afterthought, it seemed to him that Holden hadn't given him the deference that one officer accorded a more senior one. If so, it might mean that Holden knew he'd overlooked a Marine sergeant's infraction of the rules by sleeping on guard duty one night. He'd have to face the consequences of that when the time came.

"Where you going on vacation, sir?" Lena asked him when he got home. "You and Ricky need a vacation. You know, some change of environment."

He propped his left foot on the bottom stair step and let a grin play around his lips. Used to Lena's way of talking around a point when she wasn't sure of her ground, he laid his head to one side the better to observe her unobtrusively.

"In other words, there's someplace you want to go for about a week. Right?"

Laughter rolled out of her. "I declare, Colonel, if sometimes I don't think you're psychic. You young people don't do nothing but work. I been telling Audrey she gon' be dull as dirtballs."

He held up his hand. "That's enough of that. There's no reason for Audrey and me to take our vacations together."

She tossed her head. "That so? Things must've changed since I was your age. All right. There's this family reunion we have every other year. This year, it'll be in Orlando. If I'm going, I need to make my reservation right now."

He wondered if she thought she could wind him around her finger. "When is the reunion, Lena?"

"Uh . . . weekend after this one coming up."

"You may go, with my blessings. Do I still need a vacation?"

"Sure thing. But Ricky said he wants Audrey to go too."

"*Too?* You've been discussing this with Ricky?"

"Yes sir, he's a member of this family." She rushed from the room muttering, "I do declare."

He figured Ricky would nag him till he promised him a vacation with Audrey, but it wouldn't happen. He went to his room, put his cervical collar around his neck, sat down, and luxuriated in the relief he felt. Sounds of little fingers scraping across the harp in Ricky's room drew him, magnetlike, and he found Ricky standing in front of his father's harp, trying to play it.

The child ran to him, squealing his welcome. "Unca Nelson, I wanna play the harp!"

"But I thought we agreed you would learn the piano first until you got bigger and your arms were longer."

"I like the piano, and I like the harp, too."

"All right. I'll get some professional advice about this and we will act accordingly. You understand?"

"Yes, sir. When will we get it?"

"It may take a couple of weeks, so try to be patient. In the meantime—"

"I know. Miss Lena said in the meantime I have to practice the piano."

He caressed the boy's shoulder, and Ricky looked up at him, smiled, and went back to the harp. *Why,* he thought, *don't adults feel free to express love?* Ricky's smile told him more that words ever could. The child adored him. He looked at his watch.

"What do you say we drive over to the Waterfowl Sanctuary and look at the birds?"

Ricky's face bloomed into a smile, and he knew what was coming. "Can Audie go, too, Unca Nelson?"

He was beginning to wonder if there was such a thing as Powers disease; if so, both he and Ricky had a severe case of it.

"Call her and ask her."

"Nobody answers," Ricky said a few minutes later. "Can we go to her house and get her?"

The child had to learn that he couldn't always have what he wanted the way he wanted it. Nelson sat down. "Come here. A man does not go to a woman's house unless she tells him he may visit her. Understand? We'll ask her to go with us next time. Clear?"

The boy's balled fists went to his sides, and he slanted his head, as he'd learned to do watching Lena. "Okay. But I don't like that, Unca Nelson."

His action's were a parroting of Lena, but the child's facial expression reminded Nelson of his brother, and he had to push aside the moroseness that attacked him without warning.

"Do we have to go today?" Ricky asked him.

He understood that the child wanted to share the experience with Audrey, and sympathized with him. "No, we don't. We'll go one day when Audrey can come with us."

Ricky looked up at him for a minute, then hugged him. "I'm going to practice my piano lesson," he said, and ran down the stairs.

Nelson shook his head in wonder. *As thanks for my considerateness, he won't nag me about the harp, and he will practice the piano. Great! He's only five. What will he be like when he's fifteen?*

He answered his beeper, wary, his senses heightened. "Yes."

"Checkmate. Your man is in the neighborhood, seemingly out for a stroll, but he's got company."

He waited a few minutes, stood beside his bedroom window so as not to be seen and checked the surroundings. Very soon, Mustache walked by with a big black Doberman pinscher on a leash. Out walking his dog, eh? What a blessing that he and Ricky hadn't walked out of the house about that time. Suddenly, he laughed as a woman on in-line skates floated past. What a farce! This time, he knew the identity of his caller as soon as he heard the beep.

"Checkmate. Anything of consequence?"

"Not that I could tell. Talk to the old lady on the in-line skates."

"She's on the job. That canine is trained to attack."

He figured as much. "When are you going to let me know who I'm dealing with and why?"

"We should have something for you in a couple of days. A week at most. Tell your girlfriend not to drive home through Rock Creek Park, day or night. If you told her what's happening, she should know better. We're putting a man in her reception. Oh, yes, and tell your housekeeper to vary her marketing hours. So long."

He waited fifteen minutes and dialed Audrey's number. "This is Dr. Powers," she said. He gave her the gist of his conversation with Marilyn and of his now-defunct plan to invite her to visit the Waterfowl Sanctuary with Ricky and himself. "That could have been a close one."

"Right. Sorry I wasn't home; I would have loved seeing the Waterfowl Sanctuary, but it might have been well that I left the office early to attend a meeting. This other thing seems serious. How will I know the identity of the person she's sending to my clinic?"

"He'll show you his ID before he says a word. Of course, it could be a female. I work for an equal-opportunity employer," he added with a laugh.

"If this doesn't get cleared up soon, I'll have the willies."

That was only one of his worries. "You and me both."

"Where's Ricky?" Told that he was practicing the piano, she said, "He's lucky to have you in his life."

Good enough for him, but not for you, he thought and nearly voiced the words. "He's done as much for me as I have for him. 'Bye for now." She said good-bye and he hung up to contemplate his last words to her.

At noon the next day, he locked his briefcase in his desk drawer and went to meet Rufus Meade for lunch. He didn't often allow himself the time or the expense of the Willard Room, that turn-of-the-twentieth-century elegance in the famed Willard Hotel where the country's movers and shakers sealed deals over expensive lunches preceded by whatever cocktail was in vogue. To his way of thinking, that kind of elegance in the middle of the day was conducive to an afternoon of intellectual stupor. A hamburger and coffee was more to his liking.

He followed the maitre'd to the table, where Rufus Meade rose and stepped forward to greet him. A tall man, about an inch shorter than his own six-foot-five frame, Meade looked as fit as if he still raced down the field catching passes for the Washington Redskins. As an investigative journalist, the man had achieved legendary status for his meticulous, perceptive, sometimes jarring but always empathetic news accounts, which often precipitated social change. Change for the better.

Meade extended his hand. "Thanks for coming. I've been looking forward to this."

"So have I," Nelson said. "I'm very familiar with your work." He looked up at the sommelier who hovered over them and shook his head. "No cocktail for me. Thanks."

"And none for me," Meade said. "Liquor fogs up the brain."

They gave the waiter their order, each preferring a light lunch, and while they waited for the food, he observed Meade's relaxed, casual air, wondering how much of it was feigned and how much was a natural element of the man's personality. He didn't seem eager to rush the interview, but spoke of himself and what he had observed while in Afghanistan.

This man is not only a sharp professional, Nelson thought, *but he understands people and he's letting me know that he's on top of his subject, that he knows a lot about Afghanistan, the people, and the American anti-terrorist activities there. He's telling me that when it comes to knowledge of the place, we're equals.*

Meade didn't begin the interview until they had finished the meal and were sipping coffee. He had only half a dozen questions, each of them incisive and relevant.

"Here's my last question," he said after about forty minutes. "Will you go back there, and will you ever pilot another Super Cobra helicopter?"

"I'm prepared to go wherever my orders demand, though not quite so readily as when I didn't have a dependent. My late brother's five-year-old son is in my care, and I would prefer not to leave him, but I'm trying to teach him that I may someday have to do precisely that. As for that copter, I can hardly wait to get back in the cockpit. If not that, I'll take the F-16 any day." He steeled himself against the pain that shot through his right shoulder, grateful that Meade didn't notice.

"I wasn't aware that you pilot the F-16."

"Oh, yes. Well before I flew the copter. It's an exhilarating experience."

"I can imagine, and I'm glad we have men like you who enjoy it."

They walked out of the dinning room together and stood in the lobby talking. "If you have any questions, give me a call," Nelson said, "though I can't imagine there's anything left to ask."

"Thanks, I'll . . . say, can you think of a reason why a guy in black suit with a narrow lapel, white shirt, and dark tie would be so interested in us? I thought he was lip reading when we were waiting for lunch, so I made sure he didn't get anything important. Actually, I didn't start the interview until he left. Now, here he is peering over the top of that newspaper."

He could only feign ignorance as he looked in the direction to which Meade nodded. "Beats me. I didn't see him in the dinning room."

"He was behind you."

Outside, on the corner of Fourteenth Street and Pennsylvania Avenue, they shook hands and went their separate ways. Nelson turned the corner, took out his cellular phone, and dialed Marilyn's number. "Checkmate. Mustache followed me to lunch at the Willard Room."

"I know. We have a tail on him as well as on you. Not to worry. Talk later."

He was becoming annoyed with her superior attitude. If she knew something, he wished to hell she'd let him in on it. If the fellow was haunting his neighborhood with an attack dog for company, he deserved to know why. He dialed her number and told her so.

"I'm getting damned sick and tired of that guy, and if he doesn't blow off, I'm going to confront him. It isn't just me; it's my family and my—"

"I know you're frustrated and you need to vent," she said, "but please limit your venting to me. We have this well under control. Later." Maybe so, but he didn't know her definition of control.

He was standing at her door when Audrey arrived at work that morning. She stopped three feet away to await his move, but he didn't keep her guessing and, as Nelson had explained, smiled and held his official ID well out in front of him so that she could see it with ease.

"Morning ma'am, I'll just sit here and read," he said, looking around. "Right over there in that corner by the lamp. You won't know I'm here."

She would have labeled him as anything but a security officer. Handsome in an off-the-wall sort of way with fine features and a self-deprecating manner, he didn't wait for her assent, but headed for the corner, took a copy of a horse-racing journal out of his pocket, and opened it as if to read.

"Who's that man in there?" her receptionist asked later that morning. "He's been sitting in there for three hours, and he hasn't said a word to me about fitting him in."

"I spoke to him as I came in this morning," she said. Nobody had told her how to explain the man's presence. She went into her office, closed the door, and phoned Nelson on her cell phone.

"He knows what to tell her," Nelson said. "If she

brings it up again, tell her to speak to him. Uh . . . Lena's going South to a family reunion this weekend. Want to make Ricky and me happy?"

She leaned back in her chair and prepared herself for his next sally. "I'd love to make the two of you happy, but not if it involves housekeeping in any of its forms. Besides, you know I don't cook."

"Really!" His voice had a rough, jagged sound. "If I ask you to cook up something, you bet it won't be food."

Her eyebrows shot up. "Wait a minute. You don't have to get your dander up. I'm not apologizing, either."

It didn't surprise her that he ignored her last remark. She had learned that if he didn't want to engage in a topic, he didn't mention it.

"As I was about to ask, would you like to spend the weekend somewhere nearby, a place that offers swimming, fishing, a place that has good weather, trees, water, hiking—"

She interrupted him. "You make it sound like heaven, Nelson, but heaven isn't what you want right now, and I'm not sure I'd enjoy being there all by myself."

"Talk that way sometimes when I'm with you. I guarantee it'll bring results."

"Promises, promises. I want to see some action."

"When it comes to you, Audrey, I don't have a sense of humor. None at all. So don't expect laughter when we're talking about *us*. What'll it be? Yes or no?"

"I don't think so. I'm trying to get the cobwebs out of my life, and being with you confuses me. I'm trying to go about this logically."

"And getting nowhere. I'll answer for you. I've tried it, and I know it's useless. This is a matter of the heart, and hearts don't give a hoot about what is or isn't logical. You know that."

"If I could just be at peace. If I could have contentment, a warm satisfied feeling about my life and my world, I'd settle."

He was silent for a while, but she didn't mind because he always measured his words with care when he spoke seriously. "I've come to the conclusion that, together, each of us would find far, far more. So, I'm not settling for less. From now on, expect to deal with me in a serious manner. You understand?"

Stunned, she detected a quiver in her voice and knew that he did, too, when she said, "I . . . uh . . . please excuse me this weekend and give Ricky my love. You've made it through, but I'm still floundering."

"Audrey, whenever I have accepted my own culpableness in the things that have gone wrong in my life, I have always been able to put them behind me, and that's what I'm trying to do now. My father used to say that so long as we hold someone else responsible for what happens to us, we won't try to change it. I'm telling myself to apply that rigorously, and I hope you succeed in doing the same."

This man is philosophical, she thought, and then he suddenly changed his manner. "Besides, I'm a decent fellow: I'm neat and clean with my person; I hate garlic, so you don't have to shy away from kissing me; I make a good living; I say my prayers when I get scared; and I don't do drugs. I'm a real pussycat. On top of all that, I'm a lover from head to foot, and I'd like to know what the hell else could a woman want?"

By the time he finished that litany, she was nearly convulsed with laughter. *I could love him,* she thought. *Oh, Lord. How I could love this man!* To him, she said, "So now you're a comedian. Send me a notarized affidavit that you're all those things, and I'll hang my coat in your closet."

"Whoa there. Tomorrow I'll have my lawyer send you

a notarized affidavit spelling that out in detail. So if you mean what you said—"

She didn't believe him. "You do that. I've got a patient in there. This kind of joshing can get out of hand. Enjoy your weekend."

Flustered. She did not like being flustered, and that was what he did to her. She peeped in on the government's man, saw that he continued to read the racing sheet, and resisted asking him if the paper was transparent. She told herself not to get fanciful.

"What do you do for lunch?" she asked the man.

"My replacement will be here at one, and he'll stay until you close up. He'll also see you safely home or wherever you're going."

She stared at him. "If I were planning to rob a bank, would one of you tag along?"

"We're on the lookout for criminals. Any kind, regardless of age, sex, or previous condition of servitude. I believe that's the way it reads somewhere in the Constitution. Or is it the Bill of Rights?"

She figured his answer suited her question. "Sorry. I asked for that."

"This is serious business, ma'am. My office doesn't lay out this amount of resources for no reason."

"It's my intention to cooperate," she said, "but as an intelligent person, I feel the need to know what I'm in danger of."

"I'm sure you know who to ask about that," he said and let his gaze fall once more on the racing sheet, effectively terminating the discussion.

He referred to Nelson, she knew, but if he possessed that information, he hadn't seen fit to pass it on to her.

At one o'clock, man number one, as she decided to call him, introduced her to man number two, who looked for all the world like a criminal himself, and told her he'd left her in good hands and would see her the next morning. She didn't know what kind of explanation number one gave to her receptionist, but he had evidently placated the woman. When she arrived home that afternoon, her guard went in, checked the place, and left.

She prowled around the house, wishing she hadn't been so glib with Nelson and that she'd taken his suggestion of a weekend vacation seriously. Nothing claimed her attention for long. During half an hour, she spent some time in every part of her house, including the foyer and back porch, pacing from room to room without thought as to why she did it. An irritating odor brought her racing into the kitchen where she saw the charred meal that had been warming on the stove.

Call him and tell him you changed your mind, that you want to go with them. "Never!" she said aloud. She went to the phone to order a take-out meal for her dinner, and stopped in the process of dialing the restaurant. Suppose that man paid the delivery boy to let him bring the food!

"Oh, Lord," she said storming back to the kitchen to cook. "I'm getting paranoid."

She answered the telephone after the second ring, hoping she would hear Nelson's voice.

"Do you mind if I come over, sis?" Winifred asked. "I've got to talk, and Pam's starting to sound as if she's my mother. Sometimes I think she was born old."

"Of course. Say, would you bring over dinner for two. I just burned mine." She hung up at the sound of Winifred's laughter.

"What's the problem?" she asked Winifred as they ate a meal of jerked buffalo wings, stewed collards, candied sweet potatoes, and baked cornbread—Winifred's kind of food, but which Audrey considered a health hazard.

"It's Ryan. I know we've only known each other for a month, but he's it for me. Am I foolish to want to go away with him for a weekend?"

Her fork clattered to the plate, and her hand remained a few inches from her mouth as if frozen there. When she found her voice, she said, "But Wendy, honey, you're a virgin. How can you consider such a thing?"

As if she hadn't dropped that bomb, Winifred continued to enjoy her food. "I love him, and I know it's the real thing. I've known lots of guys, played around with four or five—one in particular, but I have never felt anything approximating what I feel for Ryan. When I'm with him, nothing else in this whole wide world matters or even seems real. The minute I looked at him, I was a goner. Besides, he knows I'm a virgin, 'cause I told him."

"What did he say to that?"

"His eyes got pretty big. Then he grinned and said he wouldn't hold that against me. He loves me, Audrey, and he communicates it to me in so many ways. So why shouldn't we be together?"

She took a deep breath, let it out, and tried to think. "I haven't seen you and this man together, so I can't judge; indeed, I don't know him and I probably shouldn't compare your relationship with him to mine with Gerald Latham. But . . ."

Suddenly, she remembered her turmoil before Winifred called her, her dilemma about Nelson and her lack of courage to call him and tell him she wanted to spend the weekend with him and Ricky. What right did she have to discourage her sister? Every woman had to decide for herself the man with whom she would learn to make love.

"But what?" Winifred asked her.

"But nothing. You're old enough to know your feelings, and if he's the first man you've really wanted, I take my hat off to him. You love him? Go for it."

Physician, heal thyself. Those biblical words came to her as if from nowhere. She had allowed that opportunity to be with Nelson in a different, perhaps more intimate, environment slip by, but in her present frame of mind, she didn't think she would pass up another chance. Nelson had not suggested a lovers' idyll, she recalled; if he had that in mind, he would surely leave Ricky at home. *I've got to stop being so uptight about men, especially about Nelson. If I don't get my act together, he'll kiss me off.* And that, she knew, in a moment of enlightenment, she could not bear.

"We're talking about you and Nelson as well as Ryan and me, aren't we?"

"I guess so."

"Auntie says he's a wonderful man, that he treats her as if she were his mother, and he's a good father to Ricky. He doesn't have women running in and out of there, either. Why can't you straighten things out with him? I got the impression that he thinks a lot of you."

"He does." She reached across the table and patted her sister's hand. "If this talk has been good for you, it's been a blessing to me. Pam doesn't have to approve, and she doesn't have to know you spent the weekend with Ryan. She's got Hendren, and she's happy with him."

"Yeah, and that's an amazement to me," Winifred said. "Pam doesn't believe you should make love with a guy unless you're married to him. She lucked out, but I'm scared to take that chance." She grinned. "Besides, my hormones are acting out."

"As long as you're sure."

"Not a doubt."

She looked out of the living room window, watched Winifred get into her car, and hoped her sister was as right as she was sure. Hours later, she went to bed, still at odds with herself for having rejected Nelson. It would be a long and lonely weekend.

Nelson couldn't remember when he had enjoyed so relaxing a weekend as he had the previous few days with Ricky in St. Michaels, Maryland. The boy had loved the cruise on the Chesapeake Bay, and his enjoyment of the water reminded Nelson of Joel, for whom swimming represented the peak of relaxation. Many times, he'd wished Audrey was with them, but he knew and appreciated that she needed to take her time, that for her, joining them would have been tantamount to a commitment. He walked into his office that Monday morning and closed the door.

"Please don't disturb me this morning," he said to his secretary. "I have to finish this report."

That much was true, but his reason for wanting to work undisturbed had more to do with the pain in his neck and shoulders. He had to put on his hard cervical collar to ease the discomfort, and he didn't want to be caught wearing it. By noon, the pain eased, and he removed the collar and locked it in his desk drawer.

As he left his office for lunch, Lieutenant Colonel Holden strode toward him. "You stay out of sight, Colonel," Holden said. "I take it you're over the injuries you got when you crashed your copter."

So the man had served notice that he would live up to his reputation. "I thought you knew my helicopter took a hit in the fuel tank." He ground his teeth, a sure sign that he was on the verge of losing his temper. "Yes. You do know it. Fortunately, so do several dozen other men, including my copilot. I spent a couple of months recovering, but that's behind me. See you around."

He hated being angry, especially not when he was about to eat. He got a ham and cheese sandwich, a banana, and coffee in the cafeteria and went back to his office to find his red light flashing.

He got that signal only when there was an emergency. A serious one.

Seven

It could be anything. He punched the code and waited. "Lieutenant McCafferty speaking."

Relief flushed his body with such force that he had to sit down as he realized the problem wasn't with Ricky, Lena, or Audrey. "Colonel Wainwright answering your call," he said with such calm that he hardly recognized his own voice. "What's the good news?"

"You may not think it's so good. You're wanted at Camp Pendleton tomorrow morning. Be ready to leave this evening. We have a contingent going to Afghanistan, and the officer who was to brief them has become ill. You're to fill in."

He threw up his hands and looked toward the ceiling. "My housekeeper is in South Carolina at an address unknown to me, and I'll have to either make child-care arrangements for my five-year-old or take him with me. I'll get back to you in the next hour."

He didn't recall previously having considered any aspect of his Marine Corps responsibilities as a burden. But he regarded the order that would reach him in writing momentarily as an inconvenience, and he didn't have to be told that domestic life with Ricky and Lena had pared away some of his military crust, shaved off some of his toughness and his disregard of personal inconvenience. The thought arose that Audrey may have played a role in the change he recognized in himself, but he pushed that aside.

He leaned back in his desk chair, made a pyramid of his fingers, and braced them against his chin. What were his options? Handing Ricky over to foster care even for two or three days would have a traumatic effect and rob the boy of the sense of security that he'd worked so hard to build. He couldn't do that.

"I'll take him with me," he said aloud. "Naah. That won't work; he'd have to sit with me in those briefings." He couldn't ask Audrey, because she had to work. Still musing over the problem, he answered the phone.

"Wainwright."

"Hello, Nelson. This is Audrey. How was your weekend?"

"Wonderful. I've never seen a person enjoy anything as much as Ricky enjoyed the cruise and the water. He loves the water as much as his father did."

"Where did you go?"

"St. Michaels on the Eastern Shore of Maryland. I think Ricky wouldn't mind if we moved over there."

"Sorry I missed that. I couldn't make myself call you back and tell you I wanted to go, much as I longed to."

His antenna shot up. "Are you telling me you changed your mind and couldn't drum up the will to let me know? Huh?"

"That's just about the size of it."

"Where are you now?"

"In my office. The gov's man number two is keeping watch. I was wondering if you'd like to go for ice cream or something this evening."

Her question took his mind back to the problem facing him. "I'd love that, Audrey, but I have to leave for California this evening. Lena isn't back from South Carolina, and when you called, I was deciding whether to take Ricky with me. I'm damned if I'll leave him in a foster home."

"What about me? Why can't he stay with me? Or . . . or don't you want me to keep him?"

"I thought about it, but you have to work, and I wouldn't expect you to stay away from your office in order to look after Ricky."

"He and I will work that out exactly as we did when he stayed with me before. What time are you leaving your office?"

"In about an hour. I'll pick Ricky up from day camp and take him home."

"Then suppose I meet you at your house in an hour and a half?"

"Okay. You can't imagine what a load you've taken from me. Saying I appreciate it sounds trite, but I do."

"All right. Hang up and do whatever you have to. See you later."

"I have to go to California, son," he said to Ricky, "and I may be away a few days, but you'll have a good time with Audrey till Miss Lena comes back."

"Oooh!" Ricky's eyes seemed to double in size. "I'm staying with Audie?" He slapped his hands together. "Unca Nelson, please tell her I can have all the ice cream I want. Please, Unca Nelson!"

"I think it's best to let her judge. After all, she's a doctor. I'm sure you'll get plenty of it."

He packed a bag for himself and one for Ricky and brought them down to the foyer. "I can trust you to obey Audrey, can't I?" he said to Ricky.

The boy looked up at him with eyes so like his father's, and he saw in them a sadness. He realized that much as Ricky would love being with Audrey, the child didn't want Nelson to leave him. He hunkered beside him.

"I'll be away only a few days, son, and I'll call you. All right?"

Ricky nodded, and Nelson could see his struggle to push back the tears that pooled unshed in his eyes. He drew the child into his arms and hugged him. The doorbell rang, and Ricky dashed out of his arms and ran to the door. "Is it Audie, Unca Nelson? Is it?" How like a child to embrace the sure thing.

He opened the door and gazed down into her eyes. "Hi."

"Hi."

He took her hand, pulled her inside the foyer, and into his arms. He held her as close as he dared considering that he had to leave her within the next ten minutes, and when she opened to him as a flower opens to the morning sun, he cursed his luck. There was a difference in her bearing, in her demeanor and in the way her body surrendered to him. What a time to walk away from her! Reaching deep within himself for restraint, both because he had to leave her and because Ricky had fastened his gaze on them, he pressed a kiss to her lips. She parted them, and he tasted her sweetness, just enough of her to stoke the fire that already blazed within him.

He set her away from him with care. "When I get back, we'll be together." She nodded. "Do you understand me?"

She reached up and kissed his cheek. "Yes. Be safe and hurry back." With that, she picked up Ricky's suitcase, took the boy's hand, strapped him into the back seat of her car, and drove away.

He watched until he could no longer see them. Then

he scribbled a note to Lena, picked up his bag, and
headed for Dulles International Airport.

For once she welcomed the security agent who tailed
her home. Although familiar with his car and tags, she
slowed down until she could see the driver's face in her
rear view mirror. Even so, she didn't drive through
Rock Creek Park. When she reached home, he got out
and spoke with her. "Are you taking the boy with you
tomorrow morning?"

"I was planning to do that, leave around one for
lunch, and then come on home. Is that inconvenient?"

"Not at all. I suggest you use your own car, avoid
taxis, and always make sure that I'm close behind you."

"In other words, don't drive fast."

"You got it. We're playing it close to the chest until
Colonel Wainwright gets back. I'll check out the house
for you."

"I'm going to have our dinner delivered," she told
him. She hated announcing that she wasn't much of a
cook, and maybe she ought to learn, but she didn't think
Ricky would appreciate the fare she offered. "About
seven."

"No problem. I'll be around."

Even with that assurance, she felt uncomfortable.
However, Ricky claimed his old room and made himself
at home. She found the movies she'd chosen for him
when he stayed with her previously, and he was soon ab-
sorbed in *Snow White*.

Along with their dinner, she ordered a half-gallon
each of strawberry and black raspberry ice cream. "Did
you get the ice cream, Audie?" he asked her as she set
the table. Assured that she had, he hugged her.

"I love you a lot, Audie. A whole lot."

"I know," she said. "And I love you a whole lot, too."

"I'm gonna eat all of my dinner if you don't give me too much. I have to eat my ice cream."

This child is sending me messages, she thought, after singing him to sleep. She stood beside his bed gazing down at his sweet, peaceful face and felt her heart constrict. Surprising herself, she leaned over him, kissed his cheek, and fought the impulse to gather him into her arms. At that moment, she saw her life as it was, one-sided. Empty of love and warmth. Unfulfilled.

She plowed her fingers through her hair and rushed from the room. Even with her profession and the solid respect of her peers, she deserved more than she had. "But if I got pregnant, how could I care for my patients?" she asked herself aloud. Appalled at the revealing words, she slapped her hand over her mouth. What on earth was she thinking? What had come over her?

The second afternoon after Nelson left for California, Audrey received a call from Lena. "I just got home and found the Colonel's note. You can bring Ricky home, and I'll give both of you a decent meal. Poor little tyke, I'll bet he's starved for some good cooking."

"He's been eating like a king. We had McDonald's hamburgers and fries for lunch, and I sent out for our dinners. Uh . . . Aunt Lena, if you have something to do, he can stay with me. He loves going to the office."

"I bet he does, but we got to do what the Colonel wants. Ricky can practice medicine some other time."

To Audrey's surprise, after Ricky had embraced Lena with exuberance, he started up the stairs and stopped. "Miss Lena, where's my Unca Nelson?"

She exchanged glances with Lena. Did the boy remember the time his father hadn't come back home? He ran to Lena with arms outstretched. "Is Unca Nelson coming home?"

Lena bent and hugged the boy. "He'll be home, son, just as soon as he finishes his assignment."

"When will he do that, Miss Lena?"

"Two or three days."

"Oh." He looked at Audrey. "Are you going to stay with us?"

What should she say to that? "No, but I'll come see you after I leave the office tomorrow."

That seemed to placate him, though he didn't smile. "You will?" She nodded, and he turned his attention to Lena. "I'm hungry, Miss Lena."

While Lena set the table, Ricky ambled around the house, clearly discombobulated and out of sorts. The telephone rang, and he raced to answer it.

"Hello. This is Ricky Wainwright."

Audrey watched as his face bloomed into a smile and the light in his eyes brightened. "Unca Nelson! Where are you, Unca Nelson? When are you coming home?" He listened for a while. "How many days till Saturday? Okay. Okay, I will. Unca Nelson wants to talk to you, Audie." He handed her the phone and ran to the kitchen, the picture of happiness.

"Hello, Nelson." She gave him an account of Ricky's visit with her and of her experiences with the guards assigned to secure her safety. "I'll be glad to see you. If the officials discovered anything since you left, they wouldn't tell me."

"Is that the only reason why you'll be glad to see me?"

"That question hardly deserves an answer. I miss you."

"Same here. Keep Saturday night for us."

"All right," she said, aware that he deliberately said "for us" rather than "for me."

He spoke with Lena for a few minutes. He wasn't obliged to talk with his housekeeper, but she knew he spoke with her aunt because he regarded her as a member of his family. It was such graciousness on his part that first garnered her respect and interest, and which now endeared him to her.

After they finished dinner, she read to Ricky and, using her laptop computer, taught him how to log on and access the Internet. Later, she supervised his bath, put him to bed, and sang to him until he slept.

She would miss Ricky's bedtime ritual, for it had come to represent to her a time of bonding with him, and in those times, she felt closest to him. She drove home under the watchful eyes of the number two man.

By the time Saturday afternoon arrived, her nerves had frazzled themselves. What should she do? How would she respond to him, and shouldn't she call a halt to the relationship and let them stop torturing each other?

She opened her door to him at seven-thirty that Saturday evening, and noticed at once that he'd dressed to the nines. Elegance was natural to him, but he had obviously put forth special effort to look great. Thank God she'd had the good sense to dress up. She gazed up at him. Quintessential male, and all hers—for the evening at least—if she had the sense and the guts to take him. She held out her right hand.

"Come on in. It's as if I haven't seen you in years."

He brushed her cheek with his lips, and the expression on her face must have mirrored her surprise, for he explained, "Anything heavier than that, and we probably wouldn't get any dinner. You're beautiful. What I call the perfect blend of female."

She did nothing to erase the frown that gathered on her forehead. "What do you mean by that?"

"Where your work is concerned, you're one-hundred-percent professional, but in your private life, you are all woman. You suit me to a tee."

She gathered up the skirt of her long, flowing, red dress as she walked down the steps with him, and when they reached his BMW, she said, "It's a good thing you can't see the rush of blood to my face. Thanks, though, for the compliment."

He buckled her seat belt, closed the door, went around to the drivers side, and got in. "Don't think of what I said as a compliment; I told the truth as I see it, and that includes the fact that you suit me. I don't know exactly when I came to that conclusion, but it is ir-refutable."

She didn't have an answer for that. "Was your mission successful?" she asked, in effect changing the subject.

"You bet. I wish every one of my assignments went off so easily. Lecturing is simple compared to most of the other tasks we get. What do you say we go to Kinkead's? I have reservations for eight o'clock, but we can still cancel."

Surely she hadn't heard him correctly. "Cancel Kinkead's? You couldn't be serious. I'd love to go there!" He drove to Pennsylvania and Twentieth Street Northwest, and gave his car over to the valet.

"How did you know I would dress?" she asked him.

He shrugged. "I figured that if I knew the occasion called for it, so did you."

She looked up at him and then quickly lowered her

lashes. "That kind of thinking can get you in a mess of trouble."

When she looked at him, his wink nearly knocked her off balance. "Trust me. When it's important, I leave nothing to chance." *Like tonight,* he seemed to imply.

The waiter seated them in the upstairs dining room in a cozy alcove that boasted a round table for two beneath a hanging candelabra that lent a soft glow to the setting and gave the palm trees beside it a tropical shimmer.

"Do you like it?" he asked her before the waiter left them.

"It's very special," she said, and it was. He accepted the menus and tipped the maitre'd.

After a dinner that met the highest standards, he paid the check and stood. "Ready to go?"

She guessed so, but the butterflies in her stomach demanded that she deal with them, so she decided she'd best level with him.

"My nerves are shredded," she said, "and they may not straighten themselves out. Just thought I'd warn you." She'd meant to sound flippant, but didn't succeed.

He splayed his hand on her back and urged her toward the exit. People that she suspected were notables greeted him as they passed, and not a few women gaped at him. He walked behind her, and she couldn't tell what effect that adulation had on him.

During the drive to her home, he spoke for the first time since leaving the dinner table. "Don't worry about shredded nerves; mine aren't exactly dormant. But they don't have to be calm in order for me to be efficient. You know what I'm saying?"

She did indeed, and figured she would be more comfortable with a different subject. "Any chance we'll get rid of these bodyguards soon?"

She didn't believe he wanted to talk about that, but he

answered her question. "Probably a week, at most. A few things happened while I was in California that suggest Mustache and his friends have become impatient."

She heard herself gasp. "Friends?"

"Yeah. These things are never a matter of one person. I'm told that their goal is no secret; the only problem is catching them in the act."

"But that's dangerous."

"For them, yes. Our folks are on the job."

He stopped in front of her house and cut the motor. "I'd like to come in, Audrey."

She knew that, but she appreciated his saying so. "Want to put your car in the garage?"

He shook his head. "It'll be fine right here."

"Would you like a glass of wine?" she asked, once they were inside, not as a means of stalling, but because she wanted whatever happened between them to evolve naturally.

"I'd love it, but just one."

She took that as a signal that he didn't plan on spending the night. What else could it mean? As if divining her thoughts, he said, "I don't think it's a good idea for Ricky to wake up in the morning and find I'm not there. He's not yet as secure about me as I had thought."

"I noticed that when I took him home and he discovered you weren't there. Be right back."

She slipped into the guest bathroom, brushed her teeth, then got a bottle of chilled white Bordeaux from the refrigerator and two stemmed glasses.

"Would you like a petit-four? Or, I've got some cheesecake."

He stood, took the wine and glasses from her hand and placed them on the coffee table. "Sit here with me, and tell me what you're nervous about. If you don't feel that this is right, I'll understand and we'll work toward it. But I want you to know that I don't have a single reservation. I want this with you, and I'll welcome the consequences."

"Do you know what you said?"

"Definitely. I said exactly what I meant." He took her hand and sat closer to her on the sofa. "I know a man misused your trust, that he deceived you. I've figured out that he dealt you a blow. I am what you see; if you can't trust me, tell me now and I'll be on my way."

"I've done a lot of thinking, soul-searching or whatever you want to call it, since you said you no longer consider this attraction between us as anathema, and I—"

"Whoa! I never said it was anathema, but that a deep involvement with you or any other woman wasn't for me. But slowly you got into me, seeped into my head, my heart, my veins, my whole being." He threw up his hands. "Yeah, I fought it, but I've been trained to know when I'm losing a battle." He laughed. "Baby, this one was lost long ago."

Her heart fluttered like a butterfly in the breeze, and she gave thanks that she was sitting down for, even then, a weakness crept along her limbs. "Are you sure? You're telling me that you welcome a relationship with me, that you want to see where it will lead? Is that what you're saying?"

He squeezed the fingers of her left hand. "That night when you kissed my cheek and whispered that I was sweet . . . From then on, I knew I had to test it, that you could offer what I needed."

"I'd sworn off relationships completely," she said, "and for the past five years I've kept that vow. The first time you kissed me, I knew I was vulnerable." The twinkle in his eyes was soon followed by a rumble of laughter from his throat. "What's so amusing?"

"Lady, when you start kissing, you don't fool around.

You could melt a glacier." As if fueled by his memories, his voice dropped a full register and his eyes darkened. She reached for the bottle of wine, and her shaking fingers betrayed her reaction to the desire that possessed him.

"Give me that," he said, taking the bottle from her and pouring them each half a glass. He held a glass to her lips and, after she sipped the wine, he drank from the same glass, never taking his gaze from her face. Then he repeated the ritual with the other glass, taking the first sip himself and giving her the remainder.

He set the glasses on the table in front of them, and she stared into the dark desire of his mesmerizing eyes. Immobile. Transfixed. Never had she seen his need spread so blatantly across his face. Exposed. Nothing hidden. Her nerves tingled with exhilaration, drowning her in a pool of sensuality. She crossed and uncrossed her knees, balled and released her fists until at last her bosom heaved and she had to breathe through her mouth. Still he gazed. She thought she would scream with the need to feel his hands, lips, and tongue all over her.

"Nelson," she said in desperation.

"Come here. I need to taste you."

For a split second she stared at the impassioned turbulence in his eyes, breathing his breath and smelling his heat, and then, with trembling lips and a thunderous pounding of her heart, she opened her arms to him. He lifted her into his lap, bent to her parted lips, and let her know once more the sweet torture of his tongue claiming her. Possessing her. She heard her own moans as she sucked his tongue deeply into her mouth and feasted. *More. More.* She needed more of him. His lips caressed her eyes, cheeks, and the corner of her mouth until she thought she would scream.

Jolts of electricity whistled through her veins until, caring for nothing but the way he made her feel, she grabbed his hand and plunged it into the bosom of her strapless dress. And, as if waiting for that move, he freed her breast from the confines of her dress and sucked her areola into his mouth, sending fevered sensations to every nerve in her body.

"Oh, Lord!" she cried aloud from the pleasure of it.

Heat roared arrow-straight to her feminine center, and the tugging of his mouth at her nipple plunged her deeper and deeper into the whirlpool of desire. She squirmed, crossing and uncrossing her knees until the warm liquid of love flowed from her. Beyond control now, she struggled to get to him, to feel him, to get him inside of her, and frantically grasped his belt buckle. But he stilled her hand.

"Are you sure?"

"Yes. *Yes.*"

"If I take you up those stairs, we'll—"

"It's what I want. Here. Right now."

"No," he whispered, "not here," lifted her into his arms and raced up the stairs.

Standing at the edge of her bed, he set her on her feet and stared down at her, his face a question mark, as if waiting for permission.

Without a thought as to what she did or why, she grabbed a handful of his shirt and pulled it. The fire of desire blazed in his eyes, and his breathing quickened. Her fingers worked at his belt buckle, and he allowed it, seemingly passive. Letting her have her way. And as if emboldened by his permissiveness, she threw off his jacket, loosened his tie, and began to unbutton his shirt. Suddenly, arms of steel imprisoned her body, and he plunged his tongue into her mouth, stunning her with the force of his passion.

His hot hands on her naked flesh as he sent her zipper downward released a gut-searing sensation in her and, not caring about anything but him and what he had in store for her, she unzipped him. But he stopped her, lifted her, and lay her on the bed. She threw off her bra and let him see her bare of all but the red bikini hiding her treasure.

He stepped out of his pants, tore off his shirt, and stood before her, a brown Adonis, muscled, strong, and all man. Gazing at the treasure before her, she swallowed the liquid that had accumulated in her mouth, reached out, and pulled away the tiny G-string that cupped him and let him spill into her hands. She wanted to kiss him, but he didn't give her the chance. After protecting her, he covered her with his body and wrapped her in his arms.

With his arms cradling her head, he kissed her eyes, her cheeks, neck, nibbled at her ears and, when she thought she could no longer stand it, his lips covered hers, at last giving her his tongue. He didn't linger there, but inched downward until his lips fastened on her left nipple and began that rhythmic sucking motion that made her scream for relief.

"You're nowhere near ready," he whispered. "Just let me love you."

He moved to suckle her right breast while his fingers tortured her left one, teasing and tantalizing until she thought her body would incinerate. His lips skimmed the sides of her breasts, and shivers raced through her as he adored her belly. But when his fingers teased the insides of her thighs, barely touching her flesh, she tensed. He looked up at her.

"Relax, love, I'm only going to make you happy. Trust me."

"I do. I do. But I'm going out of my mind."

"Good."

When he lifted her knees over his shoulders and parted her folds, she stopped breathing. Then the tip of his tongue fired the nub of her passion, and, as if of their own volition, her hips swung up to meet him, and he loved her until an unfamiliar throbbing began at the bottom of her feet and an awful fullness gripped her. Nearly mindless, she screamed for relief.

"Nelson, honey, I can't stand this, I'm so full. I . . . I need to—"

"Be patient, baby, and I'll give you what you need," he said, and sipped the love liquid that flowed from her. Then he kissed his way slowly up her body, torturing her senses. With one hand around her shoulder and the other beneath her hips, he kissed her cheek and pressed against her. Feeling him at her portal, she thought she'd go mad if he didn't enter, and flung her body up to force his penetration and winced at the pain.

"It's been a long time for you," he whispered. "Be patient."

He entered slowly, and, after allowing her to adjust to him, flexed his hips and let her have the powerful thrust of his loins, moving in and out of her, twisting and circling. Loving her. Staking his claim. She caught his rhythm and moved with him as if in a choreographed dance.

"Oooh!" she said as a pumping and squeezing began in the muscles of her vagina. "Honey, I'm so full, and I can't . . . I want to burst . . . please, I—"

"You will. Concentrate on that feeling. We're going to fly out of here together."

"But—"

She couldn't speak. Couldn't think. He was all around her, over her, on her, and in her. Surely she was dying. And then she sank until the bottom fell out of her as he hurtled her into a vortex of ecstasy.

"Nelson!" she cried. "Nelson. Nelson. I love you."

It was more than he'd hoped for or ever dreamed could happen to him again. He had a woman beneath him who wanted him, wanted him to know it, didn't have to fake and wasn't stingy with her loving. And miracle of miracles, she was the woman he adored. He wanted to give her everything, with no care for his own feelings or needs. He gloried in her hard, driving passion. Fired by her body's demands as well as his own, he drove into her with every trick at his command, using his strength and skill to please her. He meant to love her until he drained her of desire.

Her moans and pleas threatened to drive him to completion, and he bent to her sweet lips. Her little moves triggered in him a desire for release, but he told himself to think of something else. Anything. As he pictured the Battle of Orleans, her muscles clutched at him, squeezing and pinching him and finally erupting in spasms and shaking him to the core of his being. He held fast, until he heard the words "I love you."

"I'm yours. Yours and nobody else's!" he shouted, and poured the essence of life into her as he splintered in her arms. Her own arms tightened around him and he gripped her to him, stunned by the force of his release and of his feeling for her.

He raised up. "Look at me," he whispered. "I'm in love with you. I didn't want it to happen, but it has and I'm not sorry. You said you love me. Does that still hold now that you're back to earth?"

"Yes. It holds. That's why I'm here with you like this.

As you said, I was afraid of this, but I wouldn't have missed it for the world."

The eyes into which he gazed blessed him with a wordless affirmation of love, holding him transfixed, suspending him in a cloud of joy such as he had never experienced, not even with the woman to whom—in what now seemed the aeonian past—he had pledged his troth. His heart fluttered as he drank in the wonder of Audrey lying beneath him, and he gathered her closer, wanting to shield her from anything and everything that could hurt a single hair on her head or cause her one second of pain.

Frustrated by his inability to express what lodged so deeply and so solidly inside of him, he kissed her nose, and she rewarded him with a softening of her features into a loving smile.

After a long time, he said, "I'd move because I'm probably putting too much weight on you, but, silly as it sounds, I can't bear to stop feeling your skin against mine and your breasts against my chest. Do you mind?"

She raised both arms toward the ceiling, closed her eyes, shifted her hips beneath him, and stretched like a sated feline.

"Why should I mind? You're not putting your weight on me. Besides, you're right where you belong."

He wasn't in the mood for loose talk. He didn't want to hear nice words that would be forgotten within minutes, words that fell glibly from the tongue and not from the heart.

"I'm still inside of you. Is this where I belong? Is it?"

Her gaze didn't waver, but fixed on him almost as if in defiance. "So long as you meet the conditions for entrance. Yes. But those conditions can change."

She had never misled him and she was honest with him then. It was a trait that he prized. "I'm aware of that. It goes both ways," he said, and then repeated it to make certain that she understood him. "Is there another man in your life who is important to you?"

She stirred, either restless or impatient with the question. He wasn't sure which.

"I'm not involved with anyone else, and you have to know—"

He wouldn't let her say it. "I knew it had been a really long time for you because you were as tight as a virgin. What I want to know is whether you're willing for us to try and find out whether what we feel for each other is solid enough to build a life on."

She dragged her fingers out of his hair, and a pensive expression traveled over her face. "This wasn't easy for me. Admitting to myself that I wanted this with you, that I needed to . . . to make love with you, was a big thing for me, and I took an enormous step when I let myself follow through and accept what I yearned for. It isn't you; my reluctance has always been my problem with *me*." She took a deep breath. "I'm scared, Nelson. I don't doubt that I love you, but—"

"Then can you at least commit to giving us a chance?"

"I want to see what we've got going for us, but I can't bear the thought of ever again going out on a limb only to have it chopped off. What you don't know is that that man was the first and the only one. What he did nearly made me into a man-hater. I . . . Sorry I mentioned that. Thoughts of him send my blood pressure up."

He stroked her forehead and let his fingers caress the silken flesh of her cheek. "Will you tell me about it? Sometimes it helps to talk these things out."

"Maybe sometime. I don't want to spoil our time together, and that's exactly what would happen if I began to relive it."

"I understand, but I hope someday you'll be able to

talk to me about it. Until you do, it will be a barrier between us, a small one maybe, but an obstacle nonetheless." He raised himself up on his elbows and pinned his gaze on her eyes. "Give us a chance, Audrey. I need to know. I . . . if it's 'no,' I can take it, but—"

"All right. If I trusted you enough to lie with you in bed this way, I can take the next step."

He'd settle for that, he told himself, and he would make certain that her thoughts didn't stray far from him. "You feel all right?"

She raised an eyebrow. "Who, me?"

He almost laughed. "Yes, you. Did you get straightened out? Did you climax?"

Her eyes widened and her face took on an air of innocence, which he didn't doubt she feigned. "You mean . . . gee, was something special supposed to happen?"

"Liar. You're damned right something was supposed to happen, and it should have been extra-special."

"Really? Oh."

He'd teach her a thing or two. Looking into her eyes, he stroked her left nipple until she sucked in her breath and lowered her gaze. He rolled it between his thumb and index finger, and when she swallowed again and again he pulled it into his mouth and sucked on it until her moans filled the room.

Fully erect, he began to move, and she met his thrust with a ravenous body, the body of a woman fully cognizant of the rewards in store for her. When he felt her love tunnel begin to clutch and squeeze him, signaling the advent of her completion, he slowed down, broke the rhythm, and looked at her.

"Nothing happened, huh? You practically wrung me out of the socket, but you didn't feel anything special. Right?"

She thrashed her head to the side. "You stop teasing me. You hear?"

He kissed her top lip. "I'm not the one who's teasing. You're squeezing me damned near senseless, blowing my mind, and I'm feeling like a king. But if not a damned thing is happening to you, it's one-sided, and it's selfish of me to—"

Her fist pounded his back. "If you leave me hanging like this, I'll . . . I'll . . . Nelson, *please!*"

"Did you have an orgasm? Was it good for you? Was it?"

"You know it was. I've never felt like that before. Never. Oh, Nelson, I'm somewhere between hell and high water. Do something!"

"Then don't tell me tales. You love me?"

"Yes. Yes, I love you. But I won't if you're mean to me."

"Mean to you? Never, sweetheart. I can't even imagine it." He rimmed her lips with his tongue, wrapped his arms around her, and took her on a short, sweet ride to paradise.

Later, driving home, he thought of the commitment he'd just made, not in words but in his actions and in his own heart. And how he'd hated to leave her, to walk away from the sweetest loving he had ever experienced. He didn't want Ricky to awaken and become anxious when he realized his uncle wasn't home, but of equal importance to him was the need to shield Audrey from the all-knowing NSS. Whom she made love with was none of the government's business.

At the Fourteenth Street Bridge leading to Alexandria, he slowed down to a crawl and eased to the shoulder to give an ambulance the right-of-way. Realizing that there had been an accident, he got out of his car.

"Can I help?" he asked a police officer.

The officer shook his head. "Too late. One of these days, teenagers will learn that the automobile is not a toy."

He got back in his car to wait until the traffic cleared, and his thoughts went to his nephew. He would instill in Ricky a sense of responsibility, a respect for law and the rights of others. Bracing his arms against the steering wheel, he wondered at the level of commitment parenthood entailed. He wanted children of his own, but how could he teach them how to live if he was putting out fires thousands of miles away from them? He wanted action, always had, and he needed it. And he wanted those four silver stars on his collar. But he also needed a family and . . . and Audrey Powers.

The traffic began to move, and the policeman waved him on. But he drove slowly, contemplating his life. By the time he walked into his house he had resolved that someone in an official capacity was going to tell him why he was an agent's target. And soon.

Eight

She had always heard that after lovemaking, a woman should feel warm, cozy, and sleepy, a pile of warm mush. And loved. Warm and cozy, yes. Loved, definitely. But after daydreaming and fantasizing about Nelson, counting sheep, and even doing imaginary neck massages, she remained wide-awake. She reached inside the drawer of her night table for her copy of Donna Hill's *An Ordinary Woman* and read for an hour, but couldn't get sleepy.

What's the matter with me? I never have trouble falling asleep. She got up, went downstairs, and reclined in the chaise longue on her porch, away from the print of his body on the sheet beside her, away from his special scent, the smell of lovemaking, and the drugging reminders of how she felt when he was inside of her. Away from the scene of her capitulation to the demands of her heart, body, mind, and soul. And in the quiet of that moonlit night, she grappled with the conflict between her head and her heart. She had conditioned herself to life without the emotional seesaw that being in love guaranteed. She had learned to walk alone, to chart her own course and to follow it, but that was before she'd loved Nelson Wainwright.

He said he welcomed loving her and all that that implied, but she knew he might find that he cherished his freedom more than he cherished her. As for her, she already knew she'd have trouble living without him. She had experienced the pain and the disappointment that could puncture one's life when love soured like a jar of overripe fruit. Love him, she did, but she was going to move cautiously. Very cautiously. She had no choice.

A soft breeze and the chirping of robins and sparrows awoke her the next morning as red, gray, and blue streaks of color announced the rise of the sun. Groggy from having slept lightly, she found her way up the stairs, showered, and dressed. The phone rang as she entered the kitchen to make coffee.

"Audrey Powers."

"Hope I didn't wake you up, child, but I had to tell you I think you should come over here and have a look at the Colonel's neck. Believe me, I never saw him in so much pain. He said he'd take a hot shower and he'd be all right. I told him he was fooling himself; if water could stop pain, there wouldn't be no accupuncturists, and television would be out of business."

Sometimes her Aunt Lena could draw a straight line and get a curve. "How does television get into the picture?"

"Well, that's the way they make their money, isn't it? Aspirin, Tylenol, and Aleve. But at least you don't have to tell your doctor to prescribe them for you. Come over before he leaves for work. I declare, I don't see how a man that big can be scared of doctors."

"Aunt Lena, I can't do that without his permission. He wouldn't like it. I will call him and feel him out, though. Thanks for letting me know. 'Bye."

She made the coffee, got a glass of orange juice, and sat down at the kitchen table with that and her mobile phone. She half hoped he had left home by then, because whether they admitted it or not, her status with him had changed, and she didn't know how he would react to her cautioning him about his health. She sucked in her breath and dialed the number.

"I was just about to phone you," he said after they greeted each other. "Did you sleep well, and how are you this morning?"

She told the truth. "I didn't sleep well, and I woke up as groggy as a drunken chicken."

"*What?*"

"You wouldn't leave me alone, so I went downstairs and slept on my back porch. That accounts for my morning grogginess."

"I don't know how to take that. I thought I left you happy and that you'd sleep like a lamb."

She reached over to the stove for the coffeepot and poured another cupful of coffee. "You left me happy, Nelson. Never doubt that. How are *you?*"

"Great. I've got some readjusting to do, but that's to be expected."

What was he talking about? Her heart nearly stopped beating. "Readjusting to what?"

"To you, lady. You're causing me to rethink my life."

She wasn't sorry to hear that, but she wouldn't say so. "Oh! Well, join the crowd." Either he didn't plan to tell her about that neck pain or her aunt had exaggerated. She had to take a chance.

"By the way, I meant to give you a copy of some exercises for your neck when it gets out of hand, but we got into, well . . . you took my mind off it last night. Want me to mail them to you? Or I could drop them off."

She wondered if his silence indicated annoyance. After a time he said, "Are you suggesting that we won't see each other again before the United States Post Office can deliver a letter to me? Didn't you say you were willing to see if what we have is solid enough to build a future on?"

"I did, and I'm sticking with it." He'd pledged the same, but didn't that mean he should level with her about his health or anything else that mattered to him?

"I'll be by this afternoon with the exercise plan." She didn't doubt that once he realized that the exercises would give him relief, he would perform them assiduously.

"Good. If I haven't gotten home, wait for me."

Indeed she would, and she would give him her professional opinion about ignoring a serious health problem. He might not like it, but that wouldn't stop her.

However, Nelson's neck was not his major concern that day. He arrived at work half an hour early and began drafting alternative strategies for landing in hilly, bare, and arid terrain with three different types of aircraft. Several hours later when he studied the results of his morning's work, pride suffused him, and looking at what he'd done was like a shot of adrenaline urging him to action. He had to get back to Afghanistan, had to finish the job. But did he have the freedom to do that? Could he leave Lena and Ricky? And what about Audrey? Worst was the niggling question of whether the pain he lived with would place his men at risk.

He told himself he could handle it, and was about to ask for an appointment with the Commandant when his phone rang.

"Checkmate twice."

He lunged forward. If he had a pain then, he didn't feel it. "Yeah."

"Starbucks in fifteen minutes."

As usual, she faced the door and sat with her back to

the wall. "I take it your desk is clear and you locked your briefcase in a drawer."

He nodded, wondering where his orders would take him. "There's a car right out front, USMC issue."

"Where will it take me?"

"Home."

"What about my own car?"

"It's being examined for evidence of tampering. Now go."

He stood and glared down at her. "What the hell am I looking for when I get home, Marilyn? I'm damned sick and tired of this cat-and-mouse stuff. Is anything wrong with my family?"

"I imagine you are. You're wasting precious time. Our man has everything under control. See you."

He had no choice but to go. He got in the car, slammed the door, and said, "Step on it." He normally drove to and from work in twenty to twenty-five minutes, depending on traffic, and although his driver pressed the speed limit, the car seemed to crawl and the twenty minutes seemed like several hours.

"I'll wait for you here," the corporal said, "in case you need me."

Not liking the sound of that, he jumped from the car and ran up the walk. As he put his key in the lock, the door opened and he faced a six-foot-three stranger, a hulk of a man. But at that point nothing shocked or surprised him. He pushed past the man and would have headed into the house if the heavy hand on his shoulder hadn't given him cause to ask questions.

"Who are you, and what are you doing in my house?"

"I'm on your side, Colonel," the man said, showing his ID.

"If somebody doesn't tell me what's going on, I'll—"

"Everybody's okay. A man snatched your nephew,

and your housekeeper became hysterical and had to be sedated. A nurse is with her in her room."

"Where's my child?"

"He's in custody. Your driver will take you to get him. Clever little fellow. When the guy grabbed your boy, he kicked him in the groin, and that gave our man the chance for a clear aim at the knee. It'll be a while before he walks again, if ever. I'll be here when you get back."

He resisted calling Marilyn and giving her a piece of his mind. She could have told him that and sent him directly to get Ricky. Inhaling deeply and exhaling long breaths, he willed his heart to slow down and his nerves to return to normal. Eventually, his driver stopped at a restored turn-of-the-century mansion in Logan Circle, which, from its exterior, appeared to be the residence of a well-heeled family.

He opened the door and responded to the salute from the young marine who stood between the service colors and Old Glory. "I'm Colonel Wainwright."

"Yes, sir. Ricky's right in there having the time of his life." He pointed to a door off the entrance.

Nelson walked the few steps to what was obviously a reception room, and stopped at the door. A bucket of ice with a variety of soft drinks sat on the table in the center of the room along with assorted fruit and a plate of cookies, and he'd bet anything that his nephew hadn't told anyone there that he wasn't allowed to drink soft drinks, only lemonade and fruit juices. Ricky sat in the middle of the floor amidst figures he had constructed from Lego sets. And he had for a companion an attractive young woman, seventeen or eighteen years old, who appeared enchanted with him.

Nelson walked into the room. "I don't suppose you would consider leaving all this fun and coming home with me."

"Unca Nelson!" Part of a train flew in different directions. "Did you hear what happened, Unca Nelson? Some people came and took my picture. I kicked the man just like you taught me to do." Suddenly, his enthusiasm quelled. "But he was a bad man, Unca Nelson, and a nice man had to shoot him. And I think maybe Miss Lena got sick." He ran to Nelson and wrapped his arms around his uncle's leg. "Can we go home and see if Miss Lena is all right?"

"Sure, but first I think we ought to clean up this party you were enjoying. And don't worry about the bad man. He'll be all right."

"Heather is my friend, aren't you, Heather?"

The girl stood. "I'll take care of it, Colonel Wainwright. He's a wonderful child. Can I have a hug, Ricky?"

The boy obliged, and Nelson shook hands with Heather and thanked her for caring for Ricky. On the drive home, he wished Marilyn could have listened to Ricky's questions, every one of them to the point. Most telling was the query as to why a man wanted to take him away.

"Do you want to go back with me this afternoon, Sir?" the driver asked Nelson, "or should I come for you tomorrow morning?"

He didn't like being separated from his briefcase, but he had to check on Lena. "I'll let you know in a few minutes," he said. When he entered the house with Ricky, he went directly to Lena's room and, to his relief, found her sitting on the side of her bed talking with the nurse.

"Thank the good Lord you're home," she said. "You can go now," she told the nurse. "The Colonel will take care of everything. Ricky, honey, come here and let me hug you. I declare I never been so scared in my whole life."

Ricky's little arms locked around her neck. "I wasn't scared. I did what my Unca Nelson told me to do."

The nurse stood and saluted Nelson. "Lieutenant Harriet Ruff, sir. She's fine now. A bit upset for a while, but she'll tell you about it."

He thanked the Navy nurse and walked with her down to the front door. "Do you have transportation back to your post?"

"Yes, sir. I have my car."

"In about half an hour I'll be ready to go back to the Pentagon," he told his driver. "Would you like to stop somewhere for lunch?"

"Thank you, sir, but I can wait till I take you back to your office."

When he returned to Lena's room, he found her still sitting on the bed and Ricky leaning against her knee gazing up at her.

He pulled a chair close to them and sat down. "Tell me what happened, Lena."

She took a deep breath and expelled it quickly. "Well, I took Ricky to the supermarket with me like I always do. You know he loves running up and down the aisles in that mega-store. All the clerks in there are crazy about him. I kept him close to me like you said, and thank the Lord I did. We got to the cashier, and I was paying for the food when Ricky ran between me and the cashier's counter to grab the shopping cart—you know, he loves to push it. I looked up from counting out my money just in time to see this big fellow run around the side near the exit and grab Ricky. Good thing he was facing Ricky 'cause—"

"'Cause I kicked him right where you told me to, Unca Nelson."

"When Ricky kicked him, he let the child go and grabbed himself 'bout the time I heard this shot. I didn't know who they was shooting at. I think I screamed, but I tell you, I don't remember. Next thing I know I'm here and this nurse is telling me to think pleasant thoughts. I looked at her and said, 'Honey, you can't be serious.'"

"We came home in this great big white car, Unca Nelson, and the man said the Marines take real good care of each other." Ricky grinned, exuding charm as only his father could. "I'm gonna be a Marine."

"I'm going back to work. I'll—"

"Who shot the man, Unca Nelson?"

"Someone the Marines sent to take care of you and Miss Lena."

Ricky's eyes widened. "Gee!"

He had a few choice words for NSS, and the sooner he got it off his chest, the better he'd feel. He was an officer and, with his status, keeping him in the dark about something affecting his life and the lives of his family members didn't sit well with him.

When he got back to the Pentagon, he got a hamburger and coffee in the cafeteria, went to his office, and dialed Marilyn's number.

"Checkmate. Are you coming here, or do I go to you?"

"Slow down, Colonel."

"Either we talk now, or I'm going over your head, and I'm not walking into Starbucks again today."

"All right. I'll be there in ten minutes."

That didn't give him enough time to eat the hamburger and call Audrey, too. He'd eat the hamburger, because not even NSS—knowing what he was certain they knew—was stupid enough to keep him in the dark if anything had happened to her.

"A Lieutenant Colonel of the Army here to see you, Sir," his secretary said.

"Send her in." He stood, and the first thing he noticed when she walked in was the difference in her demeanor: less officious now that she was on *his* turf. He stood, but he didn't shake hands.

"I want to know why a man would attempt to steal my kid, why you've had a watch on me and my family twenty-four-seven, why you didn't tell me the score this morning before I left here, and why you impounded my car. Let's have it." His neck began to pain him, but his anger allowed him to ignore it.

"We were dealing with a group of crooks who steal military and commercial secrets and sell what they get to any person or government that will buy it. In spite of security, they learned that you draw up plans for guerrilla tactics and logistics, something they could make millions on. We impounded your car to see whether anyone had planted a listening device in it, because we began to suspect that as the reason Stacey wanted to visit Ricky. A five-year-old is the perfect person to hide something in your home."

"And, failing their other tactics, they figured I'd give them anything they wanted in order to get Ricky back."

"Right."

"What you did this morning was unforgivable and unfeeling. You could have told me what happened and that Ricky and Lena were safe, but you let me sweat about it."

"Sorry," she said, hardly blinking. He had to hand it to her; she must have gotten an advanced degree in composure. "I have to follow policy. If we don't know the whole story, we can't say anything, and I didn't know how Lena was."

He rolled his eyes to the ceiling, not caring if his impatience with her and the NSS showed. "Didn't it occur to the geniuses over there that I could protect those secrets more effectively if I knew someone wanted to steal them?"

"It surely did, Colonel, but I only follow established policy."

"What about the guards? Are they still tailing us?"

"Sorry, sir, but until we're sure we've rounded up everyone in that cell, the guards have to stay. And please ask Dr. Powers not to try eluding them. She's as good for blackmail as your nephew is."

"What about my car?"

"In your assigned spot. It's clean, but I suggest you park it in your garage or in Dr. Powers's garage."

Better let that pass. "Thank you for coming." He stood and saluted, terminating the conversation.

Was it over? He drove home past the house with the lion on the front lawn, and relief flooded him when he saw the boarded door and windows. At least they no longer camped in his neighborhood.

Audrey had just about reached her limit of tolerance with the assorted guards who followed her everywhere but to the women's room. Indeed, she'd stopped using the one in the hallway because the guard would position himself by the door until she came out and then walk with her back to her office. And on that day, the man stood whenever the door to her office opened and watched like a hawk until he made sure the person who entered was a genuine patient. She didn't bother to ask him about the extra precautions because she knew he wouldn't answer. A late afternoon call from Nelson— who, after loving her out of her senses the previous night had managed to ignore her for the past eight hours—did nothing to improve her temper.

"It's been a rough day," he said after their greetings,

An Important Message From The ARABESQUE Publisher

Dear Arabesque Reader,

I have some exciting news to share....

Available now is a four-part special series **AT YOUR SERVICE** written by bestselling Arabesque Authors.

Bold, sweeping and passionate as America itself—these superb romances feature military heroes you are destined to love.

They confront their unpredictable futures along-side women of equal courage, who will inspire you!

The **AT YOUR SERVICE** series* can be specially ordered by calling 1-888-345-BOOK, or purchased wherever books are sold.

Enjoy them and let us know your feedback by commenting on our website.

Linda Gill, Publisher
Arabesque Romance Novels

Check out our website at
www.BET.com

A SPECIAL "THANK YOU" FROM ARABESQUE JUST FOR YOU!

Send this card back and you'll receive 4 FREE Arabesque Novels—a $25.96 value—absolutely FREE!

The introductory 4 Arabesque Romance books are yours FREE (plus $1.99 shipping & handling). If you wish to continue to receive 4 books every month, do nothing. Each month, we will send you 4 New Arabesque Romance Novels for your free examination. If you wish to keep them, pay just $16* (plus, $1.99 shipping & handling). If you decide not to continue, you owe nothing!

- Send no money now.
- Never an obligation.
- Books delivered to your door!

We hope that after receiving your FREE books you'll want to remain an Arabesque subscriber, but the choice is yours! So why not take advantage of this Arabesque offer, with no risk of any kind. You'll be glad you did!

In fact, we're so sure you will love your Arabesque novels, that we will send you an Arabesque Tote Bag FREE with your first paid shipment.

Call Us TOLL-FREE At 1-888-345-BOOK

* Prices subject to change

THE "THANK YOU" GIFT INCLUDES:

- 4 books absolutely FREE (plus $1.99 for shipping and handling).
- A FREE newsletter, *Arabesque Romance News*, filled with author interviews, book previews, special offers, and more!
- No risks or obligations.

INTRODUCTORY OFFER CERTIFICATE

Yes! Please send me 4 FREE Arabesque novels (plus $1.99 for shipping & handling). I understand I am under no obligation to purchase any books, as explained on the back of this card. Send my **FREE Tote Bag** after my first regular paid shipment.

NAME _____

ADDRESS _____ APT. _____

CITY _____ STATE _____ ZIP _____

TELEPHONE ( ) _____

E-MAIL _____

SIGNATURE _____

Offer limited to one per household and not valid to current subscribers. All orders subject to approval. Terms, offer, & price subject to change. Tote bags available while supplies last.

Thank You!

AN093A

ARABESQUE

Accepting the four introductory books for FREE (plus $1.99 to offset the cost of shipping & handling) places you under no obligation to buy anything. You may keep the books and return the shipping statement marked "cancelled". If you do not cancel, about a month later we will send 4 additional Arabesque novels, and you will be billed the preferred subscriber's price of just $4.00 per title. That's $16.00* for all 4 books for a savings of almost 40% off the cover price (Plus $1.99 for shipping and handling). You may cancel at any time, but if you choose to continue, every month we'll send you 4 more books, which you may either purchase at the preferred discount price. . . or return to us and cancel your subscription.

* PRICES SUBJECT TO CHANGE

THE ARABESQUE ROMANCE CLUB: HERE'S HOW IT WORKS

THE ARABESQUE ROMANCE BOOK CLUB
P.O. BOX 5214
CLIFTON NJ 07015-5214

PLACE
STAMP
HERE

"and I need to spend a few minutes with you. Would you have dinner with Ricky, Lena, and me at my place? Afterward, we can sit out on the deck and talk. If that's okay, I'll be at your house for you around six, and I'll take you home later."

She wasn't so irritated that she couldn't hear the disquiet in Nelson's voice and sense in him a need for a calming force. "I'll be there when you come," she said.

Later, she reflected that the words had all but flown from her lips, and that their meaning exceeded the simple fact that she would be at home when he arrived. He may not have understood it, but she knew then that she'd told him she was there for him and would always be.

"I'd better ask my Aunt Lena to send up some prayers for me," she said aloud as she closed her desk and locked it. "I'm in deep here." *Yes,* she thought, remembering an old song, *Chest-deep in the quicksand of love.*

"Don't try to cook dinner," Nelson told Lena. "You've had a rough day, and I'm sure you're tired. I'll order dinner. I would appreciate it, though, if you'd set the table and include a place for Audrey."

Ricky nearly fell down the stairs. "Audie is coming. We're going to see Audie!"

"Yes, and try not to break your neck. Watch it when you're on those stairs."

"It's okay, Unca Nelson. The people said I'm very smart. They said so today, Unca Nelson."

"That doesn't mean you can't break your neck if you don't pay attention to what you're doing. You got that?" He ran his hand over the boy's hair in a gesture of affection.

"Yes, sir, Unca Nelson. I got it."

"I ought to be back by seven," he said to Lena.

"Meantime, decide what you'd like to eat." He hugged Ricky and headed for Bethesda.

He parked in front of Audrey's house and got an eerie feeling. Although it wasn't near dark in mid-August, the closed blinds and absence of indoor lights gave the house a deserted appearance. Marilyn had cautioned him not to park on the street, but in his or Audrey's garage. He couldn't enter the garage and had no choice but to leave the car to ring Audrey's bell, which he did with his hand on the bell and an eye on his BMW. He rang several times and waited. And waited. Finally, he went back to his car, got in, and waited there.

Six-thirty came and went, and then the shadows of trees and houses melted into the twilight. His heart began to race. Staving off fear, he used his cellular phone to call Marilyn's office but, for his trouble, he got her voice mail. He hung up and called Lena.

He didn't want to shock her by asking whether Audrey had called, so he said, "I'll be a bit late," knowing she'd tell him if Audrey had called.

"Don't worry 'bout us, Colonel," Lena said. "Ricky and me just finished some of that good old frozen peach yogurt I keep in the freezer. We ain't hungry right now."

That was the least of his worries. Lena could be counted on to feed Ricky and herself. He hung up and loosened his collar as sweat streamed from his pores. If anything had happened to her, it would be because of him, and he didn't know if he could face that. Besides, she gave his life new meaning. She was . . . He shook his head. She was so important to him.

If only he had the security code, he could find out where she was or whether she was in danger. But non-NSS personnel weren't allowed to have that code. He'd never felt so useless. Somewhere she might in trouble, needing him. He pounded the steering wheel with his fist.

In the rear-view mirror he saw the headlights of a car approach, turned on the BMW's ignition and locked his windows in case he had to move in a hurry. His anxiety increased when the car pulled to a stop behind him, and he prepared for a confrontation. A second car drove up and parked across the street, and when he saw the government seal on its side, he turned off the ignition, jumped from his car and headed for the one behind him.

As he approached, she unlocked her door. He didn't wait for her to open it, but nearly yanked it from its hinges, lifted her from the car and into his arms. "I was on my way out of my mind because I thought they'd gotten you. Baby, I've been crazy."

"I didn't have your cell-phone number, so I couldn't call you. I knew you'd worry, and I wouldn't have put you through this for anything if I could have avoided it, but I had an emergency with a patient. Honey, the guard's parked over there. Shouldn't you put me down?"

"The hell with him. If he'd experienced what I went through this past hour, he wouldn't give a damn about me, either. Besides, where's the law that says you can't kiss me if it's what I want?"

At last she smiled. He brushed her lips with his own, then stared into her face. "I think we'd better leave it at that. They're waiting for us at home, and I've got a lot to tell you, so let's go inside. Do whatever you have to do, but I'd like to leave as soon as possible."

"Am I coming back here tonight?" Her frank and open expression nearly unglued him. She would stay at his home if he asked her to, but he knew she wouldn't sleep in his bed so long as her aunt slept in the adjoining room. And he'd been tested enough for one day.

"I'll bring you home."

* * *

After dinner and with Ricky asleep, he took Audrey's hand and walked with her to the deck in the back of his house. If he had chosen that night, that time, and that place to declare his love to this woman, it couldn't have been more idyllic, he decided as they sat on the sofa that rocked like a swing. And what an awesome place to make love.

"It's beautiful here," she said. "Lovely moon, stars, and this wonderful garden. Even the freshly mowed grass smells clean and fresh."

"Don't misunderstand me," he said, "but, I was thinking, what a moment for lovemaking!"

"Hmmm," she said, and crossed her knee. "Nothing wrong with that." She locked her hands behind her head. Open. Accessible. *I'd better straighten out my mind.*

He sat closer to her. "I want to tell you about today." After relating what he knew of Ricky's and Lena's experiences, along with the story of the cell of criminals and their fate, he added, "So you may imagine what I thought when you came home an hour late. It isn't known whether there are any more members of that group, but in the meantime, we have to keep this vigil."

"I'm stunned. The entire scenario had begun to annoy me. In fact, this gal was getting a mean streak, but what you've told me shames me."

"Can't say I blame you," he said. "All I want is to know we're together. I believe we are or can be, but sometimes, like right now, I don't feel a real intimacy with you. I don't quite understand it. Maybe it's because we need to know each other better. I want that."

Her voice, soft and very feminine, melted some of his hard spots, the something within him that had always resisted being understood. Yes, and loved. He was unprepared for her response.

She seemed to consider his words for a time before she said, "Secrets get in the way of intimacy. When we know each other well, maybe you won't feel this way."

So at ease with him. Relaxed and comfortable. He wanted to . . . He wanted to lose himself in her, to give himself to her. For a brief, poignant moment, she gazed into his eyes. Then she smiled, and his blood pounded in his ears and his belly knotted into a figure eight. Her lips, full and pouting, begged for his tongue, and he sucked in his breath. Desire washed through him with stunning force, and he told himself to get it under control.

However, her lips parted and, zombielike, she moved to him, wrapped her hands around his head, and brought his mouth to her open lips. He heard his groans as he touched her and his tongue shoved into her mouth. He wanted to possess her, but she stroked his face with gentle hands while sucking on his tongue. Slow. Teasing. Letting him know what her body had in store for him. She placed his hand on her left breast, and he told himself to stop it right there, but when her fingers pinched his flat pectoral as a signal for what she needed, he thrust his hand into her blouse, released her breast, and bent to it.

"Oh, Lord," she moaned as he tugged and sucked at it.

By some miracle, he remembered where they were, sat back, and breathed deeply for a few minutes. "I knew better that to start that," he was finally able to say.

"I did, too, but I said, 'what the heck, I need it.' "

He buttoned her blouse. "I don't even want to think

about that. We'd better go or you'll have a second sleep-less night."

"Nothing's guaranteed, especially not tonight, after what we've been through today. Ready when you are."

He stood, held out his hand, and, when she rose, he kissed her forehead. "You're turning my life around, and the peculiar thing is that I don't mind. I feel good with you." When she said nothing, he asked her, "Do I bring anything special to your life?"

Both of her arms went around his waist, and she pressed her head to his shoulder. Her fingers stroked his back and she held him close. Through his jacket and shirt, with the most gentle of caresses, her lips warmed his shoulder. The tenderness. The sweetness. Pure joy raced through his every sinew. There was no desire, no passion in the way she held him. But what she felt seeped into his heart, and he knew without a doubt that no other woman had ever truly loved him, that to the woman who held him he was the essence of her life.

With his arm around her, he walked through the kitchen to the garage door. "I'm taking you home, but I want you to know that I'd rather eat crayfish. And, Au-drey, the sight of crayfish makes me ill."

Her laughter wrapped around him like warm spring breeze. "We'll have our time, or at least I hope so. I left the exercises on the table in the foyer. Okay?"

"Thanks. I'll start them as soon as I get back home." After backing the BMW out of the garage and closing the door, he looked in his rearview mirror and shook his head. "If either one of us ever gets brought up on a morals charge, the Feds will be the first ones on the wit-ness stand."

She leaned back in the soft leather seat and folded her

arms beneath her bosom. "In that case, let's give them something to talk about."

He checked out her house—though with the guards in constant attendance he didn't think it necessary—kissed her quickly before old demon desire could get a headway, and left her. Driving home, he realized that he was almost happy. He still faced some mountains, but right then, they didn't seem so rugged or so high.

Audrey noticed the light flashing on her answering machine and pressed the replay button. "What's the point in having a big sister if she's not around when you need her? Call me when you get in, no matter what time it is, or whenever tall, tan, and terrific goes home."

She recognized Winifred's distress signal and dialed her number. "What's the matter, sis? Is it Ryan?"

"I've been calling you all night. I told Ryan I'd go away with him this weekend, and now I'm scared to death. Maybe Pam's right that I should wait till I get married. But I don't want to do that. Audrey, I'm insane crazy about the guy."

She sat down beside the telephone table and kicked off her shoes. What she needed right then was a Chupa Chups. "Honey, it's my feeling that you're talking to the wrong person about this. If you're scared, the person who should know this is Ryan."

"What? Why? I don't want him to think I'm naive. Ryan's a man of the world."

"Look, you cut that out right now. Posturing is stupid. Let him know what you feel, think, want, and need. He wants to make you happy, and he can't do that if you don't level with him. How would you feel if he led you to think he was one person and you discovered he was someone else? You'd be ready to die. Trust me, I've been there."

"You mean I should let him know that I'm twenty-seven and scared to go to bed with him?"

"Wendy, if you told him you're a virgin, you can tell him anything. Pam said he's besotted with you, that the chemistry between you two is so strong anybody can see it with the naked eye."

"He does love me. I know it. It's just that I'm . . . I'm afraid I won't please him."

Audrey nearly laughed. "That pleasing business is a mutual thing. Besides, there's little chance you won't, unless you throw a pillowcase over your face and lock your knees. Call him right now and tell him you can't wait for the weekend, but you're also scared to death."

"That's true. How'd you know all this? Oh-oh. The colonel has made his mark. Right on, sis! Hmm. Thanks. I'm going to call Ryan right this minute. 'Bye."

She hung up and reached into her pocketbook for a Chupa Chups. There was something about sucking on that lollipop that was as comforting as warm water on her naked skin. Winifred had a right to be nervous; nobody had invented a way of getting a periscopic view of a man's mind, to say nothing of his intentions. Who was she to give her sister advice when she hadn't been so careful herself? And now she had once more laid herself open to possible pain and deception. What was she going to do if Nelson deceived her?

Logic had replaced feelings. Gone was the euphoric world that had enveloped her earlier as she locked her arms around her lover and told him without words that he was everything to her. Torn between the impulse to kick herself and the inclination to telephone Nelson for no reason other than to hear his voice, she did neither. She went into her kitchen, a place where she spent as little time as possible, mixed up a batch of chocolate fudge, and threw several handfuls of pecans into it. Somebody—she hardly cared who—was going to eat a lot of chocolate fudge candy.

Having worked the anxiety out of her system, she showered, slid into bed, and luxuriated in the feel of satin sheets against her naked body. Sleep came quickly.

"This is McCafferty," the voice said when Nelson punched his intercom button. "Just wanted you to know I'm working on reassignments. You're one of the officers who may be returned to Afghanistan. Just thought I'd let you know in view of all these other . . . er . . . things you're dealing with right now."

"Thanks for letting me know. Any idea how soon?"

"I'd say six weeks at the latest."

As much as he wanted to go back there, he didn't welcome that news. How could he leave his family and Audrey while they remained vulnerable to harm by criminals as yet not fully identified? He locked his office door, went back to his desk, and put on the hard surgical collar that he kept locked in the drawer. Before leaving home that morning, he'd tried the exercises Audrey gave him, and they eased the pain, but he didn't expect them to give long-term relief until he'd been doing them for a while.

Audrey. He propped his elbows on his desk and supported his head with his hands. He shouldn't go much further with her unless he meant to make it permanent. But she seemed either unable or unwilling to open herself to him. She could do that in bed, and the previous night, without saying a word she had communicated what she felt for him. But he sensed nonetheless that he didn't know her. He had no idea what was guaranteed to make her smile, laugh, dance, cry, sulk. What hurt her, and what did she want desperately other than a private practice? Had she ever done anything that shamed her, frightened her, plagued her? He wanted to open himself to her that way, but she didn't seem to need it.

The pain eased, and he returned the collar to the drawer, locked it, and then unlocked his office doors. A plan formed in his mind. He needed to spend time with Audrey away from their day-to-day surroundings and problems. If NSS wanted to follow them and stake out their idyll, let them.

Audrey looked through her drawer for a pair of sheer gray stockings that she thought suited her purple linen suit more than off-black stockings would. If she'd had purple hose, she wouldn't have worn them. As she rummaged through the drawer, her gaze fell on a packet of letters, brown with age, that she'd never forced herself to burn. Not that she was emotionally attached to them; she wasn't. She had kept them for going on six years as a reminder of her hatred of Gerald Latham. She was tempted to read once more his words of undying love and faithfulness to her. And she would have, had not the grandfather clock in her upstairs hallway warned her that she had less than an hour to dress and get downtown to the hospital.

All the way to work, she fought the hatred that seeing those letters awakened in her, and swallowed once more the bitter bile of shame she had felt when she heard his awful confession—five minutes after they had made love for the first and only time, after he had just spilled himself into her.

Still wrapped in her arms, he'd said, "I sure hope you didn't get pregnant, because I can't marry you. Maybe

I should have told you the truth, but I wanted you so badly. I'm married, and my wife is expecting our third child in a couple of weeks."

Stunned to the point of temporary insanity, she'd pushed him off her and pummeled his face with her fist. As he ran from her bedroom, she had jerked the lamp on her night table from the wall socket and flung it at him, just missing his back. She didn't know when he left her house, and when she stopped crying the next morning, she told herself that he would pay. And he would. She wasn't a psychologist, but she knew that the way she felt about Gerald stood between her and Nelson. Indeed, she didn't even let herself love Ricky with a full heart for fear that love would someday be a source of pain.

"You have a new patient at ten this morning," her receptionist said, as Audrey walked through the reception room on her way to her office.

"Thanks. Who made the referral?"

"Dr. Adams over at Children's Hospital. First time he's sent us a patient. The boy is nine years old."

Her first patient of the day had made remarkable progress in a short time because she exerted every effort to perform the exercises and took pride in her achievements. "Good morning, Ms. Hamilton. Did you follow the regimen this past week?"

"Yes ma'am. I done every single thing you told me just like you said do it. And I done them all the time, whenever I was by myself."

"Good. Would that all of my patients were as diligent as you."

"If them few exercises is gon' stop me from hurtin', I'd be plain stupid not to do 'em."

And it showed. Audrey reduced the women's fre-
quency of visits from weekly to biweekly and, as usual,
accepted one-fourth of her normal fee. The woman was
a single mother of four children and worked nights
cleaning offices at low pay. She noted the woman's condition in her file and prepared for the next patient.

Promptly at ten, her receptionist opened the door and
in walked a familiar-looking young boy and an attractive African-American woman, tall with straight black
hair, fine features, and a very fair complexion. Audrey
sized her up as fashion-conscious, wealthy, and privileged from birth.

"How do you do, Dr. Powers," she said, extending her
hand. "Thanks for agreeing to see my son on such short
notice. I'm Doris Latham."

I'm getting daffy, Audrey said to herself as she shook
the woman's hand. *Those letters I saw have me thinking
she said her name was Latham.*

"How do you do," she said aloud. "Please have a seat.
I need to ask you a few questions."

"Here's her file, Dr. Powers," Audrey's receptionist
said, as she placed the file on the desk and left the office.

She ran her gaze over the file and nearly sprained her
neck in a quick double take. As luck would have it, she
was looking away from Doris Latham when she saw the
name on the file—Gerald Latham, Junior—and the
woman didn't see her sharp intake of breath.

She glued her gaze to the papers in the manila folder,
though all she saw was Gerald Latham, Senior running
from her bedroom with his clothing and shoes in his
hands.

"Dr. Powers, is anything wrong?"

She willed herself to respond, summoning her resources as a professional and as a woman. "No. I have

to think about this," she said, her aplomb restored. "Let me study these papers, and as soon as I work out a plan for him, my receptionist will call you."

She stood to indicate that the interview was over. The woman stood, obviously nonplussed, but her breeding showed when she smiled graciously, extended her hand, and thanked Audrey.

"I hope we'll hear from you soon."

Audrey looked down at the boy and forced a smile. "Of course. In a day or so."

Mrs. Gerald Latham and her son, Gerald Latham, Junior, walked out of Audrey's office, and she nearly collapsed into the chair. She didn't believe in fate, but something approximating it was fooling with her life. Abruptly, she sat forward. Oh, yes. And it was dealing with the life of Gerald Latham, Senior, too. The chickens had come home to roost. His son's right foot had been mangled in an accident and subjected to several operations. But without proper therapy he wouldn't walk perfectly again.

"I'm not the only therapist in this country," she said, placing the file in her out box, fully aware that in Washington, DC, she was the most prominent physician with that specialty. Let him hurt as she had hurt. Let him suffer. He owed her. Why shouldn't she collect? *And why should an innocent child suffer for what you allowed his father to do?* She tried to banish the thought, but her conscience wouldn't allow it.

The next day and the next, she wrestled between her longing for vengeance and her deeply ingrained allegiance to truth and integrity and to doing what she knew to be right. She fought the boy at night as he hobbled through her dreams, stumbling on piles of bricks, falling

Nine

Nelson looked over the results of his interview with Rufus Meade, saw that it contained nothing to which he could object, and marveled at its insightfulness. He phoned Meade.

"You did what you had to do, man. Great job. I sure didn't tell you all this, so you went to the right sources for the filler."

"Glad you're pleased. I decided not to include that incident I saw tucked on a back page of *The Washington Post*."

His name hadn't appeared in connection with that article, and he wondered if Meade was fishing for news. "How'd you figure out it involved me?"

"Wasn't difficult. The child's last name was the clue. I gather he loves to identify himself as Ricky Wainwright. That seemed to amuse the *Post's* reporter."

He let himself relax. "Are you planning to do anything with that information?"

"Naah, man. I sense that's an NSS matter, and it probably shouldn't have been reported in the first place. I would like to meet that kid, though. He's a clever one."

He didn't know a lot of reporters whose company he enjoyed, but he wouldn't mind getting to know a man who'd made himself a legend both as a football player and as a journalist. "I'll speak with my housekeeper and see what she can put together. She's a great cook and loves to show off her culinary skills. I hope you'll bring your significant other."

"My wife, Naomi Logan-Meade. Just let me know when you'd like us to come. Say the words 'good cook' and I'll be right on time."

Nelson liked the man, seemingly oblivious of his aura and the high regard in which people held him. To his surprise, he found he enjoyed speaking with a man who wasn't connected to the military, that it refreshed him to meet someone as a human being and not as an individual with a rank that defined who he was.

"I'll be in touch," he said, and hung up.

After getting Lena's delighted agreement to take care of the dinner, he phoned Audrey. "You seem down, or maybe preoccupied. Is there any way that I can help?"

"Thanks, but I'm . . . maybe it's lack of sleep. How are you?"

"Me? I'm fine. I'm inviting a man and his wife for dinner Thursday night, and I'd like you to join us. Can you make it?"

"Sure. I'd love that. Aunt Lena will really pull out all the stops. What time?"

"I'd like to be at your place for you at six."

"But I can—"

"Audrey, I don't ask women to meet me for a dinner date."

"Oops! Better put on my 'tweeds' if that's the way it is."

He gave in to a hearty laugh. "I can't imagine that any woman would outshine you. By the way, when can we have that weekend to ourselves?"

"Maybe after this one coming up? Do you have any idea when these guys will stop tailing us?"

"I know it's hard on you, but try to be patient. It can't go on forever."

"And thank God for that. I suppose I've weathered worse."

She had a way of saying such things, and he wondered, not for the first time, what was behind it. She had changed the subject, and although he didn't want to put their idyll at some indefinite time in the future, he didn't question her; he was too glad that she'd agreed to go with him at all."

"Oh, what the heck, nobody's going to mistake me for a siren," Audrey said that Thursday afternoon as she stood staring at the dresses in her closet. Having reassured herself with that pronouncement, she reached for a floor-length brick-red chiffon dress that flattered her coloring and exposed so much of her back that she couldn't wear a bra. She fastened her hair in a French knot with the aid of two ivory pick-combs, put diamond studs in her ears, Fendi perfume in her cleavage, picked up the black silk evening bag that complemented her black silk slippers and strolled downstairs to wait for Nelson.

You will not think about the Lathams this night, she admonished herself. *You are going to be warm, friendly, and witty if it kills you.* She blinked back an unexpected tear. Why should she be weepy when she hadn't done anything wrong? Gerald was the architect of that hideous crime, not she.

She answered the doorbell, and earned a long, sharp whistle worthy of any hard-hat construction worker.

"Somebody should have warned me. This woman is a siren." Nelson pretended to mop his brow. "I'm in trouble, and the sun hasn't even set. When the moon comes up, I'll probably stand out on my deck and howl like a timber wolf."

She reached up and kissed his jaw. "Behave yourself. I'm about to have a meltdown, but you don't hear me meowing, do you?"

His even white teeth glistened in the smile that she loved. "Why would you do that?"

"Since you asked, nothing I get to eat at your place tonight could hold a light to you. If I don't straighten out my head, I'll think I'm Cinderella. You look . . . well . . . I hate the word, but you look smashing. Now let's go before I take it all back."

He didn't move; his eyes shimmered with need and he spoke in a voice devoid of humor.

"You're a beautiful woman, more so it seems each time I look at you."

As far as she and most people who knew her were concerned, she hadn't been beautiful a day in her life. Nice-looking? Yes. Beautiful? Definitely not.

"I'm glad you see me that way. Thanks," she said, handing him a light stole. Noticing his baffled stare, she said, "You're wearing a linen jacket. It gets cool these evenings, and when I turn around, you'll see why I could freeze in August."

He grinned. "Hmmm. You're right. We'd better go."

"Looks as if Lena decided to show off," Nelson said as they entered the house. "Good heavens! Anybody would think she's staging a seduction." A rumble of laughter poured out of him. "I should have told her Meade is bringing his wife."

She whirled around and squinted at him. "What Meade are you talking about?"

He bent over to smell the bowl of tea roses on the in-

laid walnut table that faced the living room window.
"Rufus Meade. Know him?"

"You mean the journalist? You're kidding."

He opened the bar. "No, I'm not. I see Lena has some
cracked ice here. Seems like she's planning a real party.
Soft lights, Gershwin love songs coming from somewhere, roses. I'd better go in there and tone her down.
Wouldn't surprise me if she served roast quail for the
first course."

He started toward the kitchen, but she stopped him.
"I didn't know you knew Rufus Meade. I used to scream
my head off at the 'Skins games when he was their wide
receiver. I read his stuff all the time. He's a classy guy."

"He is that. I'm sure he'll be delighted to meet a fan."

Her balled fists went to the red chiffon that covered
her hips. "Now you wait a minute. I do not gush over
celebrities."

"I didn't suggest you did. Nothing wrong with being
interested. I'm curious about him myself. That story he
did on Afghanistan and me that appeared in the weekend *Post* is as good a piece of reporting as I've ever
read."

"What're we having for din . . . ?" He stared at Lena
in a long, gold-embroidered black silk caftan, her hair
in a knot at her nape, gold bangles in her ears. "Whew!
What have we got *here?"*

"I'll have you know, sir, there ain't no flies on Lena
Alexander. We're having distinguished guests, and me
and Ricky are acting the part."

"Where is he? Never mind, I hear him downstairs at
the piano. What are we having?"

"Seven courses: coulibiac of salmon; braised quail;
peach sorbet for a palate cleanser; filet mignon roast,
fluted mushrooms, asparagus tips, and tiny red potatoes;
green salad; assorted cheeses with my special bread;

and crème Courvoisier, coffee, and mints. The menu is on the dining-room table."

Nelson pulled up his bottom lip and hoped his eyes would someday return to their normal size. "I never said the president was coming! How's Ricky going to handle this? Anything more than a hamburger disgusts him."

"Ricky is going to eat his meal, and he's going to act as if this is what he eats for dinner every day."

He inclined his head to the left. "Yeah? Which Ricky are you talking about?"

"Ours. You'll see. And wait'll you see him in his navy blue suit, long pants and all. Cute as he can be."

Nelson sat down on the stool beside the kitchen sink. "I didn't know he had a navy blue suit with long pants."

"Oh, we got it this morning." She looked toward the ceiling, her face brimming with pride. "And don't he just love it! I declare, it don't take much to make a little one happy."

Audrey risked a glance at Nelson. He was a man who inspired admiration, not pity, but right then she pitied him, for he was as nonplussed a person as she had ever seen. At that moment, Ricky burst into the kitchen.

"Miss Lena, I played the whole piece. I got it . . . *Audie!*" Miracle of miracles, she thought as his whole demeanor changed. "Hi, Audie. How are you?" He glanced toward Lena. "Uh . . . gee, you look so pretty."

She waited for him to come for his hug, but instead he *walked* over to Nelson. "Unca Nelson, hi. What time is company coming? You like my suit?"

"Definitely. I like it and I like you in it."

A grin spread over Ricky's face, then he leaned forward and whispered. "Miss Lena took me to the store this morning and bought it. I love Miss Lena."

The doorbell rang, and Nelson patted Ricky on the shoulder and went to open the door. Audrey wondered how the security guards would treat Nelson's visitors. It would certainly heighten the man's curiosity if they questioned him as to why he wanted to enter Nelson's home. Well, they'd soon know. She strolled into the living room and sat down in a beige velvet chair that didn't clash with her red dress.

Nelson greeted Rufus Meade and his wife, Naomi Logan-Meade. An elegant man with a woman who complements him, Nelson thought as he walked with them to the living loom. He looked at Audrey, relaxed and seemingly at home in his favorite chair, beautiful and queenly, and his heartbeat accelerated. She stood as he approached with his guests. He didn't know what prompted him to do it, but before introducing them, he slung an arm around her waist, breathed in the perfumed aura that adorned her and walked with her, to where Meade stood with his wife.

"This is Dr. Audrey Powers," he said, and knew at once that his act of possessiveness with Audrey was not lost on Meade, for the man lifted his left eyebrow and let a half-smile play around his mouth.

"I'm happy to meet you, Dr. Powers. This is my wife, Naomi Logan-Meade."

Nelson got through the introductions as quickly as possible because he disliked formality in intimate settings. The two women greeted each other warmly, and he realized he wanted them to be friends for he didn't doubt that he and Meade had much in common and would enjoy a warm friendship.

He excused himself and went to the kitchen. "Could you two come with me?" he asked Lena and Ricky. "I want you to meet our guests."

Ricky jumped from the stool on which he'd perched. "Is my suit all right, Unca Nelson?"

"Perfect. You look fine."

"What about my tie? I don't like this tie."

He couldn't help smiling. "It looks great, and it's properly tied. Come on."

"You look good," he told Lena. "Down right frisky, I'd say."

She treated him to a hearty laugh. "I thought I told you there ain't no flies on me. In my day, I was something else. I could get it on with the best of 'em."

It amused him that Ricky bounded ahead of them as they walked to the living room, ran up to Rufus Meade, and held out his hand. "How you doing, Mr. Meade? I'm Ricky Wainwright."

Meade's face creased into a smile, warm and friendly. "Well, Well. I'm fine, Ricky. How are you? I read about you."

"Did you see my picture? They took a lot of pictures. My Unca Nelson said you wrote something about him."

"That's right, I did," Meade said, obviously delighted with the boy. "Ricky, this is my wife, Naomi Logan-Meade."

Ricky looked from Naomi to Audrey and back to Naomi. "How are you, Miss Na . . . N . . . Naomi? Are you gonna go home with Mr. Meade?"

Naomi laughed. "Absolutely. You bet I am."

Everyone present could see that her answer pleased Ricky, who walked over and stood beside Audrey's chair. "You have any little girls and boys?" he asked Naomi.

She told him about her seventeen-year-old son, Aaron, the eight-year-old twins—Preston and Sheldon, and her four-year-old daughter, Judy, whom they'd named after her great-grandfather, Judd.

Nelson had a twinge of guilt when Ricky gazed at him pleading with eyes. "Can she come over and play with me?"

"Yeah. If she wants to." He hadn't realized that Ricky felt badly for having lost Stacey's friendship. He knew so little about the matter that he couldn't explain to Ricky why he couldn't have Stacey for a playmate, and he wouldn't lie to the child for any reason.

"We'll have a picnic at our place, Ricky, and you'll meet Judy and our boys," Naomi said.

"Trust me, it's only Judy he's interested in. I've got a ladies' man on my hands. You haven't met the rest of my family," Nelson said. "This is Lena Alexander. She looks after Ricky and me, and she's also Audrey's aunt."

"Glad to meet you both," Lena said, accepting their acknowledgments. "Y'all come on to the dining room. We're having champagne with the first course, so you'd better not have drinks, that is, not unless you want to fall out on your face."

Rufus stood and took Naomi's hand. "Works for me. I heard about your magic with food, and I didn't even eat lunch."

Nelson had never known Lena to show diffidence, or was it feminine vanity, as she did then, along with what was certainly a bit of flirtatiousness. *My goodness,* he thought, *she's a man's woman, and what's more, Meade knows it.*

He seated Audrey opposite his place at the head of the table. "What kind of message are you sending to these people?" she whispered.

"That you're my woman. You got any disagreement with that?" he asked, and placed a loving pat on her bare back. When he glanced at Lena, he saw that she'd been waiting to see where he would seat Audrey, and her expression of satisfaction didn't escape him.

Lena said grace, and they began the meal with coulibiac of salmon, pumpernickel bread, and Moët &
Chandon champagne.

"I don't drink champagne," Ricky said to Rufus.
"They won't let me." He then took it upon himself to entertain Meade as they made their way through Lena's
seven-course dinner. Nelson waited for Ricky to complain, but none was forthcoming, and he wondered what
Lena promised him in exchange for such exceptional
behavior.

He recognized in himself a sense of pride in his
home, his family, and the woman who faced him at the
other end of the table. *She's what I need in my life, but
I am definitely not what she needs. Not with the uncer-
tainties facing me. And if she knew how much pain I'm
in right now, she'd want to send me to a hospital.*

She'd been speaking with Naomi when her glance
caught his, and she stopped midsentence as if experiencing a shock. At that moment, something akin to
tremors rolled through him while he stared at her, transfixed. He knew that if they had been alone, they would
have made love. The urge to have her nearly overpow-
ered him as heat fired his loins and desire found its
target with the accuracy of a marksman's arrow. He
didn't shift his gaze, for he knew that everyone present,
including Ricky, had focused on them. He smiled as
best he could, and Audrey expelled a long breath, releasing her tension.

"We'll have coffee in the living room," Lena said,
making him fully aware of those present and giving him
an excuse to get up and walk over to Audrey.

He extended his hand to her and marveled that she
rose from the chair with the grace of a eagle soaring,
when he hardly had the strength to stand there, so hobbled was he by the currents flowing between them.

"You're so lovely . . . so . . . so warm and feminine," he said, and wondered whether he sounded foolish.

But she squeezed his fingers, reassuring him. "How could I not be feminine when I'm with you?"

"Anything you say will definitely be used against you. I'm grabbing any straw I can get to support my case."

"What's your case?" she asked, looking over her shoulder as she preceded him to the living room.

He put a heavy hand on her arm, detaining her. "Ever watched an animal eat that hadn't been fed in a couple of days?"

She lifted her shoulder in a slight shrug. "Speaking of hunger, you had your last meal when I did. You know what I'm saying?"

She would have continued toward the living room but he held her there, letting his gaze bore into her, exposing his thoughts and feelings. "I take it you understand the meaning and value of your words and that you choose words that express exactly what you intend to communicate. Right?"

"Of course, " she said, giving him a level look. "Isn't that what you'd expect?"

"You're not saying much, but you're telling me a helluva lot, and I want to keep the facts straight."

"I've never lied to you, Nelson. Never."

He stared down into her eyes. Vulnerable. Yes, and proud. How did a man deal with that kind of mixture? Her bottom lip quivered, and his hand went to her waist to bring her body close to his own.

"Y'all gon' stand there all night? You can take care of business later," Lena said, although her voice was devoid of censure.

Meade leaned against the mantelpiece sipping espresso. "A man has to do what he has to do, Lena," he said as a broad grin settled over his face. "And taking care of business gets priority."

Ricky stood beside him, looking up. "When can I come see Judy, Mr. Meade? My Unca Nelson and Miss Lena won't mind, 'cause I ate all those different things for dinner and didn't make a fuss."

Meade's laughter filled the room. "You two will make an awesome pair," he said, mostly to himself. To Ricky, he said, "We'll arrange that with your uncle and Miss Lena in a day or so. All right?"

"Yes, sir," Ricky said clapping his hands together.

An hour after the Meades left, Nelson tucked Ricky into bed and prepared to take Audrey home. He'd put the BMW in the garage as he'd been instructed to do, and they entered the garage from the hallway off the kitchen. Still on fire from the heat that began its ascent to his loins while he faced her at the dinner table, and nearly consumed with desire thanks to her admission that she wanted him as badly as he wanted her, he got behind the wheel, turned on the ignition, and headed for Bethesda. He didn't dare put his hands on her until he had her inside her house and that red dress was tumbling away from her shoulders. Nor did he trust himself to talk; feeling as he did, only God knew what might fall from his tongue.

His cellular phone rang, and he answered it thinking that Lena had an emergency. "Hello."

"Checkmate. Watch it when you get to 68 Hickory Lane. Don't let Dr. Powers out of your car until our man sweeps the place. Be in touch."

He slowed down. This was the very last time he would allow himself to be ignorant about his life and those dear to him in the interest of security or anything else. If Marilyn were on his staff, he'd fire her. He didn't care how efficient she was.

"You're so quiet. Something wrong?"

He wouldn't treat her as Marilyn did him. "Seems like it, but I've been assured we're in no danger." He glanced over and saw that she was no less relaxed than before he'd received the phone call. "Security is tight right now."

"I know a car is trailing us, but one of those guards is always either beside me or behind me, so I thought nothing of it."

He slowed down, and the car behind him did the same. Deciding to test the situation, he flashed his distress signal, and the car behind him moved ahead and pulled to the shoulder of the highway. After verifying the government insignia on the side of the car, he flashed his lights and headed for Audrey's house.

When he reached the house, he pulled up to the curve and stopped, but didn't cut the motor until he recognized the guard as the one who tailed him most often.

"All clear, Colonel Wainwright."

"What happened?" he asked the man.

"I don't know, sir, but whatever it was, it sure did create a commotion."

"Did you check the house?"

"Bomb unit checked it."

He didn't doubt that his eyes increased to twice their size. "Whatever in the hell for? And how'd they get in?"

The security officer shrugged. "Entering is never a problem, sir, either for us or for criminals. That's why we checked. I'm sure headquarters will fill you in tomorrow, Sir."

In the circumstances, he didn't dare linger with Audrey. No one had to tell him that, in addition to the protection of one or more guards, for the remainder of the night cameras would film every shadow within fifty yards of that house. And he didn't want their private lives to become a public record.

"I'd better tell you good night. I wanted more than anything to spend time with you—quality time and a lot of it—but I don't want our personal lives debated in the press."

Her voice took on a wistful note. "I was thinking the same thing, but . . . well, I hope we'll have other opportunities to . . . to be together."

"We will." He kissed her quickly and ran down the steps. If she had so much as whispered his name, he wouldn't have left her till morning. The taste of her kiss, though fleeting, had sent heat spiraling through him to his loins, hardening him into full readiness. He released an expletive, got in the BMW, and headed for Alexandria.

"Unless you give me some facts right now, I'm not cooperating in this any longer," he told Marilyn the next morning, Friday. "You interrupt my life, interfere with my plans as if you have a right to do so. I appreciate that you are protecting me and my family, but I am an intelligent human being and I know how to handle any information you give me. What was that business last night all about?"

He thought he heard her snicker. If he had been certain of it, he would have headed for her office that minute and let her have a good piece of his mind.

"You've been patient, Colonel. Remarkably so, I'd say. Last night, we caught the ringleader of that group attempting to break into Dr. Powers's house, evidently to hide there until she got back home. He tried to bargain his way out of trouble by trading information, including what he called a tip that a bomb had been placed in Dr. Powers's house. Of course, none of us believed him, because we had secured the place. Still, we had to check it out."

"Where does that put us?"

"We are reassigning your security. There is no longer any danger to you, your family, or Dr. Powers."

"You're certain of that?"

"As I am of my name. We knew who he was, but we needed a reason to arrest him. Last night, he gave us one."

He exhaled a long breath. "Thanks. You and your staff did a great job."

"No problem. That's why we're here."

He hung up and called Audrey. "What do you say we take that vacation this weekend?" he asked her after letting her know that they no longer needed security.

"What do I need to bring with me?"

"You'll go? Really?"

"Uh-huh."

"Let's go to Willow's Cove. It's a tiny place on the Chesapeake Bay off the beaten path, and we can be alone or with a crowd. You'll need a bathing suit and the most casual clothing you own. Or would you prefer another spot?"

"I haven't been there, but if you want to go, I'm game."

"Then I'll be at your place at four this afternoon. Can you make that?"

She told him she could, and he hung up, fully aware that he had turned a corner and that he couldn't backtrack, nor did he want to.

Audrey didn't entertain the illusion that Nelson planned a weekend of romantic love, moonlight, and shadows. Some of that, perhaps, but she knew he wanted to clean the slate, to rid their relationship of the rocks and boulders that could separate them later on and cause him pain and regret. He wanted to find out once and for all whether he should break all ties with her.

She was taking a big chance, gambling on his being a decent man, on his caring enough for her that he wouldn't want to make her uncomfortable and wouldn't pressure her into baring her soul. She couldn't do that, not even to Winifred and Pam. Yet she loved him and could hardly wait for the moment when they could be free with each other.

Thus, she was both disappointed and relieved when Nelson called her about an hour later to say he had to attend an emergency meeting the next morning, Saturday, at the Commandant's office. And since he didn't know how long it would last, he thought it best to cancel their weekend plans.

"I'll call you at home as soon as the meeting is over. If you're not there, I'll call you on your cell phone. You can't begin to imagine how disappointed I am."

"Me too, Nelson. Me too. If I leave home tomorrow morning, I'll have my cell phone with me. Uh, what are you doing this evening?" She hated letting him know that she was anxious to be with him, but she'd been taught that if you didn't ask, you didn't get.

"I'll be at home, preparing for the meeting, and I have quite a bit of material to review. I'll call but not till I write my brief." His chuckle relieved the gloom she felt. "You and my work don't mix well, babe," he went on. "You take over completely."

"It's no more than you deserve, mister. You make a mess of my work when you start fooling around in my head."

"Yeah? At least I have the grace to limit my meddling to your head."

"Oops! I'm not going there."

"Chicken. Maybe we can get together Sunday."

She told him good-bye and walked with lead feet to the receptionist's desk for her next patient's file folder.

"Hello, Miss Frank, I'm Dr. Powers," she said, donning her professional persona and stuffing her pain and disappointment where no one could see it. "Right this way."

She prescribed therapy for a whiplash that the young woman had received when she fell down a flight of stairs.

"Did you fall or were you pushed?" she asked, deciding that the description of the accident didn't make sense.

"Doc, if I thought that ugly little man pushed me down those stairs, you believe me when I got through with him, he wouldn't be able to sit down for months. No ma'am, I fell. Ain't *no man* pushing me around. If he tried it once, he better not get in the bed with me and go to sleep."

That'll teach me to ask questions like that one. "Doesn't matter. I want you to do these exercises." She gave her a pamphlet. "Go down the hall to Room 10-C and an assistant will give you the treatment. Please also do them at home and come back to see me in two weeks."

"Yes ma'am, and thanks a lot. If this thing don't stop hurting, his behind gon' be in trouble."

Just as Audrey had thought: boyfriend pushed or knocked her down the stairs, and her basic reaction was to hide it and protect him. She handed the woman a prescription. "Stop at the pharmacy and get this soft collar. Wear it day and night, and avoid vacuuming, cutting wood, scrubbing the floor while on your knees, and working at the computer for lengthy, unbroken periods."

When the woman headed down the hall, she breathed a sigh of relief. That was her last appointment, and if she left right then, she could avoid walk-ins. She took off her white coat, got her briefcase, and headed for home. But as she drove up Georgia Avenue, she changed her mind and called her sister Pam.

"You busy, Pam?"

"Not too busy for you. Coming over?"

She told her older sister that she'd stop by for a few minutes on her way home. Somehow, the thought of being alone didn't sit well with her. Too much time to think, and she didn't want to do that. She didn't want to start second-guessing Nelson, and her mind had already headed in that direction. Maybe he didn't want to make such a strong commitment as an out-of-town idyll with her implied. He wasn't a junior officer, so how could he be jerked around like . . .

I guess everybody in the armed services has to take orders, she said to herself, *but such a shift from one hour to the next . . . It behooves me to be careful. I don't need to learn the same lesson twice.*

She flipped on the tape deck, leaned back, and pressed the accelerator as Dizzy Gillespie's "Salt Peanuts" cleaned every sensible thought from her mind. She didn't much like bebop, but it certainly prevented serious thinking, and that was what she used it for.

"What's going on, girl?" Pam asked as soon as Audrey stepped in the door. "You look washed out."

If she had remembered that Pam could read Winifred and her like a book, she would have gone straight home. Having played the role of mother to them after their mother died, Pam was as sensitive to their needs as their mother had been. She didn't bother to answer Pam's inquiry, because that had merely been a part of her sister's greeting. When she got down to the business of asking questions, Pam could put a prosecuting attorney to shame.

"Want some tea?"

She shook her head. "No thanks." Pam believed in curing the blahs with tea, but it would take more than those little black leaves from Myramar to brighten Audrey's blues. She sat down on a stool in the kitchen because Pam had strewn the table and half the counter space with material for her lesson plans.

Pam dropped a paperweight on top of a pile of papers, pulled a chair from the table, sat down facing Audrey, and crossed her knees. "Does this have anything to do with Nelson Wainwright?"

Good old Pam. Always cut right to the chase. "Indirectly, yes."

"Want to tell me about it? I know he's the reason you're in the dumps, because you've been moon-faced for the last four or five weeks. Flying. I've been tempted to ask what's holding you up there. Never saw a woman do such a complete turnaround."

Suddenly, Pam's face contorted into a frown. "Honey, has he hurt you? I know what's happened between you two; wasn't hard to figure it out because you've been a different person ever since. If he's hurt you, I'll never forgive Aunt Lena for setting it up. Talk to me."

"Maybe I'm jumping the gun, Pam, but . . . I just don't know. He's a loving, caring man, but . . . Well . . . maybe he thinks he's gone too far."

Pam leaned forward. "Stop talking in riddles. I can't read a person's mind. *What did he do?*"

She told her about the two conversations she'd had with Nelson that afternoon and added, "He's not an indecisive person, and he spoke as if he hated to change our plans. But he's even busy working tonight. I know I have no right to penalize him for Gerald's dishonesty and treachery, but I can't pretend I don't know men are capable of such deceit."

"You and Winifred fall in love and anything goes."

"Not so, Pam. I've never let a guy think that."

"All right. I won't preach, but if you don't trust Nelson, why would you consider getting in the bed with him?"

She sighed in resignation. Nothing was as simple as Pam represented it to be. "I love him. Gerald was a product of my youthful inexperience. Not so with Nelson. I've looked at him from all sides and angles, and if he's got a trait that I can't tolerate, I'd like to know what it is because I haven't found it."

"Then why don't you trust him?"

"In my heart, I do; my head says never trust another man."

"I see. Does he love you?"

"He loves me. Look, Pam, I'd better be going. I need to do some work in my garden before it gets dark. Thanks for your ear."

"Anytime. I suppose you know Ryan took our little sister to Cape May for the weekend. One more virgin bites the dust."

At times, Pam's pontificating got on her nerves. "You wouldn't want her to live for twenty-eight years and maybe die without knowing what it is to share her body with the man she loves and who loves her, would you?"

Pam threw up her hands. "You two know it best. Stop fretting about Nelson. Mama always said that if you give a man enough rope, he'll hang himself. If he doesn't, you've got solid gold."

"Give my love to Hendren. 'Bye."

She loved her sister, but Pam's strait-laced attitude

toward men and sex belonged back in the 1930s or thereabouts. Still, that conservatism worked for Pam, who had been happily married to Hendren for ten years, so one shouldn't expect her to abandon her views on such matters.

As she drove home, she wondered what she gained by stopping to see Pam. She nursed the question until she drove into her garage and was about to get out of her car. Pam had fingered the problem. Trust. Could it be that Nelson didn't trust her or didn't have faith in a life with her?

She opened the kitchen door, went in, and sat in the nearest chair. Was he uncertain about her? Had she done anything to lessen his faith in her?

Nelson's thoughts didn't venture in that direction, however. His focus was on the plans he had drafted for guerilla warfare in differing settings. He had to defend them the next morning in what could be the biggest challenge of his career. Well past midnight, he remembered that he had planned to telephone Audrey, mostly to make up for disappointing her about the weekend. But he didn't think it proper to call her at a quarter of one in the morning. He hoped she would understand.

At a few minutes past three on Saturday morning, still wet from the shower, he dropped his nude body into bed, not even bothering to slide between the sheets. Exhaustion was an inadequate expression for the way he felt. But five hours later, he threw his briefcase on his desk and savored his first swallow of coffee for the day. Fifteen minutes after that, he locked his desk and headed for the Commandant's office.

"You've done a fine job, Wainwright," the Commandant said after Nelson presented his report.

"First-class, and I'll see that you get the recognition you deserve."

"Thank you, Sir," he said, "I'm glad you're pleased."

As the words left his mouth, his gaze caught the narrowed eyes of Lieutenant Colonel Rupert Holden, and the smirk, unmistakable, on the man's face. Holden would make trouble for him. Ratting on a more senior officer was not condoned, but the man was slick enough to engineer an investigation. The slightest hint of malfeasance could ruin him, and his failure to report an infraction as serious as sleeping on guard duty wouldn't be treated lightly. Holden knew Nelson's failure to report the marine was an act of compassion. Nonetheless, he would use the information to abort the career of an officer he regarded as a rival. Holden had no scruples.

He saluted the Commandant and was on his way to his office when Holden stopped him. "Thinking of going back to Afghanistan, Wainwright?"

"I'll go wherever my travel orders send me." He was in no mood to tangle with Holden.

"I guess you're hoping your little plan lands you a promotion to Brig General." The man showed his teeth in what passed for a grin. "Doesn't always work that way. See you around."

So Holden was declaring war, was he? Ready to ruin the career of a fellow officer in order to further his own goals. A man as ruthless as he was reputed to be always had a crack in his armor. Nelson was not going to worry about what he couldn't control.

He looked at his watch. Two-thirty and he hadn't had lunch, but food wasn't his priority right then. Although flush from his successful presentation to those who mattered in the United States armed forces, the top brass, his thoughts weren't on his accomplishments or what his performance might net him. He had to get his personal life on track, and that meant a final decision as to where he was going with Audrey Powers.

He didn't believe she'd ever lied to him, but she'd told him so little that saying she was truthful really wasn't saying much. He loved her, that wasn't in question. But could he share with her the pain in his heart, his dreams, fears, imperfections, and nonsensical habits? Did she need Mr. Perfect, and was that her reason for not allowing him to know her?

At home, he found a note from Lena. "Sure is good to be able to take off and go just like I please. Ricky and me are going to see *Snow White*. I want him to know there's screens other than those on the back door and the ones covering the TV. We'll be back at five-thirty."

He made a peanut butter and jelly sandwich, got a glass of milk, and climbed the stairs to his room feeling much as he did when he was eight years old and that was his favorite meal. He kicked off his shoes, sat on the edge of the bed, and dialed Audrey's home phone number.

"How did it go?" she asked after they greeted each other. "Are you satisfied with what you did?"

"Very much so. I couldn't ask for better. The Commandant and his cohorts thought I gave them what was needed. Are you busy this evening?"

"Gee, I'm sorry. I'm going to Wolf Trap. The Preservation Hall Band will be there, and I've never seen them. You said we'd see each other tomorrow, so I figured you'd be busy."

"Lena and Ricky went to a movie. Damn. I wish you were here with me."

"Me too. How does your neck feel?"

"Not too bad, though it gave me some anxious moments this morning when I nearly grabbed it two or three times, but then the pain subsided. It hurts sporadically."

"I know. It pains me just to think of what you're going through, but from what I've learned of you, I don't suppose it has occurred to you that your dad would understand if you couldn't keep that promise."

"Unless the matter is beyond my control, I don't welsh on a promise. My word is my bond." He bit into the sandwich. "'Scuse me, but I'm just eating my lunch, a peanut butter and strawberry jelly sandwich."

"Didn't Aunt Lena leave anything for your lunch?"

"She didn't know I'd need lunch. Anyhow, I'm capable of feeding myself. Of course, if you suddenly materialized with another sandwich and some more milk, I'd dance for you."

"While holding a knife blade in your teeth?"

"Sure, if that would make you sweet and mellow. In fact, if I could get a kiss right now, I'd dance for you holding a knife blade in my teeth and wearing nothing but my birthday suit."

"You're making my mouth water."

"I can do a better job of that."

"My goodness, you're getting naughty."

He swallowed the last of his milk. "To paraphrase Mae West: goodness doesn't have a damned thing to do with that. What time can we see each other tomorrow? I want us to spend the day getting to know one another."

"Where?"

"Back where it all started. Mount Vernon. We can walk, sit among the trees and shrubs, take a boat ride, have lunch, and dinner too, if you like. Plenty to do. And there's a riding farm not too far away, so if you like horseback riding, we could do that, too."

"I'd better go buy some Levi's. I love to ride."

"What about me? Do you love me?"

"I haven't changed since we last discussed this particular matter."

He couldn't help laughing. "Audrey, how do you come up with these clinically clean statements? A great big mouthful of words that don't say a thing. That's an art, believe me. Do you or don't you? I wouldn't ask if I didn't need to hear it."

Her laughter reached him through the wire, warming him and fanning the flames of his desire. "You don't need to know that right now, asking me cold like that." A feeling he recognized as happiness rumbled in the form of laughter out of this throat when she went on, "Is there a hot way to ask you? Uh . . . don't answer that."

He let the laughter pour out of him. "Oh, I don't mind answering that. Not one bit. Not only is there a hot way, honey, but you have demonstrated it to perfection. Fortunately, we've got roughly fifteen miles between us and you can't sock me right now. Meet me tomorrow, and I'll let you do anything to me that suits your fancy."

"Are you nuts? My imagination is already off and running. Wow!"

Was he loco? Could be. At times he wasn't sure, especially not when he was with her or talking with her. "Kiss me." He heard the sound of a kiss. "You're a sweet woman, you know that? Have a good time at Wolf Trap, and tell that Joe you're already taken."

"Hmm. I don't think I could do that, not even with the taste of your kiss still on my lips. You have to realize that I reject control even when it's in my interest."

"Yeah. Tell me about it. Didn't security lecture me about your antics? Once I know you're mine, I won't need to control you, I'll just keep you so happy that you'll control yourself."

"Promises, promises. Show me some action."

"I will, lady, and see that you're prepared for it. Till tomorrow around nine?"

"Okay."

He hung up and started down to the kitchen for another sandwich. She had the capacity to dare him into thinking dangerous thoughts and doing dangerous things. But if he did something foolish, it would be well calculated and he'd be prepared for the consequences. And yet he'd love to see how far she could drive him, and how mercilessly she would exploit his passion for her.

Ten

Nelson loped down the stairs early that Sunday morning and found Lena and Ricky laughing as though they shared a private joke. He lifted the boy, twirled him around a time or two, and set him on his feet.

"What are you two laughing about?"

"He tried to trick me into cooking waffles *and* pancakes, claiming you don't eat waffles. I'm onto him," Lena said. "He likes to have both on his plate so he can mess around with first one and then the other. Getting to be a prankster already."

"I happen to love waffles, Ricky. How was the movie?"

"I had a good time, Unca Nelson. Can I go back today and see the end? I got sleepy."

"I doubt Lena wants to see it twice. Oh, yes. Lena, I'll be away most of the day, and I'd appreciate it if you'd keep Ricky for me."

She looked at him, then at the forkful of waffle an inch from her mouth. "Don't I always keep him?" She shook her head as if in wonder, and put the waffle into her mouth. After she chewed it, she asked him, "What's so special about today? You planning to elope?"

He supposed his face had the appearance of a caricature, for he could feel his bottom lip drop and his eyes widen. When he reclaimed himself, he said, "Lena, if you're going to get fanciful, be careful about where and in front of whom you express your thoughts. I'm way past the age where that would apply anyway."

She sipped her coffee. "I don't remember hearing you deny it."

He finished eating and took his soiled dishes to the dishwasher. "I think I'll let you stew over that one," he said when he walked back into the breakfast room. "Can't you just see me getting married in a pair of jeans? Be a good boy, Ricky." He hugged the child and within minutes was aiming the BMW toward Bethesda.

Feeling as if his insides had rearranged themselves, his fingers gripped the steering wheel. So much depended on the day. He needed to spend a few minutes collecting his thoughts and calming his emotions, so he pulled off Jefferson Highway just before he reached Francis Scott Key Bridge. So much was riding on what he would say and how he acted, yet he didn't want to plan his words or even his thoughts. What he wanted for them was the truth, and he hoped it would emerge naturally, that it would be a binding force for their relationship. But he knew he might be asking for more than she could or would give. He leaned against the back of the seat with his right hand supporting his neck.

"Get it together, man, otherwise you won't accomplish a thing."

But he couldn't let their relationship remain as it was. He needed more, and he knew she could give more. If only it didn't mean so much to him! He could stand before enemy fire without the slightest hesitation; fear didn't control him in the face of danger. So why was he so anxious about what he could achieve with one woman when he had a whole day in which to do it?

I'll do my best, and what will be will be. If we split up, it definitely will not kill me. He got back on the highway and headed for 68 Hickory Lane.

Audrey shimmied into a brand-new pair of stretch jeans, tucked her yellow crew-neck T-shirt into the jeans, and zipped them up. She could think of a hundred ways to be this uncomfortable and look better, but after searching for a pair that fit her small waist *and* her hips, she had settled on those. She put on a pair of walking shoes, combed her hair down, and ran down the stairs. The doorbell rang as she reached the bottom step.

She opened the door, looked up at him, and lost her resolve to play it cool. "Hi."

He stared down at her. "Hi. Every time I see you, I'm looking at a different Audrey."

"I aim to please," she said, ignoring his seemingly serious mien and feeling the need to hold on to something solid.

"Can I come in?"

"Sure," she said, stepping back to allow him entrance, or at least meaning to. For her life's sake, she didn't know how or when her arms went around him and her head came to rest against his chest. He clutched her close, and she looked up, waiting for his kiss, but he squeezed her to him and released her.

"If my mouth touches you, I won't want to leave this house today, and that isn't what I'd like for us. Understand?"

She nodded, but she didn't understand her profound need for reassurance. Was it because Pam's question whether she trusted Nelson still worried her? She smiled to lighten the situation and flicked on the nightlight, sensing that they would return well after dark.

"Come on. Let's go," she said and, feeling him out,

added, "I feel as though something of great moment is waiting for me."

Not a smile settled on his face. "Could be. None of us can see the future, close though it may be." His fingers stroked the back of her neck. "If I have contentment at the end of this day, I won't ask for more; the price of happiness is usually too high."

She didn't want to encourage his philosophical mood, so she asked him to show her some historical places while they drove through Alexandria on the way to Mount Vernon.

"If you've got a strong stomach, we can drive along Duke Street. Some of the most notoriously vicious slave practices took place on Duke between Payne and Reinekers."

Later he pointed out the site of the Franklin & Armfield Slave Office and Pen, a headquarters for slave trading from 1828 until around the time of the Civil War. "The slave-pen walls within which slaves were herded while awaiting sale were torn down in 1870," he said, proving knowledge of the town in which he lived. "The building is known now as Freedom House and is in the National Register of Historic Buildings."

"If you ask me, there's no need to preserve that evidence of national maleficence; thirty million human beings certify that bit of history every day."

"Want to see some more?" he asked her.

"I . . . yes. I've lived this close to it and never known it was here. Ignorance is not a trait I admire."

He drove past Bruin "Negro Jail," explaining its history as the place where enslaved people were housed and from which two sisters escaped into the arms of abolitionists Reverend Henry Ward and Harriet Beecher Stowe, author of *Uncle Tom's Cabin*.

"I don't want to see any more of this," she said in a voice laced with tremors.

"Oh, it isn't all bad. Some noble African Americans contributed to the growth and development of Alexandria, including Benjamin Banneker, a mathematician and astronomer whose 1792 almanac was lauded by Thomas Jefferson. The man was a genius. Self-educated. He'd worked on the survey of the capitol and re-created from memory the entire plan for the city of Washington, DC after the original planner quit and took the plans with him."

"I always thought he lived in Maryland, over near Frederick."

"Right. He was born over that way." Nelson looked at his watch. "Think I'd better head for Mount Vernon. That okay with you?"

It wasn't as safe for her emotional state as was that excursion through history, but she didn't intend to put a damper on their day. "I'm at your command."

He let out a soft whistle. "Good thing I've got sense enough not to take that too seriously."

At Mount Vernon, they strolled through the formal gardens, and though he held her hand, he seemed content to walk in silence. After a time, he released her hand and slipped his arm around her waist. She looked around to see that they were alone among the groves and some distance from the mansion.

"I'd like us to get some food from the cafeteria, drive down to Riverside Park, and have a picnic. Okay?"

What was it that this man did to her merely by standing still and looking into her eyes? Frissons of heat shot through her veins, and she lowered her gaze.

"Would you like that?" His voice had an urgency, deep and powerful.

"I told you I'm at your command, didn't I? If you think I'll enjoy it, I will."

His big hands gripped her arms. "Don't say anything you don't mean."

She tried to get her voice, but failed. "I mean it," she whispered.

His groan sent excitement ricocheting throughout her body. She needed him, wanted him. She had to have him. "Kiss me right now," she said. "I want your tongue in my mouth. I want to feel you inside of me."

She thrilled to the sound of his groans and the turbulence of his shudders as he thrust his tongue between her parted lips. With one hand gripping her shoulders and the other locked to her buttocks, he lifted her to fit him and plunged in and out of her mouth with a promise she couldn't misinterpret.

She fought to control the kiss, pulling him deeper into her until he abruptly set her away from him, heaving short breaths, his nostrils flaring. Standing about two feet from her, he braced both hands against her shoulders and gazed intently into her eyes.

"When your passion gets a grip on you, does anything else matter? I want my woman to want me, but you just about tied me into knots there."

"Are you saying I displeased you?"

He wiped his damp forehead with the back of his hand. "No, I'm not. Far from it. I just don't want you to forget that you have to help me control this thing. Baby, you pack one hell of a wallop, and I don't want to be guilty of an indiscretion with you. Not now or ever."

If he only knew how proud she was of her ability to be free when she was in his arms! Until she fell for him, she was locked as tight as a Brinks truck. She hadn't achieved that freedom with Gerald. Far from it.

She looked at him, open, and to her amazement, unconcerned about self-image. "If I focus on control you may as well not be here. I spent most of my adult life keeping a tight lid on myself. I dropped my guard and regretted it, and I vowed never to do that again. But for some reason I shed those inhibitions when I'm with you. I don't—"

"Is that what you mean, or is the fact that you let go whenever I get my hands on you more accurate? When your mind rules, those inhibitions are squarely in place—even when you're with me. Right?"

He was pushing her, and she was doggoned if she'd let him put her on the defensive. "What you see is what you get. I don't pretend with you. If my behavior puzzles you sometimes, I understand because when it to comes to you, I often surprise myself."

He looked into the distance for a few seconds before his features softened into an almost-smile. "I believe what you said, but I hope you won't mind if I remind you of Shakespeare's words in *Hamlet:* 'This above all: To thine own self be true, and it shall follow as night the day, Thou canst not then be false to any man.' "

He brushed his fingers through his hair. "It's a problem for me that I feel I don't know you, but it looks as if you're only now getting to know some things about yourself."

"It's possible that . . . oh, what the heck. Let's go eat," she said.

This man is stubborn, she thought, watching him stand there making up his mind as to whether he would pursue that line of conversation. Either good judgment or compassion prevailed, for at last he said, "If you're hungry, of course we'll eat. Let me get the picnic basket from the trunk of my car. We'll take it to the cafeteria and have some food put in it."

In the park on the banks of the Potomac River, they ate a simple lunch and washed it down with iced tea. "I'm not letting you near any Virginia Blush wine, not to speak of champagne." He grasped her left hand in his right one. "Next time you decide to drink that stuff, I want to be looking forward to a long, quiet evening with you."

"You're not going to let me forget that, are you?"

"No indeed. I have that night to thank for some of my most cherished memories of you." He sat on the grass near her, stretched out, and lay his head in her lap. "I'd give anything to know if the woman I saw that night was the real you."

He looked up at her with eyes that were dark, that gave him a look of vulnerableness. For a moment, she resisted stroking his face and then gave in to the tenderness that welled up in her.

"You wouldn't bend over and give me a little kiss, would you?" His words came to her in a whisper. "Would you?" he asked again.

Quickly, she brushed his lips with hers. "Sometimes, like right now," she whispered, "you . . . you captivate me."

He closed his eyes and smiled, a peaceful, secretive kind of smile. "And sometimes, like right now, with your fingers running through my hair and tracing the side of my face, you seduce me to putty."

She could hardly believe he meant it, though she knew he did. "Funny how we meld so smoothly when we're . . . together this way, and the minute we start talking serious—"

He interrupted her, sitting up as he did so. "Precisely. And that's because the chemistry between us is so strong. Some couples never have it; I know I've never had this with anyone else. And that's our problem. We mate as man and woman, but not as a man and a woman who understand and accept each others foibles, warts and all. Who need each other on a deeper level. You understand what I'm saying?"

She did, and she also knew their fun time was over, at least for the day. "Yes. I do understand. You need to see the recesses of my soul. Is that it?"

"No. I want to know who you are when you're with your sisters, when you're alone. What hurts you, cheers you up, saddens you. What you need in life that you don't have, aren't getting. I want to know who you are. I'm in deep with you, but you seem content not to know those things about me. I tell you something that's important to me, but you don't probe. Don't you want to know who I am?"

She released a deep sigh. "Of course I do. But Nelson, you're the older of two children, and you had to have a special place in your family. I'm the middle of three. I suppose you've heard about the middle child syndrome. Well, it's most evident when all three children are of the same sex, as in my family. Our parents loved all of us. Indeed, I can't recall a time when they didn't try to treat us equally. But the fact remained that I was out of step with the other two.

"My sisters love me, but they're closer to each other than they are to me. My older sister, Pam, always coddled Winifred. Winifred comes to me with her personal problems because I'm not as rigid as Pam, but it's Pam she looks up to. I was a loner from the time I remember anything about myself. When I was eleven, our father gave me a little plate with this engraving: "Little cat, lit-

tle cat, walking all alone; whose are you? whose are
you? I'm my very own."

"Did he have that made for you?"

"No. He saw it in an art shop and it reminded him of
me."

"And you still remember that verse."

"I still have the little plate."

The message of that gift she'd cherished for nearly
two decades suddenly struck her as a criticism. Maybe
it wasn't. Perhaps he'd only been telling her that he understood her. Either way, she didn't want to talk about it
any longer.

"Hey, I felt some raindrops." He jumped up, fastened
the lid on the picnic basket, and reached for her hand.
"We'd better make a run for it. The clouds over toward
Washington don't look one bit friendly."

The raindrops seemed to get bigger by the second as
they sprinted across the park to his car. He opened the
front passenger door for her, dashed around to the driver's side, tossed the picnic basket to the back seat,
hopped in, and closed the door before a torrent of rain
cleared the park of picnickers.

"This doesn't look so good," he said, and she'd been
thinking the same.

"Maybe it won't last long."

"Yeah," he said, almost as if he hadn't heard her, his
entire demeanor flashing warnings. "I'm going to avoid
the expressway; cars will be backed up for miles, and
with rain pelting down like this, we could have flash
flooding in minutes."

She didn't know the region, so she said nothing when
he chose a side road that paralleled Little Hunting
Creek. Very soon, his windshield wipers proved useless,
and water rose along the road.

"Good Lord, Nelson, I never saw such a heavy down-pour. I think the creek is flooding."

"And so is this carburetor. I'm trying to make it to that incline. Then I think we'll be all right, though we may have to sit here for a while." He reached the slight hill, drove as close to a big oak tree as he could get, and cut the motor.

"If the water rises above the car, we can get up in this tree," he said. "Let's see if the radio is working." He tuned in station WRC in Washington and heard what he knew firsthand: that the southern portion of the Potomac and its tributaries were overflowing.

"You don't seem overly concerned," she said, her own nerves beginning to unsettle her.

"Oh, I am. I wouldn't want anything untoward to happen to you, especially not because of me. However, I don't think we have anything to fear." He flicked off the radio and turned to her. "Let's make good use of this time. We can't go anywhere or do anything else except talk to each other."

Here it comes, she thought. *If only I could give him what it is that he needs of me. But I've never opened up my soul to anyone, not even to my mother. He needs that, and maybe I'd be happy if I did it but I can't. I don't know how.*

"You know," he began, leaning back against the car seat, "Until I finished Buckley Academy, I was scared to death of high places. I didn't even want to get on the top of a six-foot ladder."

"But you're a pilot."

"My father was a pilot, and my younger brother intended to fly. I didn't want to be left out, so during the summer before I went to the Naval Academy, I made my way to Switzerland and forced myself to climb the Matterhorn. Every time I looked down, I got sick to my stomach, so I stopped looking down. When I got to that peak, I was so happy I cried. I flung my arms out wide and shouted at my echo for a good half-hour until I began to feel great, as if I belonged up there close to the sky with the planes crisscrossing over my head. Those were magical moments. None other of my accomplishments will ever equal that one."

"Not even earning that fourth silver star?"

He slid his right arm across the top of the bucket seat in which she sat and brushed her shoulder with his fingers. "That was triumph over myself, killing my personal demon. If I did that, I can do anything I put myself to."

And that's the key to who you are today, she thought, understanding for the first time how he could endure the pain in his neck and shoulders for the sake of a coveted goal.

"I already knew that you have an inner strength that sets you apart, a toughness that I haven't see in other men. I thought it was because you're a Marine officer, but I was wrong. It's you."

"Do you have a fear or a feeling of inadequacy that could hinder fulfillment in some area of your life, that stands between you and something you covet badly?" He asked the questions in a casual tone that anyone would have thought was merely a continuation of their conversation.

But how could she tell him she'd rolled herself up tight as a ball of knitting yarn throughout her years of college and medical school because she thought herself homely compared to the flamboyant and beautiful girls first at Howard and then at George Washington University, where she attended medical school. Girls whose fathers didn't collect tickets on Amtrak as hers did, but who were doctors, lawyers, and professors. Girls whose mothers didn't clean the women's room at the Pentagon. How could she tell him she grew up thinking she was nobody?

He waited for her answer, his hand resting lightly on her shoulder. What could she say? "Can't think of anything right now," she said, hating herself for lying to him.

He withdrew his hand, leaned back against the seat, and closed his eyes. "Soon it'll be dark, and it looks like it's going to be a long night."

His words had the impact of a blast of frigid air, and her sense of defeat was further exacerbated when he turned his head toward the window, effectively ending their conversation. She couldn't retract her dishonesty. What would he think? He, a man from a privileged family.

I knew from the start that we couldn't make it, she said to herself. *Even if I could tell him that, I could never tell him all he'd want to know about Gerald and me.* She turned on her right side, away from him. *Oh, Lord, I hurt. I hurt.* She opened her purse, took out a tissue, and slid it between her lips to stiffle her groan. She was damned if she'd cry over him or any other man. If she didn't want to advertise her background, that was her business. He had no right to demand, like some latter-day guru, that she confess all if she wanted to hang out with him.

"I won't do it," she whispered.

You're wrong, her conscience whispered right back.

"Won't do what?" Nelson asked. "Oh, never mind."

He dialed her aunt Lena on his cellular phone, explained their plight, and told her not to worry. Then he slouched down in the seat and turned his face toward the window.

In the darkness, she couldn't see whether the water

level had risen or fallen, and she didn't want to disturb him. She'd made a mess of what had been one of the sweetest, most enjoyable days of her life. If she could have forced herself to tell him something, even about her fear of the dark, maybe he'd have his arms around her right that minute.

When she heard the engine stir some time later, she realized she'd slept. "What time is it?" she asked him, noticing that the car's headlights shone brightly.

"A quarter of three. The water is down to about a foot, so I'm going to try to get out of here."

He flipped on the radio to an all-night station and didn't speak again until he stopped in front of her house.

He walked with her to her door, took her key, and opened the door and placed the key in her hand. "I went through a break-up with someone who was very dear to me but who gave me the most painful surprise of my life. I've been over it for years. I guess we broke up because I didn't understand her and definitely not her needs, and I'm not going through that again. If you want to be just friends, nothing more, I'm game. Thanks for the day. Be seeing you."

She managed to get inside the door, lock it, and make her way to the living room where she slumped into the nearest chair. He was right, she knew. If she had queried Gerald, she would have at least been suspicious of his marital status, particularly because he didn't introduce her to any of his friends. But she had been so excited, yes, and so happy that the handsome, refined man reciprocated her feelings that she hadn't let herself risk knowing more about him than he volunteered, which wasn't much.

I blew it, she said to herself, heading upstairs, *but as much as we care for each other, I can't believe it's over.* She stripped, headed for the shower, and stopped.

Hadn't he said he could do anything he put himself to? She couldn't control the trembling of her bottom lip, and after a while she stopped trying.

I did my best, and it wasn't good enough, Nelson said to himself as he rolled out of bed the next morning without having slept one minute. *I can't and I won't go any further with a woman about whom I know so little. I thought I knew Carole, but I wouldn't have dreamed she couldn't go seven days without a man. And I certainly would not have believed that she would go to bed with the man who I thought was my best friend.*

He disliked leaving home before Ricky awoke, but he had to get to his office and tackle the mound of work he'd left there Saturday afternoon.

"Good morning, Colonel. This is Lieutenant McCafferty," the voice said when he answered his intercom. "General Gray wants to know if there's a reason why you shouldn't return to Afghanistan for fifteen months. A change of command there is in the offing. If you have reasons or reservations, please fax them over to me before eleven this morning."

"Please tell General Gray that I'll try to carry out any order I'm given to the best of my ability."

"Right on, Colonel."

He knew better than to ask for consideration in any circumstance other than his health or a serious family emergency and so didn't avail himself of the general's offer to take account of his "reasons or reservations." Instead, he converted his thinking to that of a man who would soon be headed to a war zone. Ricky would be safe with Lena, but how would the separation affect his personality and sense of security? That was a risk he had to take. As for his neck, he reasoned that if he took along enough painkillers, his neck wouldn't be a problem, though the possible dangers didn't escape him.

Neither did he fail to admit to himself that he would be leaving an aborted relationship with a woman he cherished, and that fifteen months of separation would stamp it final. *I can't help it. It's over.*

However, Audrey's war with herself had hardly begun. She spent the better part of that Monday morning upbraiding herself for having gone against her good judgment and allowing Nelson Wainwright into her life, her mind, and her heart.

"Dr. Powers, that Latham case is still in my box of pending cases," her receptionist said. "Mrs. Latham has called several times. What should I tell her when she calls again?"

"I have to think about it." Audrey walked to the window and stared unseeing down on Georgia Avenue. *Why should I help Gerald Latham after what he did to me? Let him suffer as I suffered.* The words tore themselves from her, and she raised her fist to strike the window but caught herself, turned and went back to her desk. Her conscience served noticed that she would have no peace. *Is it right to make the boy suffer for his father's deed and your own folly?* It nagged at her.

Folly? I didn't know beans about sophisticated men. I was Gerald Latham's victim, dammit, she answered her conscience in an attempt to justify turning the child away. With repeated and lengthy surgery, he stood a good chance of regaining the normal use of that foot, provided he received the proper therapy. She knew what he needed and could give it to him. *But why should she?*

As if to assuage her guilt, she spent an extra half-hour with her next patient, a ten-year-old girl who had broken her left middle finger, jeopardizing a possible career as a violinist.

However, her conscience would not be placated, and that night, beautiful little girls with long braids and smooth black skin played "Jitterbug Waltz" on their violins while little black boys hobbled on crutches trying frantically but unsuccessfully to dance. One by one they fell with hands outstretched toward her. She awoke amid twisted sheets dampened with the sweat of her culpability.

She tumbled out of bed and made her way to the kitchen. As she sipped coffee, she asked herself why she should forego the chance given her by fate to show Gerald what it meant to hurt.

But the child will hurt more than Gerald, her demon conscience needled.

He'd done his dirt and walked away with impunity, unscathed. He hounded her thoughts. She couldn't look at a copy of *The Washington Afro-American* without seeing something about "socialite Dr. Gerald Latham and his lovely wife, Jemma." She got up from the table and dashed the remainder of the coffee into the sink. Gerald Latham had paid his dues and he was going to get his reward.

The telephone rang and she answered it with reluctance, still deep in thoughts of the Latham family. "Audrey, honey, do you know where the Colonel is?" The anxiety in Lena's voice triggered a sense of alarm in Audrey. "I been calling his office, and his secretary would only tell me he stepped out for a few minutes."

"What is it, Aunt Lena? What's the matter? Is Ricky all right?"

"Hold on, the ambulance is here. I'll call you when we get to George Washington University Hospital. 'Bye." Lena hung up.

"Aunt Lena!" The sound of the dial tone heightened her frustration. She didn't know whether something had happened to Ricky, her aunt was ill, or what.

She packed her briefcase, cleared and locked her desk. "I'll be away for the remainder of the day," she told her receptionist. "If you need me, call my cellular phone number." After telephoning Nelson's office and leaving a message with his secretary, she left her own office and hailed a taxi. She didn't have hours to search for a parking place. At the hospital's information desk, she learned that Ricky had been admitted and was being prepared for surgery.

"What's his problem? Why is he having surgery?"

"Sorry, madam, we give particulars only to family members."

"I'm a physician," she said, showing her credentials.

"But you're not a family member. Sorry."

She loved the child as much as if she had given birth to him, but because she wasn't a member of his family she was denied information about his condition. She went outside and walked back and forth in front of the entrance, trying to think of a way to get to her Aunt Lena. She didn't even know the floor on which Ricky was being treated.

In preparation for his return to Afghanistan, Nelson wrote a new will making Ricky his principal heir and naming Lena a secondary beneficiary and Ricky's guardian in his absence. As he signed the affidavit, it depressed and saddened him that Audrey's name did not appear on the document. Though he had searched his conscience and his heart, he couldn't find a logical reason for including her.

He rested his forearms on his desk and cushioned his

head with the back of his hands. No matter how he looked at their relationship or how he rationalized having walked away from her with that note of finality, he couldn't convince himself that she deserved it, that he hadn't been too demanding. One thing was certain: he still loved her and he didn't expect that to change for a long time.

With a feeling of resignation, he went down to the Pentagon's atrium to the law offices of R&R Blake to have the affidavit notarized and the will probated.

As he returned to his office door, he heard Holden's voice. "I see you're up for a trip back to Kabul. Afghanistan sure isn't a reward for good behavior. Whose left side did you land on?"

He stared down at Holden, enjoying his three-inch advantage in height. "I don't question the Commandant's decisions. My job is to carry out orders to the best of my ability."

"You don't say."

Nelson didn't miss the sneer that accompanied those three words. And it didn't escape him that Holden had forgotten the word "Sir" and that his audaciousness seemed more flagrant each time they met. He went on to his office where he saw the light blinking on his answering machine.

"Nelson, this Audrey. Something's happened either to Ricky or Aunt Lena, I don't know which. Aunt Lena said the ambulance was taking them to George Washington Hospital. I'm on my way there now."

He buzzed his secretary, who told him that his housekeeper had telephoned and wanted him to call home, but didn't leave a message.

"I'm going to George Washington University Hospital. Something's happened. I'll be in touch as soon as I have some information."

Outside, oblivious to the late summer heat and humidity, he hailed a taxi. At such times, with parking space at a premium, one's own car could be a liability. "GW Hospital, and step on it, please."

"Audrey!"

She heard Nelson's voice, whirled around and ran to him, and as if he had never terminated their brief relationship, his arms opened to receive her. He clasped her to him, though only briefly.

"It's Ricky," she said, "but I don't know what happened. He's in surgery."

His face ashened, the rapid movement of his Adam's apple betraying the somber nature of his thoughts and emotions. "Come on."

Within minutes, he had passes for them, and she resisted a glance at the woman who, minutes earlier, had denied her entrance.

Lena ran to them when they walked into the waiting room. "Lord, Colonel, I just been out of my mind. That child's knee is plumb near twisted backward. He fell off his bicycle and landed right into that old chinaberry tree in front of the house. Seems like he was trying to avoid hitting a squirrel. I tell you, Colonel, the poor little thing did scream. He hurt so bad."

"How long has he been in there?"

Lena looked at her watch. "I'd say about forty minutes."

"I see. We may be here for a while." He let his gaze sweep the room. "Why don't we sit over there by that window?"

Audrey felt as if she'd taken a blow to the head. What if that knee didn't respond to surgery?

An hour later, a doctor still wearing his green scrubs

walked into the waiting room. "Ms. Alexander?" The three adults rushed to the man.

"I'm Nelson Wainwright, Ricky's uncle and legal guardian. How is he?"

A smile skittered across the man's mouth. "Ricky's fine. There's no reason why he shouldn't recover completely, with the proper therapy, of— Say, aren't you Dr. Audrey Powers?"

"Yes, but—"

"He's in good hands, sir. The very best. We want to keep him overnight because he's still under anesthesia, but he can go home after eleven tomorrow morning." He turned his attention to Audrey. "I'll send you some pictures of his knee as we found it, what we did, and my proposals for therapy, although I'm sure you don't need the latter. It's routine."

She opened her mouth to tell the doctor that Ricky wouldn't be in her care, but Nelson cut her off. "Thank you, Doctor. Therapy shouldn't be a problem, as Ricky is very fond of Dr. Powers."

They walked out of the hospital into the late afternoon sunshine, and Lena grasped Nelson's hand. "It don't feel right going home without Ricky. Suppose he wakes up scared and don't know where he is."

"They'll see that he sleeps through the night, Aunt Lena. I wonder if he'll need a wheelchair for a few days. Maybe . . ." She looked at Nelson, fearing she had ventured where she didn't belong.

"Maybe what?" he asked her.

"Do you think we . . . I mean *you* ought to stop by the hospital supply pharmacy and rent one for him?"

"If you think we should, yes. Will you come with us?"

They chose one for a child Ricky's age to be delivered to the hospital the following morning, and she prepared to leave Nelson and her aunt. But the weight of the day bore heavily upon her, and she dreaded leaving Nelson.

When he asked if she drove, she shook her head, not trusting her voice. "Neither did I," he said. "Come on home with Lena and me."

She should decline what could merely be a courteous gesture from a considerate man, but instead she grasped the offer. "I'd like that, Nelson. Somehow I don't much feel like going home."

His brown eyes darkened as he focused on her, his gaze, indeed his entire demeanor, telegraphing to her what she longed to know, but didn't dare believe. Taking her hand, he said, "You belong with us. Come on."

Eleven

After a dinner that Nelson had ordered from his favorite take-out restaurant, Audrey sat with him on the deck overlooking his garden while Lena cleared the dining room and kitchen. "Am I right that you're preoccupied?" Nelson asked her.

She didn't want to share with him her dilemma about Gerald Latham, Junior, because that would be tantamount to opening a can of worms, introducing a topic she couldn't bear to face right then.

"Sorry, I have some decisions to make about a young patient, and I seem unable to get that out of my head."

"Maybe Ricky's accident, his being in the hospital and needing therapy, have something to do with it. That would certainly be understandable."

"Maybe."

"How did you happen to call me about this?"

"Aunt Lena was so excited when she called me. The ambulance arrived immediately after she began talking, and she hung up without telling me what was wrong or with whom. Just said she was going to GW Hospital. I didn't know whether, in her state, she had the presence of mind to alert you."

"I'm deeply grateful to you, not just for calling me but for rushing here to help, to be with us. I can't tell you what it means to me."

She struggled against giving in to the lump that formed in her throat. "Don't you know that I couldn't have done otherwise?"

He focused his soft brown eyes on her, and she gave thanks for the oak tree that shaded her face from the moonlight. "I . . . uh . . . think I'd better be going," she said, taking her cellular phone from her purse. "What's the number of the cab company you use?"

"I'll call the taxi," he said, "and I'll take you home."

They spoke very little during the ride to her house, and she was glad, because she didn't want superficial words, useless banalities, with him. Given a choice between silence and superficiality, she'd take silence any day.

The taxi neared her house, and the pain of their last parting invaded her thoughts, her mind, and finally her heart, the experience becoming once more fresh and biting. He opened her door with the key she handed him and stood there staring down into her eyes. Tension knotted her insides and her heart pounded with such force that she feared he would hear it.

Minutes passed, and still he gazed into her eyes, neither speaking not touching her. Unable to tolerate longer the sensation of being suspended in midair, she bit the bullet.

"Did you miss me?" she asked him. "And have you forgiven whatever I did or didn't do?"

"Oh, I missed you all right. Missed you like hell," he said in guttural tones. "As for the rest, my conscience has been telling me I demanded too much of you, but . . . well, I don't know. Are you willing to . . . for us to talk about it?"

"I think we should."

"All right. You asked if miss you. What about you? Did you want to see me?"

She nodded. "Love doesn't end so abruptly. Thanks for coming home with me."

"Don't thank me for it. I . . . I wanted to. I'll call you tomorrow afternoon. Good night."

She said good night, but he didn't move. His eyes telegraphed the message that his lips wouldn't express: he wanted her. Frissons of heat raced through her as the man in him connected with her femininity, galvanizing her with his sexual aura. Pressing her luck, she reached up, kissed him on the mouth, and pushed the door open to go inside. But arms like steel locked around her, gripping her to him, and she looked up into eyes that blazed with the fire of desire.

"Baby, I need to taste you, to love you. I'm on fire for you."

Why was he asking permission? She locked her hands behind his head, brought his lips down to her open mouth, and he plunged into her. Shivers plowed through her as he flicked and dueled his tongue with hers, darting here and there, tasting every crevice of her mouth and then plunging in and out with a growing urgency that robbed her of breath. Heat seared her feminine center and she wanted to open to him, to know again the power of his loins, to feel him driving within her. But she needed more than the physical relief she knew he would give her, and this time, it was she who halted it.

"Honey," she whispered as she fought for breath, "I don't think we should do this. As you said last week, we have other things to settle first. It isn't that I don't want you. Lord knows I do, but I realize now that I need more from you."

The smile around his lips failed to brighten his eyes. "And I from you. But this morning I thought I'd never have you like this again, and just now, I let go. You're right. We'll talk tomorrow."

She slept fitfully. Images of Gerald Latham, Junior in a wheelchair with his right knee bandaged merged with Ricky on crutches trying to maneuver with a mangled foot. By the time she fully awoke, a pounding in her head forced her out of bed.

All right. All right. I'll give Gerald Junior the treatment he needs, but not before I expose that philandering father of his. Socialite Jemma Latham is going to know what kind of man she married.

As soon as she got to work that morning, she told her receptionist to give Jemma Latham an appointment for the next day. Ten minutes later, she answered the phone to hear Jemma Latham's voice, nearly unrecognizable through tears.

"I prayed so hard, Dr. Powers. I never prayed before in my life. But God has answered my prayers, and I know he will bless you. I won't try to thank you, because I don't have words to express how I feel right now. Dr. Horne said that if you treat Gerald, he will walk like any other boy. I . . . I just want to tell you what this means to me. I'll be there with Gerald tomorrow morning at ten."

She stared at the receiver she held in her right hand. Stared and stared long after saying good-bye to Jemma Latham, who had asked God to bless her. How could she blast that woman's world by telling her that her husband had deceived her, that he had lied about his marital status and cheated on her with another woman?

She couldn't do that. Neither the woman nor her son should have to pay for Gerald's infidelity. She got the telephone directory and found the man's office address and phone number. Imagine! Eleven short blocks from her office, and she hadn't seen him in over five years.

"Dr. Latham is busy," an officious voice informed her when she called.

"Tell him Dr. Audrey Powers is on the line." She marveled that the prospect of speaking with him didn't stir in her a single emotion or feeling other than distaste.

"Audrey, my dear, what a treat! It's great to hear from you. I understand you may be treating my boy. He couldn't be in better hands."

Same old air-bag. "This isn't a social call, Dr. Latham," she said, swallowing the bile that rose from her throat. "I thought of getting revenge for your treachery by refusing to give your son the care he needs, but he shouldn't suffer for your sins. Then I thought I'd give him the care, but not before I let your wife know what you did to me."

His gasp reached her through the wires. "Please, I . . . I . . . Please."

"What's the matter, Gerald? You think you should take a woman's virginity, and a minute after you've sated yourself, tell her it's her problem if you made her pregnant, because you're already married? After you'd represented yourself as a single medical student when you were, in fact, both married and a practicing physician? You think a heel like you should escape retribution?"

"Please. I . . . I'm begging you. I'll make it up to you if you'll just tell me how. I'm up for office in the medical society, and if this gets out, it will ruin me. That was a long time ago, and you're at the top of your profession now. You're further up than I am. I'm still making it. Can't you . . . just let bygones be bygones?"

"Go ahead and sweat. You won't know when I decide to drop the hatchet, but you can be sure it will drop because I've waited a long time for this. What I didn't expect is that you would cower like an obsequious, feckless wimp." She hung up without waiting for his response. Let him worry about it, worry until he got on his knees and confessed to his wife. And he would she had no doubt of it, because she'd scared him almost senseless.

How sweet it was! In his servility, he destroyed both her pain and her anger. She dismissed him from her thoughts along with all that he stood for. Relieved of a yoke that had burdened her for years, she prepared for her first patient. Humming and darting around the office with lithe steps, she was about to question her high mood, when it occurred to her that she no longer hated Gerald Latham, that she pitied him and no longer felt a need to hurt him. Stunned by the realization, she flopped into her desk chair.

Well, I'll be damned.

The morning brightened as it lengthened and by midday she could say with honesty that she hadn't known greater pleasure in her work, that she had enjoyed it as had her patients. She got a hamburger and a bottle of lemonade from the cafeteria, returned to her office, and began her plans for Gerald, Junior. It wouldn't be easy, and he wouldn't mend quickly, but when she'd finished treating him, he would walk normally.

"Dr. Powers, Colonel Wainwright on two."

"Hello, Nelson. How's Ricky?" She laughed at herself when she added, "And you, too, of course."

"Thanks. I don't mind taking second place to Ricky today, but see that you don't make a habit of it. We're home with him. He has a little pain, hates being in a wheelchair, and wants to know whether you're coming to see him."

"Tell him I'll stop by after work."

"I had hoped you would. Audrey, I want you to give Ricky his therapy. I'm aware that you will balk at payment, but he's insured at high premiums, and the insurance ought to pay. You may send your bill directly to the company."

"Of course I'll do it. I wouldn't want anyone else to take care of him. We'll discuss that money business some other time. How do you feel? I mean, how is your neck?

"Same old, same old. I've learned to tolerate it better."

"Hmmm. I see."

"Will you have supper with us tonight?"

She didn't want to settle into a comfortable routine with him. He had opened her eyes to the shortcomings of their relationship and to what she needed deep down in a man. She wanted that, and wanted it with him.

"I'd planned on seeing my baby sister tonight, but I'd love to another time soon."

He wouldn't be put off. "Tomorrow then? There are things I want to discuss with you. Okay?"

She agreed and hung up, wondering what she had gained by not spending that same evening with him.

She left a message on Winifred's answering machine and got ready for her next patient, still floating in the afterglow of her liberation from the bondage of hatred.

"Hi, Wendy. I'm hoping we can have dinner together and swap tales over at your place tonight. If you're not busy, I'll bring some food and you won't have to cook anything but hot water for tea. Ring me on my cell phone. 'Bye."

Nelson opened the door for Audrey and had to use all the restraint he could muster to avoid touching her.

Cheerful, beautiful, and seeming to bubble with joy, she seemed to light up the room. He wondered whether he was in any way responsible for her mood and prayed that he was.

"Hi," she said, blessing him with a wink of her left eye that signified compliance with whatever he might have on his mind. He wondered if she was aware of the sexual overtones of that wink.

"Hi," he said, making certain that he kept his hands in his pockets.

She gave his flat belly a light pat as she walked on by him. "Where's Aunt Lena?" she flung over her shoulder. Who *was* this woman? Seductive. Frivolous. And oh, so desirable.

"She's in the kitchen pampering Ricky."

"Audie! Audie, I hurt my knee. I went to the hospital and I stayed there all night." He stretched out both arms to her, and she hugged him to her as closely as his wheelchair would allow.

"I know, darling. I went to the hospital to see you, but you were asleep."

"Unca Nelson told me. They won't let me walk, Audie."

"As soon as your knee heals, you can walk and run the way you used to. In a couple of days I'm going to begin giving you exercises every afternoon to help you walk soon."

"Every day, Audie? You're coming to see me every day?"

"Some days you'll come to my office and sometimes I'll come here."

"Unca Nelson," he said, "Audie's going to let me come to her office." His charm deserted him when he said, "I don't want to go in this wheelchair."

Nelson knew Ricky's protruding lower lip spelled

trouble, but Audrey placated him when she said. "Want a Chula Chup?" He took one and began sucking on it. "I give these to the children who come to my office."

Ricky took the lollipop out of his mouth and studied her. "Can I have two?"

"None of that, Ricky," Nelson said. "You do not bargain in exchange for good behavior. You always do what is right, no matter what. You understand that?"

Ricky didn't try to hide his unhappiness with the idea. "But Unca Nelson, if I'm going in this chair, why can't I have two lollipops? Audie won't mind."

"I don't imagine she will, but I mind. You're going to her office and candy is not a part of the agreement. No bargaining, Ricky. Got that?"

"Yes, sir." He looked at Audie. "Can I have two now? I can save them."

Her smile broadened, and the warmth and pure sweetness in her eyes as she looked down at the child sent his heart on a rampage, thumping like a runaway train. Love. There was no other word for it. She loved Ricky, and the boy knew it, savored it, and accepted it as normal. Suddenly, she rushed to the boy's chair and hugged him while he giggled and hugged her in delight.

Nelson had to get out of there. As he plodded up the stairs, his mind socked him again and again with the thought that Audrey belonged in his home, that it was only complete when she was in it. That she made his little circle a real family. Ill at ease in his room, his own paradise, he went down to the family room in the basement and sat down at the piano. For as long as he could remember, playing the piano had had the ability to transport him to a higher plane, a different world. A place of his own where everything was as he desired. But not tonight. He played Chopin sonatas, Liszt preludes, and some Duke Ellington funk trying to find himself. None of it gave him the solace he sought.

He ran his fingers through his hair. "This is serious," he said aloud.

"What's serious?" Audrey asked him. "I didn't know you played the piano so well. You're gifted. Anybody who plays Franz Liszt with such ease is talented. Ricky told me that you're teaching him to play."

He had no stomach for the conversation, no interest in himself.

"Thanks. It's as much a part of me as my hands. It's me. I don't get a chance to play often or as well as I'd like. Uh . . . I didn't know you were down here."

"I know that. What's the matter? You seem . . . um . . . less self-possessed than usual."

"You're discerning. It's nothing I can't handle. In any case, we'll talk things over tomorrow. What time would suit you?"

"I could come by at around five and—"

He shook his head. "This doesn't include Ricky. What time do I call for you at your home?"

She lifted a eyebrow as if surprised. "Seven all right?"

"Perfect. Let's go to B. Smith's in Union Station. I feel like some soul food. What do you say?"

"I love soul food, although I know it's rough on my arteries. Aunt Lena and Pam wouldn't think of cooking soul food, biscuits, maybe, but that's it. I'd love to eat there."

"Then we'll go. If we're in luck, they'll have a good jazz band. If not, the canned music is always great, Nat King Cole, Duke Ellington, Lester Young, all the great jazz artists."

Why was he talking so much about things of little importance? he asked himself. "I'd better look in on

Ricky," he said, not because there was a need for it, but because if he remained down there alone with her for another two minutes, they'd be in a clinch. He started up the stairs and reached back for her hand.

"I can find my way up the steps, Nelson. I know what's going on here, and I want you to know you have no need to worry."

He stopped and walked back to her. "No?" The next second, he lifted her to fit his body and possessed her mouth. She didn't deny him, but took him in and sucked sweetly on his tongue until he thought he would go mad with yearning to be inside her body.

"Unca Nelson. Unca Nelson, I have to go to the bathroom and Miss Lena's upstairs."

He settled her on her feet. "Do you understand now why I needed to get up these stairs? Do you?"

She nodded. "Sometimes I just want to give in to it and damn the consequences, but I know I won't do that."

"No. And neither will I."

"Did Audrey come by this afternoon?" Nelson asked Lena when he got home the next day.

"Yes, but she only stayed about forty-five minutes. Ricky kicked up a storm when she got ready to leave. I told him he don't own Audrey, but that don't mean a thing to him. He's in seventh heaven from the time she walks through that door. That child loves himself some Audrey, and he did from the very first."

"Fortunately it's mutual."

"Yes, sir. She loves him all right. Never saw anything to beat it. You planning on doing anything about that, Colonel?"

He let a grin flicker around his mouth and tantalized

her with a wink of his right eye. "You are welcomed to delve into Ricky's love life, Mrs. Alexander, but kindly remember that I've passed my fortieth birthday."

Her face clouded with bewilderment. "But as her aunt, don't I have the right to ask you your intentions?"

A quick shrug forecast the nature of his answer. "You'd better ask Audrey about that. I wouldn't know."

Two hours later, he faced Audrey at a table in B. Smith's, enjoying Union Station's cathedral ceiling, marbled floor, and towering Ionic columns among which nestled shrubs and flowers. Beautiful, like the woman facing him. They each ordered seafood for the main course along with stewed collards and piquant cornbread, with coconut cake for desert.

"Lena says coconut anything is unhealthy, so please don't tell her. I love this stuff."

"What's it worth to you?" she asked him.

"What do you say to some first class kisses? Huh?"

"That'll work," she said, "for starters."

The wine he had been about to swallow went down the wrong way, sending him into a coughing fit.

"Sorry," she said.

"Yeah, I'll bet. Listen, Audrey, I've got to talk serious now." He didn't like the expression of wariness that came over her.

"What do you want me to know?"

"You won't want to hear this, but I may have to go back to Afghanistan. Nothing is certain yet, but it is very possible." She folded up like a clam. "I'm an officer in the military, Audrey, and I go where I'm sent."

"What about your neck?"

"I'll face that when I have to. At least the other thing I want you to know won't upset you. I'm scheduled to receive a citation for bravery in Afghanistan. They say I

saved the lives of the men in my charge when the helicopter I was piloting crashed."

Her face brightened and her eyes glistened in that
way they had the previous afternoon when she'd looked
so adoringly at Ricky. *I am one lucky man*, he thought
when she said, "Nothing wonderful that I hear about
you will ever surprise me. I'm so proud of you."

He thanked her, but tried to contain both his remarks
and his feelings because he knew that getting that citation could backfire. Yet when he spoke, his words came
from his heart.

"When you look at me like that, I feel the way I do
when I'm at the controls of an F-16, flying high.
Woman, don't send me any messages that you won't
stand behind."

"I never have and I never will, and I expect the same
from you."

He looked at his watch. Nine-thirty. The thought of
leaving her so early didn't sit well with him, and he
didn't think it prudent to walk with her along the Mall
or around the Tidal Basin at that time of night.

"Feel like walking for a few blocks?" he asked her,
thankful that he hadn't driven his car. She agreed, and
he took her hand and strolled with her along Massa-
chusetts Avenue.

"Sometimes, like yesterday afternoon, for example, I
feel you're right for me, that you would complete my
life, and then at other times I feel as if a void exists that
needs to be filled, that in spite of what I feel for you, I
don't know you."

She released his hand and eased her left arm around
his right one. "I've often thought that if we were
teenagers, we would probably have eloped by now. It's
always great when we're together, but as soon as we
separate, I start thinking."

"Same here, but I don't want to continue this way, and I'm sure you don't either."

"No."

He slipped an arm around her waist, and they walked in silence until they reached Vernon Square, where he hailed a taxi. Telling her good night at her front door was a habit he'd begun to detest, but he forced a smile and thanked her for the evening.

"I enjoyed being with you," she said, and he wondered what she'd do if he picked her up and didn't stop walking until he reached her bed. "When will you receive the citation?" she asked, and he knew that while she genuinely cared about the recognition given him, she was nervous and making conversation.

"Tomorrow. It's a very simple ceremony." But such an important step on the way to his goal.

"Your dad would be so proud," she said, unshed tears glistening in her eyes.

It didn't make sense, but he couldn't resist. "Kiss me? Don't open the floodgates though."

Her lips, soft, sweet, and closed, pressed to his mouth. A whiff of her perfume assaulted his nostrils, and her breasts, sweet and feminine against his chest, rocked him like an exploding bomb. His vow to stave off lovemaking with her until he knew her, until she opened up to him and let him know who she was, seemed farfetched and pretentious in light of the punishing force of his need, of his almost frantic desire to have her.

With prodigious effort, he moved from her. "I know I said we'd just be friends, but I don't want that. I want us to work this out. Are you willing?"

"I want it as much as you do, and I . . . I'm willing to try."

He brushed his lips across her forehead. "Get inside. I'll call you tomorrow."

"Good luck at the ceremony."

He stood on her steps until the lock clicked and a light showed at the second-floor window. *I swore I'd die a bachelor, but I'm not so sure about that now.*

Audrey checked the messages on her answering machine and found three from Ricky. "This is Ricky Wainwright. Can I speak with Audie, please?" He hadn't mastered the problem of leaving messages. *I must teach him how to do that,* she thought, and dialed her Aunt Lena's private phone.

"Lena Alexander speaking. The Lord loves you, so stay in touch with him."

"This is Audrey, Aunt Lena. When did you start answering the phone that way?"

"When? One day last week. I read it somewhere, and I figured most people could use that little reminder. Anything wrong with you?"

"No. I got home a few minutes ago and discovered I have three messages from Ricky, so I called to be sure the two of you are all right."

"Humph. Which means you were out with the Colonel, otherwise you wouldn't know he's not home yet. Ricky thinks he owns you. I asked the colonel about his intentions toward you, and he alluded as to how he was over forty and I could ask you. Like I overstepped my bounds or something."

"He wouldn't have appreciated that question if he'd been eighteen—not with his personality. Anyway, I'm moving away from thirty and ought to be able to look out for myself. Still, thanks for the thought."

"Anything happening between you two?"

"And how! Ever been on a seesaw? Tell Ricky I'll see him tomorrow after work. Good night."

When she said her prayers, she prayed that Nelson's superiors wouldn't send him back to Afghanistan. "You and I know he wouldn't survive it intact, Lord. Please," she whispered. Still, a sense of helplessness pervaded her as she dimmed her night-table lamp and closed her eyes.

The next morning at eleven o'clock, Nelson stood in the Commandant's reception room and listened to the citation for bravery in the line of duty. "You have honored your country, the Marine Corps, and yourself," the Commandant said, "and I am happy to tell you that recommendations have been made for your promotion to brigadier general."

Nelson found his voice with difficulty, and knew from the lump in his throat that he had to guard his emotions. "Thank you, Sir. I am deeply honored and grateful."

The ceremony completed and the round of handshakes over, he headed back to his office. Rupert Holden walked beside him.

"Congratulations, man. And to think you got your ribbon pinned on by the top brass. Way to go. Uh, by the way, did you ever report that corporal you caught sleeping on guard duty in Qandahar? He could have gotten all of us killed. Man, we were close enough to Al Qaeda fighters to spit on 'em."

It was a threat, and the man hadn't even bothered to sugar-coat it. Before he could answer, Holden grinned. "You're not really expecting to get kicked up to brig general, are you? Things like that business in

Afghanistan . . . you know, that guard sleeping on duty, that always leaks out."

They arrived at Holden's office and the more junior officer gave a mock salute. "All the best, man."

"Same to you, Holden, and thanks for your good wishes." He may have fooled Holden with his attitude of nonchalance, but he could barely contain his anxiety.

Nelson closed his office door and locked it. He'd just had the wind knocked out of him, and he needed to re-group. Rupert Holden had managed to rob him of his moment of glory, refusing to allow him even one hour in which to cherish the first commendation he had received in his military career. He hadn't done anything wrong, but had showed compassion where it was justified. If that act of mercy proved to be the torpedo that blasted his career, he'd live with it. It would break his heart, but it wouldn't kill him.

When the telephone rang, he straightened up, then leaned back in his desk chair and assumed his normal professional demeanor. "Wainwright speaking."

"Hi. This is Audrey." As if he wouldn't know her voice even if he was coming out of deep anesthesia. "Congratulations. What do they do on these occasions?"

The sound of her voice raised his spirits. Enlivened him. "They said some very embarrassing things at a re-ception of sorts, pinned a ribbon on me, and told me I was up for brigadier general."

"What? You're going to be a general? I'm happy for you, Nelson, and as proud as if this were happening to me. It's wonderful!"

"Thanks. It will take some getting used to. Don't for-get, though, that it isn't a done deed. I'll celebrate that star when it's sticking on my jacket." Knowing that he might never affix that coveted emblem to his clothing, indeed that even the ribbon could be taken from him, he hadn't the will to rejoice.

"You're so subdued," she said.

"Some gave all, Audrey. And some gave a part of themselves, a part that means they can never again be normal men. It's humbling."

"You feel this way because you're not self-centered, and I like that, Nelson, but you can accept these things that happen to you as something good, maybe even your due. Be happy. If it were me, I'd be dancing on the ceiling. Barefoot. Just wait till I open my office. I'll do the wind on the corner of Sixteenth and Pennsylvania."

"What's holding it up?"

"Uh . . . I've got the money now, and the place. It needs some renovation, and that should start soon. It's just . . . I hope people will come."

What was she afraid of? It seemed out of character. "Don't be afraid of going out on your own. I gather your reputation is solid, so shape up."

"I'm going for it. I hope to hang out my shingle in mid-November."

"I wish I could say I'd be your first customer, but I wouldn't think of compromising you."

"I wish you could, too, but we both know that wouldn't be wise. Any more news about your return to Afghanistan?"

"Nothing new, and this isn't an organization in which you'd ask questions about it. We'll have to wait. Thanks for thinking about me."

"I always think about you. You spend more time in my head than all the other people I know combined."

"Is that so? Woman, you're going to have a lot to live up to when I finally get you where I want you."

"I'm definitely not asking you where that is."

He felt the racing of his blood, knew where it was

headed, and told himself to cool off. "Think of something interesting for us to do tonight, why don't you, and give me a call before I leave the office at five. Okay?"

"Right. I can do that."

He hung up, and for the remainder of the day, one thought battled with others for a hold on his mind: *If the two of us marry, I can help her open her private practice, and if I don't come back from Afghanistan, she'll be well cared for. If.* With her independent bent, she would probably refuse his help even if he was her husband. He ran his fingers through his hair again and again in frustration. Love wasn't what it was cracked up to be!

Audrey washed her hands and applied lotion to them, as she always did after treating a patient. Why was she reluctant to open her office, he wanted to know. She sighed in resignation. Just one more thing between Nelson and herself. What would he think if she told him how she dreaded his learning about the basketball player whose life she had probably destroyed?

She had known that if that player returned to the court even for one play, he risked permanent injury. But the young man had pleaded with her, swearing that he had no pain. She hadn't believed him, but she relented and allowed him to return to play. He shot the winning basket and made his college proud, but he was unable to walk off the court and, to her knowledge, hadn't walked since. If only she had held her ground and refused him permission. It was a mistake that she remembered every day.

Her colleagues and the patients who held her in high regard knew nothing of this, but she knew it and so did Patrick Jenkins, who suffered because of her irresoluteness. She didn't accept her youth and inexperience as excuses; she had known better. Now she could open her office and begin her practice, but if Jenkins should publicly accuse her, she could lose all she owned, including her reputation. Still, she had to risk it.

She checked *The Washington Post* for the program at Wolf Trap that evening, liked it, and decided that an evening of jazz and maybe a stroll on the Monument grounds, then some desert and coffee would keep Nelson and her in the company of other people, where they would be less likely to start a fire.

Audrey schemed to keep her romance with Nelson where she wanted it and where she thought he, too, would prefer it. The morning following their quiet evening together, Nelson struggled with a more profound problem, one involving both his refusal to be buried beneath the tarpaulin of Holden's one-upmanship, and his sense of decency in extenuating circumstances. He didn't want his career to end like so much excess fuel jettisoned from an overweight plane. Service to his country as a Marine Corps officer represented his life's work, and he took pride in it and in what he had accomplished. To have it end summarily because Holden enjoyed seeing his superiors fall would be unbearable. His only course, as he saw it, was to tell the Commandant what he'd done and why, and hope for tolerance.

Reasoning that he preferred to resign rather than to be relieved of duty for ignoring a service code, he made up his mind to ask for a conference with the Commandant that morning, as soon as he walked into his office.

I can't let another day go by with this uncertainty,

he told himself. *And if I've got to take bad medicine, I might as well get started on it.*

With shaking fingers, Audrey slit the envelope, then sat down and closed her eyes, dreading what she would read. The previous evening, she'd dropped the day's mail in the tray on her desk as she usually did when arriving home, but had forgotten to read it. Going through the pile of letters, magazines, and catalogues that morning, her heart had nearly stopped when she saw the letter bearing Patrick Jenkins's name and return address.

She took the letter downstairs and put it on the kitchen table while she made coffee, figuring that the caffeine would give her the boost that she was certain to need. She hadn't heard from the man in the five years since his accident, and for five years she had dreaded this moment. She couldn't afford a lawsuit or the negative publicity it would generate. Sitting at her kitchen table taking long sips of coffee, she told herself to read the letter, but the cup shook as if caught in a wind tunnel and she needed both hands to place it in the saucer without spilling the contents.

Audrey stared at the letter until it seemed to move upward to her of its own volition when, in fact, it lay where she'd placed it. Finally, she eased the stark-white linen paper out of its envelope and unfolded it with hands that trembled.

"What! What is this?" she said aloud, grabbing her chest with her hands to slow down her heartbeat. "Dear Dr. Powers," she read, "I am walking—though with difficulty—and have been for several months, but I need intensive therapy for complete recovery. You have been recommended to me as the best therapist

for what I need. Please say you will take me on as a patient. My insurance will cover it."

For the nth time, she read the words of the basketball player who had suffered a debilitating injury because of her poor judgment. She read silently, and then she read it aloud until, with her throat dry, she could hardly pronounce the words. She jumped up from the table, whirling around and around and skipping back and forth across the room until she exhausted herself. Overwhelmed with joy, through a shower of tears, she dialed Nelson's number to share the news with him.

Nelson finished dressing and had started downstairs for breakfast when the telephone rang. "What on earth is the matter?" he asked Audrey after greeting her and determining that it was she who called, for she seemed on the verge of hysteria.

"I C . . . C . . ." Her sobs tore into him. "I never dreamed . . . I—" Suddenly she hung up, obviously brimming over with emotion and unable, he guessed, to tell him what she wanted him to know.

"I'm sorry, but I have to skip breakfast," he called to Lena as he headed back upstairs for his jacket, cap, and briefcase.

She confronted him at the door and pushed a cup of coffee and a small glass of orange juice toward his face. "Unless World War Four just broke out, you drink this."

No use trying to get around her, he told himself. Besides, she meant well. He drank as quickly as he could. "Thanks. You're the best. Tell Ricky for me that I'll try to telephone him this morning. Gotta go."

The traffic crawled along George Washington Parkway until, frustrated, he got off and took the Francis Scott Key Bridge, drove over to Wisconsin Avenue, and fought snarled traffic all the way to Friendship Heights. So great was his relief when the flow of automobiles thinned at Western Avenue that he pressed the accelerator and, within seconds, heard the siren of a eager Maryland patrolman. He pulled over and stopped.

The officer walked over and pulled out his tablet of tickets. "In a pretty big hurry there, weren't you?"

"You could say that, sir," Nelson answered.

"Take it easy on the metal, Officer," the patrolman said. "You military guys are under a great deal of stress these days, but that's no reason to drive like a bat out of hell and kill yourself and innocent people. Try to stay alive." The patrolman put away his tablet, saluted, and started back toward his car.

"How fast was I going?"

The patrolman raised an eyebrow. "Sixty-two, and this is a thirty-mile-an-hour zone. So watch it." Nelson nodded and thanked the man. One more piece of evidence that he was over the line with Audrey. He parked in front of her house, jumped out, and started toward her door, hurriedly doubling back to his car to retrieve his briefcase.

Audrey heard the doorbell, but it didn't register that she should answer it as words of thanks spilled from her lips and a liquid shower of joy continued to flow from her eyes. The years of dread and of self-censure and condemnation, yes, and of guilt, and the limitations she had consequently placed on her life and her career floated through her memory. Then she heard the rapping, strong and aggressive, and quickly brought herself to the present. She rushed to the front door, wiping her eyes with the back of her left hand while opening the door with her right one.

The door opened as he pressed the bell. "Audrey, what's the matter?" He walked in and closed the door.

One look at her—face streaked with tears, hair tousled, and still in her robe when she should have been leaving for work—one look at her, and all that he felt for her surged to the fore.

"Nelson!"

He lifted her into his arms, strode inside, and kicked the door closed. "You're going to tell me what's going on with you. Why you're so bent out of shape you couldn't let me know why you called me. I'm here for you, and I always will be. Don't you know that? *Don't you?"* She could only nod her head in agreement. "We're going to talk. I'm not leaving here until we do."

Twelve

It was D-Day. He was no longer asking, but demanding, that she reach into the recesses of her private memories and let him know who she was. If she refused, she didn't doubt that he would break all ties with her, and this time there would be no reconciliation.

"I'll be back shortly," she told him. She needed a few minutes to collect herself. Knowing that he would not tolerate stalling, she didn't consider doing so.

After a quick shower, she dressed, went to the kitchen, made coffee, warmed some cinnamon buns, and fixed a tray. She brought the tray to the living room where he sat on the sofa, leaning back with eyes closed and hands locked behind his head.

"Want some coffee and a bun?"

"Love it. All I've had today are the coffee and orange juice that Lena practically poured down my throat as I was leaving. What were you crying about?"

"It's a long story, but—"

"I have time."

In spite of her resolve, it wasn't easy. She took a deep breath, let it out slowly, and told him of her role in Patrick Jenkins's crippling accident. "Patrick had wanted to get back in that game so badly he had tears in his eyes. "I knew that if he returned to the court, State U would win the championship, so I capitulated and let him back into the game. Without my approval as team physician, he would not have been allowed to play. He shot the final basket for three points, and won the game. But he collapsed immediately and had to be carried off the court."

"I wasn't fired from State U for that lapse in judgment, but I didn't get an offer for contract renewal, and without a strong recommendation it was useless to apply to another university. I was fortunate to get this job at the clinic."

"And you've persecuted yourself about it ever since. You have to get over it."

She got the letter and read it to him. "When I saw this I thought he wanted revenge or, at best, a financial settlement. You don't know how relieved I am, not just for myself, but for him especially. He's giving me the chance to help him. Oh, Nelson, I'm . . . I'm so thankful."

She wiped the tears that streamed down her face. "This time, I won't fail him. I'm going to give him my best."

"Of course you will. So you were crying out of relief and happiness?"

"That, and more. It was as if something in me burst open and began spilling out. I couldn't control it. This was the main reason why I dreaded opening my private practice. I was afraid I wouldn't get patients, that Patrick might picket my office or publicly expose me. You don't know what his letter means to me."

He slipped his left arm around her waist and urged her to rest her head against his shoulder. "You could tell me this because you've been absolved, so to speak. But there's more, and what remains is mostly what's robbing us of true intimacy."

He crossed his left knee over his right one and began a slow stroking of her arm. Unconsciously, she knew, but it got to her nonetheless. She trained her mind to receive his words.

"I understand how difficult it is to talk about past relationships that left a hole somewhere deep inside of you. I was engaged to marry a woman, and three weeks before the ceremony I walked into the apartment she and I shared and found her in our bed with my best friend, the man who would have been best man at our wedding."

She sat up straight, turned, and looked him in the face. "That must have been awful for you. Was she crazy?"

"No, she wasn't, and she admitted he wasn't the only one. I swore I'd never let another woman get close to me. As I searched myself for shortcomings on my part that could have encouraged her to fool around, I realized I didn't know her, that I knew only what I saw. Nothing of her dreams, prayers, pain, or true philosophy of life. Nothing . . . Oh what the hell—"

She raised an eyebrow. "It still hurts?"

"Naah. It's not worth discussing. I've been over it for years. Funny thing was that when I took Bradford to task about it, he admitted being jealous of me. It wasn't easy losing both of them at the same time. So much for that." He waved his hand, dismissing the matter and the topic.

As if he had peeled a film from her eyes and given her mind free rein, she understood what he was asking of her, what he meant when he insisted that he didn't know her. With his admission, she understood his reticence in regard to her and that this knowledge would help her avoid situations that would shake his confidence in her. Could she be less giving, less candid than he?

"You still haven't told me what's standing between

us," he said, "the thing that won't let you love without reservation, that makes you hold something back. Something crucial."

"I . . . uh . . . I can't say you're off-base, because you're right on target. I've never told anyone about this, and it still hurts to think I was so vulnerable."

He removed his arm from her waist and her head from his shoulder and turned to look her in the eye. "You don't trust me enough to tell me? Is that it?"

In a flash, she knew that nothing, not even her public persona, was worth losing Nelson. She leaned back, closed her eyes, and spoke barely above a whisper. "He was the first and the only one until I met you." Slowly and painfully, she tore the story out of herself, sparing nothing. "I wrenched the lamp on my night table from its socket, threw it at him, and barely missed his back. From then until last week, my one thought in connection with that man was a desire for vengeance. Vengeance as cruel as the betrayal he perpetrated against me. The hatred I felt for him was so strong that at times I was beside myself for need of an outlet."

"What happened last week?"

"I got the chance to get even. His wife brought his son to me for treatment. If he doesn't get it, he won't walk again."

"I hope you're going to treat the boy."

She told him she would, and about her conversation with Gerald Latham, Senior. "I pitied him. Groveling like an animal. I no longer hate him, and I have forced myself to see my own role in that fiasco. Like you, I didn't ask questions, and when he broke our dates or just failed to show, I accepted his excuses without question. I thought he was a poor struggling medical student when, in fact, he was a licensed physician, married and expecting his third child."

"The one you're treating?"

She nodded. "Could you ask for greater irony?"

"Hmmm. Talking about the chickens coming home to roost! This boggles the mind. Do you think you can let it go?"

"I already have. When I told him I meant to tell his wife, I realized I wouldn't do that to *her*, that I was fortunate he'd left only emotional scars and didn't ruin my life. I won't do it, but what a kick I got out of scaring him half to death!"

He wrapped her in his arms. "I can imagine what it cost you to tell me this. The man was, and probably still is, a bastard of a human being. Forget he exists."

"He means nothing to me now that I no longer hate him. Are you going to your office today?"

His lips brushed across her forehead. "Eventually. Yes. If you hadn't called, I might have been on my way out of the Marines by now."

She jerked forward. "What do you mean?"

He told her of his infraction of the rules while on duty in Afghanistan. "I was showing compassion where it was deserved. That marine had been on duty for twenty-four hours with only two half-hour reliefs. He fell asleep on duty, and I didn't report it. Now, another officer is going to inform my superiors that I didn't report that incident.

"If I'm going down, I'll go down my way. I've decided to tell the Commandant about it and take the consequences. I can always teach music."

She didn't know whether having to leave the Marines would break him, but she did know that he loved what he did and who he was, that he honored his uniform and the country for which he wore it.

"If it doesn't go your way, it will hurt you as you've never hurt before," she said, "but I believe you're right in reporting it yourself. If you don't win, you'll have the comfort of knowing the enemy didn't slay you."

He held her with both arms. "How will you feel if I have to resign?"

She let her lips brush his jaw. "I'll feel whatever you feel, hurt as deeply as you hurt, and shed as many tears as you shed. I'm here for you, Nelson. Your happiness will be my happiness, and your sorrow mine as well."

His arms tightened about her. "Do you know what you're saying?"

"I know exactly what I said. I'm not in love with your uniform; in fact, when I saw you dressed in civilian clothes, I got a shock, a very pleasant one."

He relaxed against the arm of the sofa, half-reclining, with her still locked in his arms. "I grind my teeth when I'm angry."

She snuggled closer. "I know. Would you believe that looking down at dark water make me nervous, and I sneeze five times in succession when I get angry? Oh yes, and I'm scared to death of things that crawl."

"Then we'll avoid those. Why are you afraid of the dark?"

"When I was little, my grandmother used to tell us weird stories about ghosts and goblins. Pam and Winifred loved those stories, but they frightened me, and I'd sleep with the light on. I never told her she frightened me, because she so enjoyed telling us those tales."

"I told you about my fear of high places and how I climbed the Matterhorn in order to conquer it." He kissed the side of her mouth. Soft and sweet. "I know you like jazz. Of all the greats, who's your favorite?" he asked.

"Duke Ellington."

"Mine, too. I'm glad our parents loved Joel and me.

They're the ones who teach you to love and accept love. You're close to your sisters, aren't you?"

"Oh, yes. I love my sisters. Do you think it strange that I couldn't tell them about . . . about Gerald?"

"No. You were afraid of what they would think of you. It was too personal. And thank you for telling me his name. It wasn't important, but it means you trust me."

"Do you think badly of me for having swallowed that line he handed me?"

A look of incredulity swept over his face. "What? Of course not. A single woman without experience is no match for a philandering liar, not even a stupid one. I'd love to send my fist through his face for hurting you."

"I shouldn't have closed my eyes and ignored all the mixed messages he sent me. Anyway, it's over. He's no longer important."

He traced the tip of her nose. Then he leaned forward and kissed the spot that his finger had warmed. "I like this nose," he whispered in a tone that was low, seductive, and very intimate. "You know, as a kid I dreamed of joining the cavalry and spending my days riding magnificent stallions. Funny. I haven't thought of that in years."

With her fingers, she enjoyed the smooth contours of his jaw and neck, cherishing and adoring him. "Really? When I was a teenager, I was such a romantic that thinking of it now is almost embarrassing. I dreamed of holding hands with my lover as we strolled in the moonlight and of making passionate love with him in the rain. I was caught up in my imagination."

"I wouldn't have thought it; you don't seem that way." He paused as if in thought. "Except when your libido is in control." His teeth sparkled in a grin that betrayed a wickedness she hadn't often seen in him. "I'll be delighted to help you live your fantasy. We can stroll by the ocean in the moonlight with the water swirling over our toes, offering our bodies as a sacrifice to the night, and we can make love in the rain. I've never been naked in the rain. I'll bet it's a blast."

"I'm not going there."

Laughter rumbled in his throat and spilled out, treating her to the joyous sound that she loved. "Not to worry," he whispered. "You've made so much progress today that I'm not about to let you backtrack. We've both limbered up, and we're happier for it. Are you happy, Audrey?"

She held him closer to her body. "Yes. Terribly, and I'm scared somebody or something will snatch this feeling, this togetherness away from me, because I don't feel like me."

"You're wrong. This is the real you . . . maybe with some slight modifications. Good ones. I don't care about the rest. I love you just the way you are."

She wished they could be that way always, at one with each other. She gazed up at him, breathing the air he breathed, inhaling the same scents that he inhaled, and feeling the same love he felt.

"Wouldn't it be great if life would always be this way for us?" she asked. "No misunderstandings, no reservations, and nothing separating us."

He sat up. "That would be heaven, but unfortunately, we're still wearing clothes and we both have to get to work, much as I hate to leave you."

She straightened his tie in what she knew he recognized as possessiveness. "We'll make it up to each other, won't we?"

"You bet. I've got to go deal with the Commandant. Wish me luck."

"You know I do, and I'll send up some prayers, too."

She walked with him to the door. "You haven't kissed me," she said when he turned the doorknob.

"That's all I've been doing for the past hour, honey." He kissed her cheek. "I don't need my brain fogged up with that heavy stuff you put down. Not this morning. I'll call you later." His hand went to the back of his neck. "Don't worry about this," he said, anticipating her reaction. "It's not bad right now. See you."

She watched until he drove away. Cleansed. Healed. Refreshed. Those were the words that came to mind. She thought she would burst with happiness, but as she started up the stairs, her exhilaration evaporated like steam before a flame. What if Nelson was forced to resign? Could he be happy if he'd lost all that he'd worked so hard to achieve and for which he was willing to sacrifice his health, even his life? She didn't think so.

As he drove to work, Nelson did not punish himself by pondering his fate. He knew the possible consequences, and he accepted them. He was going to tell his superiors what had happened, and leave it up to them. So he didn't let what might be a gloomy future poison his mood. He had experienced with Audrey an epiphany that allowed him to see his life as it had been, was now, and could be. The only thing separating him from peace and contentment was himself, and he didn't intend to be his own emotional executioner. He wanted Audrey in his life for all time, and he no longer had reservations about it.

His father had taught him to be honorable, to work hard, love the Lord, and be kind to others. He slipped up occasionally, but he kept that as his creed. If he got socked for it, so be it. He walked into his office to find both his intercom and his answering machine flashing red.

He punched the intercom button first. "Wainwright."

"Lieutenant McCafferty, Colonel. The Commandant wants to see you. Right now, if possible."

"On my way." This could be it. "Well, fellow," he said as he closed his office door and looked at the brass plate beside it that bore his name and rank, "it's been a great ride."

He opened the Commandant's office door and stopped as his gaze took in the marine whose career he had saved. Finding presence of mind, he saluted his superior officers assembled there.

"You wanted to see me, Sir?"

"Yes indeed. You remember Corporal Williams, I'm sure." Did he ever! He glanced to the left, saw Rupert Holden, and wondered at the absence of the man's smirk.

The Commandant gestured to the marine corporal. "Corporal Williams is receiving a medal of honor for uncommon valor in the heat of battle, for saving the lives of his commanding officer and fellow servicemen. He has asked that you pin the medal on him."

At Nelson's inquiring look, the corporal explained, "I was on guard duty and I didn't tell anyone I had a high fever because there wasn't anybody to take my place. It got so bad I finally fell asleep, and Colonel Wainwright caught me, woke me up, and gave me some water and a lecture but didn't turn me in."

The man looked directly at him. "Colonel Wainwright, if you hadn't showed compassion for me, I would not have had the opportunity to save my comrades. Thank you for doing me the honor of pinning this medal on my uniform." Nelson didn't dare look at any of his superiors while he pinned the ribbon on the marine's jacket.

The Commandant cleared his throat, getting the attention of all present. "Compassion is also a form of valor," he said, and Nelson allowed himself to breathe. *Thank God that was over!*

"This has worried me for a long time," he said to the elegant man whose shoes he might still some day fill. "Thank you, Sir."

The Commandant surprised him with a wink. "All's well that ends well, Colonel."

Several days later, Nelson received official orders to go to Afghanistan, and immediately set about getting his affairs in order. He postponed telling Audrey until after they had dinner together that same evening.

"Feel like a short walk along the Tidal Basin?" he asked her as they left the Willard Room. He wanted the best setting possible in which to introduce a topic that he knew would displease her.

"I'd love it. The moon's high and bright tonight. Is this a partial fulfillment of my fantasy?"

"If it works, why not?"

She stopped walking and tugged at his hand. "Nelson, you've been on edge all evening. What's happening? The likelihood of your having to resign no longer exists, and you received your Commandant's blessing. Our relationship seems to grow sweeter by the day. I expected you to be in a happy, carefree mood. Can I help?"

He couldn't pretend joviality. "It's . . . well, it's serious. I wasn't planning to tell you this way—"

"Weren't planning to tell me *what*?"

The only way to say it was to say it. "I'm scheduled to leave for Afghanistan in ten days, September eighth."

"*What?* Good Lord, you can't do that. It's tantamount to committing suicide. I won't . . . Nelson what are you trying to prove?"

He heard the tears in her voice. Yes, and the sound of horror. He looked down and saw that she wrung her hands.

"Audrey. Don't. Honey, don't. For God's sake, please don't cry."

"I'm not going to cry," she said, sniffing back the tears. "You're going through with this?"

"I have no choice."

Her chin jutted out and she poked his chest with her right index finger. "You have a choice. I do not oppose your doing your duty; I wouldn't respect you if you shirked it, but this goes beyond duty. I want to go home."

"Audrey, I've told you why this is so important to me."

"Nelson, I'd like to go home. If you don't want to take me, I'll hail a taxi."

He had expected her disapproval, but not such a strong reaction, not an unwillingness to listen to reason. "I'll take you home."

Hoping for a sign, any sign, that she would back down or at least concede and accept his right to do as he thought best, he parked in front of her house, cut the motor, and turned to her.

"I need to do this, Audrey. I told you I promised my father I'd go all the way to the top. Everything's in my favor. I'll only be there for fifteen months, and then—"

He watched, horrified, as her hand unfastened her seat belt and then opened the car door. Unwilling to give up, he got out and walked with her to her door.

"This is important to me, Audrey. Please try to understand."

She didn't look at him. "Speaking as a physician and an expert in joint diseases and physical therapy, and not as the woman who loves you, you don't make any sense. Even if you stayed here in Washington, DC, fifteen more months without medical care and you could be an invalid. One misstep or a fall is all that's needed. You can't go to combat duty without medical evaluation and treatment, and if you don't get it by the seventh of September, I will inform your superiors of your condition."

He gasped aloud and stepped away from her. "*What did you say?*"

She looked him in the eye. "You heard me. I love you too much too allow you to do this. I'd rather lose you than watch you ruin your life."

"You would betray me?"

"Call it whatever you like."

For a long minute he stared into the face that was so dear to him, and his heart pained him far more than his neck and shoulders.

"This is where I get off."

He trudged back to his car, got in, and sat there until he could will himself to start the motor and drive home. He headed up the stairs to look in on Ricky as he usually did when he got home, opened the child's door, and gasped.

"Lena!" he yelled, banging on her bedroom door. "Where's Ricky?"

"Wait a minute. Don't get out of joint." She opened the door and peeped at him. "Oh, Colonel, I was asleep. What's the matter?"

"What's the matter? Where the devil is Ricky?"

She tightened the robe around her and opened the

door wider. "Ricky's spending the night with Judy Meade. Such an excitement. I wish you'd 'a been here."

He let the doorjamb take his weight and exhaled a long breath. "How'd that happen?" If he was going to leave Lena with responsibility for the boy, he'd have to trust her judgment.

"You know he went to school Monday, and he's been talking about this little girl, Judy, till he just about burned a hole in my ears. This afternoon, Mrs. Meade called to tell me Judy was driving her nuts about Ricky and asked if Ricky could visit the child. Meantime, Ricky is here going crazy, so I said all right if she'd come get him. She did, and Mr. Meade brought Ricky home about six-thirty with Judy in the car. Ricky showed Judy the whole house, his room, and his precious harp. Then he took her downstairs, and they played the piano."

She looked to the ceiling and spread her hands as if helpless. "Mr. Meade was in a hurry, but that didn't bother the children none. He put his foot down, and Judy cried uncontrollably with Ricky trying to comfort her. So I packed a bag for Ricky and sent them back with Mr. Meade. I never thought I'd be glad to see Ricky leave this house without you or me, Colonel, but they were something. Hugging and holding hands and giggling and kissing. I asked Mr. Meade if he didn't think he should lay the law down to his daughter about being so forward with boys. He laughed a lot about that. I hope you don't mind."

"No, I don't, but from what you said, it looks as if we won't be seeing much of him in the future. I take it Judy also goes to Price School?"

"Yes. That's 'bout where you'd expect her to go."

He went back to his room and closed the door, realizing he'd wanted Ricky to plug up a hole that the child couldn't fill. His euphoria about the favorable resolution of his having disregarded the rules in Afghanistan and his joy that he and Audrey had finally come together as one were as nothing. Smoke in a windstorm. If she meant to report him, she'd have her chance. He began the task of sorting out his most personal items to be stored for safekeeping, listing each one for Lena's benefit if he didn't get back home. Well after midnight, he crawled into bed, limp from struggling with the vicissitudes that were his life, and slept fitfully.

"I'm not going to suffer about this," Audrey said to herself as she locked her door. "I can't in good conscience let him do it. For a short while I was happy, and I'll be happy again."

Her answering machine flashed red, and she checked the call with reluctance, knowing that it couldn't be from Nelson. After sitting down and kicking off her shoes, she returned Winifred's call.

"Hi, Sis. What's up? I just got in."

"Hi. I've been going nuts waiting for you to get home and call me. Ryan and I are going to get married."

"What? You've known him five weeks! Are you sure you know what you're doing?"

"Yep. If Mama was living, she'd die if I shacked up with a man, and for me, it's that or get married. Be happy for me, Audrey. We're crazy about each other."

"Still concerned about pleasing him in bed?"

"Good heavens, no. You were right. That was just plain silly. We have no problem with that. He's a wonderful lover. If I think about it much, I'll put on my clothes and—"

"You'll do nothing of the sort. Give the poor guy a chance to miss you."

"How's it going with you and the Colonel?"

She took a deep breath and closed her eyes. "I had a glimpse of heaven, but that's all I'll get."

"You're kidding."

"I can't go into it because I can't discuss his personal affairs, but I had a decision to make, and it turned him off. It's over."

"My Lord, you must be miserable. I'm so sorry. Does Pam know about this?"

"No. It happened a few minutes ago. But don't worry about me, Wendy, I'm satisfied that I'm doing the right thing; for me, it's the only way."

"Well, I'll be a cross-eyed donkey. I didn't believe you two would split up, and I have to tell you, I'm disappointed."

"So am I. When are you getting married?"

"New Year's Eve. How's that for style?"

She couldn't fully enter into her sister's joy, but she tried for Winifred's sake. "It's wonderful. Am I your maid of honor?"

"I'm having both you and Pam. Okay?"

"Very okay. We can talk some more tomorrow."

"Gee, Audrey. I'm being insensitive, and you're a loving, giving sister, as usual. I'll call you tomorrow."

She hung up, undressed, and went to shower. If, while showering, tears flowed from her eyes, maybe she wouldn't know it.

Nelson didn't fool himself. He knew Audrey had a point, and a good one. But she hadn't understood what it would mean to him if he could not redeem his father's sacrifices, his unfulfilled life: a life devoted to caring for the needs of his wife and children, only to lose his wife when she was forty-one, and his own life at the age of fifty-seven before he could realize his dreams. If only Audrey could have stretched her mind to see why he was as he was.

"What do you mean, Unca Nelson? You're not going to live with Miss Lena and me?" Ricky's bottom lip drooped, and tears pooled in his eyes. "Can Audie come live with us?"

He had tried for the past hour to explain. Ricky was capable of understanding, but he didn't want to. "Son, I'll be back here as soon as my orders allow it. I've tried to explain that I'm a serviceman, and I have to go where they send me."

"Then why can't I go too?"

Nelson ran his head over his hair. Try explaining war to a five-year-old. "The Marine Corps won't let me, son. If I could, I would."

"Is Mr. Meade a serviceman? Can I go live with Judy?"

"Sorry, son. That's out of the question. I have to go to work now. Try to understand."

But Ricky hadn't understood and had announced, "I'm not going to be a marine. I hate marines!"

"You know I'll do the best I can for him," Lena said, "and Lord knows I do thank you for the trouble you're going to to leave a home for me." She stunned him by reaching up and kissing his cheek. "The Lord will bless you, and you'll get back here safely." She didn't mention Audrey, for which he was grateful. "I sure do wish you'd change your mind and not go," she added in a prayerful tone.

Raising his left shoulder in a quick, dismissive shrug that belied his true feelings, he stepped out of his house and headed for his office. Once there, he began studying in preparation for the briefings that would preface his mission to Afghanistan. He had done his best to prepare Ricky for his departure, but didn't think he'd made a dent in Ricky's thinking. The boy seemed unable to contemplate a life without him. And Lena wasn't much better. He opened the manual and began reading.

A week passed and, neither having heard anything from Audrey nor learned that she'd mentioned the matter of his neck to his superiors, he relaxed and went about his daily work.

The penultimate briefing was held in the conference room of a senior general. Nelson had slept poorly the previous night and was battling fatigue while he took notes and tried to concentrate on the speaker. A door behind him opened and, as did several other officers, he turned to see who had entered. However, the abruptness of his move sent pain searing along his neck and shoulders, and he grabbed his neck with his left hand. Realizing what he'd done, he tried to recover and turn back to face the general who stood before them, but couldn't. Such excruciating pain gripped him that he closed his eyes and gritted his teeth.

Two senior officers attempted to help him, questioning him as to the source of his problem and, unable to move his head without enormous pain, he had no choice but to admit the truth.

"I'm surprised you came," he said to Audrey when he awoke to see her sitting beside his bed. "How long have I been here and what is this thing they've harnessed me into?"

"You've been here since yesterday, and the thing, as you call it, keeps your head immobile. You're also full of painkillers. Why are you surprised to see me here?"

"Are you going to say you told me so?"

She leaned over and brushed his lips with her own. "No, but I will say I'm glad it happened here where you could get proper treatment."

"I suppose I am, too. How are Ricky and Lena taking this?"

"Aunt Lena is thanking the Lord you're finally getting treatment, and Ricky is convinced you've gone to Afghanistan. Are you still angry with me?"

He needed to touch her, to know that she wasn't an apparition, that she had forgiven him and still loved him. But he had no right to ask or to expect it. He reached toward her as best he could without moving, and she grasped his hand.

"How could I be? When I walked away from you that night, I felt as if my insides had been hollowed out. Knowing you're here is . . . Let's just say I'll never forget it."

"You may be hospitalized for a while, so I'll call you and let Ricky talk with you." She looked around. "Cell phone use is prohibited in here. You don't have a phone?"

"I probably couldn't reach it without turning my head."

"Right. Mind if I come back to see you?"

Was she kidding? "I'll mind if you don't."

She continued to hold his hand, giving him hope that they could recover what they had lost. "We're talking to each other as if we were strangers. It's downright painful," he said, wondering how they would overcome it and whether she wanted to try.

Her fingers tightened around his in what he recognized as an attempt to reassure him. "I'll be back tomorrow after work."

"I'll look forward to that. If you can, would you stop

by my house and let Lena and Ricky know I'm all right?"

"Of course. I've overstayed my time, so I'd better go." But he couldn't bear to release her hand and held on to it until she leaned over and kissed him on the cheek. At his inquiring glance, she said, "It wouldn't make sense to start a fire that can't be put out."

His eyebrow shot up. "If memory serves me correctly, you've done that plenty of times."

She laid her head to one side and looked at him through lowered lashes. "There might not have been the will, but honey, there was always a way."

He laughed, and it felt good. "Touché."

"See you tomorrow." With that, she left him with reason for hope but no basis for certainty. Not the knowledge that she was his and would always be. Not the oneness they had once shared. He needed that, needed it with her, and he intended to give it his best shot.

Two weeks later, Audrey drove Nelson home from the hospital. "How do you feel?" she asked, aware that if he recovered he could leave on his mission at any time.

He pushed back the car seat to accommodate his long legs. "This is the first time since that helicopter crash that I've been totally pain-free for as long as twenty-four hours. I hope it lasts."

"It will if you do the exercises."

"Now that the cat's out of the bag, will you be my therapist?"

"We can try it, but if you don't cooperate fully, you'll have to get another doctor. Agreed?"

"Yeah. Let me spend some time with Ricky and

Lena, and if you're not busy tonight, I'd like to see you at your place."

"All right with me. Aunt Lena will want you to have dinner at home, so I'll see you around seven-thirty?"

"Great. Thanks for . . . for everything."

She drove home slowly, her mind filled with thoughts of Nelson and what he would ask or offer. If the past two weeks had taught her anything, it was that Nelson Wainwright was as essential to her as breathing. Her father always said there was more than one way to bait a hook, and she meant to test his theory.

"Unca Nelson! Unca Nelson! You came back!" Ricky ran to him with arms outstretched and threw himself into Nelson's arms.

"Didn't Miss Lena tell you I was in the hospital?"

Ricky eyes grew big and round. "You were? Just like I was? Did they give you a wheelchair?"

He hugged the boy. "I didn't need one. Where's Miss Lena?"

"In the garden doing something."

He went outside and stood on the deck. "How's it going, Lena? Just wanted you to know I'm home. Audrey dropped me off a few minutes ago."

She stopped cutting roses and rushed up to the deck. "I didn't like the looks of you in that sickbed, but you look just fine now. I don't believe you lost a single pound." She gazed at him. "It sure is good to have you home. I was so worried."

Bridging the last barrier between them, he put his arms around her and held her. "I knew you would be, and I hated those first few days when I couldn't tell you I was all right." He released her, and she stepped back, wiping her eyes as she did so.

"If I had a son, Colonel, I'd want him to be just like you."

"That's about the nicest thing you could say to me, and I want you to know you can depend on me as you would on a son. And since we have that settled, I suggest you call me Nelson or whatever suits you, but never Colonel or sir."

Before she could answer, he whirled around and headed for his room. The sound of Ricky playing the piano followed him, and the first thing to catch his eye was the stack of mail on his desk.

He sat down and began to separate real mail from junk, and his gaze landed on an envelope with the Marine Corps return address. Perspiration dampened his forehead as, with fingers that trembled, he opened the envelope. If, after all he'd gone through, he still had to resign, there was no justice. He forced himself to read the short paragraph.

"It gives me great pleasure to inform you that you have been elevated to the rank of Brigadier General. You will receive uniform adjustments under separate cover. Congratulations."

He read and reread it. When he heard Lena coming up the stairs, he dashed to meet her and thrust the letter in her hands.

"Look. Read this!"

"Well, as the Lord is my helper, I do declare! General Wainwright, you one big heap of mess. Congratulations. If I'd 'a known this earlier, you would get a dinner fit for a kin—I mean general."

He knew his face was covered in one big grin. "You're the first person to call me that. Thanks."

He could hardly make it through dinner, read to Ricky, and put the child to bed, but at last he was on his way to Audrey. Happiness suffused him, and he hoped nothing happened to dampen it. If she told him they had a chance, he'd settle for that. For now. Congratulating himself on getting there in one piece considering the speed at which he drove, he ran up the steps to the front door and rang the bell.

The door opened. "Wha . . . What's this?"

"Quit gaping and come on in," she said, in a matter-of-fact manner, as if she weren't dressed to torch an entire regiment.

He supposed his eyes appeared to be popping out of his head. "Is uh . . . that an evening gown or a night-gown?"

"Whichever I decide."

He walked around to see the back, but there wasn't any, at least none above the separation of her buttocks. He shook his head, not in disapproval but in admonishment to his libido. She turned to face him, which was certainly no help; cleavage didn't describe it. And, man, did she look a million dollars in red.

"I'd better sit down," he said. She led him to the living room. "What's this?"

"Champagne. I thought we'd celebrate your release from the hospital."

He cocked an eyebrow. She was way ahead of him, and catch-up wasn't a game he played well. "You know I wouldn't drive after drinking that."

Her shrug would have put the great Mae West to shame. "Then spend the night."

He swallowed hard. Ready for action. But his second sense told him that if he did it her way, he would win the bigger prize. He took out his cell phone and called Lena.

"This is Nelson. I don't like the idea of Ricky waking

up and not finding me at home . . . I'll get there around seven or seven-thirty . . . You bet . . . Sleep well."

"What did she say?"

"She said 'Have a good time.' Didn't even ask where I was. I can't believe it.

"We might as well get started on this stuff," he continued, wrapping the towel around the champagne bottle and easing out the stopper. She sat beside him. He couldn't glance at her without a glimpse of what he wanted in his mouth, and it wasn't the champagne.

"I'm only going to drink two glasses," she said.

"Don't I know it. A tipsy Audrey in that dress could get a man a prison term. Say, I forgot to show you this." He took the letter from his pocket and handed it to her. "Read it." He watched as she read and reread it, watched as tears streamed down her face.

"I'm so happy. You can't know how happy I am. I . . . I worried so much about what would happen to you. I'm just so thankful. So . . ." she stopped talking and covered her face with her hands when the tears wouldn't stop.

"Audrey, don't cry, honey. Please . . . I—"

She turned to him and, wonder of wonders, she was in his arms again, her lips parted to welcome his tongue. Blood roared in his head and he plunged into her, taking everything she gave as she opened to him, pulling his tongue deeper into her mouth and sucking on it until he was in a frenzy for relief. He wanted this, but he needed more—and quickly set her away from him.

"I don't need a bandage for what I'm feeling right now. I want a commitment. If you can forgive my walking away from you, knowing I was wrong, I want us to have a life together. I may or may not go overseas on duty again; more than likely I won't, but if I do, I want to come home to you."

"It's what I want, too. More than anything, I want to be with you."

"Have you forgiven me?"

"Yes. If I hadn't, I wouldn't have visited you in the hospital the first time."

"I thought as much, and prayed that was so." He poured them each a glass of champagne.

She tipped hers. "Here's to us, General Wainwright."

"Here's to us, woman of my heart." She took a sip and smiled in that special way she had when he pleased her. Oblivious to anything else, including convention about such things, he picked her up and ran up the stairs, like a homing pigeon, straight to her bedroom.

"If I have to look at you in that thing one more minute, I'll be fit for an asylum. Do you love me?"

She had his tie off his neck and most of the buttons on his shirt open. Her palm skimmed his chest, pausing to tease his pectorals. Suddenly, she leaned forward, traced his left pectoral with her tongue, and then sucked it into her mouth. He unbuttoned his shirt cuff, and she peeled off his shirt, her mouth still teasing his pectoral and playing havoc with his nervous system.

"How do you get out of this thing?" he asked about her dress, when he sensed that if he didn't call her off it would be over before it started.

"Just slip it on down," she murmured without moving her mouth from his chest.

"Audrey, honey, baby you'll—"

"I'll what?" she asked, unzipping his trousers and slipping them down, along with his G-string.

He lifted her to her feet the minute before she took him into her mouth. "Listen, baby, that's a feeling I love, but not right now. I'd be gone in a second."

He threw back the covers and lay her on the yellow satin sheet. Looking down at her full breasts with their erect nipples, he nearly lost it. She reached out her hand, urged him closer to her, and wrapped her arms around his buttocks.

"I want to kiss you."

He closed his eyes and clenched his teeth as she loved him, and a bloodcurdling sensation plowed through him, kicking his heart into runaway palpitations. Sweat poured from every pore of his body as he savored the sweet sensation of having her possess him completely. He couldn't let her take him all the way, much as he'd enjoy it; he didn't want that with her. Summoning all of his willpower, he set her from him, climbed in beside her, and wrapped her in his arms.

She knew he wouldn't be rushed, but she'd thought of nothing else since she took him home earlier that day. She opened her arms and he lowered himself into them, the hairs on his chest teasing her breasts. His lips adored her eyes and every part of her face. Why didn't he kiss her? His tongue traced the seam of her lips and at last she had him inside of her, searching, probing, and promising. She grabbed his hand and squeezed her left breast with it.

"You know what I want," she whispered.

"Tell me. I want you to tell me."

"I want your mouth on me. On my breast." He nipped an areola and then sucked it into his mouth, pulling, tugging, and sucking until she cried out. He kissed her belly and the inside of her thighs, and she began to rock beneath him, impatient for the pleasure to come. Seconds later, the warm thrust of his tongue brought a keening cry from her.

"Please!" she cried. "I'll go crazy if you don't get inside of me."

"I will. Just let me have you like this." He kissed, teased, and sucked until she rocked upward to meet his rapacious mouth, twisting and turning until he moved up her body and she felt the liquid of love flow from her.

Burning with the fire in her loins, she sheathed him and brought him to her lovers' gate; he plunged into her. Home. At last he was at home within her where he belonged.

"You okay?" he asked her. She nodded, and he began to move. Almost at once the heat seared the bottom of her feet, and the squeezing, pumping, and pulsating began inside of her. He increased the pace. Wildly, like a man out of control, he rode her. And she felt him in every muscle, sinew, artery, and vein. He was all over her, stroking her with deadly accuracy, his power unleashed.

"Honey, this is terrible. I can't . . . I want to burst wide open."

"You will. Believe me, you will."

He stroked furiously, and all of a sudden she began to erupt. Dying, oh Lord, she was dying, flying. Falling. A scream tore from her lips. "I can't stand it! I love you. Honey, I love you so much!"

Shattered by the spasms, the quaking that overtook her body, he surrendered and poured into her the essence of life, shouting his love for her. "You're mine! My life. Everything to me."

They lay for a long time without speaking. Then he asked her, "How do you feel?"

"Like a sated little night cat," she said, wondering where she got that idea. "I feel great. What about you?"

He kissed her nose. "There's no way I could be inside of you and not feel great. It's not possible."

He separated them and leaned over her. "I may yet

have to go to Afghanistan, but there's a strong possibility that I won't."

"How do you know?"

"No one told me that, but two of the generals who came to see me in the hospital said Stateside duty wasn't a bad thing, especially for a strategist, which is what I'm thought to be. So I'm guessing I won't be going to Afghanistan. That won't please me, mind you, because I left some unfinished business there. I'm just telling you what I think will happen."

"I'm with you, whether you go or stay."

He wrapped his arms around her. "That's what I needed to hear. Can we get married? Soon?"

"Would a month suit you?"

"I'll be a good husband to you, and a good father to our children."

She supposed her face lit up like a neon sign. "I don't doubt that. I'll be honored to be your wife."

"You'll be starting with a family. Lena is a fixture in my life. She's as much a part of my family as Ricky is."

"How many ways can you find to endear yourself to me? I'm glad you love my aunt."

"I work at home late some nights. Can you sleep with a light on?"

She felt her smile when it was still deep inside of her. "I always sleep with a light on. I do my pushups just before hopping in bed. Will that bother you?"

"Not one bit," he said, his eyes twinkling with happiness. "I sing while I shave, usually as loud as possible."

"Good Lord, I hope you can sing."

"Boys' choir, cross my heart. I love you, woman."

"I love you, too, General Wainwright."

He put his arms around her, rested her head on his shoulder, and went to sleep a happy man.

For a sneak peek at
the first book in the
At Your Service series

Top-Secret Rendezvous
by Linda Hudson-Smith

from BET Books/Arabesque

Just turn the page . . .

One

"Hi, beautiful, what are you drinking this afternoon?"
Smiling at the rare beauty daintily perched on a high,
cane-back barstool at the Hotel Meridian's poolside bar,
Zurich Kingdom lowered his hulking frame down onto
the stool next to hers. "I'd love to buy you a refill when
you're ready for one."

Hailey Hamilton took her good old time in sizing
up the newcomer. Her amber eyes shamelessly roved
his physical attributes with a definite spark of interest. As her gaze came to rest on his sun-bronzed face,
she decided that she loved the warmhearted smile still
pasted on his sweet, juicy-looking lips. As his smile
broadened, she got a good glimpse of toothpaste-white
teeth, all of which appeared free of cosmetic dentistry.
His twinkling sienna-brown eyes appeared sincere,
but she didn't know if she should be flattered or annoyed at the reference to his opinion of her looks. It
had slipped off his tongue a little too easily for her
liking.

"Would you like me to supply my measurements for
you?" he asked.

"That won't be necessary, since I've got twenty-
twenty vision. But you can tell me your name if you
like." She playfully purred from deep within her throat.
"I bet it's a strong one."

"Zurich Kingdom." He grinned. "How's that for strength?"

"It's packed with power and it personifies your physical make-up—tall, strong, Marine-like build—yet you seem so tender and sincere. There are a lot of manly powers packed into your six-foot-plus physique. I would be surprised if your ancestry didn't include royalty. I can imagine you running an entire *kingdom* single-handedly or commanding an entire army of men and women. Zurich brings to mind the majestic ambiance of the Swiss Alps. That thought definitely conjures powerful imagery. I can see you raising the flag of victory after your strength and fortitude has allowed you to scale your way to the very top. However, your approach needs a little polishing." Smiling smugly, Hailey was pleased to share her own brand of bull.

"Please don't stop, lady, now that you have me falling in love with myself. No, I'm only kidding, but enough about me for now. What's your name?"

"Beautiful! But I thought you already knew that since you said it when you first sat down." Her amber eyes flickered with devilment.

He nodded, smiling broadly. "Okay, okay, you got me there. Sorry for being a little overly flirtatious and forward, but I certainly wasn't lying. You *are* a very beautiful woman." He quickly arose from the stool and walked away. He only took a few steps before he turned around and came back to claim his seat. "Hi, I'm Zurich Kingdom. Mind if I join you for a drink?"

She tossed him a dazzling smile. "Hailey—with an 'i'—Hamilton won't mind if you do."

"Now that name certainly speaks to mystifying allure. I like it way more than *Beautiful*. How is it that your name is spelled like that? Isn't it different from the normal spelling?"

"I think some people spell it the same as I do."

"I don't know why, but I'm fascinated with the spelling. Is there a story behind it?"

"The story on the origin of my name is a long one."

"Am I already running out of time in your engaging company?"

"We've got a little time yet, Zurich."

"Good!"

Zurich summoned the cocktail waitress. Upon her arrival, he found out what Hailey was drinking and asked that the waitress keep both of their glasses refilled. It surprised him to learn that Hailey was only drinking lemonade, the same sort of refreshment that he enjoyed. A glass of wine or two was the only alcoholic beverage he ever indulged in, and even that was infrequently.

"Ready to tell me your name-related story, Hailey with an 'i'?"

"I guess I can tell you the story without going into all the boring details, which my parents, Martin and Marie, love to do. They lived in the small town of Palatka, several miles from the hospital in Gainesville, Florida. A horrible hailstorm had hit the morning my mother went into labor. As the conditions worsened, my father pulled off the road to help me into the world. I was born in the backseat of his car. From what I'm told, I was also conceived there. That's a longer story; another weather-related one. To finish up, my father decided to name me Hail. When it was typed into the official records, two additional letters were accidentally inserted. But I think someone felt sorry for me and decided to show some mercy, thus, Hailey."

"After hearing the story, I'm even more intrigued than before."

"Daddy wanted to change it when he first saw it, but Mom loved it. She wasn't too keen on Hail from the beginning, but there are times when she and Dad shorten it to just that."

"A beautiful story befitting a beautiful lady. In what twentieth-century year did that miracle of miracles occur?"

"In 1975. So, what's your story? What are you doing here on South Padre Island?"

"Vacationing. But I never thought I'd find literal paradise in my favorite Texas coastal city. Silky auburn hair, sparkling amber eyes, an indescribable figure packaged in a hot tangerine-orange bikini, soft-looking burnished-brown skin; all highlighted by a winning smile and a bubbling personality add up to my definition of a living, breathing paradise. Earlier I was in Dallas to honor my old football coach, Clyde Foster, during a special weekend event at my alma mater, Buckley Academy. I always make the Meridian Hotel Resort my playpen when I'm here in my great birthplace of Texas. That is, after a couple of days at my mom's modest ranch."

His loquacious description of her didn't earn him so much as a blush. Referring to her as *paradise* had awarded him the same number of points as his earlier reference to her as *beautiful*—zilch. "I've heard a lot about your alma mater. Buckley Academy is the most prestigious prep school in the country."

"So I've been told. I attended Buckley from 1981 to 1985. I also played football for the Buckley Eagles. It was sort of a reunion for all the students, especially the football team, though we were really there to honor our coach. Three of my friends, Neal Allen, Haughton Storm, and Nelson Wainwright were on the team with me. We're still the very best of friends. All of us live in different parts of the country, and travel extensively, but we always manage to stay in touch. It was good to see them again."

"I'm glad your reunion was a success. Mind if I refer to something you said earlier?" After his replying shrug she asked, "You used the word *playpen* in reference to the resort. Now that's an interesting choice of words. Do you consider yourself a playboy, a player, or just a mischievous baby boy needing a safety net in the form of a playpen for security?"

"None of the above. But that was kind of cute if it wasn't meant as an insult."

"No offense intended, Zurich."

"No umbrage taken. To answer your question, I'm no player. I came here to relax and thoroughly enjoy myself. I want to have lots of fun without any emotional entanglements. Whatever I get into in the next couple of weeks will definitely end when I leave here. I have the kind of job that keeps me moving. I'm single and I want to keep it that way, that is, until my professional obligation is stable. I wish I knew how not to come off so direct, but I don't."

"A man after my own heart. It seems like we have a lot in common; I'm here for the very same reasons you are. I like all the cards to be placed right out there on the table where I can see them. I'm leery of people who keep less-than-desirable traits hidden and then spring them on you after you've given them your complete trust and loyalty, usually based on their false representation of self. I like to refer to that kind of person as the poker-playing hustler. I don't play cardshark-like games with others' emotions and I don't allow anyone to play me, period. What profession are you in, Zurich Kingdom?"

Zurich's eyes narrowed. "That's highly sensitive information, classified as top secret."

Zurich was surprised and pleased by her mature attitude. But in no way did he think she was the kind of woman who was going to take pleasure in having a physical tryst with someone for a couple of weeks only to have it end abruptly. In his thirty-five years he'd run into every type of woman imaginable. After numerous failures to read the signals right, he had finally learned how to easily differentiate between the women who were in the game strictly for pleasure, the ones in it for money and prestige, and the ones who weren't interested in either. The kind of woman who loved without reservation, without expecting anything in return, was a rare find indeed. That's the same sort of love Zurich wanted to offer to his wife when his career finally allowed him the freedom to marry.

It was his opinion that Hailey belonged to the latter group. He'd be willing to bet the ranch on his hunch. He might be eight years her senior but she seemed to have as much savvy as he had in how the game of life was played.

"Wow, we really do have a lot in common. I have the same type of job as you do. Maybe we're both members of the FBI, the CIA, the Secret Service, or some other covert organization. This vacation is suddenly starting to look up. I never thought I'd meet a very interesting man here at the resort, let alone one as fine as you. What's so amazing to me is that you like to play by the very same rules as I do: no hang-ups, hassles, or heartbreak."

He didn't know whether she was kidding. Her expression gave nothing away, and there hadn't been a hint of sarcasm in her gentle tone. Zurich didn't know what to make of her, but he couldn't recall a single female whom he'd ever been more impressed with or totally intrigued by. Hailey Hamilton had already scored an exorbitant number of points with him, effortlessly. Zurich was truly hoping that they could spend more time together.

As he studied her alluring profile, he cursed his profession under his breath. That was something he couldn't ever remembering doing, since he was extremely proud of his chosen field. In fact, it was all he knew, the only job he'd ever had. There were countless married folk in his line of work, but he wasn't the type of man who could divide his loyalties. Plain and simple, Zurich was married to his job and he loved it as much as he could ever love a woman.

"Hailey, are you saying that you and I can hang out and have a good time without having any hang-ups or hassles when the vacation is over?"

"That all depends on your definition of hanging out."

"Dinner, a movie or two, dancing, and enjoying the sunsets. And, if I'm really lucky, perhaps we can even share in a few sunrises."

"Sounds like you're making a bid for exclusive dibs on my time. Are you?"

"As much of it as you're willing to share with me."

"That seems like a great way to spend the next two weeks. However, if at any point I decide that I'm not having such a grand time, I'm back on my own. Okay?"

"As long as it cuts both ways."

"Absolutely. I believe wholeheartedly in equal opportunity and treatment. As for the sunrises, don't count on Lady Luck. The odds aren't in your favor."

He grinned. "Don't be so sure about that. I don't have any aces up my sleeve, but I think you'll be genuinely pleased with me as a date. I'm a man who knows how to treat a lovely lady. By the way, sunrises can be enjoyed from a variety of locales. So if you're thinking I'll be trying to get you up to my room, you're probably right, but not for any X-rated activity. I only make love to a woman when there's mutual consent. Lovemaking can't possibly be the beautiful, intimate experience it was intended to be if both parties aren't willing participants."

"My instincts tell me that I'll be completely safe with you. If they somehow fail me, be forewarned. My feet are registered as lethal weapons." She winked at him as she got up.

He laughed heartily. "I thought we had more time. Where are you off to all of a sudden?"

"Up to my room to get a few winks of beauty rest before our first dinner date. I'll meet you in the main restaurant at seven. You can have the hotel operator put a call through to my room should you need to cancel. I'm registered under my intriguing name. No aliases or secret code names were used this time around. I save those babies for when I'm on a special undercover assignment." *If only he knew the truth, he'd probably run.* She laughed inwardly.

"Lady, I do like your style. You're utterly fascinating! The only call you'll be getting from me is the one I'll make if you fail to show up at the appointed time and place."

"In that case, see you at seven sharp, Zurich. It's been such a pleasure."

"You can say that again." He stood and then leaned down and kissed her cheek. "So long for now, Hailey Hamilton. This is one evening I'm more than looking forward to."

"The feeling is mutual, Zurich Kingdom."

Totally intrigued, Zurich stood stock still as he watched Hailey disappear into the hotel. The woman had certainly left him with a lot to think about. He didn't know if meeting her was luck or a curse, since their relationship wouldn't last beyond the next two weeks. A blessing was a more accurate description of his first-time meeting with one Hailey Hamilton. It had felt like the angels were smiling down on him the entire time they were together. Grinning, Zurich prayed that the angels would continue to smile on him for the duration of his vacation.

Hailey awakened to a loud knock on the door. Wondering who could possibly be on the other side, she looked at the clock. She'd been asleep a lot longer than she'd intended. The steaming-hot shower had relaxed her completely. As three short raps sounded on the door, she thought of Zurich. No, she mused, he wouldn't come to her room, not without calling first.

Quickly jumping out of the king-size bed, Hailey slipped on a loose-fitting cover-up, dashed across the room, and asked who was there. Upon learning that it was a hotel service employee, she became a little leery. She hadn't ordered anything from room service. Further inquiry let her know that the gentleman had a package to deliver.

Curious as to who'd sent her a package and why, Hailey flipped the locks and opened the door. Her eyes grew bright with surprise when the deliveryman handed her a large, white wicker basket wrapped beautifully in lavender cellophane and tied with a huge purple bow and curly streamers. Since the basket was done in her favorite color, she suspected her parents. It had to be from them. They were the only people who knew where she was. Smiling, she thanked the young man and closed the door.

The sensuous smell of Tresor perfume wafted across

her nose. Body lotion, shower gel, and a host of other fine toiletry items in that same heady scent filled the basket. The lavender heart-shaped candle touched her deeply. Looking at the accompanying card, she saw that the gift wasn't from her parents. Zurich was the one who'd sent it to her. That made her smile.

As she thought about his statement, *I'm a man who knows how to treat a lovely lady*, she laughed. He certainly hadn't been lying about that. This was such a nice way to start a first date, as well as the gift being such a lovely gesture. After all the cards had been laid out on the table in front of them, she'd felt relieved. His plans fit perfectly into hers—no hassles, hang-ups, or heartbreaks. Once the vacation time was up, she and Zurich would go their separate ways. Her next mission was far away from home; she had to be fit for duty, both mentally and physically.

Hailey didn't know if Zurich was serious about his job, but she certainly was about hers. She was so close to her ultimate goal, so near to fulfilling her lifelong dream. If all went as she hoped, a promotion was imminent. Six more weeks of intense technical training would be no problem for her. She never once regretted all the blood, sweat, and tears that's she'd already poured into her job. Hailey was extremely proud of her career.

Hailey decided she wanted to look extra special for Zurich. What to wear out to dinner wasn't a problem for her. Everything she'd brought along with her was versatile. Hailey had chosen articles of clothing fashioned in fabrics of linen, silk, spandex, or pure cotton in soft but bright colors, solids, subtle prints, and basic blacks. She could go casual, classy, or dressy by simply adding or subtracting an accentuating piece or two. A couple pairs of denim jeans, linen blazers, lightweight shells, and sleeveless tops completed her fashionable wardrobe.

Since the basket was cellophane-wrapped in her favorite shade, she decided to wear her lavender silk dress with the bandeau top, which was classy and sexy with or without the matching jacket. If Zurich had chosen the color scheme for the basket, then he just might appreciate her wearing the same hue to show her appreciation of his choice.

Hailey plugged in her portable steamer after filling it with tap water. While waiting for the small appliance to heat up, she sat down on the side of the bed and put on fresh silk undergarments. She then seated herself in front of the mirrored dressing table and applied a fresh layer of foundation to her face. Earlier, before her nap, she had given herself an herbal facial.

After steaming her silk dress, she slipped into it. Her jewelry, a pair of diamond dewdrop earrings and matching pendant, came next. The two-carat diamond tennis bracelet she had a hard time fastening was a gift from her parents when she'd recently earned her college degree. Cute lavender-and-white medium-heeled sandals were her choice in footgear. While dabbing the Tresor on her pulse points, Hailey made a mental note to leave for the date early in order to purchase a thank-you card for Zurich from the hotel gift shop. She suddenly realized that she hadn't given the delivery guy a tip. Hailey recalled what he looked like, so she could easily remedy her mistake the next time she saw him around the hotel.

There were numerous first-rate hotels on South Padre Island, but the Meridian was Hailey's choice because it was smaller and more intimate than the larger resorts; it was also easier to recognize the staff and get to know them. There would be no touring or other outside activities on this trip since she planned to stay inside the self-contained entertainment complex and get caught up on her rest and relaxation, just another of her reasons for choosing the Meridian. Her next work assignment would take her far away from the comforts of home—and her next opportunity to take a vacation wouldn't come anytime soon.

A last minute glance into the mirror left Hailey satisfied with her stunning appearance. Smiling smugly at her image, she reopened the bottle of Tresor and dabbed a bit of the engaging scent onto the base of her throat, just in case Zurich desired to shower one of her more sensitive pulse points with his affection. He seemed like the romantic type, and she couldn't wait to find out if she was right. She needed a little romance in her life; romance without the worry of commitment was the best kind. But she definitely had her boundaries preset.

The thank-you card she chose for Zurich was lightly humorous, but with a sincere message of gratitude. She had purposely looked for a card in the same lavender color he'd chosen to have her gift wrapped in. Hailey felt really lucky when she'd found the cute one done in lavender and white. Two boxes of chocolate-covered raisins, one of her favorite treats, and a roll of wintergreen Lifesavers completed her gift-shop purchases. Hailey had less than two minutes to make it to the restaurant, but it was just a few steps away and around the corner from where she was. She wouldn't have to run, but she'd have to step lively.

Zurich's sensuous smile caused her pulse to quicken. All this man wore was a crisp white shirt, dark pants, and a designer blazer that defined his broad shoulders, yet he looked the part of a highly successful business-man. Zurich also seemed extremely relaxed.

His hand came up to her face and tenderly stroked her cheek. It was an innocent enough gesture, and certainly brief, but it made Hailey sizzle. The pleasurable experience lit up her eyes like sparklers.

"You look radiant, Hailey. And I just love a woman who's punctual. Did you bring a good appetite along with you?"

She smiled sweetly. "A ravenous one." She handed him the special card. "This is for you, Zurich. I hope you like it as much as I loved the gift you had delivered. Thank you so much."

Zurich was taken by the way Hailey showed her appreciation for the gift. He raised an eyebrow. "My thanks to you, as well. Mind if I open it once we're seated?"

"Not at all, Zurich."

He took her hand. "Let's go inside and get our table. I reserved one by the window. We should have a great view of the Gulf. It won't matter once it gets dark, but we still have an hour or so of daylight left."

Zurich gave his name to the willowy, blond hostess, and she instantly directed them to the cozy, elegantly set window table. The restaurant was practically empty, but Zurich knew it would quickly fill up with patrons. With that in mind, he hadn't objected when Hailey had chosen a time for their date that was about thirty minutes earlier than the most popular dining rush hour. Le Meridian was one of his favorite places to dine when he visited the island.

Hailey gave Zurich a dazzling smile as she sat down.

"Did you arrange for this little surprise?" She picked up the placard with her name on it. "Miss Hailey Hamilton," she read aloud, "AKA Beautiful."

He seated himself directly across from her. "I'll only 'fess up if you're impressed."

"Intrigued is more precise. It's also a very sweet gesture. As I looked around at the other tables, I didn't see any other placards, so that's why I asked. When did you request this little extra nicety?"

"Right after our first date was set up. Glad you're not offended by it."

"Quite the contrary. Why would you think I'd be insulted?"

He grinned. "Earlier, you weren't too thrilled at being referred to as beautiful, so I thought I'd like to show you that I wasn't using the term flippantly. As I said earlier, you *are* beautiful, Hailey, and I am being sincere."

"Thank you, Zurich." Hailey looked up at the waiter as he appeared at the table. "Looks like it's time to order dinner." Hailey positively loved Zurich's unique way of expressing himself, as well as his seemingly romantic nature. She could hardly wait to see what else he had up his expensively tailored coat sleeve. He seemed as sweet as he was handsome.

"What do you have a taste for in the way of appetizers, Hailey?"

She picked up the menu. "Maybe I should first take a quick peek at what they have to offer. It'll only take me a minute or two. This is my first time eating here."

"Take your time, Miss Hamilton. I have no desire to rush us through our evening." Zurich looked up at the waiter. "We'd like a couple of more minutes to look over the menu, please. In the meantime, I'd like to request a carafe of chilled sparkling cider."

The waiter nodded at Zurich and then quickly moved away from the table.

As his eyes zeroed in on his lovely companion, Zurich's breath caught. Bathed in the soft glow of the candlelight, Hailey's near-flawless complexion had an angelic appearance. Her full, ripe lips were the next of her delicate features that caught his eye. Zurich imagined that a lot of women would love to have a sensuous mouth like hers. He could almost taste its sweetness.

Hailey made eye contact with Zurich. The softness exposed in the depths of his eyes made her heart tingle. "I'd like a shrimp cocktail for my appetizer, Zurich. What about you?"

"I love their stuffed mushrooms and fried mozzarella cheese. I even order the same from room service every time I stay here. This is my favorite restaurant in the hotel."

"How often do you come here?"

"Every time I visit my mom; at least twice a year. I love visiting this island. It's so quiet and peaceful here." He removed a couple of colorful brochures from the inside pocket of his jacket. "I picked these up from the hotel lobby so we can decide on a few fun things to do. I used to venture outside of the complex for my entertainment pleasures, but on my last few visits I've just stayed around here. I'm sure there have been a lot of changes on the island since then, and I'd love to re-explore this paradise with you." He handed the brochures to her.

She laid the pamphlets next to her place setting when the waiter reappeared with Zurich's beverage order. The young man removed the carafe of cider from the tray. After pouring the liquid into the crystal goblets, he set them in front of the couple.

"Are you ready to order, sir?" the waiter asked, dining check and pen in hand.

"Appetizers first." Zurich wasted no time filling in the waiter on their pre-dinner choices. Zurich then decided they should go ahead and order their entrees at the same time.

Once the waiter took the meal orders, he hurried from the table.

Hailey picked up one of the brochures and glanced it over. "I had actually made up my mind not to leave the hotel complex. I planned on catching up on my reading and relaxation. A lazy, daily stint of lying out by the pool was also on my slate of things to do. I want to get my tan on, too," she joked, laughing.

He smiled at her. "Your coloring is already perfect. But I'd love to rub the suntan oil on your body for you. Interested in my hands-on services?"

"Maybe, maybe not. However, I do have a hard time reaching my back. I just might let you handle that area for me, but only if you can control your hands and keep them from roving into the 'no trespassing' zones." Her smile was a tad smug, but the laughter within was joyful.

The waiter's arrival kept Zurich from responding verbally, but the responsive thoughts in his mind had him laughing inwardly. Controlling his hands was the easy part. It was his inability to exercise restraint over the lower part of his anatomy that had him worried. Just the thought of massaging oil into Hailey's sexy body already had him physically aroused.

Hailey hadn't expected the pink, plump shrimp to be so large. After squeezing lemon on her appetizer and then dipping one into the cocktail sauce, she bit into the seafood delicacy. Her taste buds instantly went wild. The red sauce had a tangy, gingery flavor to it, different from anything she'd ever tasted. She could barely refrain from moaning with pleasure, but her amber eyes had the tendency to give away even her simplest thoughts.

Zurich was mesmerized by the expression of utter satisfaction he saw in Hailey's eyes. "You look like you're having a divine culinary experience over there. Is it really that good?"

"Hmm, you'll have to see for yourself." Taking another shrimp from the glass rim, she dipped it in the sauce. With a slight arm stretch across the table, she held up the shellfish to Zurich's mouth. Hailey's heart rhythms accelerated when his tongue made slight contact with her fingers. Wondering if the look on his face matched the one he'd seen on hers, she laughed. "What do you think, Zurich?"

"I think I need to place another order. From the heavenly look I saw on your face, I get the feeling you may not want to share another one of those delectable shrimp with me."

Repeating the same steps as before, she offered Zurich another one of her appetizers. The totally unselfish gesture caused him to eye her with mild curiosity. This time, he allowed his tongue to linger a little longer on her fingers. His attempt to effect a tender moment between them didn't go unnoticed, nor was it unappreciated by Hailey; her smile told him at least that much. The sensuous connection had been made, and each of them was feeling it.

"Thank you. That was very generous. There are people who don't like to share."

"I guess you could say that, but since you're the one paying the bill, I can afford to be generous." Although she was joking with him, she kept a straight face.

"Oh, it's like that, huh? How is it that I'm paying

when you're the one who asked me out to dinner? Or was I mistaken in my assumption, Hailey?"

"I know I don't have amnesia, but you're remembering something that I'm not."

"I distinctly recall someone saying they were going to their room to rest before our first dinner date. Does *I'll meet you in the main restaurant at seven* ring a bell?"

Hailey couldn't have lied even if she wanted to. There was no denying what he'd remembered. Her own words rung in her ears with such familiarity. "Well, in that case, it looks like this dinner is my treat. But I don't mind if you order another appetizer. What's a few dollars when you're having a wonderful time?"

His eyes fell softly on her face. "It's nice to know you're enjoying yourself, Hailey. And I wouldn't think of having you pay the check. I realized you were joking when you made the statement about me paying. The laughter in your eyes allowed me to ignore the poker-bluffing look on your face."

"Oh, so you think you can read me that easily, Mr. Kingdom?"

"No, but I'd like to learn how." His expression turned pensive. "I know you and I have already set the ground rules, but what happens if one of us falls in love?"

She raised an eyebrow. "One of us? Why can't it be a mutual thing?"

He shrugged. "It can be. It happens all the time. I didn't come here looking to fall in love, but I didn't know I was going to find you here, either. We said a lot of things earlier about what we are and aren't looking for during our vacation time and what we're going to and not going to do. I'm now wondering if perhaps we made a mistake by doing that. What's your take on it?"

"We made those comments because we both knew that we weren't in a position to look back when it's time to go our separate ways. I think we're the type of people who have to keep it real. I know that every comment I made earlier about my life was an honest one. What about you, Zurich?"

Zurich gave Hailey's comments a minute of thought. "It has often been said that I'm too honest. But in my opinion, honesty is the only way to fly. The story will always be the same when you're telling the truth. Lying is the most confusing to the one doing it. You're right about keeping it real. It's easier that way. To answer your question, I was honest with you."

Zurich definitely knew how to keep it real. But what he didn't know was if it was going to be so easy to leave Hailey Hamilton behind without looking back. Their imminent separation might indeed be a hard one to pull off, especially without bringing about some sort of a change in him. For the better or the worse? He just didn't know. But this woman was truly different.

"*I wish I knew how not to be so direct, but I don't.* Do you remember who said that?"

He cracked up. "Sounds just like me. Well, here comes the waiter. We'll have to get deeper into this conversation after we eat. Okay with you?"

She nodded. "Fine, but what about ordering another appetizer?"

"It was good, but I really had enough. The main course is here now, so I'll be just fine. Thanks, Hailey."

Zurich quickly picked up the envelope he'd received from Hailey. He then opened it and read it. The simple words of thanks put a smile on his face. "This was really nice of you. I appreciate the way you show your appreciation. You're very thoughtful."

"I'm glad you like the card. It was the least I could do

to show how much your gift meant to me." She stretched her arm across the table and put her wrist under his nose. "How do you like the perfume on me?"

His heart raced as he traced her wrist with feathery kisses. "It smells divine on you. It looks like I picked out the perfect scent for you. You two were definitely made for each other."

Seated across from one another in one of the popular lounges inside the hotel, where a live band played top-forty tunes, Hailey and Zurich had yet to experience an awkward moment as they enjoyed getting further acquainted. It was a little difficult to communicate above the loud music, but they somehow managed to converse despite the noise level.

His lips grazed her ear as he spoke into it. "Do you want another ginger ale, Hailey?"

"That would be nice. While we're waiting for the waitress, I'm going to slip into the ladies' room." She stood and reached for her purse.

Smiling, he got to his feet until she walked away.

After coming out of the stall, Hailey washed her hands. She then stood in front of the mirror as she freshened her lipstick and dusted her nose with corn silk. A slight smile appeared on her full lips as she thought of the good-looking man waiting back at the table for her. Zurich came off as a very genuine person, and she had to admit that she already liked him a lot.

Too bad they only had two weeks to click with each other. She could really get into Zurich, but when duty called she had to be ready and all set to go. Even if they did make a love connection, they'd still have to go their separate ways. Each of them had laid down the ground rules from the start: two weeks of fun in the sun and then it would be all over for them. The fact that Zurich thought they might've made a mistake in laying down the rules surprised her. Sighing with dismay, Hailey picked up her purse and left the ladies' lounge.

For a sneak peek at
the second book in the
At Your Service series

Courage Under Fire
by Candice Poarch

from BET Books/Arabesque

Just turn the page . . .

Prologue

Ronald Taft wore dress blues. Although his wife couldn't see the shoes, she knew they were spit-shined black.

The officer's dress blues were his favorite Army uniform. He wore them with a sense of pride and honor for his country and for the fact that he—a black man who came from little—had progressed so far. He loved the Army and even more, he loved his status as an officer.

Arlene Taft remembered when Ronald had taken her to her first formal military function. Since it was his ball, she'd elected to wear a blue gown instead of her dress uniform.

Just a smattering of African-Americans had been in attendance.

"We'll go far in the military," he'd said to Arlene. They were both stationed in the Washington, D.C. area. Although it was unusual to get assigned to the same location for years, he'd lucked out with his posting at the Pentagon. Since she was a nurse, staying in one location wasn't unusual for her. She'd been at Walter Reed Army Medical Center for years.

As the years passed, Ronald's postings required more and more travel—so much, in fact, that it was easy for him to take a vacation with a mistress without his wife's knowledge.

Arlene sat through her husband's funeral with

strained emotions. What was she to feel except betrayal, disillusionment, and a deep burning anger that she couldn't appease?

Her mother-in-law sniffled and moaned her grief beside her. She held on to the woman's hand, perhaps too tightly at times, but Nancy Taft didn't complain. She was swallowed up in her own grief and she didn't even notice. The nurse had already revived her once with smelling salts. Ronald had been Mrs. Taft's only child—a truly beloved son. And somewhat spoiled. But she didn't blame Mrs. Taft for being a loving and giving woman. She'd accepted Arlene into the fold as if she were her own child. Nancy was a rarity. She seldom spoke a disparaging word against anyone.

Arlene's father was present with his new wife, a woman who was merely a few months older than Arlene. She was so unlike Arlene's mother that Arlene wondered what he saw in her except for the obvious appeal of a younger woman. Arlene's mother had died three years ago, and Arlene supposed this was his way of moving on. He certainly dressed younger. His wife stood out in her lavish black attire. The skirt was higher and tighter than Arlene thought appropriate, but who was she to judge? She only wished she could see more of her father. Their relationship hadn't been the same since her mother's death.

The preacher's words droned on. They could have been disjointed ramblings, because Arlene didn't hear any of it. She didn't know why she was grieving.

Her husband died on a boating trip with his lover—a lover Arlene must have subconsciously known had been out there. Did she have blinders on? The reality that he spent so little time with her should have been one clear indication. Randy army officers rarely went without physical pleasures. She'd only deluded herself into thinking that her man was made of sterner stuff.

Arlene shook with his betrayal. She wondered if his army buddies who laughed and joked in front of her knew of his exploits behind her back. Had their wives, who called themselves her friends, also been privy to the information? The military community was small. People knew each other's business, and they told. Yet no one had seen the necessity of informing her.

Somehow Arlene got through the funeral. She barely startled at the gun salute, and made polite conversation at the reception held after the gravesite service. Her father and his wife left.

Arlene stayed on for a few days to console her mother-in-law. Then she flew back to Washington, D.C., telling Mrs. Taft that she would stay in touch and that she would send her mementos of her son.

It was Friday night when she unpacked her suitcase in the row house she'd lived in for years. The message machine was beeping. Ignoring it, she stood under the shower a long time, then went to the closet to pull on a robe, even though the outside August temperature hovered in the nineties.

Ronald's suits and clothes hung in the closet beside hers. What happened next seemed to be outside of her control.

She came back to her senses when she heard the doorbell ring. Shelly Bailey, her girlfriend since kindergarten, stood on the cement steps, a suitcase beside her.

Arlene glanced around the room. It was a disaster. Every piece of Ronald's clothing was flung about the room. A stack of black garbage bags was hidden under more clothes on the cocktail table.

Shelly glanced at Arlene's ravished features. Then she

One

Some days were better than others. Arlene wanted to pull the covers up to her neck and spend the next few hours in her warm bed.

At nine she made an effort to rise, but never made it up. She dozed again, off and on for two hours. A siren blared from afar, but that wasn't so unusual in the city.

The clock closed in on eleven when she finally considered actually getting up. She didn't feel too guilty. After all, she'd worked the eleven-to-seven shift at the hospital the evening before.

Arlene contemplated calling in sick—perhaps to spend the rest of what was left of the day in bed. Half of it was gone anyway. This was totally out of line for her. She'd never called in sick when she wasn't. But many things had changed in the last month and she didn't feel quite herself.

Suddenly the phone rang, a loud and unwanted sound in the quiet of her bedroom. Lazily she reached out a hand, plucked up the receiver, and barked out a groggy "Hello."

"Lieutenant Colonel Taft, we need you here stat!" the hospital scheduler told her.

Now! Was that woman crazy? Arlene wanted to avoid the day altogether, but she wouldn't dare say so out loud. A soldier was on call twenty-four-seven. If they needed her, she'd have to go.

"Due to the disaster, we need more nurses, especially specialists," the woman said.

"What disaster?" Arlene asked.

"Haven't you seen the news?"

"No. What happened?" Sitting up in bed, she reached for the remote. It was too far away. Now that she thought about it, she had heard more sirens than usual, but it hadn't pierced the fog that had settled on her.

"The Pentagon has been bombed. And both towers of the World Trade Center are gone. And that's just the beginning."

"Gone? *Impossible.*"

"Just turn on the TV. Every station is broadcasting. We need you here. Now."

"I'll be there as soon as I dress." Arlene fumbled the receiver back onto the hook and scrambled for the TV remote to press the power button. Every channel focused on the tragedy. It didn't take long for her to get the gist of the earth-shattering disaster. A deep sense of dread and sorrow flowed through her for the suffering these people were experiencing and that someone would dare do this in America. She saw it in the news when it happened in Europe and Israel. *But here?* The U.S. seemed isolated from all that, but global involvement had brought the entire world closer—for the good as well as the bad.

With a quick prayer, she rushed out of bed so fast her head swam. Tugging off her nightgown and thrusting it aside, she headed to the shower. After taking the fastest shower in history, she listened to the news as she quickly donned her uniform. Her new hairdo of short red curls only took a moment to rake a comb through. Turning off the TV, she paused only long enough to grab a bagel and cream cheese to eat in the car as she drove the short distance to the hospital. Depending on the number of injured, finding time for a break once she arrived could be next to impossible.

At the hospital, she was quickly directed to the trauma section. It was a beehive of activity.

"Lieutenant Colonel Neal Allen is one of your patients," she was told. "He has multiple fractures, scorched lungs and throat, and internal injuries. Right now we're trying to keep him breathing on his own to clear his lungs and increase his chances of survival."

Arlene recorded his vital signs on his chart. He was still heavily sedated from surgery.

Neal Allen. That name was indelibly etched in her mind. Could this be the Neal Allen who lived next door to her in middle school? Arlene shook her head at the foolish thought. It couldn't be. Of all the people for her to run into.

The Neal Allen she'd known back in Texas had been the bane of her existence. She would never forget the time he'd taken her red-and-white panties off the clothesline, attached them to a piece of cardboard, scribbled her name in huge bold letters across the front, and hung them on his father's flagpole. Her panties had flown for hours where the man had so proudly flown his American flag. All because she wouldn't walk to the movies with him. She'd already accepted a date with someone else, but even if she hadn't, she wouldn't have gone out with Neal. *What was that boy's name?* she wondered. Perhaps she hadn't been the most diplomatic with her refusal, but she didn't deserve that.

As Arlene looked at him, she realized he was that Neal Allen. Determined to find something to dislike about him, she noted his physical appearance had changed a lot in the last twenty-one years from the gangly youth she'd known.

It was immediately evident that he worked out regularly. His relaxed state failed to mask his underlying strength. His chest and shoulder muscles were amazing. She felt the steel beneath soft skin when she attached the blood-pressure cuff. His dark lashes covering his closed eyes were much too attractive. His hair was cut short, yet still managed to look striking. As Arlene gazed down on him, she wondered if his character had changed as much as his appearance.

She shook the memories away and got back to the business of keeping Lieutenant Colonel Neal Allen alive.

The next day, when Arlene reported to duty, the patient was looking better. She wondered if he remembered her.

"How are we feeling today, Lieutenant Colonel Allen?" Arlene asked him as she slipped the pressure cuff on his arm.

"Good to be alive," he whispered in a raspy voice she could barely hear. It was tinged with the smoke and heat damage from the fire.

"Oh, you'll be feeling better in no time." After making a notation of his blood pressure, she slid the thermometer into his ear, then recorded his temperature. It was only slightly elevated.

"How did the others—"

"You saved quite a few people. They've been calling about you."

"But—"

"Don't try to talk. Save your throat." She smiled. Whatever their past, he was her patient and she was determined to give him the best care. "You're a hero."

"No . . . So much destruction. So many people injured—" he whispered.

"And many generous people who are out there offering help. You did your part; now let us help you."

"It wasn't enough."

Arlene patted his hand, wanting to ease his distress. "You gave all you could. No one could ask for more."

He closed his eyes.

Arlene didn't know if her words had had any effect. She only hoped they eased his pain.

She kept peeking at him as she attended to his injuries. His concern for the others touched her more than she wanted. Could he have changed so drastically from that obnoxious kid she knew so long ago?

"Well, Little Miss Leave-Me-Alone."

Arlene stopped in her tracks, her hackles rising. She forced herself to present a calm front. "We must be feeling better."

"Thought I'd forgotten you, didn't you?"

Arlene had hoped so.

"Were you trying to hide your identity?" His voice rose barely above a whisper. She strained to hear him, but she heard nevertheless. His cute brown eyes were dancing with merriment for the first time. Even though it was at her expense, she was glad for it.

She'd hoped he'd forgotten about her past, darn it. After all, she couldn't look the same, and her last name had changed. Back then, he'd loved to tease her. "I don't have anything to hide. My life is an open book. I see you haven't changed from that obnoxious kid who lived next door to me."

"In some ways—in many, many ways—I hope I have. Changed, that is."

"Hummm." He had changed, all right. Even with his numerous injuries, she hadn't missed the striking proportions of his body. As his nurse, she'd seen all of him, and to her chagrin, she liked what she saw.

"We'll just work on getting you healed right now, okay?"

His smile faded. "How are the others who were brought in?"

"I don't know. I'm sorry. They were taken to hospitals all around the area." She pulled the sheet up to his chest. "I want you to rest your voice. Your throat is still raw. It must be painful for you to talk."

He clasped her hand in his, imprisoning it with a grip that belied his condition. "I need to know."

"I know you do. Believe me, we're all doing our best for all the injured. Trust me."

"Can I trust you?" The seriousness of his tone surprised Arlene.

"Why wouldn't you?"

His stare was intense, as if his eyes spoke words he wouldn't say aloud. Then suddenly he glanced away from her to the picture beside his bed.

She regarded the photo, which a nurse had found in his pocket. A pretty young girl with two thick pigtails. Arlene had brought a frame for it and put it on his bedside table, hoping the photo would give him pleasure. From her conversations with his mother, who called often, she'd garnered that the child was his niece, a cutie named April.

"Your mother and your niece have called several times. They're very concerned about you."

"What did you tell them?"

"That you're better, and that we're taking excellent care of you. As soon as your voice heals, we'll let you talk with them. But right now, I want you to rest your vocal cords."

He glanced at the clock. "It's time for you to leave?"

"Yes," Arlene said. "My shift is over."

"Can't you stay a little while?"

"Why?"

"I don't know. To talk about home. To read to me. Something—anything. I can't sleep."

She stopped the urge to stroke his forehead. "They'll give you something to help you sleep," Arlene said softly. "You need your rest."

"I don't want any more medication."

Arlene knew very well that she had nothing to rush home to. Her husband was dead—had seldom been around when he was alive. Since his death, things hadn't changed that much, actually. Except for the expectation of his arrival. When she looked back on her marriage, she saw that it hadn't been that great. She'd been complacent. And that was sad.

Arlene had nothing to go home to.

"All right. I'll read to you. What kinds of books do you like?"

"Anything will do." Neal just wanted to listen to her voice. Her soothing voice intrigued him, not the story. He was disgusted with himself for wanting her near. Most of his waking hours were spent watching the disaster on TV. His unit would be one of the groups dispatched to Afghanistan. He was disappointed that he wouldn't be among them.

Now he was punishing himself by listening to Arlene's voice, even though he knew she'd been responsible for his sister's, and thereby April's, unhappiness and pain.

But Ronald Taft *had* been Arlene's husband. He'd already been married, and Bridget had no right to him.

Arlene smiled—a smile he remembered so well from when she was up to mischief. "Would one of my romance novels work?"

He smiled, and the image was amazing.

"How about a mystery?" Arlene amended, knowing the skewed notion men had of romance novels. "I'll find one that will keep your heart pumping for hours. Or I might get you something soothing enough to help you sleep. What's your preference?" She found herself stroking his hand even though she'd cautioned herself not to.

"Excitement, please."

There was that smile again—the one he'd used just after he'd teased her in middle school. Back then, Arlene had hated that smile, but now she found it sexy. She chuckled. "I'll be back soon," she said, and went to meet with the nurse who would replace her.

"Arlene, we're transferring a call. This kid insists on speaking to you and only you."

For a change, Neal was sleeping peacefully. Arlene's hand hovered over the phone so that she could catch it before the ring woke him.

"Nurse Taft?" a young voice asked in a firm tone.

"This is Lieutenant Colonel Taft," Arlene responded.

"Good. I'm calling about Uncle Neal. I'm worried about him. When can he come home? I miss him. I *need* him." The little girl sounded as if she were near tears.

"Are you April?"

Silence greeted Arlene. Then a hesitant, trembling voice said, "Yes."

"Your uncle is much better, April. He's responding well to the medication. But he needs time for his body to heal. It might take a little while."

Arlene heard sniffles on the end of the line, and her heart cracked.

"Is your grandmother there, or your mother?"

"My mommy's dead. Uncle Neal is supposed to take care of me now."

"I'm so sorry, honey." Arlene's heart went out to the motherless little girl. She remembered Bridget well, and was saddened to hear the young woman was dead. Neal seemed to be the child's security blanket.

"Grandma's worried about Uncle Neal. She wants to come there but Grandpa's too sick. Grandpa wants to come, too. But he can't."

"It won't be easy catching a plane right now, anyway. Maybe it's best they stay home. Anytime you're worried about him, just call me, all right?"

"Will you tell me the truth?"

Arlene closed her eyes, moved by the hope in the child's voice. "Always."

"Uncle Neal's really doing better?" she asked with a skepticism too old for one so young.

"Yes, he's much better. I promise." That much wasn't a lie. Arlene wouldn't lie to her.

"He's really not going to die? Grandma said he wouldn't, but I thought she was just trying to make me feel better."

"No, he's definitely not going to die. I wouldn't lie about that."

"Thank you."

"You're very welcome, dear. Did you get your grandparents' permission to call?"

"Uncle Neal gave me lots of phone cards so I can call him anytime I want to."

"And you know how to use them?"

"Sure," she said with a confidence that belied her age. "He showed me how to use them. And I've been reading for years. I can read directions."

Arlene smiled. "You're a big girl, aren't you?"

"Yeah. I can do lots of things."

When Arlene hung up the phone, she caught Neal's steady gaze as he watched her. He was always watching her in that strange way. Why? What was he looking for?

"I didn't know you were awake," Arlene said finally. "I'm sorry I woke you."

"It's okay," he whispered. But a deep sadness seemed to steal over him. She understood some of what he felt, only her grief was different. Her sorrow was tinged with adultery, mistrust, and hurt. The loss of a beloved sister was so much worse.

"I'm so sorry about your sister," Arlene told him.

He nodded and turned away from her. Nothing could be said to ease the sorrow of a loved one's death. She wouldn't even try to ease what she couldn't anyway.

She thought of Bridget again. She'd been five years younger than Arlene. They'd known each other, but their ages were too far apart for them to run in the same circles. But Bridget had looked up to Arlene. And Arlene sometimes baby-sat for Mrs. Allen. Bridget had been as full of energy as her precocious brother, but not quite as mischievous. Their mother was practically useless when it came to handling two such active kids. Sometimes it seemed she didn't even try.

Arlene glanced at the photo on Neal's bedside table. "April is very pretty. She resembles you."

"You think so?"

"Yes. Although she also reminds me of Bridget at that age. She definitely has your nose and your smile."

His smile was not filled with humor.

"Are you comfortable?" Arlene asked, straightening his covers.

He nodded.

With nothing more to offer, Arlene touched his hand and left the room.

* * *

Considering the meticulous care she gave him and the gentle comfort she offered his family, it was difficult to believe that Arlene was the vindictive woman who wouldn't give her husband a divorce, even after she'd already agreed to do so, simply because she discovered another woman was pregnant with his child. According to Ronald, his relationship with his wife had been over years ago. He'd finally decided to end it, and she'd agreed. Then, when she discovered Bridget was pregnant with his child, she refused to give him the divorce, threatening to ruin his career if he tried to get one.

Ronald and Neal were both Army career men. The threat of adultery could damage a black man's career in a heartbeat. White officers could sometimes get away with unsavory behavior. Even with the barrage of publicity, only a few cases actually amounted to anything. The press usually died down after a short while. Besides, officers protected each other. Today as much as in the past, black men lived by a different, more cautious code.

Another worry nagged relentlessly at Neal. He was responsible for raising his niece. Would he heal well enough to return to his post so he could properly care for her? He wasn't ready to retire. But if his body betrayed him, he would have no other recourse. He wanted to expose her to the world. There was so much for her to learn—so much to see.

April had lost a mother and father only a month ago. And now her guardian was in the hospital. His parents were too infirm to care for a rambunctious eight-year-old. And April had always been full of energy. Every week since his sister's death, his mother had called to tell him about some mischief April had gotten into. He'd lecture the child, but her deeds weren't that serious, and Neal didn't put that much energy into the lecture. She'd

lived through enough traumas. He wouldn't make her
life any more unbearable than it already was. He needed
to be with her.

Neal had paid for a live-in nanny to care for her until
he could take the responsibility for her.

She was on her third nanny so far. The second one
had been frightened away when April put her hamster
in the woman's bed. The woman had woken in the middle of the night to find the hamster crawling up her
leg.

Neal had hoped to get April in a few weeks. Now,
there was no telling when he would be able to return to
the real world and care for her.

He could imagine the frightening thoughts running
through her head, especially with his accident so close
on the heels of her parents' deaths.

It was Saturday. Neal had been in the hospital for two
weeks now. It was Arlene's day off, and she debated
going in to visit him. He expected to see her every day.
They had fallen into a routine of sorts, although sometimes his mind seemed to wander. Some deep, dark
secret from the past, perhaps. Arlene got the feeling he
didn't like her for some reason. But she certainly
couldn't be part of whatever troubled him.

When she arrived, the phone in his room rang. By
now it was second nature for her to reach for it.

"It's time to send Uncle Neal home," April said, when
Arlene answered it.

"He's healing very nicely," Arlene told her. "But he
isn't quite ready to return home."

"But I need him *now.*" Every situation was urgent as
far as April was concerned.

"He misses you, too, sweetheart."

"My nanny is a witch." A long, labored breath followed that pronouncement.

Arlene smothered a laugh.

"How so?" Arlene couldn't help but ask.

"She doesn't understand me."

"Maybe if you explained your problem to her—"

"She doesn't understand, though. She's too old. I need help!"

"Honey—"

"Can you believe she got mad because my guinea pig got out of the cage and went to her room?"

"It just happened to get out?"

Silence greeted her. Arlene surmised the rodent had had plenty of help.

"I may have *accidentally* left the door open when I took her out to play with me. Maybe I didn't latch the door good enough. But it was an *accident.* Everybody makes mistakes. Why can't I make them?"

"I see," Arlene said. Evidently Nanny didn't like little animals scurrying around the house.

"And my hamster won't stay in the cage. Nanny keeps calling it a mouse and threatening to kill it. Can you believe she'd kill my hamster? I told Grandpa on her too. He told her not to kill my animals. She's a mean old lady."

"Let me get this straight. The hamster gets out of the cage on its own. You didn't give it any help?"

"No. Never."

I just bet it did, Arlene thought.

"Is it my fault he keeps getting out? I do everything I can to get him to stay in, but every morning when I wake up he's gone. And he stays away until he gets hungry. Then he comes back looking scrawny and starved."

"So after the hamster got out of the room on its own, it found its way to your nanny's room, too?"

"What can I do about *that?*" April asked, affronted.

"He got out on his own. It's the hamster's fault. Why doesn't she blame him?"

"She can't exactly talk to the hamster."

"I talk to him all the time. But does he listen when I tell him to stay in a cage? Nanny's mean. He's got to be careful around her, and I told him that, too. But Grandma says that's a man for you. They never listen."

Arlene couldn't contain her laugh.

"And then there's my dog."

Did the child have a zoo in that house? Arlene wondered. "A dog?"

"Nothing worth getting mad about. It just chewed on her raggedy old house shoe. And then it peed on the carpet in her room. But that was her fault. She shouldn't have scared him. If I was a baby, I would have peed too if that old hag had frightened me. It's just a puppy."

Arlene peeked at Neal to make sure he was still sleeping. "I take it she doesn't frighten you."

"Not really. I hate her!"

"Have you spoken to your grandparents about this?"

"They don't understand because the mean witch always gets to them first before I even get a chance to tell them *my* side." A long, defeated sigh came over the phone. "Now I'm stuck in my room until I learn to behave. I'm going to spend the rest of my life cooped up in this room. Can I come to Uncle Neal? Please? Please? I'll take care of him. I won't bother him. I promise to be good."

Arlene's heart clenched. April desperately needed her uncle. "Sweetheart, you *are* good." She was just an eight-year-old acting her age.

Early Monday afternoon, General Ashborn presented Neal with the papers and eagle for his promotion to

Colonel. He also received a special commendation for his rescue efforts.

Arlene borrowed a disposable camera from one of the nurses and snapped pictures.

"Congratulations, Colonel," Arlene told him once the general had left.

"Thank you," he said.

"This is absolutely wonderful."

He studied the commendation as if it held the secrets to the universe. "So many people were hurt far worse than I was. So many lives lost. I don't feel I deserve this."

"That doesn't mean we can't recognize our heroes. You deserve your commendation, Neal. You have something to be proud of."

Neal's phone rang, and Arlene picked it up as if it were her own.

"My hamster's dead!" April wailed over the phone.

"What happened?" Arlene asked, ready to go to battle with the mean old nanny who had the nerve to kill a child's animal.

"My dog bit it."

"Your dog?" Arlene pressed a hand against her chest to still her quickened heartbeat.

"It got out of the cage again. It wouldn't listen to me. And Pickles ate it. He was bloody and dead on my carpet this morning. I didn't even hear him last night."

"Oh, I'm so sorry, honey."

"I want Uncle Neal. Please can I come?"

"Honey, your uncle is improving daily, but it will take some time before he's ready to come home. You can't stay in a hospital."

"I'll be good, and I'll be quiet, too. I promise."

Arlene's heart ached for the little girl. "Who will keep your animals if you leave?"

"I'm mad at Pickles. She ate my hamster."

"It's not quite Pickles's fault, honey. His natural survival instinct encourages him to eat animals. Dogs are made that way."

"It's mean."

"It seems like it. But those instincts keep them alive when they don't have someone special like you to take care of them."

"I feed her. I even give her food from my plate sometimes, even when Nanny gets mad."

"I'm sure you take very good care of her. And you must continue to do so until Uncle Neal is well. Okay?"

A few sniffles came over the wire before a weak, "Okay."

"Good."

"I buried him in a shoe box in the back yard. Grandpa said a prayer over his grave."

"That's good."

"I made a cross out of some sticks, and planted a flower by his grave. My mama's flowers were prettier. You think he'll like the flowers?"

"I'm sure he loved them."

"I miss my hamster and I miss my mom."

"I know you do, sweetheart." Arlene struggled to hold back tears.

A couple of sniffles preceded, "My friend Keanna has a boyfriend. I'm never going to date a boy."

Arlene smiled and swiped the wetness away from her eyes. "You might feel differently when you enter high school."

"They're so hardheaded. Grandma said that's why my hamster's dead. Because boys are hardheaded. They're the devil's spawn, she said. They always do what you tell them not to. I don't want any hardheaded boys. It hurts too much. I'm not getting any more boy animals."

"Oh, sweetheart. They aren't all bad." Thinking back on Neal when he was a boy, Arlene thought April wasn't too far off the mark.

"Grandma says they are. Nanny agreed, but I don't believe anything she says. She wanted to dump my hamster in the trash. Can you believe that? She wanted to treat him like he was trash."

This woman was toast if Arlene had anything to say about it.

"Grandpa wouldn't let her. He made her keep him so we could bury him."

Arlene closed her eyes briefly. So much grief for one so young. First she buried her mom. Now her pet. Arlene's own pain seemed minuscule in comparison.

"What's the devil's spawn? Nanny called me that, and I'm not a boy."

"You're not the devil's spawn. Put your nanny on the phone."

"She'll be mad at me."

"Right now."

A few seconds passed before an older woman answered the phone. "Hello?"

"Mrs. Carter, I'm Colonel Allen's nurse. He has asked me to speak to you about April."

"She's a handful, I'll tell you that."

"All little eight-year-olds are handfuls," Arlene said.

"Mine weren't."

Did the woman think she'd raised angels? They were probably just good around her. "You do understand that she's just lost her mother, and her uncle who is now her guardian is gravely injured. He would appreciate it if you can keep things calm for her and give her a little consideration."

"He wants me to spoil the child?"

"Consideration means not calling her bad names that

might label her for life. Children are very sensitive about that. She also loves her animals. If you could be a little generous toward them, he would be grateful." Arlene chose her words carefully. After all, Neal couldn't search out a new nanny in his condition. Still, the nanny should show some kindness toward the child. No child should be labeled the devil's spawn. Of all the nerve!

When Arlene hung up, she wondered if she'd overstepped her authority. She glanced at Neal. He was watching her, his emotions unreadable. Even regarding his illness, she couldn't always read him. He hated taking pain medication. He was so good at hiding emotions that she couldn't always tell when he was in pain. What else was he covering up?

"I hope you don't mind," she said.

He shook his head.

Neal seemed always to be thinking, always considering some matter. Arlene wondered what was going through his mind. Sometimes she felt he was measuring her, and wondered why. She wondered if she came up lacking.

Near the end of Arlene's shift, as she recorded Neal's vital signs on a chart, a gorgeous, honey-brown–hued woman wearing an Army uniform entered Neal's room.

"Hello, Neal. I was told you were improving," the woman said as she walked to the bed.

He nodded.

"Just ring the bell if you need anything," Arlene said to Neal, and prepared to leave.

"Hello, I'm Natasha, Neal's wife."

Wife. A ring hadn't been among his possessions, and he'd never mentioned a wife.

"Nice to meet you," Arlene said, and left the room.

Neal's wife *would* be what men considered a knock-out. Why hadn't Natasha visited him before? Or called him? Perhaps she was stationed elsewhere and had trouble getting to D.C. April called every day. Surely the wife could have called him once.

For some indescribable reason, a shaft of disappointment swirled through Arlene. *You weren't falling for your patient, Arlene. So what's going on?* She took a deep breath and continued the last of her duties of the day. Neal was thirty-six—certainly old enough to have married at least once.

Neal watched Arlene leave the room, surely thinking he'd lied to her.

"Why are you here, Natasha?"

Natasha approached his bed. "I know this is bad timing, but the sooner we get this divorce moving, the better. If you sign the papers now, the divorce will come through in six months. I got the papers a couple of weeks ago, but I wanted to give you some time."

"How generous," he whispered. His voice was a little stronger than it had been, but not much.

"Give me the papers."

Natasha took a manila envelope out of her huge purse and retrieved the papers.

"The lawyer tagged the areas where you should sign," she said.

Neal activated the remote for the bed so he could sit up.

"I'll help you with that."

"I have it," he shot back. If he could handle a divorce, he could damn well handle a remote. He scanned the papers, making sure he wasn't signing away everything he'd ever saved. A five-year marriage that only halfway worked for the first three years wasn't worth everything he'd ever worked for.

Now Neal was grateful Natasha had insisted on a prenuptial agreement, fearing that if things didn't work out, he'd end up with the little her father had left her. He knew very well his assets amounted to more than hers. He wanted to keep it that way.

Neal signed the papers and handed them to her.

"How is April?" she asked, as if she really cared.

"She's fine."

"Good." Natasha checked the clock. "Well, I have an appointment. I hope everything turns out well for you."

"You, too," Neal told her, knowing very well that she was rushing off to be with her new boyfriend.

Now uncomfortable with him, she quickly left. A part of Neal's life was nearing a close. He shouldn't feel anything, should be grateful to see the last of her. Still they had been married for five years, and parting wasn't easy.

He glanced at the clock and wondered if Arlene would stop by once again before she left. He was falling for her, just as he had as a lovesick thirteen-year-old. Every time she came in the room, his system went into overdrive. He had to work at keeping his emotions contained. She was forever leaning over him or touching him in her warm manner. And her touches set his heart thumping. He watched the clock, waiting for her to return.

She didn't, and he was even more disappointed than he'd been with the ending of his marriage.

Arlene had the next two days off, and for the first time since Neal had arrived, she didn't go by the hospital to visit him. They were the longest two days of Neal's life.

She returned on Thursday. When she came into his

room, she was very businesslike. She did the chores she usually did, and was about to leave the room when he grabbed her arm.

"What's going on?" he whispered.

"Nothing. Did you have a good weekend?"

"I expected to see you."

"Wasn't your wife with you?"

Neal sighed. He needed to clear the air. "We're separated. She brought the separation papers by for me to sign."

With an unbelieving glint, Arlene's eyes widened. "She brought you papers while you're in the hospital?"

Neal shrugged. "They needed to be signed. My marriage has been over for years. We're just getting it done legally."

"I'm sorry, Neal."

"I'm not."

"Are you okay?"

Neal nodded.

Arlene squeezed his hand and went about her rounds, wondering at the cruelty of people, or was it just that they didn't care anymore as long as their needs were taken care of. She hoped she would never be that uncaring.

April had called practically every day since Arlene's conversation with the nanny. Somehow, the energetic child brought Arlene out of her own grief.

"Are your bags all packed?" Neal asked.

"They are. Most of my things have been shipped to Korea," Arlene said. Korea was her next tour of duty. She was scheduled for a short stay there.

"Aren't you going to miss this place?"

Arlene nodded. "I'm definitely going to miss the D.C.

area. The beautiful old homes. The rhythm of the city. The museums and activities on the Mall. The theaters. Cherry blossoms in the spring. The restaurants. But it's time for me to see other parts of the world." The things she'd mentioned were only a few of the activities Arlene would miss, but the day after she returned to work after burying Ronald, she'd asked for a change in location. She realized she'd grown stagnant. She was pleased the change had come through quickly.

Neal was leaving the hospital today. He was taking a flight to Dallas to finish his recuperation near his family. April needed to see that he was still alive and recovering. Arlene had halfway fallen in love with the child over the last few weeks. She would miss their lively conversations. If she'd had a child, she would have wished for one like April.

She would also miss Neal. Darn it. Tears clogged her throat. How had she fallen for him so quickly? She hadn't fallen in love with him or anything stupid like that. It was just . . . in their month and half together, they had formed a bond of sorts.

Neal, too, had mixed feelings about Arlene. He'd grown to respect her skills, and had even fallen in love with her a little over the last several weeks. It was difficult to reconcile the vindictive woman Ronald had described to Bridget, with this tender, caring woman who dealt so well with April, his parents, and his concerned friends.

Perhaps Ronald had been wrong. It was possible that Arlene had refused to give him a divorce because she was in love with him. After all, he had been her husband. She had first dibs on him. Bridget, the baby sister whom Neal had loved so much, had found her happiness on the dregs of another woman's lost dreams.

It hurt to think about his sister. The two of them had

always been protective of one another. It seemed his connection to family stability had been broken with her death. Family was special to him. Sometimes he thought the only thing keeping his life in perspective was April, simply because she needed him.

For the last month she'd called almost daily, wanting him home with her. The doctors wanted him to stay in D.C. another week or so before he went to Texas, but he couldn't. He was going home.

Arlene drove him to Dulles International Airport. The trip on 66 West was almost bumper-to-bumper traffic. Normally he would have flown from Washington National, but their full flight schedule hadn't resumed yet. From Dulles, he wouldn't have to change planes.

From the passenger seat he assessed her. He was accustomed to seeing Arlene in her nurse's uniform. She was beautiful today in dark blue slacks and a matching V-neck top and gold necklace. She looked elegant and fetching.

"Thank you, Arlene, for all you've done for me and my family."

"You're very welcome," she said.

Words couldn't express his gratitude. He'd received many letters of good wishes from the families whose loved ones he'd saved, and his friends from Buckley Academy had called him often—even sent flowers and cards. But Arlene had been his steady champion. And he couldn't think of the words to express how indebted he felt.

When they arrived at the airport Arlene let him off at the terminal and requested a wheelchair. He went through check-in while she parked the car. The lines were long due to increased security. Although he could stand for short periods, he was glad she'd insisted on the wheelchair, as much as he hated it.

An athletic man his entire life, an Airborne Ranger, even, he found it humbling to be pushed through the airport to his gate while Arlene walked beside him carrying his cane. He shouldn't complain. After all that had occurred, he was grateful to be alive, and well enough to even take the flight.

"Can I get you anything?" Arlene asked him. "A sandwich, maybe?"

"Nothing. Thanks. Just sit and relax."

She sat in a chair by his wheelchair. He took in the beautiful elegance and warmth of her face, the tenderness in her eyes, and wondered if he would ever see her again. He hoped that another twenty-one years wouldn't pass before their paths crossed again.

He started to ask for her phone number—ask if he could visit her once he healed, but decided against it. April was his responsibility now. And he couldn't ask Arlene to be a part of her husband's baby's life, to have her pain thrown in her face on a daily basis.

The fact that he had gotten custody of April had been the final breaking point of his marriage. Natasha had made it clear that she didn't want a kid of her own, much less to take care of somebody else's. He certainly couldn't expect Arlene to care for her husband's child.

This would be their final good-bye.

Preflight boarding for his flight was announced, and Arlene started to stand. Neal caught her hands, leaned toward her, and, with a gentle tug, pulled her toward him until their lips touched.

He expected her to jerk away from him. When she didn't, he swiped his tongue over her lips. Her sweet essence mingled with a touch of perfume and the sweetness of the kiss was almost painful.

She opened her mouth to him, and for the first time in his life, he kissed the lips that had tempted him as a horny fourteen-year-old, standing on the cusp of tomorrow without a clue about how to deal with the girl who'd snubbed him. Even now she enticed the full-grown man. The emotional distance between them seemed as palpable as it had years before.

With a pressing need to touch her, he captured her warm face in his hands, tasted her, felt her soft skin—knowing this was all they would ever share. The realization was heartrending. A knot rose in his throat.

"Thank you," he whispered, while gazing into her eyes. There, he saw the same need that held him in its grip. Slowly, he slid his hands down her arms. Holding both her hands in his, he carried them to his mouth and gently kissed her knuckles, closing his eyes against the strength of his need.

They had come so close once again, only to have the future snatched away. When she opened one hand to caress his cheek, his gaze jerked to hers. All that he felt was reflected in her pretty brown eyes. There was so much he wanted to say, yet he felt compelled to remain silent. With hundreds of words left unspoken between them, the attendant wheeled him away.

He'd been given a commendation for courage, but he felt far from courageous when he caught one last glimpse of Arlene looking after him. The attendant whirled the wheelchair toward the gate. He didn't dare glance back with longing for what he could never have. Dear Lord, fate would have it that he could only move forward—toward April.

For a sneak peek at
the third book in the
At Your Service series

The Glory of Love
by Kim Louise

from BET Books/Arabesque

Just turn the page . . .

Prologue

Franklin "Amadeus" Jones had gone completely mad.

Carl Baer stared at his lifelong friend with a rancid mixture of pity and revulsion.

"What do you think, Carly?"

Carly! He hated being called that. But he'd put up with it for the twenty-five years that they'd been friends. Carl swallowed, forcing a bitter rise of bile back into his stomach. Yes, he admitted; he'd put up with a lot.

Carl's nerves flickered with unease. "I think it's time to get him back before the toxident wears off."

Amadeus cackled, then strutted around like a peacock, as though the world were in his hip pocket, as though they all weren't living on borrowed time.

There were three other men in the motel room. Amadeus's muscle looming quietly in the shadows. They had helped to incapacitate and carry the soldier. After they got him on the bed, they bound him so that Carl could *do his thing*. The injection had taken only seconds to administer, and the man on the bed started talking soon after.

Amadeus had hurled a barrage of questions at the soldier. Pulling out his innermost feelings had been like extracting a tooth, and Amadeus played the masochistic dentist role to the hilt—drilling, picking.

Needling.

He acquired more information from the soldier than he could ever use.

"Look at him, Carly. A warrior. A killing machine. They don't come any better than Chief Storm, here. He'll be perfect. Don't you think?"

Amadeus hadn't lost *all* of his faculties. He was right about that, at least. A Nubian king. The hard detachment of a warrior. Bulky. The guy tied down on the bed looked as though he could rip a man in two with his bare hands and had probably done so on several occasions.

"He will be formidable," Carl admitted. It was one of those times that he couldn't stop staring at his friend. Pillsbury Dough Boy complexion and bright yellow hair. He was the only individual with albinism Carl had ever known personally.

Drool glistened at the corners of Amadeus's mouth. "What about the sample?"

Carl pulled a long, thin syringe from a case. The surgical steel glinted angrily in the harsh overhead lighting. As a scientist, what he was about to do had thrilled him once. And God help him, aspects of it still did. But the implications of his actions felt like hands choking him sometimes, made him physically ill.

Amadeus turned to him before he had time to mask his wave of repugnance. The pale man drew closer. Just a soft whisper above skeletal, his body gave new meaning to the word gaunt. He always dressed more like Beethoven than his namesake, and Carl could smell the scent of mental decay rising like rotting flesh from Amadeus's pores.

He closed in. That thin mouth and those tiny teeth grinning. Desperation sparked inside Carl and he slapped Amadeus quickly across the face. Knowing his own strength, he was sure the blow sounded much worse than it felt.

To no avail. The grin was still there. Still moving toward him. Carl closed his eyes for his punishment, but what he received was a cold kiss on the cheek from lips that weren't quite there.

He shuddered.

He'd always been afraid of Amadeus, especially the light flickering just behind his eyes that made him look like a wolf on the verge of being rabid. He hadn't wanted this friendship. But they were *both* freaks. They'd been outcasts since birth, and had found each other.

Like the man lying on the bed, their fate was sealed.

One

He would need surgery soon. Commander Haughton
Storm lay low in the dry night air, obscured by brambles
and thin, lifeless bushes. Just when he thought he'd be
going home, his squad had gotten an order for recon in
Gabon.

The pain slicing across his lower back stemmed from
an old football injury. In the past, if he'd ignored it, the
pain would give up and go away. This time he'd had it
for a week and it only gotten worse. Soon he might be
forced use a hot pack or buy, God help him, Icy Hot.

He squinted his eyes against the darkness. The heat
of the tropics began to cool. Storm's search-and-rescue
unit had been stalking for hours. The inch-by-inch crawl
toward their target would have sent ordinary military
forces packing for home, but his team of highly trained
Navy SEALs was the best at what they did. As SEAL
operators, they consumed a regular diet of search and
rescue, demolition, and recon. The kind of dirty work
he lived for.

He listened, and slid forward another inch. His re-
cent-issue fatigues could barely be seen beneath the
leaves and twigs he'd covered himself with. Any poten-
tial sweat or shine from his face was obscured by the
black hue of burnt paper he'd covered his face with.

Another inch and they would be in range.

A twinge of pain vied for his attention. It had been years since he'd had any serious lumbar problems. Years. The slow, dull pain felt more like a warning, a premonition of bad things to come. On mission after mission, he'd learned to trust what his body told him. By the pounding, his body was preparing him for something out of the ordinary. He summoned his training and turned his mind from the ache. Just like a switch, he shut the pain off.

En route to the target, four of Storm's seven men swept the perimeter in preparation for their seizure of the building. They would ensure there were no outside threats.

Almost there now. He and his men inched closer and reached for their assault rifles, which they'd kept tucked beneath them. War in slow motion, he thought as each man drew up his weapon and took aim.

First, they would take out all personnel they could see, both inside and outside the building. Then, in a swift rush forward, they would advance.

Storm gave a barely perceptible nod. A thunderstorm of shots bombarded the still night air. Guards fell like targets on a shooting track. And those who didn't, ran into the hills after seeing the bodies of their comrades shatter and explode in the barrage.

A short whistle, a sweeping hand, and they attacked. Scouts, patrolling the perimeter, covered them as Storm and three of his squad took snake formation and entered the building single file.

Storm moved in first. Their mission was to search and secure the building where an American scientist was being held, and bring him home.

Checking corridors. Checking rooms. Searching. Looking. Hands on weapon. Mind on mission. Haughton Storm had never lost a man during a mission and had had very few wounded. His gut told him to make this quick or that fact might change.

His operators called out from above and below. "First floor, secure!" "Third floor, secure!" Check hallways. Check doors. Gunfire! He was being shot at. Storm got off a round, ducked behind a door, and slapped in another magazine. One operator was on his left. He signaled him to go around to the other side of the hallway and into the holding room.

The picture they reviewed in the mission briefing had not done justice to the man they'd been sent to rescue. The photo was bad, but this guy looked worse. Storm could tell he was African-American. The problem was he looked as though a vampire had come along and drained all the blood from his body.

His second in command took out the last guard in the room.

Storm ran toward the pale man. "Are you injured?" he shouted.

The man shook his head and his eyes widened and seemed to dance a bit. Storm registered that the man had one gray eye and one ice-green eye.

"Then down on the ground! Now!" As per his training, he treated all rescued personnel as hostile.

The man did as he was told.

"Put your hands behind your back!" Storm had drawn his nine-millimeter handgun and had it pointed toward the man's head. He patted the man down on all sides. "Are you armed, or concealing anything that can be used as a weapon?"

"No," the man said, with what sounded like a smile in his voice. Storm was immediately distrustful. While one of his operators trained his weapon on the man's head, Storm put him in handcuffs and yanked him up.

"Let's move!"

Again, his men maneuvered into snake formation. This time, the hostage was in the middle. With eyes like eagles, each one of his men checked side to side, above, and below. Their movements were precise like the internal workings of the finest watch. The enemy could be anywhere.

When they reached the lower level, three men from his squad fanned out to sweep the area for their departure. They took the hostage with them.

There was a rhythm to mission deployment, something a few soldiers tuned into like a sixth sense. Sensing like a hawk or panther exactly when to move, when to strike, when to retaliate. Many of his men said he had it—the rhythm. He wasn't sure what he had, but he knew it was like a pulse in the earth pounding in his brain. A tremor only he could feel sometimes. It told him when to strike, when to stay put, when to lie low, and when to take risks. And that tremor was telling him now that his squad was in danger. Maybe something in the orders they'd received was off, but the game had changed within the space of the last few minutes. And suddenly the whole thing smelled like rotten flesh.

Storm made a series of gestures with his hand. Closed fist. Open. Open. Point north. Three fingers, two circles. Closed fist.

They had to get out of there now.

The message traveled quickly, and the men of Cobra One fanned out one by one and pulled back from the edge of the enemy camp.

Storm's skin prickled. Closed fist.

Footfalls in the jungle. They were in trouble.

Shots fired. They hit the deck, each man rolling and scampering behind the shelter of the dilapidated building. The familiar surge of adrenaline charged through Storm's body as he barked orders through his headset.

As customary, his team was in perfect sync. They followed his commands as if they had read his mind before he could think his thoughts.

Back out.

T-formation.

If he could get the men back to the perimeter, they could return to the extraction point and be lifted out by helicopter.

"Alpha Six this is Cobra One!"

"Alpha Six, over."

"Need extraction! ETA ten minutes!"

"Copy that."

Over a dozen enemy soldiers scrambled from the shadows, guns drawn.

Storm tagged a guard, who buckled with the impact and went down.

Gunfire filled the jungle night. Explosions lit up the sky like an erratic strobe. As his men fought for their lives and their country, Storm defended himself and swore that whoever was responsible for setting this trap would pay.

"I'm hit!" a voice said, slicing through the thunder of gunfire.

"Sharky!" Storm shouted, recognizing the call of his second-in-command.

A sniper pinned Storm down in a thicket. If Storm didn't take him out soon, he'd never get out of there to help Sharky.

Storm jerked himself against a tree for cover. His pulse pounded loud and hard. Jungle shadows provided some cover for him. His eyes swept the perimeter quickly. Bullets whizzed by on both sides of him. The enemy was behind them, stationary, not following—yet. He had to get to Sharky before that was no longer the case.

The footfalls and suppressing fire from his unit told him they were regrouping, but not fast enough. Without his men to cover him, he would have to run unprotected to where Sharky lay, at the foot of a thick bush, unmoving.

He could see one leg. The rest of his comrade's body was motionless. A bolt of pain struck Storm in the middle of the chest, and he sprinted toward the man's location.

For years he'd trained against letting the sight of injuries, wounds, or blood affect him. Every SEAL had. But for a millisecond, he lost his training as a sliver of remorse slid though him. Then it was gone and he knew that the man, shot in the side but still reaching for his gun, needed and deserved every bit of military training Storm could summon to get them out of the ambush.

"Just get me on my feet and put my gun in my hand," Sharky said, stark determination making him seem much older than his thirty-two years.

"You got it, soldier," Storm replied.

More shouts and bootfalls as the SEAL Team Cobra One aborted their reconnaissance mission. Storm hefted Sharky up and handed him his weapon. With a nod from the injured man, they scrambled toward the extraction point, arm in arm, rifles drawn and blazing.

"SEALs, we are *lea-ving!*" Storm shouted when his unit had regrouped.

The enemy was following close now.

"Alpha Six this is Cobra One, over."

"Alpha Six, go ahead."

"Zone is hot. Repeat, zone is hot, over."

"Roger that, Cobra One. What's your ETA?"

Storm tightened his hold on Sharky.

"Two minutes, and we got injuries, over!"

"Two minutes, Chief. We'll prep for medical, over."

"Copy that. Cobra Out."

"Alpha Six, out."

Storm's breathing matched the pace of his run with Sharky through the heat and brush. He sensed the anxiety of his team. "Cobra team sound off."

"Sandman, on your six, Sir!"

"Hardgrove, side by side, Sir!"

"Mills, on the move, Commander!"

"Fox, still in the pocket, Chief!"

"Tuxedo, kickin' up dust, Sir!"

"Faison, bringing up the rear!"

Good. His team was intact. He'd be damned if he'd lose any men to an ambush, which is what this was.

As the sound of gunfire grew behind him, he realized that what they'd experienced was a brush-off. If the guards had wanted a confrontation, he and his men would have had to do a lot more fighting than simply retreat.

Why did this feel like a test?

When they arrived at the extraction point, the chopper flew in, cannons blazing. All seven of his men were by his side, and ready to lift out.

"Go! Go! Go! Go!" Seconds into the helo, and Storm issued the command to leave.

The helicopter lifted up and away sharply, guns still blazing.

"What happened back there?" one of the pilots shouted.

"Ambush. Somebody set us up." After making sure the hostage was secure, Storm knelt beside his teammate. He and Sharky went all the way back to Hell

Week in BUDs training. They had endured every horrendous test thrown at them. He was the closest thing Storm had to a brother.

Sharky was getting worked on pretty good by Raymond "Doc" Collins, the best med tech Storm had ever worked with. If he couldn't save Sharky, no one could.

Doc looked up. "Punctured lung. I'm going to intubate and patch to keep his lung from collapsing. He's bleeding like a stuck pig, but I'll get it stopped and he should be okay."

Relief slowed Storm's raging pulse.

Sharky trembled on the floor of the helicopter. His eyes widened. It was the first time Storm had ever seen anything close to fear in his eyes in all the years they'd served together.

"Suck it up, soldier!" he barked. "That's an order!"

He touched Sharky on the shoulder. "You're gonna make it," he said.

"I gotta . . . gotta make it," Sharky replied, heaving with each word. "Or else there'll be no one who can keep . . . keep your . . . sorry carcass in line."

Storm grinned and nodded. Sharky was going to be fine.

Relieved, he sat back, reflecting. At the beginning of each mission, Storm would take a mental snapshot of his platoon. Every time, he etched their faces into his memory.

Failure is not an option to a Navy SEAL. Each mission is carefully planned and rehearsed to be successful without casualties or injuries. If either occurs, the commander has made an unacceptable mistake.

His head rocked back and forth against the cold metal of the chopper. Vibration from the propellers strummed inside the vehicle like the heartbeat of a giant bird.

He shifted, as his back sent out another twinge for

THE GLORY OF LOVE 377

good measure. The hostage hadn't said a word. Not "thank-you." Not "much obliged." Not "kiss my behind." He only sat in silence with a strange grin that gave Storm a jolt of unease.

He knew his men. Their body language was clear. Seven men, twitching and snorting like nervous bulls. The inside of the helicopter was uncharacteristically quiet, and their gazes moved to and away from the man. Something about the man they'd rescued put them all on edge.

Storm closed his eyes and wondered why his green-faced warriors, a platoon of the most highly skilled soldiers in the U.S. military forces, were spooked by a tiny little man.

Dear Reader,

Neither my editor nor my publisher could have dreamed that this book and the other three in the "At Your Service" series would become a homage to our servicemen at a time of real battles in real armed conflict. I chose a marine as my hero, because marines have always represented towering strength and extraordinary courage and valor. If you've read many of my stories, you know that is the kind of man I admire.

I hope you enjoyed Nelson Wainwright's struggle with himself and with his love for Audrey, as he put loyalty and honor above his personal desires and needs. As I wrote his story, he became real, alive for me, and so often I had to stop writing because I hurt for him when his pain would become almost unbearable. And through it all, I kept thinking that those of us who find a love as strong and as solid as theirs are truly blessed. At the end, I was loathe to tell him good-bye. I hope you felt the same way. If you need something else to read, pick up my latest mainstream, *Blues from Down Deep*.

Thank you all for making *Once in a Lifetime* so successful. I have been so encouraged by the hundreds of letters and e-mails I have received about the book, and I want you to know that I am paying attention to your requests. In a few weeks, I shall begin Russ Harrington's story, as yet untitled. After that, Drake will get his story. You may write me at P.O. Box 45, New York, NY 10044, or e-mail GwynneF@aol.com. Please also visit my Web sites at http://www.gwynneforster.com and http://www.tlt.com/authors/gforster.htm.

Warm regards,
Gwynne Forster

ABOUT THE AUTHOR

Gwynne Forster is national best-selling and award-winning author of two best-selling books of general fiction *(When Twilight Comes* and *Blues from Down Deep). When Twilight Comes* was a main selection of Black Expressions Book Club, and both novels received excellent reviews. She is also author of thirteen romance novels and five novellas, and is winner of the Black Writers Alliance 2001 Gold Pen Award for *Beyond Desire*, best romance novel. *Beyond Desire* is a Doubleday Book Club, a Literary Guild, and a Black Expressions Book Club selection. Others of her novels selected by the Black Expressions Book Club include *Blues from Down Deep, Scarlet Woman,* and *Once in a Lifetime.* Romance Slam Jam 2001 nominated Gwynne for three Emma Awards and for its first Vivian Stephens Lifetime Achievement Award. Gwynne has received many awards for her books, including The Romance in Color internet site Award of Excellence for *Against the Wind* and citation as 1999 Author of the Year. Gwynne's books won the *Affaire De Coeur Magizine* award for best romance with an African American hero and heroine in 1997, 1998, and 1999.

Gwynne holds bachelors and masters degrees in sociology and a masters degree in economics/demography. As a demographer, she is widely published. She is formerly chief of (non-medical) research in fertility and family planning in the Population Division of the United Nations in New York and served for four years as chairperson of the International Programme Committee of the International Planned Parenthood Federation (London, England), positions that took her to sixty-three developed and developing countries. Gwynne sings in her church choir, loves to entertain, is a gourmet cook and avid gardener. She lives with her husband in New York City.

She is represented by the James B. Finn Literary Agency, Inc., P.O. Box 28227A, St. Louis, Missouri 63132.

The Arabesque At Your Service Series

Four superb romances with engaging characters and dynamic story lines featuring heroes whose destiny is intertwined with women of equal courage who confront their passionate—and unpredictable—futures.

__TOP-SECRET RENDEZVOUS

by Linda Hudson-Smith   1-58314-397-1 $6.99US/$9.99CAN

Sparks fly when officer Hailey Douglas meets Air Force Major Zurich Kingdom. Military code forbids fraternization between an officer and an NCO, so the pair find themselves involved in a top-secret rendezvous.

__COURAGE UNDER FIRE

by Candice Poarch   1-58314-350-5 $6.99US/$9.99CAN

Nurse Arlene Taft is assigned to care for the seriously injured Colonel Neal Allen. She remembers him as an obnoxious young neighbor at her father's military base, but now he looks nothing like she remembers. Will time give them courage under fire?

__THE GLORY OF LOVE

by Kim Louise   1-58314-411-0 $6.99US/$9.99CAN

When pilot Roxanne Allgood is kidnapped, Navy Seal Col. Haughton Storm sets out on a mission to find the only person who has ever mattered to him—a lost love he hasn't seen in ten years.

__FLYING HIGH

by Gwynne Forster   1-58314-427-7 $6.99US/$9.99CAN

Colonel Nelson Wainwright must recover from his injuries if he is to attain his goal of becoming a four-star general. Audrey Powers, a specialist in sports medicine, enters his world to get him back on track. Will their love find a way to endure his rise to the top?